The Vein Openers

RICHARD MOOR

C000117283

DEDICATION

The Vein Openers is dedicated to the men of all nations who took up arms to fight for their countries during the Revolutionary and Napoleonic Wars that raged from 1792 to 1815. They were not always heroes and they were not always brave, but their efforts became part of history giving us such battles as Trafalgar, Marengo, Austerlitz, Auerstadt, Aspern-Essling, Borodino, Leipzig and Waterloo. My focus in a series of books, of which The Vein Openers is the first, is on one British unit - the 29th Regiment of Foot, the Worcesters. The 29th had a remarkable history and its trials, successes and tribulations during the Peninsular War will make for compelling reading.

ABOUT THE AUTHOR

Richard Moore is an award-winning journalist and photographer whose passion for the Napoleonic Era began in childhood. In 1998 he created The Napoleonic Guide (www.napoleonguide.com) an online encyclopedia on the Napoleonic Wars.
Originally from Australia, he has worked for news organisations around the world. They include the British Broadcasting Corporation's World Service, Radio Australia, The Age newspaper in Melbourne and owns a number of websites. His most recent position was as editor of the Cook Islands News on Rarotonga.

The Iberian Peninsula
1808

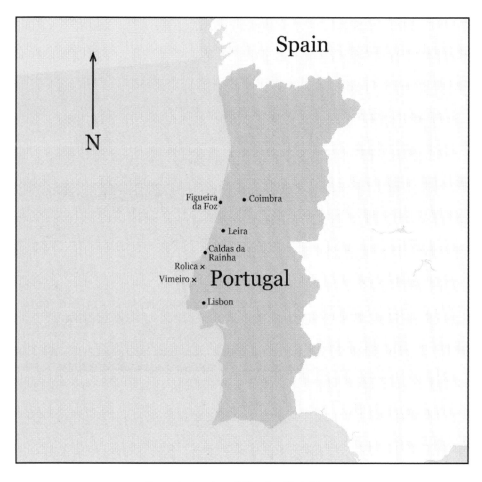

Cover Artwork and Map by Chris Rowe

Prologue

Joshua Firth watched as the smoke from a score of clay pipes seeped through the hot air, rising slowly before halting near the yellow-stained ceiling.

A roaring fire added to the closeness of the atmosphere, aided by the body heat from a large party of revelers whose raucous, ale-released shouts mixed cheerfully with the surrounding laughter.

Across the dark-panelled room a barmaid playfully slapped an over-friendly hand and, when it didn't stop its exploration, she good-naturedly poured a jug of Whitby's finest ale on to the head of its owner.

More laughter erupted.

Moving away, the maid moved to a small, well-worn table where Firth sat with another youth.

"Shame, Master Joshua, your tankards are nearly empty," the barmaid softly chided, then murmured as she refilled the pewter mugs.

"Those gentlemen have been asking questions about you."

Firth glanced across the room to where three dark-blue coated Royal Navy officers were sitting at a corner table.

Having noted the men in question, Firth returned his gaze to the drunk fishermen celebrating the record catch of the season.

"What did you tell them, Mary?"

"Only that you're a merchant's son, your friend Samuel Brook's father is a chandler, and you're both off to join the army in Portugal; wherever that is."

"Did they say why they wanted to know about us?"

"No, they gave me a penny to keep my mouth shut. A penny, the cheek! And them all in uniforms that are worth more than a year's pay to me!"

Firth smiled. "I'll give you a shilling for telling me."

The barmaid stopped. "No, I don't want any money from you Master Joshua … you're …" she stopped.

Firth smiled again, he knew the barmaid had a soft heart for him and he had, on occasions, wondered about discovering how soft.

Brook interrupted, "Don't worry Mary, I know how you feel about him. So he's rich and good looking, what else can he offer?" he joked as he turned away smiling.

Captain Jonas Ricketts had been watching as the trio talked. "Never give a woman money to keep her mouth shut," he muttered, "she'll always open it for more."

Shame, he thought, she's a damn fine-looking woman. A little old, maybe 30, but he knew a few shillings held her way would get the usual welcoming response from her sort.

Looking at his First Lieutenant, Ricketts pressed his lips together and stared with black eyes.

The younger officer shifted nervously under the hard gaze and then began: "They seem to be well known locally sir. Don't you think we might have a problem if we take them?"

"The law is on our side, Reynolds. If we get 'em, we'll keep 'em."

The Captain spoke with the arrogance of success. They had just captured a French privateer that had been attacking English vessels. Their small 20-gun sloop, the Audacious, had brought its prize into the Whitby harbour where it sat shackled alongside the northern docks. The French had put up a fight as the English swarmed aboard and Ricketts had lost several men in the melee. His task that night was to press some replacements, willing or not.

"Get outside Mr Walker and make sure the men are ready," he instructed the young midshipman sitting by Reynolds. "And don't get noticed."

The young man stood and eased his way through the jostling throng and out of the smoke-laden atmosphere.

"Ay up, I sense something's amiss," observed a now-watchful Firth. "Those officers have mischief on their minds. All these fishermen would be pretty useful in the Navy."

Brook looked up alarmed. "They'll not take them … it's against the law."

"Well, Sam, I don't think that matters much to the Royal Navy. They've a job to do and most turn a blind eye as to how it is done."

Outside in the cool night air Walker strode up to the main street where he signalled to a junior midshipman at the head of a dozen sailors waiting outside a small tailor's shop. The Tars, led by a massively built seaman, were all armed with clubs and heavy cutlasses. Their short blue jackets were covered in pitch and the months at sea had taken a toll of their loose-fitting trousers, all of which were patched and grimy. Looking at his gang Walker said to his young colleague. "The Captain's chosen well, these lads would scare Beelzebub himself."

"I feel sorry for them," the lad replied, "The food is rotten."

"Then there's the floggings," Walker added, "and Captain Ricketts is a whipping man. I've seen more than enough of the cat these past 18 months to last me a lifetime."

Back in the Duke of York some of the carousing fishermen were calling it a night. Five staggered to the door and, after several bawdy farewells, headed into the dark. Ricketts watched them go, hoping the youths would not leave before his men had dealt with the fishermen. But, within a minute the pair stood, picked up their bags and moved to leave. That was when Ricketts saw they both had sheathed swords in their hands. He hadn't noticed the weapons before. They must have been lying beside the table. It was an added problem, but the Captain was sure his men would be able to handle it.

As Firth and Brook made for the door a chorus of cheers began and the patrons good-naturedly thumped them on the back and wished them well.

Mary ran up to Firth and grabbed him and gave him a kiss for good luck. "You be careful now Master Joshua, the Frenchies are evil men."

The young man smiled. "From what I have been told Mary, so are some of ours. In a few weeks we'll be in Portugal having the time of our lives."

"But Master Joshua, Bonaparte's Frenchies are killing nuns and eating babies. They roast them, it is said."

"Calm yourself, Mary, we'll be fine. In a year or two you'll be handing us ale and listening to how we taught the Frogs some manners."

"Come on Joshua," Brook said, "before this gets even more embarrassing!"

The pair opened the door and walked briskly down the path between the tavern and

Whitby's southern moorings.

There was a moon rising and, together with lamps in the windows of several houses, the pair found the way to the main street well lit.

"I want to have a last look at the abbey," Firth said. "It was my mother's favourite spot."

Brook nodded sympathetically. "Do you still think about her?"

"Every day, Sam. Every day for eight years."

Brook thought it better to leave the issue there and walked on up the street towards the imposing sandstone structure that sat as a crown on the cliffs overlooking the town.

Both he and Firth had spent many summer hours lying under the abbey's arches taking in the fresh sea breeze and dreaming of adventure in foreign lands.

Brook chuckled: "Do you remember when we found that piece of Viking helmet near the ruins?"

"Viking helmet?" scoffed Firth, "It was a horn Sam. The only exciting episode that thing was ever associated with was avoiding a randy bull. And the only rampaging it saw would have been for fodder."

Firth quickly patted his friend's stomach and added: "It was not the only thing that likes its food, eh?"

The pair strode up the rise and the stillness of the night allowed them to hear the sounds of a fight ahead.

Breaking into a run, Firth reached the corner first and saw the fourth of the drunken fishermen falling under a blow from a club.

In an instant the man's belt had been removed and the waistband cut to prevent him running away.

A fifth man, who had escaped the sailors' clutches, ran south towards the centre of the town.

One of the Royal Navy men looked up from tying a pair of hands and shouted a warning.

Walker turned and pointed towards Firth. "You there, we are acting on behalf of the Impress Service. You are to come with us."

Firth didn't even bother looking at Brook before he challenged the order: "We are about to join His Majesty's Army in Portugal, we have commissions and we won't be joining you."

"Yes," Brook laughed, "but thanks for the offer."

"Perhaps, you don't understand," said the Midshipman, "You've no choice. You will come with us."

Despite the young man's obvious nervousness, Firth could hear the threat and drew his sword.

The leading sailor approached with his weapon raised and aimed it flat-bladed at the side of Firth's head.

Closing inside the left-handed man's reach, Firth jabbed his arm forward stabbing the assailant through the fleshy part of his forearm.

As the blade bit the sailor screamed, dropped his weapon and crumpled to the ground.

The ring of blade on blade to his side told Firth that Brook was also fighting, but his main thought was to see where the next attack was coming from.

5

To his front and left came the largest sailor, warily moving behind the cutlass.

His attack, when he made it, came fast and the power of the man sent a shock through Firth's sword and into his arm.

He leapt backwards and thrust the sword forward. It hit nothing, but was enough to momentarily check his assailant.

A second lunge passed close to the face of the man, who countered with a wild swing. The cobblestones made the footing uncertain, but Firth maintained his balance as he avoided the blow. A third sailor, moving around the side, drew his wooden club and waited.

The leading hand attacked again, grunting with each effort.

He must weigh 18 stone, thought Firth, as he again found himself forced backwards. A cry of pain sounded to his left, but the continuing clashing of swords told him that it was not Brook who was injured.

"Come on whelp," the sailor panted, "I'm going to geld you," and laid on with renewed vigour.

In a way, Firth thought, it was just like practice. Just keep your feet, watch for openings and stay out of reach.

His sword ranged out again slicing through the sailor's baggy checked shirt. Again he avoided a roundhouse swing but, instead of moving backwards, he aimed a short jab at the man's thigh. The blade missed and gave the sailor time to regain balance and attack again.

He charged at Firth, parried a slashing stroke at his head and grabbed the youth's arm. Firth could smell the man's appalling breath and the sweat from his clothes. He knew he was giving away at least six stone in weight and had to move quickly.

Unfortunately, it was not fast enough and the sailor, a veteran of countless gutter fights, brought his forehead down on to Firth's head.

The blow knocked him backwards, the cobbles seemed to move under his feet and he landed in an awkward half crouch with his left leg splayed. The blood from his split eyebrow ran into Firth's right eye and, within an instant, his view filled by the sailor looming over him with his cutlass raised.

"Right you little bastard, you're ...," but he didn't have time to finish the threat as Firth's sword ripped up and through his thigh, slicing easily through the flesh before glancing off bone.

As the man fell screaming a hand grabbed Firth by the shoulder and hauled him upwards.

"Let's get out of here," Brook urged.

The remaining sailors had halted, not sure how to approach the spirited pair. Swords in hand, the friends backed towards the lane leading to the Duke of York.

The sudden appearance of the naval officers blocked that route to relative safety and so they changed direction and headed up the steep hill towards the ruins of the abbey. Running past the two-storey houses, Firth was working out how to avoid another confrontation. He knew it was an offence to resist the Impress Service and, by wounding three of the sailors, the pair had bought themselves serious trouble.

The ruins would offer them some chance of escaping detection, but their hunters would outnumber them by at least three to one. The small church and graveyard on their left meant the abbey was close, but so were their pursuers.

Pointing towards the headstones Firth made for a shadowy area at the base of the square church tower.

"It's not a bad place to hide," Brook agreed, patting the stone wall, "and this'll be good protection for our backs."

"I'd rather they just didn't see us. They'll string us up for a flogging if we're taken."

The crunch of boots from the roadway made the pair shrink closer to the stone.

The sailors halted 60 paces away and two of them were sent to search nearer the abbey. The officers moved among the graves as Ricketts paced in frustration.

"Find those damned boys quickly, sirs, or we'll miss the tide. Find them and tie them, and don't be gentle about it."

He cursed himself for not bringing along his Marines, but redcoats marching in the streets of Whitby would have been too easily spotted and those damned canny Yorkshiremen, sober or drunk, would have quickly melted from a naval party that screamed Press Gang."

"Mr Walker! Stop chatting to Mr Reynolds and check that church," Ricketts bellowed. "I'm damn sick of your dallying. Are you moonstruck sir? Does the thought of forcing these soft townspeople into serving their King and defending our shores offend you? Grow up sir, it's how we keep those bloody Frenchies at bay!"

The chastised officer moved to within 10 paces of where the youths crouched.

"Too many damned shadows," he muttered to himself. "The Captain should let them go ... they'll only jump ship at the first chance."

Walker poked at the base of a gravestone with his sword, brushing aside the long stalks of grass that were sprouting unchecked. Moving again towards the church the officer kept his eyes low, fully expecting at any second to spot the youths sheltering behind the monuments. Closing to within three paces of their haven, his attention was suddenly diverted by the sound of hooves clattering up the steps from the town.

All the naval officers turned towards the approaching horses.

"What now?" Ricketts spat and called for his men to join him and await the riders. From the indistinct outlines they presented, he was sure they were a patrol from the local militia. He had always sneered at men who were prepared to join a volunteer home-defence force but were not made to endure the hardships of overseas duty. Soft men, he thought derisively. Soft men safe with their women and families while others did the King's work. He always got riled by the special status given to the militia who did not have to leave home shores, had their families supported by the district parishes and could prance around in uniforms pretending to be soldiers. These militiamen, Ricketts mused, would not hold up a King's naval officer for long.

There were 12 riders in the patrol, all wearing single-fronted, red jackets with green facings around the collars and cuffs. Unusually for mounted troops, Ricketts thought, they had tall black infantry-style shakos.

Each carried curved, light-cavalry sabres at their sides and a brace of pistols held in saddle buckets.

All the riders sat well in the saddle and all, Ricketts noted, seemed a cut above the usual collection of country yokels.

The gray-haired officer in charge urged his mount forward and halted it next to Ricketts. Both men held each other's gaze for several seconds.

"Good evening, sir. Fine night for it. It's unusual to find Navy men wandering around a church at this time. May I inquire as to your ... business?"

Ricketts straightened. "Sir, I am Captain Jonas Ricketts and I am searching for two deserters from my crew. They are sheltering hereabouts and I wish to return them to my ship. They injured several of my men."

"Yes, we know about your wounded, we came across them in the town. We will help you search as we have an interest in them ourselves."

"That's much appreciated sir, however, my men will manage them. I can assure you of that."

As if to prove the point a shout sounded near the church. The sailors who had been sent to search the abbey were roughly pushing Firth and Brook through the gravestones.

"As you can see, sir, my men can handle them." Ricketts found himself smiling, both at the thought of his success in front of these locals and the punishment he would hand out to the youths who had caused him such inconvenience.

"Bring them here ... quickly now," he called to his men, who responded with a series of hearty shoves, the last of which sent Firth sprawling at Ricketts' feet. The Captain motioned for the sailors to tie the pair.

"I hardly think that is necessary, do you Captain?" the mounted officer asked.

Ricketts turned. "I don't really think that is a concern of yours, sir."

"Well, I'm afraid it is ... sir," the officer stressed the last word in a way that made Ricketts' hackles rise.

This country gent was beginning to rile him. He barely managed to control his anger and tightly asked "And just who are you?"

The man ignored him: "Are you all right lad?" he asked Brook.

"Yes sir."

"And you?" he inquired of Firth.

Ricketts broke in, "This is none of your damn business ... these men are my ..."

"I heard you before Captain, and now I'm listening to the boy. Are you all right lad?" Firth looked up at the man and nodded. "I am. Thank you ... father."

Spinning around Ricketts saw both boys grinning. They were mocking him and the authority of his rank. His own men shifted uneasily, somewhat cowed by the dozen riders around them.

"To answer your question Captain, I am Colonel Denholme Firth of the North Yorkshire Militia. I command the local forces here and take very unkindly to seaborne raids on the local population - particularly by my own side.

"I was told of your presence by one of my fishermen who, unluckily for you, escaped your charming invitation to life in the Navy. I think you should take your men and return to your ship. You will find your wounded have been treated and will be on board by now. You may go ... sir."

Ricketts' eyes blazed at the impudence of the man. How dare he dismiss him like a commoner? Did he not know that one of his brothers was a Member of Parliament, had the ear of influential people. Damn him, he silently screamed. "You will regret this," he threatened the Colonel.

"And you will doubly do so," he shouted at Firth.

Ignoring Ricketts, Colonel Firth looked down at his son. "You had better get back to Clifton Hall. There'll be hell to pay unless I can get a gift to the Duke of York to calm the waters. He does so hate getting offside with the Navy … but I suppose he'll turn a blind eye for a dozen bottles of champagne liberated from Calais just last month. Don't worry Joshua, by the time you get to London all will be well."

The young man responded: "Thank you sir, we'll make you proud of us."

Colonel Firth gave a broad smile and nodded. "Of course you will. But, lad, I think you'll make me even happier by getting back home and getting yourself cleaned up."

Firth agreed. "A good soak in a bath will see me right, father."

"Just remember, Joshua, you are an officer now and people will look up to you. The 29th is a fine regiment and will ..."

He stopped suddenly as a cry came from Ricketts. The Captain had been moving away, but had immediately halted and turned.

"The 29th? He's joining the Worcesters?"

There was a slightly hysterical note in the naval Captain's voice as he put the question. He stood there, hands on hips, threw his head back and sent out a laugh that seemed unnervingly suitable in a graveyard. Then Ricketts looked at Firth.

"We will meet again. Mark me. You will pay for tonight."

And Firth, suddenly chilled, had no doubt at all that he would.

Part One: Smelling the Powder

I

Mondego Bay, Portugal, 1 August, 1808.

The Fortune sat wallowing at anchor like an ageing duck that was too full to swim. Stripe-shirted sailors swarmed over her sides as they ran out lines and winches to speed the off-loading of supplies to the shore.

To Firth it was the most beautiful place he had seen. Standing at the rail of the old merchantman his eyes feasted on miles of golden sands that disappeared over the northern horizon amid a haze of spray thrown up from the large Atlantic breakers.

To the right lay the southern bank of a narrow entrance to the Mondego River that, according to a map he and Brook were looking at, meandered its way past the city of Coimbra. From there it flowed almost up to the border with Spain before turning upon itself like a fishhook. On the north bank he could see a village called Figueira da Foz, a score of fishing smacks, and a small stone fort.

On the deck around them soldiers were relaxing, trying to forget the oppressive heat that stifled the cooling effects of the breeze. Some played cards, others clapped and tapped their feet as lively country tunes were played courtesy of tin-whistles. More men just sat smoking with their backs leaning against their packs.

Firth and Brook were dressed in long-tailed red jackets that had the yellow facings of the 29th Regiment on the collars and cuffs. A silver-braided yellow epaulette on their right shoulders showed their rank as lieutenant. Their breeches were white and each had black, knee-length boots with brown fold-down tops.

"Well, Joshua, your dream has come true … you're overseas and wearing a red coat."

"Yes," Firth smiled at his friend and nodded. He had long thought about donning a uniform and now he had achieved it. Persuading his father had not been easy, but Firth had a stubborn streak that made him almost impossible to move from his chosen course once he'd made up his mind.

It had taken a while, but eventually Denholme Firth had relented. He had seen his son's dedication at sword practice. He would wield the weapons for hours each week and then, when his young muscles could take no more, would retire to the manor's library where he read histories on Julius Caesar, Hannibal and Frederick the Great.

"It's hard to believe, isn't it Joshua? And we're lieutenants too!"

"Well," said Firth, "That was our luck and the misfortune of others."

"How?" asked Brook.

"We should really have been ensigns. Horse Guards – the body that runs the Army - has just introduced a regulation forcing new officers to spend two years as ensigns before being promoted to lieutenant. But just before my father looked at buying our ensign commissions two lieutenants drowned and so their places were available and he bought them."

"Oh," said Brook.

"As I said, our luck and someone else's misfortune ..."

Brook changed the subject. "I wonder what sights and adventures we'll see?"

"I don't know, Sam, but if you jump up and down any harder you'll capsize us."

Brook stopped and looked at Firth: "Go on, you're excited too ... aren't you?"

"I am that, Sam, I am that," he laughed.

"But not as excited as you were after you met that girl in Portsmouth. What was her name again?"

"Constance."

"Yes Constance. She was beautiful. But a bit thin for me."

"She was full in all the right places from what I saw, Sam, and those eyes ... I've never seen such a green colour."

"I didn't look at her eyes much."

Firth laughed. Sam was more interested in other parts and would point out buxom women whenever he saw them.

"I think she eventually took a bit of a shine to you Joshua, after that - how can I put it - rather unfortunate meeting."

Firth flushed. "All right, all right don't keep reminding me. It wasn't my fault she wasn't watching where she was going."

"She wasn't watching? Lord, Joshua, you were ogling that preacher's wife and you walked straight into the poor girl. Knocked her parcels everywhere."

"Oh shut up, Samuel Brook, I apologised."

"Yes you really did knock her off her feet, didn't you?"

"Sam ..." Firth said with a rising note of annoyance.

"Okay, okay ... but it ended well didn't it."

Firth silently agreed. After helping her to stand and picking up her packages he had managed to elicit a smile from Constance that almost took his breath away. He would never forget those luminescent eyes.

Firth was brought back to the moment by Royal Marines noisily climbing down the side of the ship and into two longboats. The boats were moving vigorously with the swell that surged several feet up the side of the Fortune dousing their occupants with white spray. The Marines were sitting silently, their musket flashpads safely wrapped in oiled cloths to keep them dry. Agile sailors, standing at each end of the tossing boats, held on to the rope netting that had been slung over the rail of the transport to allow easy access to the boats. Others were using oars to keep the smaller vessels from smashing into the solid-oak planking that towered above them. A Royal Marines captain was steadily negotiating the net down to his men when Firth yelled down to him.

"Don't suppose we could join you? Our regiment doesn't arrive until the second flotilla and we're ... well ... somewhat at a loss."

The Captain looked up and gave a wave. "Glad to have you. The more the merrier, eh?"

"Watch yourselves," the Captain called, "you've no idea how many people have ended up in the water. Keep your sword scabbards pointing out otherwise we'll be pulling you from the drink."

Firth and Brook did as advised and, as they neared the water level, they turned side on and waited for the lead longboat to begin its rise on the wave before stepping in. Settling in beside their host, Firth nodded to him and held out his hand.

"Joshua Firth, the 29th. This is Samuel Brook."

"Charmed, I'm Wren, Christopher Wren ... and yes, he was a relative. My great-great grandfather's third cousin twice removed four times, or something like that. I don't design buildings, but I do sketch a bit. Not too bad at it if I say so myself," he said, smiling, and then turned his attention to shore.

"My job is to secure that fort, such as it is. See the black flag, that belongs to a bedraggle of students from the university of Coimbra who have taken it upon themselves to rid the area of the Frogs. Damn silly idea, but they did it, or so they say. Surprised the garrison, took over and here we are ... off to check it out."

"How many French?" asked Firth.

"Not sure, but 30 Marines should be able to deal with them. My men are itching for a scrap ... been on the boats too long. Who are you with again? The 29th? Well, they've been floating about as well. Round and round the Mediterranean since late last year. When do they arrive?"

"We don't know. Sam and I joined up after they left for Sicily and, according to the Fortune's captain, they're just about to leave Cadiz and are due here soon," answered Firth.

Nodding, Wren looked back towards the shore. The boats were about to enter the entrance to the estuary and were quickly being picked up by the confused currents created by the clash of sea and river. Calmer water lay closer to shore and the sailors strained to pull the heavy longboats free from the water's grasp and towards the fort. Brook handed Firth his telescope and pointed to the walls of the brown-stone strongpoint. "There's a few men with muskets on the ramparts ... but no uniforms I can recognise."

"French or Portuguese?"

"Don't know, but they're dressed in brown ... not French blue."

Firth focused his eye through the 'scope and selected two figures to study. Both had red-brown jackets with white crossbelts and their hats were black with the left side pinned at right angles. "Could be the students. What do you think Captain?"

"Whoever they are we're vulnerable until we secure our landing area so we will be treating them as the enemy until we know differently," Wren said decisively.

"We'll advance off the shore in skirmish order. That will give them less of a target if they are to play dirty. We'll move double quick to the fort and then see what's up."

Despite the heat, the sweating faces of the rowing sailors were unchanging as the speed of the longboats picked up though the estuary. Under the watchful gaze of a hard-looking sergeant, the Marines unwrapped the cloths from their muskets and attached 18-inch, triangular-bladed bayonets. Firth noted not one of them looked nervous, all sat expressionless, concentrating on the job at hand.

As the longboats moved into the shallows two sailors from each prow jumped into the water helping to drag the vessels ashore. Wren's boat touched first and his Marines fanned out. The second landed and the men formed around their officer.

"Sergeant Henly, move the men off. No shooting unless fired upon. And keep your eyes open."

The Sergeant repeated the order and the landing party quickly headed off the sands and towards its objective.

Moving to the walls Firth could hear the sentries shouting down to the courtyard.

Ahead of them was the fort's main gate.

Standing the height of two men the wooden planks of the double gates were well-weathered and strengthened with sheets of iron. Firing holes had recently been added on both sides of the entry way and Firth thought how lucky the students had been to have caught the French unawares.

If they had tried to storm the building, against even a small body of prepared troops, he guessed they would have lost many men.

The gates began to swing back and Wren ordered a halt.

From out of the darkness of the gateway came six men who, despite their moustaches and unshaven faces, walked with the confident air and grace of gentlemen. They all wore red-brown jackets and breeches, which were tucked into grey socks that rose above brown gaiters. Each carried a musket slung across their right shoulder with the barrel pointing down.

The group moved to the English officers and one man, smiling broadly, strode forward. His hair, which was tied in a tail, fell below his shoulders and the warmth of his smile almost took one's notice away from a badly scarred face that was the legacy of smallpox.

"English, welcome English. I am Bernardo Zagalo and would like to present Fort Figueira to you."

Wren nodded: "Thank you, to both you and your men. I'm Captain Wren of the Royal Marines and this is Lieutenant Firth and Lieutenant Brook. I have the honour of accepting it on behalf of His Majesty George III, although I have to ask Senhor Zagalo, how did you manage to take this place?"

"It was easy, English. We the students of Coimbra, decided to strike a blow against the French invaders. One hundred of us arrived here last night as the French were sleeping. They had few guards, we were many. It was easy."

"Where are the French now, Senhor Zagalo?" Wren asked.

"They are dealt with ... come with me."

Firth moved next to Zagalo as the British and Portuguese moved into the fort. "Your English is very good, Senhor Zagalo. Where did you learn it so well?"

"Coimbra, of course. Its university has a long and fine reputation for languages. Spanish, Latin, English and that cursed French. But come, the invaders are this way. We have put them in their own barracks," he said again, flashing white teeth.

Zagalo spoke as he led the way across the dirt courtyard to the largest building in the fortifications. "These barracks were designed 500 years ago as the last refuge against attack from pirates. It was formidable against swords and arrows, but is not so strong against cannons."

Entering the dim shadows of the cool interior Firth's eyes took a few seconds to adjust to the different light. He and Brook followed Zagalo as he moved to a score of French soldiers talking at tables. Firth noted that four showed signs of wounds, two of them with head bandages, the others with bruised faces and surmised they would have been the unfortunate men on guard at the time the students arrived.

The French looked calm, all were awaiting the arrival of the British and the chance to be paroled home. Looking at the prisoners Firth was surprised at their age. He had expected the enemy to be the grizzled veterans who had overrun most of Europe, but only two looked older than he was. An officer and a sergeant stood out by the heavy growth on their faces.

The soldiers rose as Zagalo approached and smiled, a little tentatively, at the newcomers. Zagalo motioned them down with his hand and turned to Firth and Brook.

"These men are from the 32nd line regiment belonging to General Loisin. He is currently burning his way across the land east of here. He has been trying to put down disturbances in our north ever since your countrymen reinforced the Spaniards at Cadiz.

"He has not had a lot of success. He is a proud man and is not happy with being made to look foolish in front of his commander, General Junot.

"And he has not spared the rod - I think that is one of your sayings, is it not? - on our people. Many homes have been burned and village crops stolen, but still he cannot claim to control the area."

Turning to the blue-coated French, Zagalo said: "There have been reports of women being violated and killed, but these men are not responsible. We have been watching them at this place for some time and they have done nothing, so we will send them to your England and your prisons."

"Once the landing has been completed these prisoners can be moved to the ships," Wren said.

Firth hoped prisons didn't mean the awful hulks that dotted England's shores. He had heard tales of the old, unseaworthy ships that were towed into swamps and permanently anchored as floating jails for enemy soldiers. The conditions were appalling and slow decay into death was likely.

"Senhor Zagalo ..." Firth began.

"Bernardo please, Lieutenant," Zagalo said. "I would be on friendly terms with you all."

"Thank you, Bernardo, how close is the main body of French?"

"General Delaborde is to the south with about 5000 men and to the east is Loisin, he has 9000 troops. I do not know how far away he is now."

"Cavalry?"

"There is not much with the generals, but there are large patrols out in the countryside. Often up to 200 men. They search areas very quickly and hope to catch our people by surprise. They are very good soldiers."

"Artillery?" Firth asked.

"Yes, they have cannons - the tyrant Napoleon's favourite toys."

"Bernardo," Wren interjected, "with your permission I'd like to have my men prepare the fort in case the French arrive. This place will be very important should they get here before we've fully disembarked."

Zagalo looked quizzical.

"I mean before we have fully got off the ships and on to shore."

The student nodded and smiled. "Ah, your vernac ... alar confused me."

"Sorry, Bernardo, our vernacular even puzzles many Englishmen. But if the French attack us while we are coming ashore then we will be at a severe disadvantage. We may not even be able to remain here."

"I take it more of your men will be here soon?"

"Yes, I'm to report back to my ship and we'll have 100 Marines here in no time. That means very soon. They'll stop any Frogs. Ah, French that is."

Firth broke in. "Well, Brook and I will stay and watch the landings, if you don't mind. Maybe we could be of some help here."

"Fine by me," Wren said. "I'll leave a sergeant to organise this place. Well, better be going. Gentlemen," he bid farewell, smiling, and walked towards the doors.

Turning to Zagalo, Firth said: "What will you do now, Bernardo?"

Taking two cups of red wine from the table, the Portuguese offered them to the young officers who happily took them. "My men and I were planning to return to Coimbra, but we may ride south for a day before we do. We have lost a great many messengers to French cavalry and our reports are not as recent as we would like. "Delaborde and Loisin are on the march and if we locate them that would be good for you British, would it not?"

Firth and Brook nodded and quickly finished their cups - the light-red liquid was cool and refreshing with a slight hint of pepper - and they were pleased to accept a second from their host.

"It is good yes," Zagalo beamed, "Douro Clarete from near Oporto. Very fine."

Neither of the pair disagreed and so a third round was served. Perhaps it was the wine, or maybe the chance of adventure, but Firth could not pass up the opportunity to see a bit more of the country before his regimental duties began.

"Bernardo, perhaps we could join you. Only for a day, just until our regiment arrives. What do you think, Sam?"

"Good idea. But we'll need horses, ours are on the transport."

"But we have horses for you," Zagalo broke in. "There are many French ones here. Good beasts too. I've had my eyes on a couple for myself. Come," he said standing, "let us see them."

Firth and Brook followed the student out into the courtyard. Their boots crunched over the stony ground leading to the stables where a group of students was noisily appraising the quality of the French mounts. Zagalo moved to a pair of beautiful long-tailed grey mares that were busily eating hay from feeding boxes near the stalls.

"Magnificent are they not? And they are yours. They were due to be given to General Junot, but better ridden by friends than by the French, yes?"

"Most certainly," agreed Brook, "They are lovely animals, Bernardo. But you wanted them did you not?"

"I did, but my family is very rich and I have too many already. Besides, I think they will suit your uniforms better. It is important in my country to have good horses, particularly for officers, it creates a good impression. Maybe one day you can be generous with me."

"We'll have to be generous indeed to match this gift," Brook said.

"Think no more of it," said Zagalo, "There are saddles and bags in the stables, and food is being readied. We will leave in mid-afternoon for a town 30 of your miles south of here called Leiria. We have friends there who will be able to tell us about the French."

With that he strode off towards the main stairway that led on to the ramparts above the gateway, leaving the friends to prepare their mounts.

"Must have been a cavalry unit here recently," Firth said as he indicated towards a score or so saddles and bridles along the longest wall of the building. "You've got to say the French certainly have style. Look at those."

Brook looked past Firth outstretched finger to a row of white horse-cloths with red shark's-tooth edging hanging on pegs. Taking one of the shabraques each they fitted white sheepskins over them and finally the black cavalry saddles. Being good horsemen, Firth and Brook then adjusted the stirrups and reins to suit the way they preferred to ride.

Ten minutes later they walked the animals to a rail near the barracks and set off to find Zagalo. One of his men pointed out his position and they climbed the stairs to the top of the low walls. The sight was spectacular.

Out to sea sat six yellow-and-black hulled Royal Navy warships that guarded the score or so transports. The merchantmen were buzzing with activity and longboats plied a regular convoy of soldiers and supplies to the beach.

It was chaos on the shore as troops rescued comrades from the waves as longboats overturned in the surf, or settled down to cups of tea made by the select few women allowed to join their husbands on foreign shores. The artillery had not yet been moved, but Firth could see the preparations for its landing going on the nearest ship.

"There are a lot of men, English. A lot of men."

"Yes, Bernardo, 10,000 of them, and more to come. We'll teach Bonaparte a lesson."

"Many have tried, English, many have tried," Zagalo sighed. "But, maybe, this time it will happen," he added. "Now, my men are ready so we should go."

Taking a last look at the beach Firth glanced at Brook. Was it wise to go? Probably not, he thought, but the chance was too good to pass up and they did not officially begin their duties until the 29th arrived. The reasoning seemed good - to him.

"Ready?" he asked Brook.

"Lead on, my friend," came the reply.

II

Lavilho, 1 August.

Captain Hippolyte Rey was in a foul mood. It had begun 12 hours earlier when he had been woken just after midnight to deliver an urgent order to General Loisin.
Keen to show he was ever willing to do his duty for Emperor Napoleon Bonaparte he'd smiled at the aide who delivered the leather satchel and had hurriedly dressed.
Within half an hour he was galloping north through the cool Portuguese night.
Now he was stomping about a small village waiting for a dullard of a Polish major to point him in the direction of "Old One-hand", General Louis Loisin.
Despite his anger Rey was more than a little wary of the Major. He had a look about him that indicated he was not a man to be crossed. Rey tripped mid-stomp, causing another waft of dust to cover his once immaculately shiny boots.
"Damn dust," he cursed, "and damned country. Who wants it?" Unfortunately for Rey, who loved the society balls of Paris, his Emperor wanted Portugal. Rey didn't care that the country was Britain's main entry point to a Europe dominated by France. Or that Portugal was one of the few nations to defy an imperial order and continue trade with the English. But the Emperor did and so he was here.
Rey remembered nine months earlier, when he and 20,000 Frenchmen had marched across the Pyrenees, through Spain and then into Portugal, leaving behind the glitter and conversation of their capital to silence a nation of superstitious peasants and bring them to heel.
It had been an easy task. General Jean Andoche Junot had marched straight for Lisbon, the only city worth a sou in the country, and had captured it with just 1500 men. Rey had been one of those soldiers who had arrived exhausted, but triumphant, and had ridden through Lisbon to "arrest the government and claim the land back for the Portuguese people".
The French discovered they had only just missed capturing the fleeing Portuguese royal family and Rey had watched from the docks as the king and queen sailed down the Tagus River towards the Atlantic Ocean and the safety of the distant-but-wealthy shores of the colony of Brazil.
Since then, Rey thought, it had been a fairly pleasant life in Lisbon with plenty of noblewomen eager for the company of dashing officers in elegant uniforms.
Even the wine was good, although it could not compare with the subtleties of France's sublime vintages. Yes, life had been acceptable in Portugal … until the past few months.
Rumours of an imminent British landing had been whispered around the countryside and many peasants ignored French decrees and refused to pay taxes.
In the north, open hostility had been shown to the Emperor's soldiers and when Loisin went to restore order the minor disturbances turned into a small revolt.
There had been several incidents that Rey knew of where things had got out of hand and the French, infuriated by the murder of lone soldiers by peasants, had begun

reprisals against villages.

It began as looting but, as casualties mounted, the army decided to put entire villages to the torch. That, in turn, had provoked the population into more assassinations and the soldiery into heightened violence. Rey stopped and shook his head, now the troubles were here.

Only yesterday he had been forced to abandon his own escort of 20 troopers as they had fought off a large group of ambushers and he was now keen to quickly deliver his papers and return south to the relative safety of Lisbon.

The hamlet of Lavilho was located in an expanse of luxurious, ancient olive groves that appeared to have been lovingly tended.

A finger-tip taste indicated to Rey that the oil was of very high quality and the locals had obviously grown rich on the proceeds. He could see the wealth of the place in the unusually good condition of the white-washed buildings, the clean water sprinkling from an elegant fountain in the square and the wandering herds of fat goats. The sky was a deep blue with only a few small wisps of cloud floating serenely by. It was going to be another beautiful day, Rey thought, and the villagers would no doubt have been preparing to tend trees and animals at a leisurely pace with barely a care in the world.

But that had been before Major Stanislaus Zapalski arrived with his 200 Polish cavalrymen.

Rey had met the Poles earlier in the morning and had joined them on their ride towards Loisin's base. Four of their number had gone missing while the others slept near Lavilho. A search had found the men two miles away.

They had been tied to trees and their throats had been so deeply slashed that the weight of their heads had almost ripped them free from the necks.

Great pools of blood had dried at their feet.

Worst of all, their eyes had been picked out by large crows that had flown from the bodies as the cavalry rode up.

The discovery enraged the Poles who swore revenge against those who had so basely killed men of the Vistula Legion. Their reaction was such that Zapalski did not need to urge speed from his men as they cut their comrades down and buried them.

The villagers of Lavilho had only just finished their midday meals as the blue-coated Poles, distinguished by their square-topped czapka helmets, arrived.

Two troops of men remained mounted while the rest proceeded to round up villagers on foot. Using the hilts of their swords to hammer on doors, the cavalrymen forced their way inside houses and manhandled the occupants into the square.

Mothers tried to comfort crying children and the men walked as bravely as they could between their women and the soldiers.

Once in the square they were herded together.

Zapalski paced in front of the Portuguese until the entire population was within earshot.

Knowing the people in front of him could not possibly understand his native tongue, the major began in Latin – the language of priests - they'd surely know that.

"What is the name of this place?"

It was a phrase that the inhabitants had learned to fear over the past few months and no-one wanted to respond. Better not to stand out when these Frenchmen were clearly upset about something.

"What is the name of this village?" Zapalski asked again.

The villagers remained silent and continued to look at the ground. The only sounds in the square were sobs from children whose mothers held them in closer to their bodies.

"I will ask again, what is the name of this place?"

The blond Major waited for 30 seconds staring into the crowd. His eyes fixed on a grandfather at the front and he smiled at him. It was a charming smile, one that could put nervous people at ease and entrance women. It was open and warm, but did nothing to thaw the coolness of his blue eyes.

"Old friend,'' Zapalski gestured to the man, "Come here."

The villager reluctantly moved forward, his unsteady gait kept his movements slow. Stopping in front of the officer he bowed his head. "Senhor?"

"Does anyone here speak French well, old friend?"

The man nodded, three of his nephews were students at Coimbra and one had just returned to help in the groves.

"My nephew, he understands."

From out of the crowd a short young man moved tentatively. He crossed to his uncle and touched his shoulder.

"I speak French, sir."

The Major nodded. "Good, translate for me."

"What is the name of this village, old friend?"

"It is Lavilho, excellency," the old man responded.

"Lavilho. It is lovely. You are lucky people to live in such a place."

As Zapalski spoke the man nodded and tried to avoid looking at the Major's face.

"People of Lavilho, you have a problem," the Pole announced. "Last night four of my soldiers were killed and their belongings were stolen.

"I want to know who committed such acts and, because you are the closest village, you are the suspects."

The Pole waited for the translation and watched the faces carefully as they digested his words. The ones he examined showed surprise at the mention of murder and then fear began to creep over their features.

"I want those responsible to either come forward, or be brought forward. If this does not happen then Lavilho will suffer."

"Senhor," the student said, "We know nothing of what you talk about. This is a village that does not care about politics. All we do is make oil. You are welcome here."

Zapalski turned to one of his lieutenants and issued an order for the village to be searched. "Welcome we may be … now," he said through the interpreter, "but last night is a different matter."

"Sir, you will find nothing to condemn us."

"I hope for your sake, that we don't."

For more than an hour the troopers searched. Every home was turned upside down, but nothing incriminating was found. The heat of the day had peaked and several elderly people left standing in the shimmering glare found it too much and fainted. Children cried as their thirst mounted and even the soldiers on guard were irritated by the length of the search.

Rey thought it obvious that the village had done nothing, otherwise some evidence would have been found long ago. Still, the Major was sure they were guilty and that was enough.

Rey walked over to Zapalski. "It seems, Major, that the villagers may have been telling the truth. There is nothing here to show they killed your men."

"That may be, Captain, but I am not convinced."

As Rey was about to make a further point shouts came from a group of soldiers inside the village church. They had found a hidden vault under the wooden altar and when they emerged a sergeant carried four cavalry carbines to the officers.

Zapalski picked up one of the short-range firearms and turned it around. An imperial symbol was pressed into the side of the barrel along with the inscription "Vistula Legion." It belonged to his men.

A growl went up from the Poles. To die in battle against soldiers was one thing, but to be murdered by villagers was intolerable.

Zapalski held his arm up and the murmuring stopped.

"How do you explain these then, translator?''

The student quailed. His face had gone white under his tan and his hands shook. "I cannot, sir."

"And you, old friend," he said to the uncle. "Can you?"

The grey-haired man looked straight into the major's face. Gone was the feigned subservience and his eyes were bright and defiant. "Brigands left them here to hide. We did not have anything to do with the deaths of your men."

"I do not believe you, old friend."

"Believe what you will, Frenchman."

When it came the speed of the blow surprised everyone.

Zapalski's right hand snapped across the villager's face knocking him to the ground. The muscular officer then bent and dragged the man up. He smiled as he straightened the old man and then struck again. The slap staggered the man and blood began to pour from the left side of his mouth.

"I asked you about the carbines ... answer me."

"I have nothing to say."

Zapalski stood back. "Sergeant, I want a gallows here, four metres high ... and four barrels of oil."

The old soldier nodded and moved off taking a squad of troopers with him. It took them fewer than 10 minutes to dig in the side posts and tie on a four-metre cross beam. The Sergeant then ordered eight men to roll the large casks into position. When four ropes were thrown over the bar above the barrels Zapalski turned to the crowd.

"France finds this village guilty of rebellion and murder," he said coldly. "Four of you will die for the deaths of my men. Begin Sergeant."

While a troop of cavalrymen separated off the crying women and children, scores more moved in to seize all males who looked old enough to carry guns. They slapped and pushed them until the men faced the crude structure.

Four young men were then selected and dragged, struggling, towards the nooses.

Rey was confused, he understood the need to execute murderers - once they had been legally tried - but he did not consider this legal. And why had the tops from the oil casks been opened? How would they support a man before being pushed from under his feet as a make-do trapdoor?

He moved to Zapalski's side.

"Major, I must protest. These men may not be guilty, they should be given a chance to defend themselves."

Zapalski looked at the expensively uniformed Rey and curtly said: "Listen messenger, don't question a fighting officer. These people have killed my men. After today they will think carefully before murdering any more real soldiers."

The Major had spat the word fighting out. He was sick of overdressed poppenjays in the Emperor's armies.

Rey bridled. "Sir, I will point out that I fought at Austerlitz and after Auerstadt was promoted by Marshal Davout himself. I have seen as much fighting as you and would urge you to reconsider these actions. This is not the way to win over a people."

"Neither is by being killed by them, Captain."

But Zapalski's voice had softened a little. Being promoted by Davout was praise indeed, particularly at Auerstadt where 26,000 Frenchmen had routed 70,000 Prussians.

"There is only one way to deal with these peasants and that is fear. Fear, or terror. Continue Sergeant."

The Poles moved quickly to tie the nooses around the feet of the prisoners. They were then hoisted over the barrels before slowly being lowered.

The eyes of the youths were bulging with fear and each was crying out for help. One had wet himself and the urine poured down his stomach and chest. As the tips of their heads dipped into the oil all four let out soul-wrenching screams.

A moan rose up from the villagers, but the troopers held their charges tightly, giving them no chance of acting. The screams of the dangling men were replaced by splutters as the cold oil covered their eyes and ran into their upturned noses. Their mouths contorted as they desperately tried for a last breath before their heads were fully immersed.

Rey looked away as the suspended bodies struggled futilely against the inevitable.

By now all the youths had soiled themselves and the thick, clear oil began to froth and slop over the sides as their heads frantically moved from side to side.

It took more than a minute for the last one to stop moving – an eternity for the horrified villagers.

Zapalski was carefully watching their reactions and when he was sure terror had overtaken them he spoke again.

"In case you didn't learn from that there is another lesson we want to teach you. No Portuguese will raise his hand against France without punishment. Continue Sergeant."

The male inhabitants were too numbed to react as the Poles pushed them to the top steps leading to the church and then on to their knees.

The nearest one was dragged forward and a cord was wrapped around the fleshy part of his right hand. A squatting trooper pulled the cord back and the villager's arm was stretched out, his wrist taut.

Bewildered, the man looked wildly around at his neighbours and did not see the axe fall. He screamed in disbelief after the blade had severed his hand and fainted as blood spewed freely from the stump.

A Pole used a red-hot scythe blade to seal the wound.

The smell of burning meat soured Rey's stomach.

The next Portuguese was quickly thrown forward and the axe bit again.

More screams, more burning flesh.

Three men broke free but were expertly killed with single sabre thrusts. Rey rode out of the village after the third hand had fallen. He was sickened by what he had seen. It was not war.

Behind him the maimings continued late into the afternoon and by late afternoon 80 fly-encrusted hands were piled on the steps. Many of their former owners would die from shock or infection, but the Poles carefully bandaged the cauterised wounds. The punishment would be far less effective if the victims died, better they lived long lives and every day remembered the vengeance of France.

The only man in the village who was not maimed was the defiant old grandfather. Zapalski had told him the burden of being the only able bodied man in the area would add to his punishment.

When their task was over the Poles set fire to each building in the village, with the exception of the church. Zapalski had ordered that to be left alone. The drying pools of blood that stained its white steps also would remind the villagers. They left Lavilho as the sun was setting, their saddlebags filled with food and wine. They would find a campsite away from the smells of the village and eat. They had built up quite a hunger.

III

South of Leiria, 3 August

Firth rolled over on to his side and spoke in quiet tones to Brook and Zagalo who were crouching just behind him.

"He's not far away."

Through Brook's telescope Firth had been watching the rider's approach for the past half-hour. The man had kept his horse to a walk along the road that wound beside a slow-moving stream and was now only 500 yards from where the group hid. He appeared preoccupied and, despite the perfect weather and pretty scenery, clearly was not taking much interest in his surroundings.

Beautiful uniform, Firth thought as he inspected the enemy's green clothing in detail. Firth guessed by the amount of gold lace on his uniform that the Frenchman was an officer in the Chasseurs a Cheval.

So this was one of Bonaparte's elite, Firth mused. Well even the best can be caught by surprise.

He had suggested to Zagalo that the spot in which they lay was a good place to waylay the rider. Splitting the party in two, he placed Zagalo and six men on the lower side of the road while he, Brook, and the rest of the Portuguese concealed themselves in the rocky bank above. The group's horses were being tended by three students 50 paces behind Firth.

It hadn't taken long for the two young officers to name the horses given to them by Zagalo. The decisions were made while at dinner in Leiria, where the inhabitants got their first look at their new British allies and offered a marvelous feast in celebration of the landing at Mondego Bay. It was after endless rounds of toasts that the pair had selected the appropriate names.

Brook had taken a fancy to Ghost, while Firth had called his Ricketts, after the Navy Captain in Whitby.

"But you can't," Brook had objected, "She's a mare."

"Well, so was Ricketts after my father had finished with him," Firth had laughed.

Smiling at the memory, Firth readied himself. The Frenchman was now only 200 paces off and the waiting men tensed as the sounds of hooves got louder.

The first thing Rey knew of the danger was when a tall red-coated figure stood to his right and shouted an order in French. He had been busy thinking about the Portuguese village and the nightmares that had woken him the previous night. He jumped at the sudden movement and flash of colour, but his training had him preparing to spur his horse forward when he was surrounded by men armed with muskets. As barrels pushed at his chest and back, Rey shrugged and nodded towards the redcoat. "Parole, m'sieu."

Firth jumped down and walked to the mounted man. His French was basic, but he hoped he could make himself understood. "You are our prisoner, sir. Do you give your word not to try to escape?"

"Yes, m'sieu. Parole."

By giving that promise, Rey knew he could keep his sword and would be well treated by his captors until an exchange with an officer of equal rank could be arranged. However, honour now demanded that he not try to escape - it was unworthy.

Rey's mind worked quickly as he tried to work out who his captors were. There were now two officers in red beside him and the uniforms were definitely not Portuguese. Their bicorne hats had no badges, but the officers' gold gorgets, which hung loosely from their necks, featured a crowned wreath surrounding a standing lion. The initials GR stood out. George Rex, Rey thought - these men were English! Their faces were pale, but touches of sunburn meant they had not long been in hot weather.

So, France's old enemy had finally arrived. He looked at the officer who had first appeared near him. "I am Captain Hippolyte Rey, m'sieu, and I must say I regret to make your acquaintance."

"My name is Lieutenant Joshua Firth and the pleasure is all mine, sir. Would you be kind enough to hand over your dispatches."

Grudgingly Rey slipped the black-leather strap from around his neck and handed over the gold-embossed courier bag to Firth.

"Where were you travelling to, Captain?"

"I was heading north monsieur, towards Coimbra."

"To meet with General Loisin?"

Avoiding a direct answer, Rey said: "I was travelling north."

"Well, we're heading that way ourselves so we can escort you."

"I am most grateful," the Frenchman said through clenched teeth.

As the horses were brought down to the roadside Zagalo fell in to the left of the Frenchman while Firth sat to his right. For the next few hours the party remained silent. Rey was furious with himself for being so stupid as to be captured and neither Firth nor Zagalo wanted to intrude upon his obvious embarrassment.

Firth spent his time surveying the countryside south of Leiria. It was fertile and the Portuguese appeared to be farming it well. The steep hills were dotted with olive groves and orchards that had been planted on terraces to take advantage of the best land. Water was drawn up by the ridge-top windmills and channeled through crude clay pipes into the trees and crops. Here and there flocks of brown chickens noisily flapped and jumped, while in the shade of the trees the riders could see bored goat herders lazily sitting in the early-afternoon heat.

It was good for farmers, Firth noted, but tough country for soldiers. There was plenty of food, but the roads were poor and men on the march would quickly slow as tired legs forced their way up yet another series of hills. The well-treed ridges and rocky outcrops added to a soldier's troubles as they provided good cover for enemy troops.

Firth remembered listening to one of his father's servants, an old regular soldier, who would indulge a young boy with tales of war as he pottered about the gardens. His stained, broken teeth would show as he smiled at the memories of his own youth in the Indian Wars against France. Badgered to distraction by the 10-year-old, the groundsman would sit down, wipe his bald head and talk about soldiering.

"Keep your eyes open," he would say, "Watch for places where soldiers can hide." The young Firth would then try out his ambushes on unwary birds and rabbits in the sprawling woods next to his father's home. The old man's yarns sparked Firth's interest in the army and led to him spending many a day on his bed reading accounts of long-ago wars.

Firth smiled at the memories and tucked into a hasty lunch in Leiria with gusto. On the final leg back to Figueira, their French captive was in a more talkative mood and, much to Firth's relief, spoke remarkably good English.

He had been in Napoleon's army for five years and had crossed swords with soldiers from the biggest empires in Europe during some of the bloodiest battles ever fought on the Continent.

He had been at Austerlitz three years before when Napoleon Bonaparte had lured the Austrians and Russians into a trap and had annihilated them. Rey told them he had been with Marshal Davout's III Corps and they could hear pride in his voice as he talked of men who rivalled the famed Imperial Guard.

He told of the sickening pace of a 70-mile march from Vienna to Austerlitz – and how III Corps had arrived to bear the brunt of the allied attacks.

"It was brutal fighting," he told Firth, "and many, many good men died."

"What was the worst of it?" Firth inquired.

Rey fell silent for a moment as if wondering whether to go on. Then he steeled himself and spoke.

"The enemy began to retreat across a frozen lake called the Saatchen – it was their only hope of escape. Marshal Davout ordered our army's guns to smash the ice from under them to make sure none escaped."

"And what happened?"

"He succeeded ... few escaped. We heard the cracks of the ice over the sound of our cannons and saw whole artillery teams just sink instantly without a trace. Perhaps they were the lucky ones as many who fell into the water and managed to get out froze to death over the next few hours."

"My God," Zagalo whispered.

"I think more than 5000 men drowned."

Firth could not quite believe what he was hearing. "You drowned those men? Five thousand of them?"

"Maybe more, lieutenant. It was terrible, but war is war," Rey said.

"But so many ..."

"Do you think, lieutenant, that they would have behaved differently? They want to destroy us. We have been fighting the Russians, Austrians and Prussians for 16 years. You English have rules of war that are fine when you sit on the sidelines. How will you be in five years, will you have the same standards?"

Firth couldn't answer that. It was true that Britain could afford such gentlemanly notions because Admiral Horatio Nelson had smashed the French and Spanish navies at Trafalgar three years earlier and since then there was no threat to home shores. But if Britain were landlocked with hostile neighbours always plotting to destroy it would we be as squeamish? Probably not, thought Firth.

"You may be right, Captain," he conceded, "But I like to think not."

The flat countryside and the good roads north of Leiria allowed them to move more rapidly towards the north-west and Figueira. Ten miles short of the Mondego River the riders saw a column of cavalry kicking up dust as it cantered south.

Again borrowing Brook's telescope, and yet again promising his friend he would buy his own at the first opportunity, Firth studied the horsemen. It was a troop of light cavalry, about 90 men, but he could not be sure whose side they belonged to. They had indistinctive blue jackets, but did seem to be wearing the British black-fur crested Tarleton helmets. Another clue for Firth was that the horses' tails were docked short. "They're ours," he said confidently.

The commander of the patrol saw the group of horsemen to his south and ordered his unit to close. The cavalry covered the distance in short time and then eased down to a walk as they approached the party. The elegantly dressed colonel with an orange turban wound around the base of his black leather Tarleton urged his mount forward with a slight movement of his legs and stopped in front of Firth. He was a fine-featured man in his mid-30s, Firth estimated, with a shock of prematurely greying hair and side whiskers.

"Strange place to find British officers, sir," he commented. "You are?"

"Lieutenants Firth and Brook of the 29th, sir," he told the Colonel.

"The 29th?" the officer queried. "They haven't arrived yet. How is it that you are riding around the Portuguese countryside?"

"We arrived on the Fortune, sir, and joined the Marine landing at Figueria where we met Bernardo Zagalo," he said indicating towards the student, "who had captured the fort from the French."

"You have papers?"

"We do, sir."

"I'll see them later. I'm Colonel Charles Taylor of the 20th Light Dragoons and I have to say I find this most irregular."

Suddenly noticing Rey's uniform he exclaimed: "Good God, is that a Frenchman?"

Firth shifted in his saddle, "Yes, sir, this is Captain Rey of the Chasseurs a Cheval. We captured him just south of Leiria. He has dispatches for General Loisin."

"You captured him?"

"Well, we caught him by surprise sir. I'm not sure he was expecting us in the area," Firth said modestly.

Quickly looking through the papers Taylor said: "You seem to have done well, Lieutenant. We'd better get these to headquarters as quickly as possible."

"Yes sir."

"Tell me, did you run across any other Frenchies on the way?"

"No sir, we didn't sight anyone other than the Captain."

"Very well, I'll send a detachment back to Lavaos with you. Sir Arthur Wellesley was moving there yesterday. You'll have to report to his aide-de-camp. What are your names again?"

"Firth, sir, and Brook."

"Well, gentlemen, I wish you well. Cornet Finlay, take care of these men until they reach headquarters."

With a brisk salute, Taylor wheeled his mount and rode off to the south. Finlay and his men took the vanguard and began to move off.

Spurring their horses forward Firth, Brook and Zagalo set off to meet the commander of Britain's army, the man his enemies called the Sepoy General, Sir Arthur Wellesley.

IV

"Horse Guards!" came the bellow. "Bloody, bloody, Horse Guards." The accompanying sound of smashing china, heavy objects hitting walls and more curses reverberated into the corridor. A dozen men in gold-laced jackets shifted nervously while servants scurried past at an unusually rapid rate.

"Benton!" came another roar, followed quickly by an even louder one. "General Benton!"

At the last shout a short, grey-haired officer steadied himself, straightened his uniform and touched his sword hilt.

"Wish me luck, gentlemen," he murmured before making his way towards the dark mahogany doors. He knocked once and then entered.

"This is not going to be a pleasant day," said a cavalry colonel.

"I'd rather face Bonaparte and 30,000 men than go in there," added another.

"Why is Wellesley in such a tiz?"

"Seems he's been promoted over, Sir Harry Burrard is to take over."

"Old Betty? No wonder Nosey's in a vapour."

"So, who's first then?"

The officers looked around and spotted two young candidates standing by the entry. The Colonel took the nods of his fellows as permission and walked across to Firth, his spurs jangling on the tiled floor. "You sirs," he said importantly. "You fellows here to see Sir Arthur?"

Standing to attention Firth said: "Yes sir, General Benton told us to report here."

"Good, good," the Colonel smiled, "Well, you'll be first in. You're not here with bad news are you? Hope for your sake you're not," he laughed and returned to his friends. "All settled chaps, no doubt he'll take it out on them."

The laughter from the senior officers did nothing to ease Firth's nerves. He had arrived well after midnight and had spent most of the intervening four hours telling Benton about what he had seen and the capture of the dispatches.

The urgency of getting the information to the commander meant Firth had little time to freshen up, a bowl of cold water to throw over his face was deemed sufficient. Still, he had seen a wonderful sunrise. More brilliant than any English one and he had been surprised at how quickly the temperature had climbed.

Standing in the same room as the freshly polished headquarters aides was making both Firth and Brook uncomfortable. They had been on horseback for more than a day and the dust and grime from the roads had darkened their white breeches to a mottled brown. Exhaustion showed in their eyes and Firth hoped that it was Brook who did not smell as fresh as he might.

Firth looked at Brook: "Well, Sam, this could be interesting. I get the feeling we're being served up for breakfast, don't you?"

"Please don't talk of food, I'm starving. Is that your stomach, or mine?"

"Probably yours, mine wasted away hours ago."

The doors to the commander's office opened and Benton walked briskly over to the pair. "Sir Arthur will see you now. Keep your answers brief and to the point, he's in a fury. Come on," he said, almost apologetically.

Firth followed the General and ran his fingers down the silver buttons on the front of his tunic checking that all were done up. As they passed the cavalrymen he caught the words "lambs to the slaughter" and then flushed as laughter burst out. Then he was through the door.

Like the outer lobby the room was cool and their boots clicked disconcertingly loudly on the blue-and-white tiles as they walked to a beautifully carved desk. It was bathed in light from a large window and strewn with parchment maps. On top of two charts lay the dispatch case that had been taken from Rey. Its contents lay unwrapped next to a neat pile of pottery shards that had once been a fine tea set and plate.

"So these are the deserters, eh, Benton?" came a well-toned voice from behind Firth. "Left their posts to go gallivanting about with the enemy, eh?"

"Yes, Sir Arthur, Lieutenant Firth and Lieutenant Brook."

The friends could hear the commander pacing about and then the steps clicked closer. "What am I to do with junior officers who take it upon themselves to go where they like, when they like? Can I countenance that, sirs?"

Firth and Brook stood statue-like as the voice stopped just behind them. "Well, lieutenant?"

Taking a quick breath Firth uneasily replied: "No, sir."

The clicking started again: "Can I allow junior officers to endanger themselves with hare-brained trots into enemy territory? Eh?" he asked sternly.

"No, sir."

Moving around into view Wellesley strolled to the window and looked out. Firth thought the silhouetted general was smaller than he had imagined, probably a good half-head shorter than he was, with a tousle of light-brown hair that sat up at the front like a wave about to break.

He was dressed in a dark-blue tunic with a high collar and white neckerchief. The only decoration on the uniform of Britain's leading soldier was on the left breast, a large silver star signifying the Order of the Garter. Turning, Wellesley revealed a profile dominated by a hawk-like beak. It gave the commander a hunter's stare. Despite the grace of his movements, Wellesley looked like an athlete. To Firth he looked very much like a soldier – and a successful one. The young man had keenly followed newspaper reports of Wellesley's time in India where the general had saved British interests by defeating the French-backed princes. Firth had imagined himself as Wellesley leading his men into the fortress of Seringapatam and ending the life of the sadistic Tippoo Sultan. How he would have loved to have been the first Englishman to touch Tippoo's famous mechanical tiger that growled as it ate a screaming redcoat.

And now Firth was looking directly at his hero.

"What am I to do, eh, with junior officers who operate outside of orders? What do you think Benton?"

"I would suggest that if they had left their posts they should be cashiered, Sir Arthur."

Firth forgot about the commander's nose.

"And if they had not yet joined their regiment and managed to capture vital documents?"

"I would think the situation ... a special one, Sir Arthur, and perhaps one could look the other way."

"But the discipline, Benton, what about discipline?"

"It would be good for morale, sir."

"True, true," Wellesley said as he turned his piercing blue eyes on to the pair. He could see the discomfort in their faces, particularly in that of the dark-haired youth. The taller of the two, while not at ease, had a confidence about him that Sir Arthur recognised. As a young officer he had had that same look. He knows he's done well despite bending the rules, Wellesley thought. He smiled and sat down behind his desk.

"Tell me more about your ... how shall I put it? ... patrol. What's in front of us? What's the terrain like?"

Firth spent the next 20 minutes describing the countryside towards Leiria amid a host of interruptions from Wellesley on matters such as rivers and strongpoints. Initially somewhat awestruck, Brook took some minutes before he croaked out a reply but then warmed to the conversation with a series of interjections that broke Firth's concentration.

"Aha, you've woken up at last lieutenant?" Wellesley laughed, letting out a whoop that made both jump. "Now, gentlemen, tell me about yourselves."

Brook told the General of his family's business as boatbuilders for the fishing fleets of Whitby, the largest of which was owned by Firth's father, who also owned the chandlery and large tracts of land.

"Sounds like you should have joined the Navy," Wellesley said.

"We almost did, sir," Brook replied, before a withering glance from Firth told him to keep quiet.

"Aha," said an intrigued Wellesley, "sounds like a tale in this. Go on."

"Well, sir, we were attacked by a press gang and well, we sort of declined their offer of life at sea."

"Bribery?"

"Oh no sir, we fought them off."

"You did what?" General Benton spluttered, "You fought them off?"

"Yes sir," Firth took over. "Seven of them attacked us and we defended ourselves. With minimum force," he added.

"Minimum force, lieutenant? Meaning?"

"We downed three sir, but they were not seriously injured."

Another whoop erupted from Wellesley who almost leapt to his feet in glee. "My God, Benton, we've a fine pair here. If they're not intercepting enemy dispatches they're cutting up some poor Jack Tars. These boys'll do us nicely."

For a moment Wellesley turned serious.

"Gentlemen, the papers you captured are invaluable and will give us just the start we need against the French. They tell us there are two enemy forces moving to our south and east to hold up our advance while Junot brings up the main French army. They will link up within two weeks and we must not let that happen."

It was a fortnight, Wellesley knew, that would give his men already on shore, and the soon-to-arrive reinforcements, time to rest and organise.

"Thank you for the information and a welcome respite from the more incompetent of my officers.

"Dear Lord I have a bad day ahead. I have to knock some sense into the thickest of heads - those of my cavalry commanders - and order men flogged for leaving the camp without orders. Keep that in mind, gentlemen," he said pointedly.

"I do hate the lash, but if I don't use it my fine soldiers will turn back into the scum of the Earth quicker than a bishop will have your purse. Now good day, I have no doubt that we will meet again."

Firth and Brook quickly stood and followed Benton to the doors where he ushered them out and then called in the group of waiting officers. The doors closed and the youths allowed themselves quick grins. They had gone about four paces when more shouting broke out in the office.

"What do you mean we've no horses?" thundered the voice from inside. "You're cavalry, you need bloody horses! Don't you?"

Knowing there was a time to stand and a time to walk away, Firth and Brook did the latter and headed at an as seemly a pace as possible towards the main entrance eagerly seeking the baths and beds that Benton had arranged for them.

V

Lavaos, 6 August

Firth stirred as the gentle knocking became increasingly more persistent. He opened his eyes, saw that the room was light and reached for the silver pocket watch lying on a chair next to his bed. Eight o'clock, he registered, and slowly pulled back the coarse woollen blankets. The knocking grew louder and it seemed Brook, too, finally heard it. His snoring stopped, started and then ceased again.

"Yes, what is it?" Firth called.

The door opened and a corporal appeared. "Beg pardon sirs, breakfast is about to be served. Punishment is in an hour and orders are for all officers to be at the parade ground by 10 to nine."

"Thank you, corporal," Firth yawned. "What's punishment?"

"Floggings, sir. Four today. I've had your uniforms cleaned, sirs, and managed to locate your belongings. A Captain Wren had seen to them."

"Thank you, corporal ..?"

"Todd, sir, Corporal Todd. I've been told to look after you until your regiment lands."

"If you need anything special sirs, just ask," he added with a wink.

Easing his stiff body out of the bed, Firth threw his heavy pillow at Brook. "Come on, Sam, time to be up."

Brook dressed gingerly and when it came time to haul on his close-fitting boots his back protested against bending over so far.

"I feel I've just hauled in three tons of fish, Joshua, I can barely move."

"Come on, that bath should have fixed you."

They had soaked in the steaming iron tubs for an hour, fussed over by elderly Portuguese women who cackled and grinned while they firstly poured pans of water over the pair and then scratched what felt like layers of skin off their bodies with rough cloths. Pale they might be, one grandmother had said lewdly, but they were tall, a head taller than the townsmen, and were well built. Another chorus of cackling and toothless laughter. The mirth had done little to disturb the youths who had been fighting to keep their eyes open. Within 20 minutes Firth was in a rickety, but clean, bed and by the time his mind registered that his head was on an uncomfortable pillow, he was asleep. Brook succumbed second, but only by a snore.

"I'm sure the bath helped but I'm still aching."

"Too sore to eat?"

"Never. Bring on the bacon," Brook said as he bolted for the door in a rather ungentlemanly way. "Bags the bigger plate."

"You swine," Firth grinned as he lunged after him, failing by a whisker to catch hold of his friend's yellow coat tails.

Never had food tasted so fine, they both thought as they sliced into another thick rasher of bacon and tore off more chunks of bread to dip into the eggs. There were no other officers in the room so the pair had their choice of servings. Firth felt full after two plates but Brook, against the warnings of his groaning stomach, finished four. He was just finishing his second mug of tea when Todd entered.

"Beg pardon sirs, time for parade."

"Why isn't anyone else eating?" Brook asked.

"It's the flogging sir. It's very nasty and very messy. Most officers don't like to eat before one ... in case they bring it up."

"Oh, I see," said a worried-looking Brook.

The officers followed Todd the short distance from the inn, which had been commandeered as part of the British headquarters, to the town's old stone walls. Firth noted that the Quartermaster had been busy organising accommodation and had left chalk markings upon the faded and flaking light-blue paint of the doors, assigning each building a crowd of military officers and staff.

A detachment from the Royal American rifle regiment stood guard at the southern entry to Lavaos. Two of the dark green-uniformed riflemen paced about watching those passing through the gate while the remainder sat to one side cleaning their Baker rifles.

Beyond the gates sprawled the hundreds of Bell tents that sheltered Wellington's army. Each regiment had been placed around the perimeter of a large parade ground with its encampment centred on a large Union Flag and its own Colour. Usually they flew proudly, but today they would be furled and sheathed in their leather cundums so they would not be shamed by the punishment of absconders.

As Firth, Brook and the Corporal moved down the brown, dry slope towards the clear ground the drums began to beat. Orders were barked and lines of red uniforms were formed, bayonets shone in the sun. Sergeants moved slowly with their spear-like, 10-foot spontoons to the Colours and, with great ceremony, wrapped and then covered them.

To the beat of the drum they slow-marched into the centre where Wellesley and his staff officers sat unmoving on their horses. Regiment by regiment the British trooped to the edge of the dusty area and stopped at attention. Not a word came from any of the men, not the oldest of hands, who had seen this many times before, or youngest of recruits, who had yet to witness such an event.

As if to be at one with the solemn mood that pervaded Lavaos, the sea breeze dropped away leaving the gathering silent but for the echo of drumbeats. Twenty paces from where the general staff gathered a triangle of spontoons had been lashed together.

Four of the half-pikes were used to create the frame, three forming a hollow pyramid while the remaining one was used as a crossbeam. When all the regiments had settled the order was given and the prisoners were marched - stripped to the waist - out from their jail in the township.

Corporal Todd whispered to Firth: "That first fellow was absent without leave. He's getting 50 scratches of the cat-o-nine-tails.

"Them next two were drunk as well, they get 100 each. But the last beggar'll be lucky to survive his flogging. 400 he gets, for stealing food from a house. Lucky he weren't hanged."

Firth had seen the results of floggings on the backs of many of the fishermen in his father's fleet. Even years after the men had finished serving in the Royal Navy the scars still stood out noticeably.

"Nasty things," said Todd. "Them things are made so one stroke will send nine lengths of knotted cord across some poor bugger's back.

"Mind you, they're lucky today," he continued, "They've just got young-uns to whip 'em. If you gets a man doing it then the back'll be mince meat within two score lashes."

The drummers were eight young boys drawn from each of the regiments. Their reverse-colour uniforms of red on yellow and red on olive clashed vibrantly in the bright sunshine.

Firth and Brook had positioned themselves to the right of Wellesley and his staff and stood next to Bernardo Zagalo and his men. The students had been allowed to watch the punishment to witness the fact that the British would not tolerate crimes against the Portuguese people.

"What will happen?" Zagalo asked.

Firth shook his head slightly. "I'm not sure Bernardo. I think the drummers get turns at whipping the man."

"Turns?"

"They change over. I guess it's to stop one getting too tired to hit them hard enough."

"Barbarism," said the Portuguese student with some feeling.

The drums stopped tapping as a private from the 5th Regiment walked to the triangle. The trio could clearly hear the charges being read out.

"He was trying to buy wine from a tavern," Brook whispered.

They watched as the man moved steadily to the triangle and raised his bound hands to its apex. A corporal moved in to give him a leather patch to bite down on.

The first drummer was a tall, thin boy from the man's own regiment and the soldier gave the youth a wink as if to say that the imminent infliction of pain would not be held against him next time they met in camp. Acknowledging the signal with a pitying smile the drummer readied himself. The officer overseeing the flogging looked to Wellesley and, receiving a nod, barked "begin."

The cat-o-nine-tails slowly rose over the head of the drummer and then came down in a whistling arc to slap upon the exposed back. The soldier barely moved, he just tightened his grip on the cords binding his wrists and stared ahead. The second blow came a second later and then the third. By the 15th the back was reddened and sweat was pouring into the drummer's eyes while dark patches soaked across his olive-green coat. By 25 lashes he was straining to put any energy at all into the whipping and the next boy took his place.

From the Norfolk Regiment, the fresh, yellow-jacketed arm rose and fell quickly, the first crack split the private's skin.

The second was harder and the already weakened flesh gave up its hold on precious blood, which slowly welled out of the cuts and began trickling down into the victim's pants. The trickle became a stream under further whipping and a low murmur went through the ranks until it was silenced by the looks from hovering sergeants and corporals.

At the 50th stroke the private bowed his head slightly, but then straightened as his wrists were untied. His back was blazing with pain but he had survived his ordeal without betraying any sign of it.

"He's not given the goddamned officers the pleasure of seeing him break and sing like a nightingale," came a voice from the ranks behind.

"Aye and he'll get a dollop or two of brandy as well," said another.

Turning quickly Firth did not see who had made the comment as all the soldiers glanced at the ground.

The second soldier had to be dragged to the triangle by two corporals. He was very young and was clearly terrified by the thought of what was about to happen. Whimpering as his hands were tied above his head he lost the leather wadding between his teeth and begged to be released.

One of the corporals moved to him and after shoving the mouthpiece back in whispered savagely "Shut your noise you bloody Moonraker. You may be stupid enough to think you can pull the moon out of a pond, but your back won't allow that for a while. Now shut your bloody noise or I'll promise you true suffering!"

Shaking like an old drunk, the private braced himself for the shock of the first blow, but even then the stinging slap made him gasp. By the 10th tears were rolling freely and after 15 he was sobbing "please, please."

The drummer boy, again from the victim's regiment, was embarrassed by the performance and began to really put his back into the strokes. His pitted face twisting with the force he was generating. The screams started after the youth's skin split and blood poured from the criss-cross wounds.

The private fainted after 70 strokes and, after a quick examination by someone Firth presumed was the surgeon, he was carelessly hauled away.

"He's lucky," said Zagalo.

"Not really," Firth replied quietly, "he'll get the last few dozen when he's fit enough."

Firth watched as the third man was brought to the triangle. Despite the violence of the punishments and the touch of sadism at having men whipped in front of the entire army, he had no problem with floggings. The offenders knew the rules of the army and had been warned against straying from camp. They also knew the consequences of flouting army rules.

"Better them than us, hey Sam? Sam?"

Firth turned to his friend and immediately saw that his face had changed to a very unhealthy shade of grey and he was quietly taking deep breaths.

"You okay?"

His friend gave two barely noticeable nods, as if to do more would be to risk the control he was currently fighting to hold over his body.

The whistle and dull crack of the cat continued in the background as Firth watched Brook's internal battle.

"The flogging ... and too much breakfast?"

Brook nodded and turned his attention to a small, mangy dog that was moving into the parade ground.

A mongrel of some sort it had a torn ear and two bald spots on its back where sores oozed a clear liquid from red-raw flesh. Surprisingly unbothered by the thousands of men in the area and the noise of the whip, the dog zigzagged its way to the triangle and began to lap from the pool of blood at the feet of the flogged man.

Brook's stomach contracted at the sight and he could feel himself sway. It was so damn hot, he thought. The nose of the dog was by now covered in red and one of the guards pushed it away with his foot. The starving dog was not about to be put off by so easily and returned to the pool where its feed continued.

Infuriated, the guard took a moment to steady himself before planting a boot into the side of the dog, which yelped and slunk off.

"Hold on Sam, you must think about something else."

By now, the victim's back was cruelly cut and quarter-inch deep furrows had appeared like a crimson spider's web across its width. Every stroke added to the blood that poured on to his pants and in to his boots.

Brook thought he was able to cope with the scene in front of him, but his stomach maintained its churning. His attempt to use mind over matter was going well but it became a losing battle when a pea-sized piece of flesh, sliced into a rough triangle by the haphazard spread of the tails, flew from the man's back and landed on Brook's cheek. A second plopped on to the bridge of his nose, together with several globs of blood.

Brook looked as if he had been struck by a club.

Through sheer willpower he forced himself to stand steady and then moved several paces backwards before quickly walking, hand over mouth, towards the nearest building. Turning behind a wall he emptied his stomach's contents next to an old barrel collecting rainwater. Dipping his hands into the mosquito-larvaed water he washed his face and rinsed his mouth, trying to rid it of the bitter taste of vomit. He sagged, one-shouldered, against the wall and listened as the crack of the cat continued apace. Brook guessed the man's quota was just about over when the soldier began to cry out. The brave fellow had lasted a long time, probably 12 dozen lashes or so, and then Brook forgot about the event as his stomach began to heave again. Slumping into a crouch with his back planted against the wall and his bicorne between his knees, he bowed his head in his hands.

It took five minutes for him to feel steady enough to stand and compose himself before the embarrassing walk back.

Moving into the flattened-earth roadway he was almost run down by a horseman galloping towards the British troops watching the last man's punishment begin. Brook thought he recognised the rider as one of Zagalo's student militia and quickened his pace. The man dismounted while his horse was still moving and half-fell, half-ran to Zagalo.

Firth watched as the student leader listened to the rapidly speaking man, punctuating the flow of Portuguese with single-word questions. It looked to the young officer as if Zagalo had received some news that he was not willing to hear.

The men's conversation stopped just as Brook made his return to Firth's side. A sheepish smile told his friend that he felt okay. Zagalo made his way to the pair. "My friends, I have just had some bad news."

"What is it Bernardo?"

"I can't believe it, but this man says there has been an atrocity in my home village of Lavilho. A French patrol hanged four people and cut the hands off all the men."

"It can't be true, Bernardo, the French are not like that," a shocked Firth said.

"Not against your people, my friend, but against us they are animals. I must go to my village now, but I pray you will visit me sometime."

One of his men moved up with his horse and Zagalo mounted.

"Keep well, my friends," he said as he spun the beast and shouted "Death to the French!"

VI

Chapter 8 West of Lavaos, 7 August

Sergeant Thomas Needham had a terrible thirst. The walk from the landing site at Figueira had brought it on and it was now raging in his throat. He wiped a grimy hand across his lips and felt the stubble on his chin. Better shave before the colonel saw him, otherwise he'd lose his stripes again.

He had been a Sergeant on three occasions, but each time he'd risen to that lofty height he had been caught out on a camp search of rum.

Rum his great friend. Rum, that pleasing fluid he was now thinking so much about. Still, there'd be plenty of grog just over the hill in Lavaos and that would not take too long to root out.

Well then, there was only one thing, in Needham's book, to help cure dryness and that was a song.

"All right lads, here we go," he called.

"*When I was bound apprentice in famous Worcestershire,*" he began in a strong baritone that fitted his large frame.

"*Full well I served my master for more than seven year ...*

"*Till I took up to poaching as you will quickly hear ...*

The marching men beside him took up the jaunty song. "*Oh 'tis my delight on a shining night, in the season of the year ...*"

With each pace more and more of the veterans of the grenadier company joined in singing *The Lincolnshire Poacher*, the regimental marching song adopted by the Worcesters. It had a catchy beat and lively lyrics, and Needham knew it kept the men's feet marching in the most trying of conditions. Today, however, the march was not testing and the men of the 29th had an automatic spring in their collective step as all were looking forward to setting themselves against the French.

"*As me and my companions were setting of a snare ...*

"*Twas there we spied the gamekeeper, for him we did not care ...*

"*For we can wrestle and fight, my boys, and jump o'er anywhere ...*

"*O 'tis my delight on a shining night, in the season of the year.*"

Needham acknowledged that but, for himself, the regiment looked in very fine fettle. Well, time for a shave, he decided and began a trick he had become famous for among his comrades, that of shaving on the march.

Using a splash of water from his canteen he wet his jawline and then smeared a small cake of soap over his ginger bristles, gently massaging the film of white until it felt evenly applied. Taking a wicked-looking knife from his linen side bag he brought the first strokes down from beside his ear and then down his jaw and on to his neck. He repeated the moves on the right of his face and then scraped the blade to the point of his jutting chin. Another quick splash of water and another smear of soap and the final touches were done.

"Well done Sarge, didn't miss a bit," said a voice from behind.

"Thank you … private," Needham genially said to a quick-witted poacher from Kent named Garret Dalton. "Now shut your trap and sing, it was written for you."

The grenadiers burst into laughter and the verses continued.

"Straighten up and sing lively lads, here's the Colonel."

Needham looked ahead to the head of the column and saw Colonel the Honourable George Lake sitting imperiously on his horse, Black Jack. The steed stood an impressive 17 hands high.

Though small in stature Lake had an aura about him that demanded respect. He sat on his giant mount in a tailor-made uniform that looked worth every shilling of the thousand pounds he was rumoured to spend on it each year. A deep scarlet, it had solid silver epaulettes decorated with a crown and star on each shoulder and large silver buttons on both sides of the high yellow collar.

As Lake turned to comment to one of the regiment's majors, Needham could see the Colonel's long queue of powdered hair flick around. The old army style was now unfashionable but looked spectacular. Lake's queue fell past his shoulders and was tied with a strip of black silk. It gave both officers and men a more military appearance, Needham thought.

"*As me and my companions were setting four or five ...,*

"*And taking on 'em up again, we caught a hare alive ...,*

"*We caught a hare alive, my boys, and thro' the woods did steer ...*

"*O, 'tis my delight on a shining night, in the season of the year.*"

Next to Lake sat Major Gregory Way, an officer who had fought for many years in India and the Low Countries. Tall and thin he had the tell-tale yellow-tinged skin of a man who had suffered through the ravages of fever. He looked almost 50 years of age, but Needham knew he was closer to his own 39 years.

Way was a cool head in battle, the Sergeant freely admitted, and an officer who thought well of his men. There should be more like him. Yes, Way was the best of the silver-wearers.

The Worcesters also had one of the least pleasant officers in the army but, fortunately, he was away with the Quartermaster organising supplies.

Well, Needham interrupted his own thoughts, the tents were back on the transports and he and his other Swaddies would be sleeping under the stars. A dozen pack mules had been safely off-loaded at Mondego Bay, together with the 29th's cooking pots, so at least there would be hot food.

Wonder if there are any spare chickens around, he pondered? Anyway, he had managed to have two small kegs of rum placed on the baggage animals, enough to tide a man over 'til the army sorted out the daily rations.

"*I threw him on my shoulder and then we trudged home,*

"*We took him to a neighbour's house and sold him for a crown,*

"*We sold him for a crown, my boys, but I did not tell you where,*

"*O, tis my delight on a shining night, in the season of the year.*"

My delight, all right, he chuckled.

He had stolen game and many fowl from men like the Colonel, country squires with little more to do than hunt and fish. Boredom, that's why most officers joined the army. It was either that, the church, or politics.

Different for the Swaddies, they had little choice. Prison, hanging, deportation, or the army ... those were their options. Thieves, thugs and no-hopers ... well, before they joined up.

Now they were Sergeant Thieves, Corporal Thugs and Private No-hopers.

Smiling at his own wit Needham looked up the files of marching men towards his old 6th company.

There were not many of his former comrades left in it, some had been pensioned off while others had died of various complaints - pox and drink being the most common.

Still, there was Jonathon Siddle, a private who had been old when Needham was young, so the bugger must be ancient now, he thought. He and William Sweeney, who walked straight-backed at his side, had joined up together and had shared the army life for more than 40 years. Good men both.

Then there was Absalom Barclay, a sergeant, who had joined the company just before Needham left for the grenadiers six years before.

A good-looking lad he had been forced to join up because he'd got two girls in trouble at the same time and had to flee their vengeful brothers. He'd done well and even had himself a wife.

The last man he recognised was William Good, who was the most inappropriately named person Needham had known. He had a flat-nosed face that always had a sullen set to it. If ever a man was a nasty piece of work it was Good, Needham thought.

A thief and a cutthroat he had admitted, while in his cups, to murdering seven men with a knife and two more with a club. Always willing to brawl and steal, his vicious temper had his comrades warily looking over their shoulders.

"*Success to every gentleman that lives in Worcestershire,*

"*Success to every poacher that wants to sell a hare,*

"*Bad luck to every gamekeeper that will not sell his deer,*

"*O, tis my delight on a shining night, in the season of the year.*"

Aye, they were a mixed bunch. Farm boys, criminals, English, Scotch and Paddies. Eight hundred of them. Well trained and drilled into first-class soldiers by a collection of top-notch sergeants, one of whom was approaching from down the head of the column.

"Your bacon-bolters are looking and sounding good, Thomas," Sergeant-Major Richard Richards said to his friend.

"Thanks Dick, and it's not just my grenadiers - the whole regiment looks bang-up, so it does," Needham responded.

"It has to, the Colonel wants to impress Wellesley. He's raring to be at the Frogs and wants to get first crack at 'em."

"He's an eager one, all right."

"A little too eager, maybe, but that's not for us to think on."

"True, have you seen The Twins?"

"They're around somewhere, I'm not sure they've got over their adventures at sea yet, poor buggers," Needham laughed.

The Twins were the regimental surgeon's assistants and had been known by their collective nickname for so long that the soldiers had forgotten their real names.

The pair had been badly wounded 10 years before at Aboukir in Egypt when a French cannonball had passed in between them and had taken off Twin One's right arm and

Twin Two's left arm, both at the elbow.

Their lives had been saved by the quick work of Dr Geoffrey Guthrie who stopped the bleeding with tourniquets made from crossbelts and later neatly trimmed the skin around the stumps. Marked for return to England the pair approached the doctor who, taking pity on them, took them on as his assistants and kept them with him when he joined the Worcesters.

Life had been comfortable for The Twins with the 29th until the regiment began its seaborne journey around the Mediterranean, when it was discovered they became heartily seasick in the slightest swell.

As they had sighted the surf off Mondego Bay the pair had rejoiced that their suffering was over - until the longboat they were in overturned throwing them into the sea.

"You should have seen them Dick. They couldn't work out whether to paddle or raise their hand for help," Needham laughed.

"It was priceless. I almost wet myself. We got them tho', me and a couple of lads swam out and got 'em."

Richards smiled. "They seem okay now, Thomas. They even see the funny side. Mind you, they refused to go back to the ship to get Guthrie's equipment."

"I'm not even sure we'll get them close enough to water to have a wash from now on Dick."

The pair chortled.

"Well, Thomas, we'll be in a place called Lavaos by noon … in plenty of time to get meals organised."

Nodding, Needham agreed. In plenty of time, he thought, to find some rum.

VII

South of Caldas da Rainha, 7 August.

The screams of the Frenchman filled the leafy hollow by the side of the road.

They began somewhere deep inside him and slowly worked their way through his throat and out of his blood-and-vomit-covered mouth with an intensity that suggested mortal pain.

But for Citoyen Charles Tabbard, imperial notary for Estremadura, it was not his own agony that caused him to release such an unholy noise. His suffering had been momentarily eased by the death of the nerve endings in his feet as the fire beneath them ate through his flesh.

He had been dangling over the flames for more than half an hour but it had only taken 10 minutes for the heat to sear his skin sending awful signals of pain to his brain. That had been when he had bitten through his tongue.

After 20 minutes the flesh began to smoke and with horror he realised that his blackened feet were actually cooking. Since then, however, the shrivelling nerves had dulled their cries of danger, leaving him with what he found to be a tolerable level of agony.

So Tabbard's cries were actually for his wife and daughter who were being raped in front of his eyes.

Dozens of men had taken their turns in violating them and the two most precious people in his life now lay semi-conscious as the *cochons* began their tortures again.

His beautiful wife had fought with all her strength before one of the men hit her with his musket butt, caving in her left cheekbone and breaking her nose.

His 15-year-old daughter had, fortunately, fainted with the horrors she was witnessing and had barely been conscious throughout her ordeal.

An exquisite child with raven-black hair that fell to her shoulders she had been deflowered by the leader of the wretches.

Through his waves of pain Tabbard had heard the bastards call that devil The Chef. The notary screamed again as the flames reached previously untouched skin and his calves began to char. "Please God, please, let this end soon," he prayed.

Ten paces away from Tabbard's torment stood The Chef and five of his senior men. Wearing gaudy, feather-bedecked hats the group of leaders was easily recognisable.

His band had been brigands in the area for years and had switched from attacking rich merchants and royal coaches to robbing the French.

It was all for Portugal, The Chef had told his guerrilleros patriotically, although many local merchants still had the discomfort of handing over all their goods when forced to stop.

There were 80 men under his leadership and the time was right to strike a blow against the invaders.

The occupants of the coach deserved their tribulations, The Chef thought, for had not Portugal been raped and burned by France? Anyway, they were not the main target.

That would be here soon.

Clapping his hands he called his men from their pleasures.

"Now is the time, set fire to the coach and take your places."

"Do we kill them?" his second-in-command asked.

"No, leave them, they will add to the confusion."

"Miguel reports French horses on the road from Caldas, 20 of them."

"Good, they will see the smoke and come. We will be ready for them."

The clearing, he knew, was a perfect spot for an ambush. On the far side of the road there was woodland made impenetrable by a high undergrowth of thorns, while the rough dirt road could easily be blocked by his men.

In front of the treeline on the fourth side, where he now hid with most of his followers, there was a large clear space that made a perfect killing ground. They had ambushed and killed some 30 Frenchmen in the past month, some of whom had taken a very long time to die over the fires. Behind him was a steep cliff that dropped into an evil-smelling bog so foul and treacherous that no one entered it.

The smoke from the ornate wagon was now rising quickly into the blue sky and the crackle of burning wood covered the sounds of his men taking their positions. Miguel had said the French were only minutes away so their arrival was imminent.

When they came it was with extreme caution. Three blue-coated troopers warily entered the glade, their short-barreled carbines resting at the ready on the saddles. Unusual helmets, The Chef thought, they had square tops.

Another four horsemen moved into sight and approached the bodies of the two dead coachmen. Next came an officer, who dismounted and drew his sword before moving quickly to Tabbard and his family.

Lieutenant Dezydery Chlapowski recoiled at the sight in front of him. "My God, they've burned his feet off...," he said to no-one in particular. Fighting his horror at the sight of the dangling man he kicked away the wood from under the victim and ordered two men to cut him down. Crossing to the two females he muttered a curse on the animals who would do such a thing. Both women were alive, but only just.

"Quickly, get these poor people away from here. Be as gentle as you can," he said and winced as Tabbard screamed at being moved. "But do it quickly."

The young Lieutenant felt eyes watching him as he scanned the trees and knew he had very little time to effect a rescue. "Hurry Sergeant, hurry."

"Ready, sir," said the NCO, who held the girl close in front of him, not knowing if she was able to draw any comfort from his arms.

As the Lieutenant was about to order a withdrawal a Portuguese voice sounded. The already hazy clearing disappeared in clouds of smoke as scores of muskets belched out from the wood in front of the cavalry. At least six of his men fell hit by musket balls, two more were struggling to free themselves from their fallen horses.

"To the north, go north," the Lieutenant hollered, pointing his sabre towards the road they had come down. "Go, go, go," he shouted and then reeled from a heavy blow to his thigh. A second thump spun him sideways but he managed to hold on to both sword and horse. He could see a dozen men blocking each of the exits and more enemy coming from out of the woods. "Go north, cut your way through."

His troopers had reacted well after the initial shock and were now forming up for a charge at the northern blocking force. The Portuguese muskets continued to bang away, but were less effective because powder smoke obscured their targets. A bayonet snaked up at the Lieutenant who parried it and then split his assailant's head, sending blood and brains across his horse's hindquarters.

Urging the mount on he crashed into three men who had driven their bayonets into the creature's neck and chest.

Whinnying in pain and fear the horse lashed out with its front hooves felling the men and giving the officer a precious opening to force his way clear.

There were fewer than half the blue coats left in the saddle, and five of them were hampered by the injured civilians and wounded soldiers they were carrying. If only they could break the ring around them.

The Lieutenant, screaming in rage, slashed and cut at any heads he could see. Another trooper toppled, clutching his innards as if by pushing them back into the gaping wound left by the swordstroke he could stop himself from dying. A knife thrust ended his efforts.

We're all going to die, the Lieutenant conceded to himself, killed by these animals. At least they would go down with honour and glory. "Vive l'Empereur, long live Poland," he shouted.

"Long live Poland," his small band responded.

Then came a welcome sound – a massed shout of "Vive l'Empereur, long live Poland."

The Lieutenant spun around to see a wall of blue coats sabreing their way through the Portuguese to the south. More were spurring in from the north.

In an instant the guerrilleros had turned from victors to a panic of men. They were outnumbered almost two to one by the horsemen whose charge carried them effortlessly through the enemy. Within seconds at least 50 of The Chef's men were dead or maimed and a dozen more only escaped killing thrusts by falling to the ground.

"To the woods," The Chef called, "Flee!"

There was safety in the woods and once down the cliff the French would never follow them into the marshlands. "To the woods."

Not waiting to see if he could help his stricken men, the guerrilleros' leader and his cronies ran towards the trees. As they got to within five paces of shelter they were stopped in their tracks by the sudden appearance of more French uniforms at the woods' edge. "They're behind us," gasped a disbelieving Chef.

"Long live Poland," a grinning Zapalski roared and leapt into the fray with 70 men, mud-stained from crossing the boggy ground. Running towards the bandits in the feather hats he flat bladed his sword across the head of one, knocking him senseless to the ground. A second was spitted with his sword and a third was shot in the neck with his pistol. "It's you I want," he said and placed his sabre at The Chef's throat. "Surrender, pig. Or I will cut you to pieces here."

The Chef didn't understand a word that was said, but the menace in the voice of the blue-eyed officer made him drop his sword.

He could not believe what had happened. Less than half a minute had elapsed since the French reinforcements had entered the fight and already his men had been wiped out. Here and there one would appear being pushed forward by cavalrymen and the moans of the wounded were beginning to grow.

Zapalski saw the young Lieutenant, bleeding heavily from two wounds, and his troopers moving towards him. "Well done Dezydery," he called, "You did well."

"Thank you, Major. You set a brilliant trap, but I feared we were dead."

"Yes, Dezydery, I'm sorry. We moved up the cliffs as soon as they left the woods but it was harder going than we expected. How many men did you lose?"

"I think eight dead, Major and as many injured. But … we did save three hostages, although one is unlikely to live. They did terrible things to them."

"They will suffer for it, Dezydery, they will suffer." He patted the younger man on the shoulder. "See that your wounds are cared for."

Zapalski walked slowly through the tangle of bodies to the spot where the Tabbards had been carried. Gang raped by the look of them, he thought.

It was just as the Austrians had done to the women of his town during one of their invasions.

Zapalski could tolerate many things, soldiering demanded that, but rape was one weapon he did not think real soldiers should use. He had seen too much of it in Poland. He knelt down in between the two females and placed his hands on theirs. They were in extreme shock and would probably not hear him but he had to say something.

"It's over now, mesdames, you are safe. God will help you."

He looked over to where the notary lay moaning. "You poor bastard," he said quietly, the man's legs had been burned almost to his knees and would need amputation. "You may survive, but probably not. Filthy Portuguese bastards."

Zapalski had already decided the fates of the surviving bandits and they would regret their actions this day. His troopers were in the woods preparing stakes. Others were building horse-litters on which to transport the wounded home.

"How many of the scum live, corporal?"

"About 20, sir."

"Round them up, strip them and gag them."

"Yes, sir."

The Poles had worked quickly to cut down and sharpen 23 stakes. Each was some two metres long and five centimetres across with roughly hewn points. Holes were dug two metres apart and the spears were laid next to them. The prisoners were marched to the stakes and were seized by four troopers, one holding each limb.

"Rape is an evil," Zapalski said loudly, "you made these women suffer and now you will know what it's like. Begin."

The Portuguese were forced face down on the ground and their legs spread. The fifth Polish cavalryman at each stake picked the wood up and roughly rammed it into the rear of the prisoner. Despite the gags the screams of the men were horrendous. Using shoeing hammers the troopers belted the stakes until their points had disappeared well into the bowels of the victims, who shrieked and struggled wildly. The Poles holding the arms then slowly lifted the spitted victims so that the body's weight was forcing itself down on to the wooden spike pushing it through intestines, lungs and finally the heart.

As he drifted in and out of reality, Citoyen Charles Tabbard could see The Chef weakly twitching as his life's blood poured down his legs and on to the ground. He was still squealing 10 minutes after being impaled. Unfortunately for the brigand leader his stake had lodged between his ribs and, despite breaking several of them, had yet to hit a mortal spot. The man's excruciating pain was easy to see in his eyes and movements.

"I can die an avenged man," Tabbard whispered.

And did.

Lavaos, 7 August.

Firth slid off Ricketts and quickly tethered her to a post. He gave her a pat on the neck before unlooping the reins to Lass, the horse he brought to Portugal, and hitching her as well.

Brook dismounted and did the same.

Then the friends surveyed the scene.

Two flags waved delicately in the slight breeze - a six foot square King's Colour, better known as the Union Flag. In the middle of its striking colours of red, white and blue was a stitched "XXIX Regt" surrounded by a horseshoe-shaped wreath of roses and thistles. Next to it stood the Worcesters' regimental Colours - a blazing yellow standard with a Union Flag in the top left and its number "XXIX Regt" centrally placed.

Firth stopped and looked at the emblems of both his country and new regiment and felt a surge of pride.

"Don't hang about too long lieutenants, it doesn't do for officers to be seen standing around uselessly," came a voice from behind them.

The pair turned and looked at an officer who stood hands on hips in a style he took to be the latest fashion in London.

"I'm sorry, sir … Captain," Firth corrected himself when he saw the man's uniform. "We were just looking at the Colours."

"Impressive aren't they," the Captain said in a light voice.

"They are," Firth said and Brook enthusiastically added "and we are here to defend them."

"No, lieutenants, you are here to die for them," and with that the Captain turned on his heels and moved towards the tents.

"Well, he's a charmer," said a surprised Firth, but Brook only shrugged and stifled a half-yawn.

"I am so tired Joshua, that trip with General Wellesley today has almost done me in." Firth smiled, it had been a long day. Up at 4am and, within an hour, on the road with Wellesley and his senior officers over part of the route to Leiria.

Again Wellesley was full of questions, but even while undertaking the serious work of reconnoitering the terrain he couldn't resist a chase of a wild pig and time out for lunch. The British commander loved the hunt and whooped as he careered along on his thoroughbred. The fact that they had not managed to catch anything didn't seem to bother Wellesley, as the thrill of the chase seemed enough.

Firth was fascinated at the dryness of the countryside and its marked difference to the rain-sodden fields of Yorkshire - through which he and Brook had galloped after foxes.

As riders they were among the best in the area, although much of their reputation came down to more-sensible participants refusing to chase them on their death-defying leaps across dry-stone walls and thorn-entangled hedges.

There had been more than a fair share of broken bones between the pair although both had laughed them off as being the price of having good fun. There were few such fences to jump in the Portuguese countryside, but it was still a pleasant outing.

After the hunt, Firth sketched a rough map of the areas they had covered, penciling in the main roads, large hills and streams. As they were finishing a fine-bodied madeira wine served with cheese and bread, a messenger arrived to inform the commander that the reinforcing regiments had landed and were preparing for an inspection. Eager to finally join up with the Worcesters, Firth begged Wellesley's indulgence and asked to return to the main camp. The General, mouth full of cheese and port, cheerfully waved them off before turning to read a pile of papers placed on a rock next to him.

The pair put their hands and heels to their mounts as they sped towards Lavaos, sending up a trail of dust on the unmade road.

"If we time it well we may be back at the camp in time for dinner," Brook said.

Several times along the way they had met small British cavalry patrols moving out on scouting duties and stopped to help with directions.

It was late afternoon by the time they saw Lavaos in the distance and slowed their horses to a walk to allow them to ease down from their exertions. Moving through the crowded streets of the town they had stopped at their temporary lodgings to bathe, change uniforms and pick up their belongings.

It was nearing 7pm by the time they had loaded their horses and had ridden down to find the Worcesters.

"Oh stop yawning Sam," Joshua said in an annoyed tone. "It's contagious, you know," he added, holding his jaw tight to stop himself.

"Look after your horses, sirs?" a young, yellow-jacketed drummer boy interrupted.

"Certainly," replied Firth.

"The gray's a real beauty sir, what's her name?"

"It's Ricketts ..."

"What sir?"

"Ricketts."

"Ricketts, sir?"

"That's right, and that's Lass. Lieutenant Brook has Ghost and Blackie."

"But that one is called Ricketts, sir?" asked the disbelieving lad, breaking in to a huge grin.

"That's her. Is this the Worcesters' headquarters?"

"Yes sir, the Colonel's in now, sir. Officer of the day is Captain Hodge, that's him there sir."

Firth turned to Brook and motioned towards the officer seated at a table outside one of the large tents. Two grenadiers stood silently at the entrance. "Well, let's pay our compliments."

The Captain stood as the pair approached.

"Good evening to you sirs. You are?" he asked.

"Lieutenants Firth and Brook, sir. Reporting for duty," replied Firth.

"We were expecting you this morning, Lieutenant."

"Yes sir, we were unexpectedly detained, sir."

"Never mind now," said Hodge, "Better get inside. Regimental meals are at 8 o'clock and I expect Colonel Lake would like a word before we eat."

"Yes sir," the youths replied.

"I'm glad to see you have your swords, we never sit for a meal without them. Regimental tradition, you know. By the way, I'm Captain Peter Hodge."

Taking out an expensive-looking pocketwatch he flicked its elaborately carved top open and looked at the time.

"Time for you to have a tasting of sherry before we dine. Well ... let's be in then."

Hodge was only an inch or so shorter than Firth and, after stopping to remove their hats, all three officers had to stoop while entering the tent. Firth and Brook followed the Captain into a small canvas ante-chamber that was divided off from the Colonel's quarters by a muslin drape. Four wooden chairs sat in pairs on two of the canvas sides of the tent and Hodge motioned for the pair to sit. He then coughed gently and tapped twice on an exposed tent pole before pulling back the partition and walking in.

Firth and Brook heard him say their names and then he reappeared and beckoned them inside. The scent of roses and lavender greeted them as they pushed through the gauzy material.

"Ah, gentlemen, I bid you welcome," said a small figure as he crossed from an easel with a map pinned to it.

"Very pleasing it is for me to meet you. I'm Colonel Lake."

Standing at attention Firth said: "Lieutenants Firth and Brook sir, and may I say we are very pleased to be here at last."

Brook nodded his agreement.

"Splendid, young fellows, splendid."

Turning to the Captain, Lake asked: "A drink, Peter?"

"No, thank you sir. I'm duty officer for another hour." He excused himself and made his way out of the tent.

"Have a sherry?" the Colonel inquired and smiled genially as the friends nodded their assent. "Don't usually serve the stuff myself," their new commander said, his dark brown eyes moving rapidly between the pair, "But officers can see me in the hour before we dine and I find sherry helps the conversation if we don't have rankers hanging around."

Softly clapping his hands, he moved to a delicate waist-high table and filled three narrow glass flutes with honey-colored fluid poured precisely from a crystal decanter. Passing the drinks to the youths, he sat down and indicated they should do the same on two carver chairs. Taking a sip of sherry, he leaned back and examined the pair.

"Well, tell me about yourselves. Where are you from and why did you join the army. Not escaping from anything are you?" he asked lightly.

"We joined to fight Bonaparte, sir," piped up Brook.

"To fight Boney, eh?" Lake's eyes narrowed.

"And for the adventure, sir."

"Adventure, eh? Well splendid, splendid," the Colonel smiled, his face crinkling around his eyes as he did so. "I think you will find plenty of adventurous spirits in the 29th. We are a fine old regiment and have given the French many good thrashings in times gone by. Now, we are going to do it again."

Lake's brow creased with a sudden frown. "Damned impertinent fellows the Frogs, just walk into other countries and steal what they want. What is worse is that they then preach their appalling brand of freedom - and I use that word advisedly. What does a Frenchman know of freedom? Nothing!"

"Captain Rey seemed to, sir," Brook said.

"Who? Who is Rey?"

"He's a Frenchman we captured sir," said Firth.

"You captured a Frenchie? Upon my soul." Turning to Firth he asked "How?"

"Well, sir, we were riding back from Leiria, that's to the south, and laid a trap for him. We captured some dispatches too."

Leaning forward Lake asked: "Do you still have them?"

"No sir," Firth answered, "We gave them to General Wellesley."

"Wellesley, eh? Good man that. Likes to be up and at 'em. A bit like me. Always attack, I say, that's something you lieutenants will have to remember. When in doubt attack with the bayonet - puts the fear of God into the enemy."

"Yes sir," the pair said in unison.

"So you met Wellesley?"

"Yes sir, twice," said Firth, "We went scouting with him this morning."

"Did you now?"

"Yes sir, almost down to Leiria. We'd been across that country before and so General Wellesley asked us to guide him."

"Well, well. More sherry?"

"Thank you sir," Firth responded.

Lake stood and refilled the glasses.

"Now, what do your families do?"

Firth told the Colonel of his father's estate and businesses and then Brook did the same.

"So, you'll have enough money for the mess bills then, gentlemen," Lake said, gently pulling their legs. "We employ several very fine cooks for the officers' meals. It is most important to get good food. Eat hearty, fight hearty, eh?"

Lake continued: "Well, we are known for our fighting skills, courage and, most importantly of all, our style. Our regimental dinners are the best and we have the finest band in the army. Hired a troupe of musicians, you know. Even have black drummers - they're damn fine boys with the sticks."

"Blacks, sir?" asked Firth.

"Yes, had 'em since 1759 when the regiment was in Ireland. The commander's brother was an admiral stationed in the West Indies and sent him 10 blacks he thought would make excellent drummers. Never has someone been more right, they and their descendants have been a credit to the 29th."

Lake stood and placed his glass on the table. "Well, gentlemen, time to dine."

The pair got up and followed the Colonel from the tent. More than two dozen officers now waited talking around the mess marquee and all stiffened to attention as Lake passed among them.

Inside, tables had been placed end on end in two rows running from a master table. Down the lengths of the forms were folding, canvas-backed chairs and there were enough settings for all of the regiment's officers and a dozen or so guests.

"It's rare for so many of us to gather together, but I decided to have a large formal meal to celebrate the start of the campaign," Lake informed them.

The Colonel took his place in the centre of the head table and signalled to Firth and Brook that they were to sit at settings near him. A thin yellow-faced major nodded and smiled and several captains welcomed the pair. After the Colonel was seated the rest of the officers sat down and the mess attendants arrived with bottles of port for one of the three glasses at each place.

"Gentlemen," Lake said as led his officers in standing, "The King."

"The King," came the toast.

The small glasses were refilled and Lake spoke again.

"Gentlemen, the ever-sworded 29th."

"The ever-sworded 29th," again a loud, chorused response.

When everyone was seated Lake introduced Firth and Brook.

"Gentlemen, we have two new officers - Lieutenants Firth and Brook - I bid you make them welcome. Stand, sirs," he said to the pair, who rose blushing, unsure of where to look. Firth set his eyes on the Captain who had been so abrupt to them earlier. He was lounging back in his seat with locks of wavy brown hair dropping over his eyes. The man gave him a sneering smile.

"Lieutenants, you have joined a proud regiment and we expect you to uphold its honour at all times. In this tent are your brother officers. Gentlemen all of them, particularly Lord Edmund McGuire there," he said of the Captain who languidly gave a small bow, much to the amusement of the gathering.

Smiling, Lake continued. "I bid you welcome sirs."

Then the meal was served, spit-roasted beef with potatoes baked in the meat's juices. Loaves of Portuguese lanches bought from the town were placed in baskets in the centre of the tables. Firth was delighted to find that each of the sweet-smelling loaves had been stuffed with sliced ham. The claret went very well with the meat but despite its exquisite taste Firth declined a third glass from one of the privates.

"Don't drink much do you?" came a drawl from McGuire, who was quickly into his fourth.

Firth looked up. "No, sir, not tonight."

"Weak stomach?"

"No, sir, I don't mind the drink, but we've had a long day."

"Hard to find the place, eh?" the lord snorted.

Firth was finding it very difficult to be civil to McGuire who he immediately supposed to be a wastrel. The man's uniform was straining slightly around his midriff and the puffiness around his eyes suggested he liked a drink. Still, McGuire was a superior officer and Firth knew he had to hold his tongue. He watched with interest as McGuire finished another glass and stared at him.

"Tell me Lieutenant," he began belligerently, "What does your family do? Is it in the trades?" he sniffed derisively.

Ignoring what he knew to be a barb, Firth replied: "Yes, sir, my father is a merchant."

"I suppose he has money?"

"Yes, sir. He has enough."

Draining his glass McGuire stared at Firth. He was the richest man in the regiment drawing a huge income from his family estates and enjoyed seeing new officers squirm at the mention of the sum.

"And how much is enough, lieutenant?"

Firth could sense the officers seated around him, including the Colonel, taking an interest in proceedings.

"As I said sir, he has enough."

"And I suppose you do too, hey, Lieutenant?"

"Yes, sir, more than adequate thank-you."

"Well, tell us then. Five hundred pounds a year? That'd be good money for a trader? Don't tell me 1000? How many pounds a year, Lieutenant?" McGuire invited with an arrogance that made Firth bristle.

"I think Mr Firth's income is his business, Captain," the gaunt Major Way broke in quietly.

Firth turned to the Major and said: "Thank-you sir, but I am prepared to tell Captain McGuire … if he will first inform me of his."

"Glad you asked, old boy," McGuire laughed, sweeping back another tendril of hair that had fallen across his forehead, "Glad you asked."

Leaning forward, he took his time to build up the effect of the amount. "Five ... thousand ... pounds!" he declared triumphantly.

Firth took a moment. "That is a lot of money, sir."

"Now, Lieutenant, how much do you get?" McGuire insisted, "Loudly now."

The tent had fallen silent as the officers waited for Firth's answer.

Firth took a breath, stared into McGuire's hazel eyes and delivered his reply slowly. "Five ... thousand ... pounds ... sir."

"Upon my soul," the Colonel said, somewhat taken aback. Here and there low whistles could be heard among muffled comments.

"My father, sir, gets much more," Firth added, directing the comment at McGuire, whose grin was quickly vanishing from his face.

Laughter erupted around the tables and hands were pounded on the wooden tops.

"Well done lad," Major Way said, "Is that how you can afford such beautiful horses?"

"Horses, sir?"

"Yes, the ones outside. The brown and the gray."

"I suppose so sir, although the gray was a gift."

"She's magnificent. What's her name?"

"Ricketts," said Firth, too pleased with his display over McGuire to notice the tent falling quiet again. "It's Ricketts and she's named after a naval captain."

"Upon my soul," said a stunned Lake. "I think, Lieutenant, that maybe you should change her name. Sooner, rather than later."

"Sir?" queried a confused Firth.

"Because it's my name too," came an angry voice behind him. He spun around to see who it was and found himself looking straight into a strangely familiar face with jet-black eyes and hair.

"I, Lieutenant, am Major Edward Ricketts and I am glad I have arrived in time to meet you at last. My brother," he added ominously, "has written me all about you."

IX

Caldas da Rainha, 15 August.

The blazing sun beat down on the column as it wound like a giant red millipede over the series of high ridges leading down the road towards Lisbon. A salty breeze blew over the soldiers' right shoulders and the dust kicked up by those in front swirled around before caking on sweating faces and equipment.

Labouring under the weight of his pack Private William Slater trudged on, thinking only of the next rest and a mouthful or two of tepid water from his blue barrel canteen.

"Damn these blasted flies," Slater cursed. The annoying host of buzzing creatures was adding to his discomfort. "They just won't bloody go away," he grumbled as he tried to wipe away a defiant one refusing to move under even the most energetic waving of hands.

"Are you all right, soldier?" Firth asked.

Slater immediately straightened. "Yes, sir. Fine, sir. But these flies ..."

"They are brutes aren't they?" Firth agreed. "What is driving me mad is the noise from those wretched wagons. They screech. Don't the locals know about greasing them?"

"They say it's to keep evil spirits at bay, sir."

"They'd certainly do that."

For Firth, riding on the quickly renamed Boadiccea, the heat was bearable but even he was looking forward to rinsing his parched throat. He had felt like opening his own canteen several times since lunch but resisted the temptation knowing that he had to set a good example for his men.

Soon after joining the regiment he and Brook had been assigned to different companies. Their placement was left to Ricketts and the Major had taken the opportunity to attach Firth to the 6th Company under the stout Captain Robert Gell. The amiable Gell welcomed him in a friendly manner and eased the doubts Firth had after being told that the 6th was the regiment's worst company – filled with drunks, criminals and skivers. Brook had been very pleased to have landed the better posting with the highly rated 4th Company and was currently riding somewhere to Firth's rear.

It had taken the army five days of difficult marching to come within sight of Caldas. The first two days were the worst for the soldiers who, having been ship-bound for many weeks, were not in the condition needed for such exertions in the heat. There were plenty of grumblers around, Good being the worst, although none had been silly enough to make comments within earshot of the new Lieutenant.

On the first day they had managed 20 miles and had slept where they had fallen out, too exhausted to bother preparing food or shelters. Some fortunate ones had managed to drop into patches of tussocky grass, but most just placed their gray greatcoats on the rock-strewn ground and had slept dreamlessly until first light.

For Firth, however, it was not to be a night of rest. The Worcesters were in the vanguard of the army and so Ricketts had ordered a foot patrol to scout the road well in advance of the regimental picquets.

Accompanied by Sergeant Major Richards, Sergeant Barclay and 12 men, Firth had walked for three uneventful hours before returning for some desperately needed sleep. Four hours later he had been woken by the shouts of the corporals as they moved along the sides of the road kicking and prodding the soldiers into action.

It did not take long for Slater to start feeling his aches and pains, but after an hour on the march the stiffness began to ease from his legs. That day the army – much to the 18-year-old's relief - only managed eight miles and reached the large market town of Leiria by mid-afternoon.

The site chosen for that night's camp was beyond anything he had ever dreamed of in his home village. It was a large, richly scented garden that spread out in a blaze of colours below a towering royal castle, the walls of which rose as a sheer cliff above the township's terracotta rooftops.

After orders arrived from Wellesley that each soldier was to receive a pint of wine and pound of meat that evening, Colonel Lake suggested all officers take the opportunity to explore Leiria.

Unfortunately, for Firth, Ricketts decided to keep him on duty as officer in charge of the baggage carts, an onerous task at the best of times but one that was particularly chaotic during a march. Having partially sorted out the mess with the help of an experienced corporal, Firth then was greeted with another night patrol, courtesy of Ricketts, and barely had two hours sleep before recommencing
the move south at dawn.

Soon after a brilliant sunrise rumours flew around the camp that Wellesley and the Portuguese commander General Freire had not agreed on how the campaign should be fought and the two armies were to move apart. The general thinking in the ranks was splitting forces was not a sensible move, particularly with the French somewhere nearby, but while he agreed Firth kept his own counsel.

The British and a battalion of Portugal's sharp-shooting Cacadores now continued along the coastal road to stay close to naval supply lines, while the main Portuguese force moved inland.

For most of that day Firth had spent his time chasing after the Quartermaster for requisition slips. The man was slippery as an eel, the Lieutenant thought, as he was never able to locate him when he needed to do so.

On the 13th the army stopped in the shadows of a magnificent abbey at Batalha. Sharing a crusty loaf with a Portuguese officer from the Cacadores, Firth was told in broken English that the hermitage had been built near the battle site of one of Portugal's greatest victories over its domineering neighbour Spain.

"It was in 1386," the gap-toothed Captain began, "and was the first time you English and we Portuguese fought side by side.

"Your archers from Lincoln were very deadly and killed many of the Spaniards. But, for shame, there were too many enemy.

"We fought until we could fight no more and were near the end. Our leaders called for one more attack and prayed for heavenly support, offering to build the greatest abbey in the world if they lived to see victory."

Firth was caught up in the man's story of the legend and noted his eyes light up in its telling. "The miracle occurred," the officer whispered, "and with the Spaniards routed our king immediately called the best craftsmen in the land together to create one of the glories of Christendom."

Firth wondered if it was indeed divine intervention, or just plain pride and desperation that had given the Portuguese victory?

Whatever the reason for its construction, Firth thought the abbey a glorious achievement and one he wished Wren could be there to sketch.

When the sun rose bright and fiery it quickly illuminated the thick wall of dust that rose from the British as they took to the roads in search of the French.

Firth was again on patrol ahead of the regiment and this time was accompanied by Captain Gell.

Firth liked Gell most of all the regimental officers. He was prepared to take the time to show a newcomer how the army wanted things done. Not only that, Gell was an expert on the regiment's history and happily told Firth of its earlier campaigns in North America, Ireland and the Low Countries of Europe.

"I'm delighted you are so interested," Gell said. "You are very keen Joshua, that's good to see."

"Well, Captain, I find there are so many interesting things to learn about in history. It is exciting to me."

The Captain looked at his new officer and wished he had more men like him in not only his regiment, but the army itself. Intelligence was needed, but also a willingness to listen and learn. Young Firth impressed him.

"Look Joshua, don't take Major Ricketts' treatment of you to heart. Just keep handling it as you are and it will get better."

Firth wasn't so sure. He was exhausted from being constantly on night patrol.

But Firth's stubborn streak was now engaged and he was determined to put up with whatever Ricketts had in store for him. I'll show that bastard, he thought.

At the top of another rise Firth stopped and called "Captain Gell, I think we've found them."

Riding up to where Firth was halted, Gell paused and studied the horizon with a brass telescope.

"That's a hell of a dust trail, Joshua," he said, focusing on the base of the cloud. "It's the French all right, I can see blue uniforms. Moving back by the looks of it. Well, we've seen them at last. Have you a glass?"

"No, sir, I do keep promising to buy one but haven't had the moment."

"Take mine," Gell said passing over the shiny tube. "Over there, just under the horizon ... how many would you say?"

Firth did a quick count of the men within the scope, found them again with his naked eye and then multiplied that section of the column along its length.

"Looks like several thousand men sir, but it's a bit hard to make out. They are just leaving the town."

"That's a brigade, it's probably General Delaborde's men. I have little doubt of it," Gell stated, snapping the telescope shut. "Well, better be off and tell the Colonel. He'll no doubt want to inform General Wellesley and hope to be the first at them."

"Action today, sir?"

"I doubt it. They are moving so fast we'd be lucky to catch the main body ... maybe the rearguard, but only if it's infantry and baggage wagons. We'd never catch cavalry."

Gell was right about Lake who, upon hearing the news, sent a dispatch to Wellesley asking for permission to close with the enemy. It did not take long to get the reply back and from the dismay on the Colonel's face it was in the negative.

"Damn! We are to follow them, but not close. It's disappointing, gentlemen, but that's the way it is."

Within 10 minutes the 29th had formed into column and had set out towards the town of Caldas. The light company took the vanguard, the dark-green tufts on their shakos moving up and down as they strode off at the quick march - 108 steps to the minute. Next went Brook's 4th Company at a more sedate 75 steps and Firth managed a wave to his friend as he passed by. Always one for show, Lake ordered the band to strike up the official regimental tune and the fifes and drums began the lively *Royal Windsor*. Gell's company was in the rear of the long line of men, just ahead of the grenadiers. Firth thought the Worcesters made a most impressive display as they headed into Caldas and was filled with pride at his new regiment's style.

The streets of the town were empty when the light troops entered, unsure of the reception they would receive. The skirmishers spread out and began to check the houses for enemy troops who may have remained to ambush the pursuers.

They checked two abandoned French wagons in the main square for barrels of gunpowder or other traps and helped themselves to any easily carried foodstuffs they found. Soon their long-haired goatskin packs were crammed with bread and hunks of cheese and so they moved off to continue searching.

Within half an hour the rest of the regiment arrived and, by mid-afternoon, the entire army had passed through Caldas and was nearing its intended campsite three miles beyond the town. The British were desperately short of horses, but Wellesley threw a small cavalry screen ahead of his command to prevent it being surprised if the French doubled back.

Infantry picquets took positions a mile south of the main force also to give early warning of a sneak attack. Despite the presumed proximity of French troops the British rested well that evening, having cold beef, ship's biscuit in place of the yet-to-arrive bread ration, and either a pint of wine or a cup of rum.

Firth sat with Gell and an older lieutenant called Coker just off the main road in a shady vineyard. A pile of stacked branches served as their seating and they ate their meals off three silver platters the Captain had brought from England.

"Well here we are gentlemen," Gell said moving his hands, "our eating quarters ... such as they are."

Finishing a mouthful of rum Firth asked: "Captain Gell, where did the name the Ever-Sworded 29th come from?"

"It dates back to 1746, in the American colonies. Our Indian allies decided to switch sides and attacked us while the officers dined. They were beaten off, but it proved to be a very savage lesson as only a captain and two lieutenants were left unwounded.

"It means that when we are not on campaign - even in the safety of Worcestershire - we always wear our swords Joshua."

Taking up a pistol that he had laid next to his bicorne, Gell reversed the weapon and pounded the handle on to a pale biscuit he was intending to eat. It took three blows to crack the inch-thick slab and another six to break it in to pieces small enough to more easily absorb the wine that he was now pouring over it.

"This is the only way to eat this infernal stuff," Gell said with distaste. "At least it isn't full of worms. We had some awful food while at sea, Joshua, I don't know how the Navy puts up with it."

"I imagine that most are so sea sick, sir" said Coker, one of the few regimental officers actually from Worcester, "that they don't feel like eating."

"Could be, Thomas, but the only time men can bite into it is when the stuff is so rotten with maggots that it breaks before your teeth do."

"It certainly isn't the bread we used to get from old Evans down in Broad Street sir. We used to say that if Boney were to invade he'd make straight for Worcester and Evans' bakery. Best bread in the world," Coker said disconsolately, before making another attempt to bite off a corner of biscuit. "Best in the world it is."

The trio sat quietly eating for a minute or so and watched as their company ate, smoked short clay pipes known as chin burners and greedily downed their mugs of wine. Firth saw one old private try to swap a small bag of tobacco for a drummer's drink ration and then move away cursing when his attempts failed.

Feeling somewhat intimidated by the rich, new Lieutenant, Coker was determined to show Firth that he was the senior of the two and that he knew more about the regiment than most.

"Of course, Joshua, as well as the Ever-Sworded 29th we have a couple of different nicknames," he said proudly.

"There's the Guards of the Line, for our first commander, Colonel Farrington. He raised the regiment after leaving the Guards."

Gell joined in: "I think it's also to do with the fact that we are among the most disciplined regiments in the army."

"There is another," a nodding Coker went on, "and no doubt you will soon hear it. We only use it on active duty."

"What's that?"

"Well, it has been said that we started the American Rebellion after the regiment was attacked by a mob of troublemakers at the Boston customs house. We ended up shooting several of the buggers. Oh, there was a trial and most of the men were found not guilty. Two, I think, were convicted. Funny thing was that the defence lawyer went on to become America's second president."

"The name?" Gell prompted gently.

"Oh, yes. It's the Vein Openers. You can see why we usually keep it for overseas duties."

Moving the conversation on, Gell said: "By the way Joshua, you didn't get duty last night."

"Thank goodness, sir. I was resigned to another long night, but Colonel Lake had sent Major Ricketts to Alcobaca and so Major Way organised the patrol. I have to confess I slept like a log."

"Well, I'm not surprised. You've done more than enough extra duty, I would have thought."

But the Captain had spoken too soon and a voice came from behind the diners.

"Ready yourself, Lieutenant Firth, you've a foot patrol to lead."

Firth stood and turned to the black-haired Major. "Yes, sir. Twelve men, sir?"

"Correct, Lieutenant. I daresay you're getting the hang of this patrol work," Ricketts said mockingly.

"Sir."

"Well, do your duty Mr Firth."

X

South of Caldas da Rainha

By the time the patrol had marched a mile from camp the sun had set, leaving a pale-orange cast on the horizon that lit the small white clouds and gave them a warm glow. To Firth's right the eastern sky was darkening already allowing a few bright stars to announce the arrival of another cooler, clear night.

At Sergeant-Major Richards' suggestion he had divided the patrol on each side of the road and the men went forward warily with their muskets held ready across their chests.

Firth recognised some of the dozen privates from the previous patrols although it seemed to his tired mind that it was only he and the Sergeant-Major who had been volunteered for every one. Not that he minded, the patrols gave him a good opportunity to see how the men of his company behaved and talk to the veteran Richards who was fast becoming his right-hand man.

Richards enjoyed himself on the marches. He had accompanied the young officer to keep an eye on him and see whether or not he would make the grade. So far, he had not made any bad mistakes and his only fault, if it was one, was that he was keen to talk to the ranks.

Could he be a bit soft? Richards asked himself. It was a bad thing in an officer. The men didn't respect softness, Richards knew, and that's why Major Ricketts was the most respected silver-wearer in the regiment. Hard man that, Richards granted, too hard maybe. Among the troops he was known as the Flogging Major and at last count had ordered almost 100 men to the triangle during his five years with the Worcesters.

"Moon's coming up, sir."

"Thank you Sergeant-Major. We'll go on for another mile or so and then return. I don't want to move too far from the picquets," Firth said.

"I think that's a wise plan sir, there'll be Frenchies about tonight."

In the strengthening light of the moon Firth could see a small wood ahead and immediately saw it as a good site for the enemy to lay an ambush.

"Sergeant-Major, I'd like two men to move ahead and push 20 or so paces into that wood. They are not to move further on until we close. They are just to keep lookout."

"Sir."

Richards tapped two men on the shoulder and sent them forward. They set off at the trot but slowed as they got within 50 paces of the trees. Keeping on separate sides of the road the pair eased towards the shadows knowing full well that they would be very visible to anyone hiding there. When they reached the cover of the trees Firth waited for 30 seconds before giving the order for the rest of the patrol to move.

Slater was one of the forward men and edged slowly through the trees. Never keen on the dark, he found it difficult to concentrate on looking out for French skirmishers while the shadows from trees twisted and threatened his vision. He could hear old

Siddle moving slowly in the undergrowth to his right and while that gave him a small degree of comfort the knot remained tight in his stomach.

"John," he whispered loudly. "John."

The rustling near him continued.

"John."

"What is it lad?" came the response.

"I can't see anything."

"Just keep looking, lad, and keep your noise down," the voice sounded impatient.

Stumbling over a branch, Slater knocked his knee and gave a stifled yelp.

"Quiet!" came a hissed command.

Regaining his footing the youth pushed on. He jumped as a bird gave a call to his left and whipped around as something cracked behind him. Ahead he could make out a large patch of light and knew it meant a clearing. His feet seemed to pick every small twig to stand on and break. Each snap seemed unnaturally loud to his ears and sent his heart pounding even harder in his chest.

"Open space ahead John," he warned in what he wanted to be a whisper but his nervousness spat it out as a half-shout.

"Quiet, lad, I'll join you soon."

Just as Slater reached the edge of the copse one of the few clouds in the sky passed in front of the moon, plunging the area into darkness.

Pushing through a tangle of branches, the private's right foot caught on an exposed root and he half fell into the clearing and rolled down a slight embankment hitting his head on several hard objects.

An appalling smell smothered his nostrils and he quickly sat up and pushed his shako, which had fallen across his eyes, off his face. Above him loomed dark shapes that were impossible to make out. Having lost his musket he scrabbled about for it and, grasping the stock, hurriedly brought it to bear on the nearest shape just as the moon broke from behind its cover.

Slater gasped at what he saw and let out a terrified cry. Surrounding him were dozens of dead men, impaled on stakes. Unable to take his eyes from the nearest face the cowering youth blindly reached out to push himself off his knees and recoiled as his left hand pushed wrist-deep into sticky, rotting flesh. The smell was disgusting and Slater's stomach heaved.

"John," he whimpered as another stream of vomit spat from his throat between his outstretched arms that were locked on to the musket. "John."

Suddenly he heard a movement behind and spun around, his eyes bulging with fear. One of the shapes was moving and making guttural noises. Then it began to move towards him. It proved too much for Slater who shouldered his musket and fired.

Firth had heard the shot and drawing his sword had doubled his men forward. Reaching the clearing he stopped short at the smell and sight that greeted him.

"My God," was all he could manage to say.

The rest of the patrol thundered past him before also stopping abruptly.

"Jesus," breathed the Sergeant-Major, who was stunned at the horrific scene. He quickly recovered his senses and spaced his men out.

Among the dead bodies Firth could see two figures on the ground. The larger was on his knees muttering something incomprehensible and trying to pull the other up by the lapels of his uniform.

"Where's Slater, Sar-Major?" Siddle said as he ran into the clearing.

Richards turned around and, pointing to where Slater lay, demanded: "Well, if that's not you, Siddle, who the hell is it?"

The group watched as the figure lurched to its feet, swayed and then half-flopped forward to tap the lad across his face.

"You're a bad shot lad, here have a drink," it said forcing a bottle of brandy into Slater's mouth and pouring in a large mouthful. The boy spluttered, swallowed and then coughed as the fiery spirit rushed down his throat.

"That's right, my lad, drink away."

Suddenly Richards recognised the shambolic figure and called: "Sergeant Needham, leave that man."

Needham did his best to straighten, but his balance was not what it should have been and as soon as he released the private he fell over.

Walking to the man, Firth asked: "Who is this, Sergeant-Major Richards? He has the uniform of the 29th."

"It's Thomas Needham, sir. A good man. A brave man. But he does like the bottle."

Hesitating, Firth took Richards aside.

"He is a friend of yours?"

"Yes, sir, he's a friend and very well liked in the regiment."

"What does he face?"

"A flogging, sir, if he's charged. And if I may say, sir, it would be a shame to lose him with the French just over the hill. He's a good fighter, sir."

Firth chewed at his lip and thought before going on.

"Can you sober him up quickly?"

"I can sir."

"Right, he's in your charge, Sergeant-Major. No one will care about him when we tell them of this," Firth said, counting the impaled corpses. Who could do such a thing? And, Lord, this place stank.

He brought his sleeve up to cover his nose and mouth and walked to a sign hung around the neck of the front body. A gaudy hat lay at the base of the stake spitting the man who, by the agonised look that had been frozen in death, had obviously taken a long time to die. On the sign were words written in French. "Poles take no prisoners."

With the exception of Richards, who was trying to get Needham to throw up by forcing him to drink a mug of water laced with two cartridges of gunpowder, and Siddle, who was picking up the pack and musket of an ashen-faced Slater, the men of his patrol stood looking at the corpses.

It was the first time that any had seen men killed in such a way and their reaction was one of interest rather than horror. Apart from the smell, which was too disgusting to think about, the main talking point was how far the stakes had gone through the victims' bodies.

In two cases, the sharpened points actually came out through mouths causing some comment and not a little humour among the soldiers.

"Must have taken good aim," grinned the skinny William Good, whose callous mirth was quickly stifled by a glance from the new officer.

"Better watch that one," Good said softly to the man next to him, "he doesn't appear upset at all by the appearance of so many bodies."

While Firth would have been cheered by Good's assessment he was shocked by what he saw. It was savagery beyond his wildest imaginings but he was determined to put on as much of an air of nonchalance as he could in front of his men. Stay above the men, the Colonel had advised him, in word, bearing and deed.

"Sergeant-Major," he called. "Let's return."

The march back to camp was slowed by Needham's inability to walk in a straight line. His mind, too, wandered along straying from thoughts of the night's drinking to women, food and bed. The buzzing in his Needham's ears was getting louder and Richards' shoulder was becoming increasingly more supportive.

"Bloody good night, Dick," he breathed boozily.

"Shut up, Thomas, and right now it's Sergeant-Major to you. Grog-soaked sot!"

"No, no, no, it was a good night, right up until I got into that clearing. Almost scared me sober it did, Dick. Almost scared me sober."

Needham paused for a moment and chuckled slowly, shaking his head. "No, I could never be that scared, not tonight."

"Nor for the next week by the smell of you. You're lucky it's Mr Firth and not Major Ricketts. If it was that one you'd lose three stripes from your arm and get 300 on your back."

"I'll be fine, Dick, I'll be fine," Needham slurred.

The patrol passed through the British picquets and made its way to where the Worcesters bivouacked. Firth dismissed the men and was about to report the discovery of the massacre site to the Colonel when he saw Ricketts swaggering towards him.

"Well, Lieutenant, anything to report?"

"Yes, sir. We didn't see any French, but they've been around." He went on to explain to the Major about finding the bodies, leaving out the part about Needham, who Firth could see being escorted away to his left.

"What are you looking at, Mr Firth?" Ricketts demanded.

"Nothing, sir."

Ricketts moved and shouted out to Needham who was doing his best to disappear into the shadows.

"You! Sergeant! Come here!"

The grenadier stopped and looked. "Me, sir?"

"You. What are you doing?"

"Just going to the privvy, sir."

Ricketts' eyes narrowed and he moved closer to Needham.

"You've been drinking," he said, spinning back towards Firth. "You allowed this man on patrol while drunk, Mr Firth."

"He was not part of my patrol, sir. We ... found him at the clearing, sir."

"Have you charged him?"

"Not as yet, sir."

"Then do so. Sergeant-Major have this man guarded, he'll face the Colonel tomorrow. I will deal with you, Mr Firth, myself," said Ricketts with a canine-like grin.

XI

Caldas da Rainha, 16 August

Black Jack stamped the ground impatiently as Colonel Lake waited for the prisoner. A slight squeezing of his knees quieted the stallion and Lake continued to watch the silent lines of his regiment. He looked aloof and impassive, but inside he was fuming. The court-martial had been brief, fair and decisive.

Needham had been found guilty, demoted back to the ranks and would receive 100 lashes for being drunk on duty. The Colonel had barely controlled his temper during the hearing although he would have dearly loved to have shouted at the Sergeant for being so stupid.

The regiment would soon need his experience on the field, but it was more important that the men were shown that regulations had to be obeyed.

The tapping of the drums fell silent as the popular redhead was brought to the triangle. Thank God, thought Needham, for whatever awaited him it could not possibly be worse than the pains that shot through his skull every bang of the drum. The bright sun was blinding his half-closed eyes and his mouth was as dry as the dusty ground. I'll never touch another drop again, he promised himself, feeling desperately sick at the thought of grog.

"Good luck Tommy," a corporal called Jones whispered into his ear as he gently tied Needham's hands. "The calfskin fiddlers have been told to lay on easy. You'll be all right."

When the miscreant had been tied Lake edged Black Jack forward.

"Men of the 29th," he began in a clear voice, "tomorrow we will be moving against a strong French position just to our south. We are to be among the first regiments to be at the enemy, an honour I take very seriously.

"Each of you should take it as a compliment that our regiment is held in such high regard. Tomorrow you have the chance to prove yourselves in battle.

"You will stand like true Englishmen and deliver the Frenchies such a blow that they will regret taking the field against us.

"Mark me, it is an honour we have been given but it is one that still needs to be earned. Honour has a price and on the morrow we may pay it, but we will do so whole-heartedly for our King."

Shifting his gaze down the assembled lines he stopped on the Colour Party.

"There lads are the Colours. They should be flying proudly at our head but, instead, are covered because of one man. His actions have brought dishonour to himself and to our regiment.

"Tomorrow we can wipe the stains of disgrace away, but this man will not. It is to his shame that he will not be standing with us as we show the damned French how to fight.

"He," Lake indicated towards the pale figure on the triangle, "will have to confess to his children that he was not one of those heroes of the 29th who beat the Frogs bloody in Portugal."

Standing with his company, Firth could feel the power of the Colonel's words. If any man had disagreed with the flogging before Lake's speech he was sure that none did now.

The Colonel looked to Ricketts and gave the signal.

"Begin," the Major ordered with relish.

Needham had prepared himself for the first blow and its accompanying sting. Focusing on a large tree that he could see through his extended arms he kept telling himself over and over that his back would never be as sore as his head.

It wasn't until the 50th stroke that he began to doubt his optimism. The pain started to exert its influence over his brain soon after he felt his skin split and the blood run down to his britches.

Needles, he thought, it felt like someone was slapping him and then pressing hundreds of needles into his flesh. The stinging worsened, momentarily bringing tears to his eyes, before he regained control and returned his gaze to the tree. He had no idea what kind it was, but a brightly coloured bird was settling itself on to a high limb.

The slap of the cat-o-nine-tails brought his mind back to the triangle.

"Seventy," continued the duty officer's call of strokes. Only 30 more, Thomas, he reminded himself, just a few more. The hard work's done.

Firth watched the beating shamefacedly. He felt sorry for Needham who, by all reports, was one of the best men in the regiment, but he was furious at himself.

He had been bawled at by Ricketts in a most ungentlemanly way over the incident and had been told that he was to obey regulations to the letter.

The Major, currently smiling at the punishment being meted out, had told him he was soft - "a soft boy with too much money."

Firth bridled at the memory. The anger rose in his throat, but he willed himself to forget the insults, vowing to never put himself in that sort of situation again. Stay distant from the men and keep it by the book.

He looked at Ricketts and saw a face beaming with malevolence. The only good thing about this flogging, Firth thought, was that Brook was not there to witness it. The pair had met briefly that morning just before his friend had been sent with the wagons to bring back ammunition from the main supply train lurching along the roads somewhere between Alcobaca and Caldas.

Brook had laughingly admitted that the officers of his company had heard the story of his being ill at a flogging and had given him the nickname of Gurgling. Firth had burst out laughing and even now, at a whipping, had to stop himself smiling. Gurgling Brook, what a name he thought.

"Ninety-eight ... ninety-nine ... one hundred," said the duty officer, taking a pace backwards. "Punishment complete, sir."

Two corporals supported Needham as they released his hands and then carried him towards Dr Guthrie's wagon.

"Dismiss the men," a stony-faced Lake said curtly to Ricketts before wheeling Black Jack around and walking him away.

"Sir! Parade dismiss!"

The ranks broke up and instantly began talking among themselves about the possibility of fighting. The soldiers had been given a clear indication by the Colonel that they would be going into action tomorrow and so made their way back to where they had left their kits.

For the next two hours sergeants and corporals hovered as muskets were cleaned and bayonets sharpened.

Firth went to one of the armourers and asked for his sword blade to be honed.

The private took the weapon lovingly in his hands and treadled the stone up to top speed. Wetting the steel he gently pressed it on to the spinning disc sending a small number of sparks into the air.

"Nice blade, sir," he admired, "doesn't need much work. We'll just give it a bit more of an edge. The point's fine."

The man's brow furrowed as he concentrated on his work. Checking the edge with a grimy thumb he looked up and smiled at Firth. "Sharp as a shrew's tongue, sir. That'll teach a few Frogs a lesson."

Reaching down he picked up a soft cloth and, using long smooth strokes, rubbed oil from an old canteen into the shiny surface. Placing the sword on his small wooden table the soldier wiped his hands on a second rag and then, picking it up again, offered it to Firth.

Taking the sword Firth examined the man's worksmanship.

"It's better than anything we had in Whitby. You've done a fine job."

Taking a shilling from a small pocket inside the top of his breeches, Firth handed the coin to the man who was surprised by the generosity.

"Price is only tuppence, sir."

"I'm happy to pay for good work, private ...?"

"Reardon, sir, Private Reardon."

"Well, thank-you Private Reardon. And please take the shilling, you've earned it."

"Much obliged, sir. If you need anything just come to old Denis and I'll fix it."

Firth slipped the blade into its scabbard and walked to where Gell and Coker were in conversation.

"Ah, Joshua," Gell greeted, "we were just discussing the benefits of pistols. Thomas likes them, but I must say I don't hold with them. Not accurate and tucked inside a waist sash they play havoc with your ribs. What do you think?"

"Well, sir, I've never had reason to wear one, but my father swears by them."

"Good shot is he?"

"He's regarded as such, sir. He spent a summer teaching me how to use personal arms and told me that as a pistolier I'd make a fine swordsman."

The Captain and Lieutenant laughed at the self-deprecation. Firth had fitted in well, Gell thought. The Sergeant-Major had spoken highly of him and that was a good sign.

"Well, Joshua, you'll be pleased to know that you won't be patrolling tonight. The green-jackets of the 60th Royal Americans and the 95th Rifles have gone out ahead to clear French picquets from the next village.

"A good friend of mine, Lieutenant Bunbury, is lucky enough to be going with a company of them into Obidos. He'll have some excitement soon while we, I'm sure, will see action tomorrow."

The Captain's usually smiling face became serious for a moment.

"Colonel Lake has told me to advise all the men, officers included, to ready their affairs this evening and expect to march before first light."

In a series of small rooms close to where the officers talked, Twin One and Twin Two were doing their best to gently lie Needham face down on a bed in a makeshift surgery.

They tried to avoid getting gore on their clothes but the difficulties of holding such a large man steady with only two arms between them was causing problems.

Already the white cuff on each of their shirts was stained red and their fingers were almost too slippery with blood to grasp the soldier's arms. Needham moaned every time their attempts jarred his body and finally had enough.

"For God's sake leave me be!"

Grimacing as his movements stretched and tore at the drying blood that was already crusting over some parts of his lacerated back, Needham slowly eased on to the rough cloth sheet covering a gray-wool blanket that was tucked around a thin cotton mattress. A large cup of brandy had dulled the pain temporarily and a second brought by the kindly Twins sent him towards sleep. I'll fight tomorrow, they'll not stop me, he thought, and began drifting into slumber.

Four hours later he was woken by a commotion outside. Men were shouting and the squeal of wagons pierced the small window above his bed. Pulling himself on to his knees Needham looked out through the glass and saw dozens of bloodied, wounded men lying on the flat trays of the carts. Most were calmly waiting for an examination by the surgeon but one man, with his hands pressed on to his stomach, was writhing in pain. Poor bugger won't last long, Needham told himself.

The Twins were helping Dr Guthrie and so he was alone. Getting down from the bed he crossed to a large chest and took a swig of brandy from one of the bottles packed in its wooden partitions. For medicinal purposes only, he excused himself, taking another gulp for the road.

Those men outside need the bed more than I do, he reasoned, and my company needs me. Finding his uniform he carefully pulled on his shirt and jacket, wincing at the discomfort his arm movements caused to the torn flesh on his back. Christ it hurt. With a farewell mouthful Needham replaced the bottle and closed the lid, before shuffling to a side door and into a quiet lane.

The commotion that the return of the troops sparked brought Firth out of his tent where he had been reading *Tom Jones, a Foundling* one of four books he had brought to Portugal. Men were standing in groups talking excitedly among themselves. To his right, Firth could see Captain Gell sitting with his head in his hands.

"Sir, are you unwell?"

Gell looked up with eyes that appeared about to burst with pent up tears. "I'm all right thank you Joshua. It's just that John Bunbury is dead … killed by a French voltigeur as we took Obidos."

"I'm very sorry, sir," Firth said.

"You know, Joshua," Gell went on in a faltering voice, "we grew up together. My wife is his sister. What will I tell her? It's a sore loss, Joshua, he was well loved." Gell stood and rubbed his eyes with his hands.

"It will be a hard morrow, Joshua, we may lose many friends. Make sure you have written to your family," he said and moved off.

Firth stared after the sad figure and felt sorry for his Captain. He had penned a letter to his father and now needed to find Brook. If he fell tomorrow, then his friend could have his belongings.

XII

Columbiera, 10am, 17 August

General Henri Delaborde limped with difficulty up the crude wooden stairs inside the windmill. Its internal workings squealed and rumbled, driven by the four, two-storey sails being pushed by the strengthening breeze.

The noise irritated his ears, but he tried to ignore it as the building was the tallest in the village of Columbiera. Climbing through a window on to a narrow balcony, he could see north down the valley to where the British columns marched from Obidos. To his left was a low hill that, despite being only 20 metres high, still dominated the dusty, brown plain.

Delaborde brushed his right hand through his short hair, which was styled forward in the ancient Roman way to cover its slow recession, and watched the enemy's manoeuvres.

"It's not a good position is it Antoine?" the middle-aged General asked without expecting an answer.

"It is not General, but we've had worse," said the aide.

Delaborde smiled at the Colonel, who had served with him on four of his campaigns. It was true, he thought, the position was unsound. His 4500 men were outnumbered by at least two-to-one by the soldiers of Wellesley and he was sure there were more British troops in the area.

His men blocked the road to Lisbon, although their ranks could be skirted by an enemy commander sending troops around their flanks.

"We need to hold them off for as long as possible Antoine. This is just a delaying action … nothing more, and the longer the better."

Delaborde knew that somewhere across the rugged hills to the south, his colleague General Loison was marching to him with enough men to even the odds.

Unfortunately his cavalry patrols had seen nothing of the reinforcements, so he would have initially to meet the enemy alone.

As the sounds of fifes and drums reached his ears, Delaborde had to admit the Redcoats were impressive.

Through his spyglass he could see enemy officers bringing their troops into line. The changing of formation was carried out with a style and precision that made him think of a parade ground.

Those men could rival the Imperial Guard on the Champ de Mars, he thought. It certainly was eye-catching and Delaborde knew that was exactly what the British wanted. They will try to hold me here against those men while they send others out round the hills to surround us.

A hussar with jingling spurs moved out on to the balcony and presented two dispatches. Taking the pieces of paper Delaborde scanned the looping handwriting and gave a grunt. It was as he thought, enemy troops were marching to his west, hidden from view by the steep-sided hills that formed the rim of the valley. A larger force, with as many men as he had in his entire brigade, was advancing around to the east.

Never mind, the French commander thought, it was all going to plan.

"Well Antoine," he said to the aide, "they are now four to our one. Those men will be around our flanks by noon so we will need to time this very carefully."

Snapping shut his telescope Delaborde moved inside and began a precarious descent. His chronic rheumatism was playing havoc with his right hip, making it difficult to walk, and he thanked God for the heat of the Peninsula. Better here than in some snow-swept town on the Rhine.

"Someone should have fixed a rail to this cursed stairway. It's more like a ladder," Delaborde growled impatiently as he almost lost his balance. "Do you want me to break a leg?"

Outside the General mounted his horse and, followed by several more aides, rode towards the blue uniforms of the 70th line regiment drawn up on the hill.

From his new vantage point Delaborde could see the British beginning to advance again. Riding down the triple ranks he called out to his troops.

"Here they come men. The leopards of England. They think they have us, but we will give them a little surprise. Vive L'Empereur."

After the men's shouts faded, he turned to a colonel and said quietly. "We will wait until they are within cannon range."

Again to his men he cried "Vive L'Empereur" and the return roar echoed through the valley.

XIIa

The shouting made Firth look around. He was standing within two miles of the French lines and had halted with the other companies to allow the men to prime and load their muskets. In the distance he could see the French waving their hats and cheering. A bit different to our silent ranks, he thought, and returned to the task at hand.

He had been kept busy all morning and was very glad about it as his mind had been kept from thinking about the coming battle. He did feel nervous and hoped that others felt the same, though no one showed it. The officers paced calmly in front of the ranks putting their men at ease.

"This'll be easy boys," a captain predicted.

"The Frogs'll never stand, my lads," another said with certainty.

Occasionally a cough, or the whinny of a skittish horse, sounded but down the long, red-coated lines the soldiers waited for the order to advance with no sound.

Firth's stomach gurgled. He had not been able to eat breakfast and he wished he had drunk another mug of tea. His mouth was very dry. Two companies down he could see Brook and wished he could talk to him, but a distant smile was all they could manage. Again turning to look at the enemy he heard boots crunch next to him.

"Permission to speak, sir?" asked Richards.

"Of course, Sergeant-Major."

Looking a little reticent, Richards struggled for the right words. He had seen the

Lieutenant silently looking at the enemy and knew he must be thinking about the coming fight. From experience he knew that a man's first battle was one of the most terrifying things to face. He himself had puked his guts up as a private before the attack at Valenciennes some 15 years before.

An old private had picked him up, given him some water and told him the worst was over. Fear was the biggest enemy, he had said, and the trick was to regard yourself as being dead already and only think of spitting a Frenchman on your bayonet.

Bloody stupid advice, Richards recalled, as the private died screaming after a blade had ripped open his stomach.

"Well, sir, if you don't mind me saying ... before your first battle and all ... that fear is the biggest enemy."

"Sergeant-Major?"

Flushing bright red Richards shook his head. "No, no, that's not right ... beg pardon for not putting it properly, sir, but I'm not a man of learning. Except army learning, of course."

Coughing in his hand, he began again.

"What I'm trying to say is that my job is to make the men following me believe I am not afraid of whatever is ahead. It's even more important for officers."

"And?"

"Well, sir, as we walk towards the Frenchies I'll be telling myself that when I hear a musketball whirring by me then it has missed. It's a nice sound sir, tells me it's been and gone and there's no point in ducking. Helps me show the lads behind me that I'm not worried. Gives them confidence."

"So if I hear it, I don't worry?"

"Yes, sir, there doesn't seem to be much point. Do you follow me, sir?"

"I think so, Sergeant-Major, and thank you for your concern."

"Sir," Richards came to attention.

"By the way, do I look that nervous?"

Richards laughed. "No, sir. You look the picture of calm, but everyone has nerves sir. All except the Colonel, that is."

Firth looked over to where Lake sat facing the regiment as Major Way rode up to the commander.

"All in readiness, Gregory?" the Colonel asked.

"The men are eager, sir, and raring to do some damage to the French."

"Excellent, Gregory, they are good fellows and they are looking damn fine today," Lake said, extremely pleased with the cut of his men with their hair freshly powdered and queued.

"That they are, sir." Way agreed, noticing that his Colonel was dressed from top to toe in a brand new uniform. "May I compliment you, sir, on your regimentals today."

"Thank you, Gregory, it's an entire new suit. Cost me a fortune, but I have kept it away until our first day of action. New jacket, boots, leathers ... the whole kit. Even got a new feather!"

"Well, sir, you look as if you are about to be addressed by the King himself."

"Upon my soul, Gregory, if I am killed today I mean to die like a gentleman."

Edging forward, Lake halted 10 paces from his troops.

"Gentlemen, display the Colours," he called.

The flag bearers took the leather sheaths off and the great standards stirred gently. Wheeling Black Jack around the Colonel ordered the advance as the fifes and drums struck up *Heart of Oak*. Shoulder to shoulder and with the bayonets gleaming the Worcesters started their march towards Columbiera.

XIIb

Posted just below the hill with a voltigeur company, Florian Bellegarde tapped his brother on the green epaulette decorating his shoulder and pointed out a magnificent black charger at the head of the first British regiment.

"Hey, Ugo, I want that Englishman's horse."

"Merde, Florian, you are always looking for loot. Can't you see it is a horse for a general, not a poor *sous-officier* like you."

"But Ugo, if we get that horse you will not remain a private for long. Think of it, it must be worth 5000 francs. How many years pay is that?"

"We could live well on that," his brother agreed, remembering the tough times they had as farm labourers before joining the Emperor's armies. "They are getting close, I hope the General knows what he's doing."

"He's one of the best, Ugo, one of the best."

The pair watched the British close within a kilometre of their lines. The faces of the approaching red ranks were still indistinct, but now the defenders had recognisable human forms at which to jeer. They knew their shouted insults calling the attackers sheep buggerers and boy lovers would not be heard above the music, but it certainly made them feel bolder.

The Bellegardes and their fellow voltigeurs were there to disrupt the British lines by sniping at the advancing men and reducing their numbers as best as they could. The pair knew it was dangerous work – particularly if the British sent out their own skirmishers - those green-clad "Grasshoppers" with rifles. Then it would be hot work, Florian thought, caught in a battle within a battle.

"Here they come Ugo," he said to his brother.

"Are the Grasshoppers coming?"

"They are brother, although we've twice their number. Keep close to me and watch my right, I'll look after the left. Remember, move fast and don't stand still – I've seen what the Austrian jaegers can do with a rifle and it is very nasty."

Sous-officier Bellegarde gave the younger man a loving pat on the back and smiled. "Don't stand still or stop. Follow me and stay close brother."

XIIc

Moving forward with his sword over his right shoulder, Firth kept looking over the blade and then to his left to make sure he and the men who followed him were in line with the rest of the regiment. Coker was marching 20 paces to his left with Gell in between them. The stoney ground made it difficult to keep one's footing, but the advance continued with parade-style precision.

As the band changed into *The Lincolnshire Poacher* Firth felt a shiver of pride running up his back and through the nape of his neck. He gave an involuntary shudder and hoped no one took it to be a sign of fear. His nerves had settled and all he felt marching to the sound of drums and fifes with this body of men was exhilaration.

Sir Arthur Wellesley was also excited. Sitting on his horse Copenhagen among his aides and senior officers in the centre of the British force, the commander whooped with delight as the pincers of his army reached around to cut off the French.

"We've got 'em, gentlemen. Once those wings join they'll never get out. General Benton," he called, "Lake's up forward is he not?"

General Benton peered at the leading regiment and nodded.

"Yes, Sir Arthur, it's the Worcesters."

"Just the ones. Lake is not one for caution and this is just a matter of getting in and at them. Courage of a lion, that man."

XIId

From his hill, Delaborde took a last look at the enemy who were now within 500 paces. A solitary cannon could be heard firing to his right and on the left white-coated Portuguese cacadores were moving down a well-worn track from the valley's sides. It was time to move.

"Sound the retreat," he called.

The French drummers beat out the recall for the voltigeurs and, as they melted through the lines, changed their rhythm into that of the retreat.

The sudden withdrawal caused Wellesley, to stand up in his stirrups and give a curse. "Bloody hell, he's moving!"

Quickly calculating the distance between his closing wings and that of the running French he knew the trap would not spring in time. "Bloody, bloody, hell," he fumed. "They've gone, they've bloody escaped."

Watching the disappearing enemy he knew it had been a waste of an entire morning. Now, he would have to start again and hope that the delay would not give the French reinforcements time to arrive.

XIII

Rolica, 1pm, 17 August.

It could not have gone any better Delaborde congratulated himself. Having left the surprised British behind, his men were now busily preparing their second stand of the day on the ridge high above Columbiera near the village of Rolica.

The General allowed himself a smile and eased into a chair at a small table set with cold chicken, olives and a vintage bordeaux. This was a fine defensive position and one that would cause the enemy many headaches.

Half of his troops were placed behind a low stone wall that ran for a kilometre along the top of the ridge. From the wall they could overlook the only three routes to the top of the hill - narrow, rocky gullies that at times shrank to allow only a handful of men at a time to pass through.

His remaining men were hidden along the tree-lined walls of the passes and would add to an attacker's woes by being able to fire at them from almost unseen positions. Delaborde's biggest decision had been whether or not to level the village of Columbeira, which lay in front of the passes. That small collection of white houses could decide the outcome of an attack against the heights. His aides had argued that the village would offer too much cover for the attackers and had suggested flattening it with gunpowder, but Delaborde had decided against that hoping the British lines would be disordered as they were forced to move around the buildings.

Taking a gulp of red wine he washed it around his mouth enjoying the flavour. As he placed the glass back on the table a drop of wine fell on to the white cloth, staining where it landed a dull red. Yes, Delaborde thought, there would be much British blood spilt at this place if they try to force the passes.

XIIIa

At a hastily convened meeting well out of cannon range of the French, the British senior officers were considering how to take on the enemy's new ground.

Wellesley, still barely able to hold his fury at being outmanouevred by his opponent, was pacing about like a caged tiger. With one eye on his commander and the other on a report from the right wing, Benton was biding his time before speaking.

Wellesley kicked at a rock sending it skidding under a dispatch rider's horse that jumped and almost unseated a young Ensign.

"Well, Benton, what are we going to do?"

"Sir Arthur, we have a report from Colonel Trant and his Portuguese. They are in good order and will continue their flanking march on your orders. The left wing is also ready to move."

Looking at the hills Wellesley had to commend Delaborde. "He's chosen well, that will be a brute to assault from the front. How many guns does he have?"

"Five that we can sight, Sir Arthur. All defending his left wing behind that village, Columbeira."

"So what do you think, Benton? Try the same again?"

"It may be the best way, sir."

"All right, gentlemen," Wellesley announced, "we will try to encircle him again. This time his ground is perfect and so he is unlikely to move.

"In the centre here we have three ravines to move up. Major-General Hill," he said addressing a solidly built man with red cheeks. "You will take the right-hand pass. "Major-General Nightingall, your brigade will advance through the middle.

"Brigadier-General Crauford your men will use the western pass. Let's be done with it, gentlemen, and show these French that we are not to be trifled with."

Moving out of Wellesley's earshot Miles Nightingall, a thin, whippet-faced brigadier-general, said to the older and heftier Crauford: "Those gullies look like devils, Catlin. Hard devils at that."

Crauford nodded. "That they are, and it looks like you have the toughest of them. Your lads up to it, Miles?"

"With the 82nd and the Worcesters I could take Paris," Nightingall boasted. The pair burst into laughter.

"Glad to see such high spirits," Hill said, joining them. "We will need some spirit, gentlemen, if we are to move the Frenchies off their backsides. If things go wrong up there we can expect to lose a great many men."

"Oh Rowland, you're such a daddy to your boys," Nightingall teased, knowing of Hill's great concern for his men.

"Better to be safe than sorry. That Frenchman up there knows what he doing and he's had time to prepare for us. This will not be a walk up some easy mountain track, Miles," he subtly chided as he mounted his horse.

Nightingall and Crauford watched him go.

"Did I say Daddy Hill? More like Granddaddy Hill," Nightingall snorted. "Well, all the best, Catlin, I'm off for a quick round of sherry. See you at the top."

Crauford waved his colleague away and looked again at the heights. Unlike Nightingall, Crauford could not help a feeling of foreboding as he went to join his brigade.

While the staff officers' meeting was being held, Brook had sought out Firth. As soon as they saw each other the pair broke into instant reports of the past few days, neither stopping to see if the other was listening. When it was clear that Brook wasn't hearing a word that he was saying, Firth patiently let his friend finish.

From what he could gather, the 4th company was a fine bunch of fellows, except for Captain Lord Edmund McGuire. He'd left Brook alone, but could often be seen talking with Ricketts. Just as Brook finished his news the senior officers were summoned to a meeting and he had to return to his post.

"Best of luck Joshua," he said, already moving away.

"Same to you," Firth said, hoping that the over-excited Samuel had heard his farewell. Just ahead of him lay the village of Columbiera, its whitewashed houses long deserted by the owners who had seen the armies approach, picked up whatever they could carry and fled.

Beyond the dwellings a series of brown fields and green groves spread through several small stands of trees before stopping at the steep faces of the cliffs.

Firth thought the imposing rock barrier resembled a clenched fist, with knuckle-like promontories sitting atop the entrances to three deep ravines that split the walls like the gaps between fingers. There was an almost constant twinkling along the ridge as the sun, having broken out from behind some low clouds, glinted off burnished metal. He could see a long line of Frenchmen standing behind a wall running the length of the heights and supposed that more were waiting within the passes themselves.

They'll be able to shoot down on us and there won't be anything we can do about it, he thought.

Firth shifted his weight nervously to his right foot and, lost in thought, watched the enemy positions.

He had a strange feeling in his stomach, a familiar one that he had not had for some years.

It brought back the smell of old leather-bound books, musty rooms and the kitchens of Eton, where the mouth-watering aromas never managed to appear as anything edible on the schoolboys' tables. He had spent 18 months at the prestigious school - a year-and-a-half of a hell that started when he was 12.

His studies had been excellent, all the masters had said so, but the problem Firth had was with some of the older boys. It was known he had money and had several times been stood over for a bag of coins by five or six of those in their senior years.

The acidic taste that rose into his mouth had been a constant companion for months as he tried to avoid the bullies. Then, shamed by his inability to fight them, Firth had secretly asked one of the gardeners, a former bare-knuckle boxer, for lessons.

The worst, and largest, of the boys was the son of an MP who would bash Firth given any excuse or opportunity. The bullying continued and despite being increasingly able to do so, Firth did not fight back. He did not think himself ready.

One winter's day he had no choice but to defend himself as his nemesis and four cronies had it in their minds to hold him over one of the great fires in the students' quarters.

Months of fear and frustration erupted into physical violence as Firth at last stood up for himself. As the bully went to hit him Firth stepped forward and landed a right jab in the solar plexus. Instantly he hit the same spot again and then launched heavy nose-breaking blow. With tears and blood streaming, the bully shouted to his friends to grab Firth, who was already closing on them. Before they knew it, the well-aimed fists of their usually passive victim had downed another and were starting on a third member of their circle.

Through the fog of his anger, Firth was telling himself to keep punching. Right, left, then right. The thrill of paying back his attackers back helped him ignore the pain of his bruised knuckles and even when return blows began to rain in, his mind was still seeking out the weak spots on his opponents' bodies.

With five against one the fight was never going to last long and by the time a passing master had been attracted by the shouts and cheers of a large crowd of onlookers, Firth had been badly beaten. His right eye was closing and blood poured from his nose and a number of cuts on his face and knuckles. Despite the pain around his ribs he felt ecstatic. He had stood up and proven himself.

Recovering in bed Firth had a week to think things over and had realised he no longer cared about the physical pain because it couldn't compare with the relief of having conquered the fear of being hurt.

His enlightenment didn't help him in front of the headmaster, however, and both he and his assailants were expelled.

Unexpectedly arriving back home he had been marched into the study by his father's manservant, who handed over a letter from the school. Denholme Firth read the note silently, pausing occasionally to look up at his son. He asked for an explanation and, upon hearing the tale, stood and walked to a cupboard.

"They won't have you back there, so now I have to get you a tutor young man. And, I'm afraid I'm going to have to punish you. Come over here."

Firth had no idea what to expect. He looked into his father's face and saw a smile, then a shiny, well-oiled sword was taken out. Running his hand through the boy's hair Denholme Firth presented it to him.

"Here, Joshua, this is for a fighter. Your punishment is to take sword lessons every day - on top of your studies. When you are big enough you can have this." Smiling again, he added: "I'm proud of you."

It had been three years before Firth could handle the weapon properly and he spent each night polishing it, getting to know it like a friend.

Looking up at the heights of Rolica, Firth ran his hands over the smooth wooden grip, drawing comfort from such a familiar object. Fear of injury, he told himself, is worse than physical injury. Lord, I hope that's true.

A chorus of orders was sung out, interrupting his thoughts, and the junior regimental officers were told to get the troops into marching order.

As the units formed, a slow-walking figure attached itself to the end of the grenadier company.

The unmerciful rubbing of the heavy pack against his back was giving Needham second thoughts about rejoining his unit. The goatskin knapsack was far more comfortable than the new wooden-framed canvas ones that had been issued to the battalion companies, but it was still an agony to wear for a man just off the triangle. You're a bloody idiot, Needham, he cursed. You could be sitting in a nice bed with some grog to ease the pain and instead you're marching to a fight. Oh, well Thomas, you always were a bit soft. Careful, here's the silver-wearers.

Riding silently down the sides of the column, Lake waited until the troops were silent and then returned to the front of the formation. Coming to a halt he looked among the men before him. Slowly moving his gaze, the Colonel smiled.

"Soldiers, we are in the lead of our attack and I shall remain in front of you. The enemy in the hills is waiting with cannon and musket but we will go forward, always forward." Lake paused for effect.

"You may be nervous, but those scoundrels are terrified. They know that they are faced by the best regiment of the best army in the world and that scares them. The Frogs fear our bayonets as their fathers feared our fathers' blades."

"Our orders are to drive the skirmishers back and, upon my soul, we will do so." Standing up in Black Jack's stirrups he exhorted: "Close fast, lads, and remember that the bayonet is the only weapon for a British soldier!"

Turning with great deliberation Lake started off towards the village of Columbeira at a slow walk, Black Jack's tail swishing in time to the pace. The fifes and drums sounded and the advance of the Worcesters began.

XIV

Rolica, 2pm.

Ugo Bellegarde shifted carefully trying to get the circulation in his right leg running again. He had been sitting on the same rocky patch of ground for an hour and the pins and needles that had started in his foot had slowly worked their way to his backside. Behind him was a large prickly bush that scratched him every time he leaned back, and to his front was a drop of about 10 metres to the ravine's floor.

"Merde, this is a terrible spot. My arse has gone numb."

"You could be sitting up there," his brother Florian said, indicating the rocky outcrop on their right, "good sitting, but there's no shade. We, Ugo, have a comfortable spot so stop your moaning,"

The younger Bellegarde nodded. It was true that the trees kept out most of the sun and the heat was bearable. Even so, the sweat was pouring from under his arms, through his already saturated blue jacket and down into the top of his off-white trousers. He wiped at a gathering of droplets that had formed on his skin under the thin and wispy moustache he had been growing for some months. He unslung a flask from over his shoulder and poured some of the liquid from it down his throat. Looking at his brother he could not help but admire the way he put up with the hardships of a soldier's life without complaining.

"What are you thinking Florian?"

The *sous-officier* indicated down and to his left.

"There's that horse again."

Scrambling over to the edge of the cliff he looked down to where the brown finger was pointing out the magnificent beast as it paced with its officer at the front of the red ranks.

"We must get it, Ugo."

"How?"

"One of us kills the officer while the other takes the horse. There are some large rocks just there, and we should be able to climb down them. If we're fast enough we can be the first to grab it."

"When?"

"Wait until the officer has passed us. That horse is worth a farm for us in our old age, remember that, brother. You know that one near Vianne. It could be ours. Now watch their beautiful marching and rest. It's getting too hot to waste energy."

XIVa

Brook was feeling the heat. The buildings of Columbeira were acting as a breakwater that split the regiment and forced it to flow around them, making his job of keeping his centrally placed men in line doubly difficult. The right flank of the 5th company, his previous mark for holding the line to the left, had manoeuvred away and he was now concentrating on quickening his pace to keep his men in line with them as they wheeled in the opposite direction.

"Come on lads, keep the line," he said in a stern voice that he hoped did not sound too forced. The men responded well, as they had at all the drills Brook had attended, and easily lengthened their strides to stay with the ranks to their right.

An explosion to his front jerked his head around and he could see a puff of smoke settling around a point on the high-above ridge. A sound like material being ripped passed overhead. A second cannon fired and again the strange sound flew by followed by the pitiful scream of a wounded horse.

"It's roundshot, Samuel," said Major Way, "and the ripping you can hear is the ball hurtling through the air. Nasty things, bowl the men over like skittles ... still, the Frenchies are firing way too high to worry us."

Brook had not known the Major was behind him and wondered what gave him the courage to sit calmly on a horse in full view of the enemy. He was about to acknowledge Way's comments when two more artillery pieces belched flame and smoke. The gunners clearly had not changed their range and the shot roared overhead.

"We'll be within musket range soon, Samuel, and expect the Frenchies to start yelling and firing as loudly and as quickly as they can.

"If their aim is like their artillery's, then we need not fear much. But watch out for their skirmishers, that goes for you, too, my Lord. They'll be after all officers and they are bloody good shots."

Both McGuire and Brook nodded.

"The orders are for us to stop 50 paces from the base of the cliffs. We will have to clear those damned skirmishers away before moving back to the left and into the pass. Now remember, do not fire until I give the order."

Glad to have an experienced officer nearby, Brook smiled as the Major gave him a confident wink and drew his sword. The advance continued and puffs of smoke from the voltigeurs' guns became more frequent. The first shots seemed to have little effect but men began to stagger and fall as the British lines moved to within 100 paces of the enemy.

McGuire was about to say something when he spat out an oath and lurched backwards. Falling to a half crouch he stared in shock as a red trickle moved freely down his sleeve and on to his sword hand.

"Good God, I've been hit. Don't just stand there Brook … give me a hand up, damn your eyes!"

With the assistance of a private, Brook managed to haul the heavy Lord to his feet. The blood was moving more quickly now and even a thick, folded handkerchief could not stop the flow.

"Better get off to the surgeon, my Lord," Way said. "That looks nasty."

"Sir," McGuire replied shakily and staggered off with the soldier.

As the Redcoats closed another 50m paces Major Way ordered the junior officers in front of the lines back to their companies and the NCOs took up his command to ready arms.

Standing shoulder to shoulder the front rank of infantrymen brought their muskets to bear on the smoke-dotted cliffside, while the second row held the heavy weapons steadily between the heads in front of them.

Brook knew muskets were inaccurate at anything over 50 yards and rare indeed was the man killed by a ball aimed at him from 100 paces. However, in two ranks and at close range, his company could deliver a devastating wall of musketballs into the enemy.

"Aim for the smoke," he shouted, hearing the order echoed along the lines by his fellow officers.

"Steady now, keep steady 29th," Major Way yelled as several men in front of him were hit as the voltigeurs' musketballs fell just short. "It's almost time, lads."

Receiving the signal from Lake, the Major raised his sword and then brought it down. "Fire!"

Jumping at the sudden deafening crash of muskets, Brook was immediately enveloped in a choking cloud of smoke that cut the enemy from sight as if a canvas curtain had been lowered.

"Reload!" he called, and the men quickly began to recharge their weapons.

Eager hands flipped open covers to the black boxes at the soldiers' right hips and sought out the waxed-paper cartridges containing the musketball and powder.

Tearing the tips off with their teeth, the men poured a small amount of powder into the priming pan before closing the cover and grounding the musket butt. The rest of the cartridge's powder went down the smooth barrel before the ball was dropped in and tapped in to place with a ramrod.

Brook still marvelled at the precise way the movements were carried out. It was almost second nature, although the enemy's shots, whizzing overhead, reminded all that this was no practice.

"Ready," came the call, and the muskets of his half-company were brought to shoulder.

"Fire!" Way yelled.

Again the air clouded, stinging the eyes of the men as they reached for the next cartridge. Bite, pour, close, ground, pour, drop, tap, they all mentally repeated the drill.

"Fire!" Brook could hear the 4th's other Lieutenant shout to his half-company before they too disappeared in a bank of smoke.

"They're moving back, Mr Brook and Mr Robinson, so it's one more volley each, reload and then it's off to the left and up that ravine. Don't stop ... as the Colonel wants the bayonet used," Way shouted.

The roar of the last volley subsided and when the smoke cleared the southernmost French regiment had withdrawn from view. Colonel Lake galloped along the lines urging his men on as the right-hand companies began to move left, towards the entry to the gully.

"The bayonet, lads. Give 'em the steel," Lake whooped as he passed.

The regiment cheered and followed the lead of their commander. Brook now found his company at the head of the advance and he began to search for a clear path through vineyards to his front. The fields were crossed with sturdy-looking fences from which the vine leaves and ripening grapes hung in abundance. The dense growth that cascaded on to the farmer's narrow work tracks would hinder the troops and slow movement down to a crawl. He was trying to work out best course when Lake and Way reined in next to him.

"Well, Mr Brook," the Colonel began, "up and at 'em, eh? The light company will go first and then the 4th." Swinging around in his saddle, Lake looked towards the other half of the Worcesters, marching from his left flank.

"Come on, Major Ricketts," he muttered, "move those men more quickly."

Turning to his second-in-command, he pointed to the paths through the groves. "Up there, Mr Way. Forget about stopping to deal with any Frenchies behind us, let's get to the heights. And send someone to speed up Major Ricketts. Tell him we can't wait all day!"

Way nodded to a Captain who immediately kicked wicked-looking spurs into his horse and set off at a dash across the half-mile gap that separated the two wings of the Worcesters. A gap, thought the Major that appeared to be widening as the forward companies moved away from Ricketts' men.

"Sir, we've driven off their skirmishers," Way said, "should we not wait for the remainder of the regiment to arrive?"

"And risk them reorganising? No, Major. Better we press on. Always attack, eh?"

Way did not in fact agree with Lake, but he could see the Colonel's dander was up and nothing would hold him back. Watching as his men began their arduous climb through the vines he hoped they were not walking into a trap. With only just over half the regiment present, under 450 men, he did not think it was wise to proceed up the pass as the unseen enemy still lined most of the length of the ravine's walls. Taking off his bicorne and running a handkerchief over his perspiring forehead, Way looked again towards the left-hand companies. Those men were desperately needed and he prayed Ricketts would realise it quickly.

Urging his horse on, Way thanked God it was dry ground as the men would really struggle if the conditions were slippery. Already he could see several men of the light company, who were clambering over rocks near the gully entrance, losing their footing and stumbling. The disruption was not great but the flow-on effect as the following Redcoats also slowed to pick their way over the rough ground caused a considerable delay. At some parts the path beneath the cliffs narrowed so that only five or six men could move through it at once.

Way was surprised that his men had not yet received any fire from the French, but he was exceedingly grateful for whatever was delaying that initial volley. The first of the Worcesters were now turning into the ravine itself and began disappearing from view. Within a minute he, too, had entered and for the first time had a chance to see exactly what the regiment faced. Instantly, he knew the pass would be a nightmare. It was narrow with a rocky and uneven floor and the walls, covered in olive trees and jutting boulders, rose steeply to the plateau. On that ridge, Way knew, the French were waiting. It was 400 paces away through some of the worst terrain he had seen. Now we're for it, he thought, and dried his brow again with a careful wipe. This is where it gets nasty.

The Bellegardes had just settled into their new position half way up the ravine when the red-jacketed infantry moved into sight. The British volleys had forced them to withdraw from their original vantage point and they had quickly moved over the ridge and down to where they now crouched. Ugo was frantically rubbing his lower arm on a tuft of long grass trying to remove a sticky mass from the back of his hand.
"Will you sit still," his brother ordered. "And what the hell are you doing anyway?"
"I was standing next to Alois when I heard a horrible noise. Merde, it was like an unripe melon being cracked with an axe. I felt this on my arm and then saw he no longer had a side to his head. He didn't make a sound."
"Unusual for him," Florian replied, "He loved the sound of his own voice."
"He was a very fine singer, though."
"True, but didn't he let everyone know it. And he owed me 20 francs. Did you clean his pockets?"
Shaking his head the younger man finished his task and looked up.
"No, I did not. I was too busy getting out of the range of those damned British."
Moving across to the boy, he ruffled his dark hair.
"Too bad, but we'll make up for it with that horse, heh?"
Smiling, Ugo nodded. My, he thought, how Florian wanted that animal. He had never seen his brother this determined on something and that meant one thing - the officer riding the black horse was a dead man.
At the sound of approaching boots the pair seized their muskets and brought them to the ready but they soon relaxed as the moustachioed face of Gaston Lambert appeared around a tree.
"Here they come, friends. Let's welcome them."
Again fighting off his brother's attempts to mess his hair, Ugo half-stood and followed his sibling as he formed part of a ragged chain of skirmishers above the heads of the advancing enemy. The waiting French could hear the curses of the British and the clatter of metal on rock as muskets scraped across large boulders just below them. Hidden by overhanging olive trees, the redcoats were moving towards a small grove and would be in sight in another few moments. The voltigeurs' fingers tightened on their triggers, they would give these Englishmen a shock.

XIVc

Lake was enjoying himself. The excitement was bubbling through him and he urged his regiment on with a rousing voice. This was living, he thought, congratulating himself on rejoining the regiment in time to lead them to the Peninsula. It certainly was more important than living on his family estate and dabbling in politics.
The wars against Napoleon had given him the opportunity to spurn life as the local Member of Parliament, a task made easier by his complete contempt for self-serving politicians and their hangers on.
No, better to be here with men who, though they might not be any more honest than the men of Westminster, were a deal more loyal.

As the 3rd company passed one of the soldiers shouted out.

"Colonel, why do the light men get first crack at 'em. We can do it as well as them."

Laughing, Lake called back. "Never mind, my lads, let the Light Bobs lather them first, we will shave them later."

That brought a bellow of laughter that was almost instantly drowned out as the French finally opened fire. The roar of Charleville muskets and the mass of smoke erupting out of the bushes sent Black Jack up on his hind legs, almost tipping off its rider. Lake instinctively shortened his reins and regained control of his mount. At least a dozen men were lying unmoving on the ground. A further score were trying to rise after being hit. Their moans combined with the chatter of French voltigeurs as they picked more targets among the enemy.

To his rear, the Colonel could hear Way shouting orders, yelling at the men to double the pace. Another ragged series of shots told him their assailants were not formed infantry firing volleys, but rather skirmish troops whose role it was to whittle down his force before it reached the ridge. He could see more men being thrown to the ground by the force of the lead musketballs that flattened as they hit bone after bludgeoning their way through flesh.

Screams echoed around the gully and Lake looked away as a sergeant, his arm severed at the elbow by a ball, slumped to his knees desperately trying to stop the gushing blood that soaked his trousers. The officer was surprised at how silent the man was as he struggled to wrap a rag around his upper arm before a comrade crouched down to tie it tightly for him. Opening the sergeant's canteen for him, the soldier patted the wounded man on the shoulder before moving quickly forward to where Sergeant-Major Richards was encouraging the men on.

"Hurry, boys, get to the top. Don't stop, now, keep going," he called.

Grabbing a stumbling private by the white crossbelts Richards steadied him and pushed him onwards.

"Keep your feet boy, or the Frenchies'll have you. Hurry, lads, hurry."

The urgency in Richards' commands, together with the French fire, spurred the troops on and they struggled with renewed vigour up the track, momentarily forgetting the burden of their cumbersome packs.

Towards the rear of the regiment, Brook was also urging his men on. Ahead he could see the puffs of smoke from the French muskets and knew it was his duty to force his men into and through the enemy fire. He would have loved to order the men to shoot back.

"I know what you are thinking, Samuel," said Way as he caught up to Brook, "but it will slow us down. We have to ignore those men and get to the ridge. The men must move, and quickly, Lieutenant."

The Major turned in his saddle and looked back down the gully. Where was Ricketts? Damn him, cursed Way. We need those men!

XV

Rolica, 2.45pm

The sound of musket fire in the ravine took Wellesley by surprise. He had seen the skirmishers cleared from the front of the heights and knowing that Nightingall's brigade was under orders to then stop and wait for reinforcements he switched his attention to the left wing. Now it was with some worry that he returned his spyglass to where the 29th was supposed to be holding.

"Benton, what the hell has happened to Lake?"

The General nodded. "Sir Arthur, I fear Colonel Lake has gone in ahead of time."

"What!" Wellesley exploded, "he's only taken … half of his strength with him. Is he mad?"

The British commander did not expect an answer to that and his active mind was racing as he worked out the best way to handle the new situation. The sounds of battle poured from the gully and a cloud of smoke began to rise above its ridge.

"Christ almighty," he swore. "Well, Benton, that damned man has forced our hand. We'd better make the best of it and throw everything at them. Send the orders, General."

Shaking his head, Wellesley watched as the rear companies of the 29th neared the gully. For once, he was not in control of what was going on in a battlefield and he was furious about it. Whether it be by honest error or stupidity, Lake had led his men into a trap from which they may not escape.

"I'll kick Lake's arse when I get hold of him. Bloody fool will be lucky to stay in this army. He's likely sentenced those men to death." Indicating the men moving towards the gully, Wellesley turned to Benton. "And more of the poor devils are marching to join them."

Firth was one of those poor devils and, by the look on Ricketts' face, he knew he was in for a hard time. The Major was fuming at the orders given to him by the dispatch rider that he, correctly, took to be a slight on his handling of the men. Lake had not phrased the request for speed subtly and the Captain delivering the message, who had little time for Ricketts, did not bother to couch it in more diplomatic terms.

"Sir, Colonel Lake requests that you move your men more quickly in the direction of the enemy and assist him in the carrying of the pass."

Ricketts' black eyes blazed at the implied criticism that he thought bordered on accusing him of incompetence, or worse - lacking courage. Giving the smiling Captain a dark scowl he turned around to Gell.

"Smarten your company up, Gell, and that includes Lieutenant Firth. You will double forward and reinforce the Colonel."

"With only one company, Major?" Gell queried.

"Just do it, Captain."

Gell stood to attention and, motioning to the lieutenants, led the 6th forward. The Captain waited until his men had jogged out of Ricketts' earshot and then spoke quietly to Firth.

"Joshua, I believe that man has just given you a good lesson. And that is how not to support an attack. Never weaken your force. If the Colonel is in as much trouble as those shots indicate, then our 100 men will not help much. The Major should have kept our companies together and moved as one."

"Will we be able to help Colonel Lake, sir?" Firth asked.

"Only, Joshua, if we can get to them fast enough ..." Gell paused as more shots rang out from the gully, "and you may be thankful we are not in there at the moment."

Firth anxiously looked towards the ravine's mouth and prayed for Sam to be kept safe. He had no idea what they would find as they entered, but it would only be a matter of minutes before they were able to do so. Gell's line of advance veered off from Ricketts' course along a path, and he pushed on across a rough stone fence and through a thick wall of shoulder-high shrubs. Beyond the initial obstacles lay a steep rise that would halve the time to the entrance. The boots of his men scuffed up small clouds of red dust as they made their way up the brown, stubble-grassed slope.

Firth could hear some of the older men's lungs hauling in the air as they increased the pace, but he could see no-one was prepared to slow as their comrades lives could depend on their quick arrival.

His own strong legs were easily pushing him along but he could see from Gell's face that the overweight Captain was struggling.

"Not far to go now, sir," Firth encouraged, "only another 50 paces or so."

"I'll make it, Joshua, don't you worry. I may enjoy my food and wine a little too much but I refuse to let it hold me back. Whew," he added, puffing out his red cheeks, "it's hot work this."

The smile that comment drew on Firth's face was almost instantly lost as he reached the top of the slope and looked into the gorge. There were red-coated bodies lying everywhere. Many were moving, but too many were still. They looked as if they had been flung around the area like the tin soldiers of a temperamental child who had grown bored and had swept them away with his hand. Some had fallen on the track, while others were entangled in thick, spiky bushes at the sides of the pathway. A few paces in, Firth passed a middle-aged private who was propped uncomfortably against a rock. The man had been shot in the chest and each time he took a laboured, choking breath, red bubbles rose from out of his blood-filled lungs and dribbled from his lips. Barely able to haul his eyes away from the dying man, Firth edged forward, and almost fell over the form of a soldier whose face had been punched in by a ball. The dead eyes were wide and staring and below them there was little else.

"Come on, lads" Gell urged, "It's no time to be gazing. Our friends are ahead and in need of us, quick time now!"

The company continued its grim progress, passing through the cluttered boulders and into the olive grove where the small clearing was choked with even more bodies.

Firth was not the only one to be shocked by the scene, his Captain, too, was stunned, as were the rest of the 6th company.

"My God," was all Gell could manage. It was appalling, he thought, there must be half a company here alone. "For God's sake, boys, hurry!" and led the way forward at a trot.

Each man was by now moving as quickly as his equipment and the body-strewn ground would allow. Their leather pack straps squeaking as they bounced with each crunching step. The urgency of their advance was made more obvious by shouts coming from the ridge at the end of the gully.

"Joshua, there'll be no time to reload so hold fire until we know what's going on." Turning another twist in the track the Captain ran headlong into four blue-coated soldiers who were crouched down removing valuables from the dead British.

Seeing the overweight, British officer, one of the robbers shouted a warning to his accomplices, dropped the razor with which he was slicing open pockets and levelled his musket. The enemy was too close to miss and even without seeing the shot strike home, he knew from the grunt he had hit his target. By now more of the enemy had arrived and the Frenchman thrust his bayonet savagely at another officer, who deflected the point with his sword and then countered in an instant with a strike of his own. The last thing the voltigeur felt was the pain as the blade sliced through his right eye and deep into his brain.

The remaining trio of Frenchmen threw down weapons and raised their hands but all were cut down in an instant by vengeance-seeking Redcoats who took great pleasure in hearing the bayonets punch into their enemies with a popping sound and the fleshy sucking as the triangular blades pulled clear.

As soon as the last Frenchman was down, Firth turned back to where Gell had fallen. The Captain was being cradled in Sergeant Barclay's arms as a private tried to put a pad of cloth gently on to a stomach wound. His mentor's white face twisted in agony as the pad pressed home but he didn't make a sound. Kneeling, Firth gripped Gell's hand.

"Don't stop, Joshua, don't stop. Keep the men going. You ... ," Gell stopped as another wave of pain went through him and his hold tightened on Firth's hand, "You must get to the Colonel." The Captain's face again contorted, "Sweet Jesus it hurts." Pausing to compose himself, Gell stared into Firth's eyes. "Hurry now, Joshua, I'll be fine."

Fighting back tears, Firth nodded at the lie, then stood and looked at the men around him.

"Sixth company, move forward at the double. Do not stop, do not slacken and do not fire until told to." With one last look at Gell, Firth moved off after the lead elements of the 6th.

Ahead of them the noise of battle worsened and he prayed he would not be too late.

XVI

Rolica, 3pm

For Brook it was a nightmare of smoke and noise and the figures around him seemed to be moving in slow motion. All except Major Way, who was yelling orders and waving a broken sword from on top of his horse. His weapon had been snapped in two by a musketball as he rode over the crest and into a wall of fire from the defenders at the top.

The disordered Worcesters needed somewhere to reform and the Major had spotted an area behind some trees that offered modest shelter from the French fire.

"To the right," he shouted, "29th to the right."

Continuing to take casualties, the regiment pushed right towards the left flank of the French positions. Brook heard musketballs humming overhead and several men fell around him. Grabbing one wounded man around the waist he hauled him along behind the Major. About 100 yards off he could see Colonel Lake calmly ordering the arriving men into line.

Another volley of shots had Brook ducking and then he was almost knocked flat as a ball ripped through his bicorne, snapping its chinstrap and tearing it from his head. Brook regained his balance and, not stopping to pick up the mangled hat, continued on. As he got close to the steadying lines he could hear Lake calling.

"Don't fire, men, don't fire. Wait a little, we shall soon charge!"

Brook hoped the Colonel was only trying to keep spirits up because from where he stood, the much-reduced ranks of the regiment did not appear capable of charging the French. He guessed that maybe half of the force that entered the gully was missing. Still, if anyone could turn the situation around, it was their commander, he thought.

It may have seemed like hours, but it only took two minutes for the Worcesters to ready themselves. The resplendent figure on the black stallion rode along the newly formed lines encouraging and exhorting his men, disdainful of the increasing French musket fire.

"Soon now, my boys. Soon." he called, "Don't let these Frogs think they have the measure of men from Worcestershire. Wait a little, wait a little, we'll soon charge."

Suddenly, Lake twisted, and put his hand to the back of his neck. It was plain for all to see that blood was flowing over his fingers. Holding up his hand, the Colonel shouted.

"See, my boys, they won't stop us. Upon my soul, they can't even shoot straight!" and he grinned as the regiment roared its approval.

One hundred and 20 paces away the elder Bellegarde cursed.

"Merde, Ugo, you should have done better than that. How many shots is that?"

"Six, brother."

"Idiot! You are supposed to be better than me. Now, it's my turn."

Florian Bellegarde slowly drew back the hammer of his Charleville and aimed his musket at the enemy officer's back. Despite the fact that Lake was within close view it was not an easy shot. But there was no wind to push the ball off target and he could count on the projectile to rise slightly. Mustn't hit the horse, he thought and then berated himself for losing concentration. Think of the horse later, now wait for the right time.

That moment arrived almost immediately as Lake turned Black Jack to again move down the lines. The Frenchman gently squeezed the warm trigger and, flinching slightly at the discharge of smoke, prayed the shot would be good. The ball flew out of the smooth barrel and did not waver in its flight until it was too close to Lake to matter. It entered the Colonel's body just under the right arm and, gouging its way along the length of his ribs, tore a gaping wound under his left armpit as it exited. The shock of its impact threw Lake over the neck of Black Jack who, terrified, reared wildly before fleeing from his master's body and galloped away from the British lines.

The regiment was stunned. Way leapt from his horse and ran to Lake's side, where Sergeant-Major Richards was already trying to stem the flow of blood from the entry and exit wounds. Both men instantly saw that the wound was mortal, the telltale red froth confirming their worst fears. Lake's red-stained mouth was opening and closing as he fought for breath but the damage to his lungs was too great to survive. He was drowning in his own blood.

"Doctor Guthrie will be here soon, Colonel, you'll be fine," Way said.

Lake stopped gasping for a moment and what passed for a smile flitted across his face.

"Upon ... my soul, Gregory," he whispered with difficulty, "the damned Frenchies have done for me."

"No, sir, no."

"Yes, they ..." Lake would have gone on but a fit of coughing wracked his body. He tried again to speak but all that came from his mouth were pink pieces of lung. A final vomit of blood stained the front of his uniform and then his eyes widened, momentarily, before stopping in a frozen stare.

Way stood slowly and covered Lake's body with the Colonel's gold-laced, blue cloak.

"Stay with him, Sergeant-Major."

A murmur of anger started in the ranks and built into a growl. Sensing the men's mood, Major Way turned from Lake's shrouded body and pointed to the French positions through the trees.

"There are the killers, boys, there are the stinking, garlic-eating bastards who have done this to the Colonel. I want to kill them all ... are you with me?" he screamed.

An angry acknowledging roar came back at him and, almost as one being, the men of the Worcesters levelled their bayonets in the direction of the French.

XVII

Rolica, 3.30pm

As he advanced Brook could see the sleeves of violet-coloured jackets being waved about in the French lines. Above them their owners' mouths opening and shutting like a silent choir. To his rear the strains of the regimental march were lilting via the fifes and drums and yet, just paces to his side, lines of Redcoats strode in silence, their rage clearly showing in their grim faces. Iron-willed discipline now held them quiet.

"Have you picked your man, sir?" a soldier asked him.

"What?" Brook replied, nonplussed.

"I've got mine. So's Jones here. I'm going to kill that Froggy bastard with the saggy pom-pom on his shako there. And Jones is going for the one next to him."

"Um, why?" asked Brook.

"Dunno, sir, just don't like the look of 'em. Everyone does it, they're probably doing the same to us."

Brook hadn't picked an enemy to kill, but his anger was rising over the death of Colonel Lake.

Again he marched into a pocket of sound and heard Way, who was still brandishing his broken blade, yelling: "Don't stop to fire. Just get in with the bayonet ... this is sticking work!"

Then the now crimson-cheeked Major voiced the vitriol that so many others felt. "Pay those frog munchers back with a belly full of steel for the Colonel, lads."

Brook felt like cheering but he held himself and the lines continued the menacing advance.

Ahead the French waited and as he moved forward Brook suddenly thought that what he had taken to be jeers, were instead cheers. His hand loosened on the grip of his sword. Something was not right.

"On, on," Way urged, knowing his men were now within range of even the most poorly aimed musket.

Stomach muscles tightened and some troops burped out nasty-tasting mouthfuls of vomit-tasting air. Fear was taking a hold. For the killing volleys were about to be spat at them, leaving them dead, or worse – left with horrible injuries.

Brook steeled himself as moved more quickly. Any second now, he thought, any second. Lord, I love my family and please make it mercifully quick. He hoped his prayer had been silent, but saw around him other lips moving as they mouthed comforting phrases.

"Halt!" Came the command and the British lines pulled up. The regiment was now only some 30 metres from the murderers of Colonel Lake and when the volley came it would bring complete destruction to the front rank of the 29th.

Brook, positioned where the first shots would surely hit him, felt rivulets of sweat pouring down his forehead and neck. He resisted the desperate need to wipe the stinging drops from his eyes, mindful of the expectation that he should show no sign of fear.

"Prepare!" Came the order and 250 bayonets sparkled.

"Forward the 29th!"

Now was the time to scream the famous British "huzza" and launch towards the enemy. But suddenly a white flag was raised in the French positions and the troops began to sing a hymn.

"Damn me," muttered Way, who was spring-tight and set to unleash his men.

Just as suddenly an officer, with shako on an upraised sword, climbed on to rocks and shouted in heavily accented English.

"Britishers, we are Swiss, do not fire."

Stunned, the ranks of the Worcesters watched as the supposed enemy piled their weapons and waved to them.

"Down with the tyrant. Down with Napoleon."

The bewilderment was shattered by Way's barking of an order to secure the position. Within seconds the Redcoats had crossed to the Swiss and taken their muskets.

The looks of puzzlement on British faces and the smiles of the Swiss, mixed with a huge feeling of relief, had Brook laughing loudly. Even Way allowed himself a momentary look of pleasure that instantly hardened.

"The task's not done, Mr Brook, look to the front, sir. The French are still behind that wall overlooking the gully."

A scuffle broke out next to Brook as an angry corporal pushed over a young officer and began to hit him with his musket butt.

"Why did you kill the Colonel, why?" he shouted and was set to crush the boy's skull when Brook grabbed him and hauled him off.

"Easy man," he said, "Easy."

The Swiss spat a small dollop of blood out of his mouth and protested his treatment.

"We have not fired a shot, m'sieu," he said, "the one that killed your officer came from those trees, not from these lines."

Brook helped him to his feet and looked him in the eyes.

"Where did that shot come from?"

"There m'sieu, over there," pointing to the copse on the Worcester's right flank.

"There are French there."

Brook clambered on to some rocks and looked towards the trees. He could see no sign of anyone, but the news had him worried.

"Major Way," he called, "This man says there are French in those trees."

"No, they're to your left, Mr Brook, so keep your eyes open. Watch for any cavalry … and make sure those men are disarmed."

The wooden clatter of musket butt on metal barrels increased as the weapon piles grew. Occasionally, the last thrown on to the heap would clatter as it slid down the heap. Nearby, ammunition pouches were neatly placed in lines ready to be gathered by the regimental Quartermaster when he arrived on the ridge.

Still concerned at the woods being full of French, Brook again stood on the rock wall and studied the treeline. He reached for his 'scope and then remembered he had not got it back from Joshua. In the mid-distance he could see Major Way dismounting to talk with a captain and an ensign.

Way was pointing towards the Colonel's covered body, still under the watchful guard from Sergeant-Major Richards, and as he spoke the ends of the more junior officer's bicornes moved up and down as they nodded. It was then Brook noticed a small sparkle over their heads. It may have been the light, or nothing at all, but something was not right. Again the sparkle came, and then another. Through the trees, he thought, the same trees that the Swiss had said contained French.

"Major Way," he called, shading his eyes with his arm. "Major Way, sir, there's movement behind us."

Thank God he's listening now, Brook said to himself, as the senior officer turned and then stopped, somewhat stunned.

It was then Brook saw blue uniforms coming from cover.

"Form line," he shouted. "French behind us."

Drawing his sword, Brook ran towards the Major as Redcoats scrambled to form a hasty defensive line against this unexpected threat.

It was too late, however, as the surprised British were outnumbered by four to one and were within seconds overrun by the charging French.

Brook's only thought was to get to Way and although he was just 20 paces away the crush of bodies made it difficult to get there. The clash of blade upon blade rang out and the screams of injured men followed. He could see a French soldier pushing aside the Major's broken sword and ramming the butt of his musket into the side of Way's head. Immediately Sergeant-Major Richards bayoneted the man and stepped over his unconscious officer's fallen body. Surrounded by at least six Frenchmen, Richards courageously fended off the probing enemy weapons, shouting abuse at them as he did so. As he closed, Brook could see Richards' jacket had been sliced open in several spots by bayonets and blood was darkening his jacket. He had almost reached the Sergeant-Major when the attacking French drew back several paces. He's fought them off, Brook thought, but then was shattered to see that the enemy had only moved to allow muskets to be levelled at the devilish British soldier. Brook saw the powder flashes and smoke plumes and watched helplessly as Richards was thrown off his feet and was dead by the time he hit the ground.

Hacking at a blue coat, Brook found the French had almost cut off those nearest Way from the remainder of the 29th. "Rally, rally," he cried and then was dropped to his knees by a blow on his head. With his world spinning, he half raised himself and jabbed his sword out at half strength. His blade was smashed downwards and another butt caught him a glancing blow above the left eye. Falling he could see a blue figure standing over him with his bayonet raised. Brook felt fear, an incredible pain and then nothing.

XVIII

Rolica 3.30pm

Firth could hear the cheering on the ridge away and above to his right and wondered what was causing the commotion. It must be the regiment, he thought as he leapt over a corporal lying in a large pool of blood. The breathing behind him was coming in loud gasps and with the ridgeline fast approaching he needed to slow down to allow the men behind him to form into as near as a line as they could.

Turning, he saw Coker 10 or so paces behind him. Now the senior officer, Coker would undoubtedly want to take the lead, but Firth saw him wave his sword towards the ridge.

"Take them on, Joshua," he shouted, "Don't slow down!"

The ridge was looming quickly and judging by the number of fallen soldiers at its lip, was likely to be heavily defended.

"Come on men, the Colonel needs us," Firth called. "Don't fire, form lines at the top, but don't fire."

Then he was at the top and found himself within 20 paces of a low stone wall behind which scores of Frenchmen were levelling their muskets. Forcing himself to present his back to the enemy he called the Worcesters on.

"Form line, form line!" he yelled, pointing his sword to first his left and then right. "Two ranks, men, two ranks."

Behind him Firth could hear the French officers bellowing orders. He knew what was coming but didn't dare stop and interrupt the Redcoats forming up. Coker was now with him and had just opened his mouth as a commanding voice screamed out "*Feu!*"

Firth flinched as a massed volley from the French roared out behind him. Something tugged at his jacket and to his left and right men were suddenly thrown backwards. Coker's open mouth now changed shape and he fell screaming as a ball tore into his right leg, chipping his shinbone and tearing through the calf muscle.

Momentarily stunned, Firth gathered himself and spun around. "Keep going," he yelled, "form ranks."

Knowing that a second volley would come from the defenders within half a minute, Firth steadied his men.

"6th company, front rank kneel."

The red line did at it was commanded.

"6th company, present."

Almost 100 muskets came up to the men's shoulders.

"Wait men until they stand to reload after their next volley. Then it's one shot and in with the bayonet. Wait, for it," Firth called.

He flinched again as another eardrum-pounding discharge spat from the French muskets. More cries and curses followed from his troops and the sound of bodies and weapons hitting the dusty ground.

"6th company, fire!"

In an instant Firth's view had been swallowed up by a mass of smoke that stung the eyes. "Charge," he roared, "Come on men."

With a resounding "huzza" the troops leaped forward and burst through the wall of smoke. They had no idea of how many casualties their shots had caused but it didn't matter. All there was to think about was the distance they had to cross to reach the enemy.

The speed with which the stone wall loomed astounded Firth, who was looking at a young blue-coated Frenchman in the process of pulling out his ramrod. Reaching the pile of stones Firth thrust out his arm and his blade whipped into the man's forearm, forcing the hand to drop the rod.

His next target was the man to the left of the now-yelling victim. He was about to raise his musket as Firth's sword snaked out at his face. Recoiling from the steel the man tripped and was trodden on by his comrades who were retreating from their attackers.

Firth leapt the wall followed by several men on each side. French officers were beating men with the flats of their swords to keep them from running and the more experienced troops met the British with extended bayonets.

He watched a large red-headed figure take on two Frenchmen and put them out of the action with a brutal stab into one's stomach and a skull-breaking blow with his musket butt for the other. Without pausing the figure then jabbed his bayonet into a Frenchman's chest. The triangular blade got stuck between the screaming man's ribs and when several pulls and twists failed to free it, the Redcoat kicked the falling man in the chest and wrenched it free. His next victim was a small soldier who took one look at the charging man and threw his musket down. It didn't save him as he was run through the side by a stab that punctured his kidney and then ripped open his stomach. The sight of the almost berserk Redcoat was enough to have all but a brave few fleeing. They, however, were soon cut down and within seconds the British set off after the running French.

"Hold men," Firth yelled, "hold!"

Looking for, but unable to find a sergeant, Firth grabbed the sleeve of the redhead and slightly turned him. The man's face was covered in specks of blood and powder stains, but Firth recognised him.

"Needham! What are you doing here? Never mind, you are a now an acting sergeant. Reform the men here. Understand?"

The big man nodded. "Reload!" he bellowed. "And 'ware the front."

Firth now turned to his right, towards the main body of the regiment and saw a scene of utter chaos. Scores of bodies lay on the ground, wounded soldiers in blue and red raised their arms or called weakly for assistance. There were no French troops standing so he presumed they had been pushed away. At first glance he could not see Brook, nor Colonel Lake, nor, for that matter, Major Way.

Looking left he saw a body of red-coated men arriving from another gully. Their light-yellow collars told him it was the East Norfolks who had advanced in support of the Worcesters. At least their left flank was now temporarily secure.

Firth left Needham and walked with a deliberately measured pace towards the recovering troops on his right. He hoped there was a more senior officer among them, but until he saw one he had to give the impression of being completely in control. He nodded to the men as he passed them and let them get on with collecting weapons from the captured and wounded French.

Ahead he saw a fair-haired sergeant directing troops to stand-to at the wall and moved towards him. What was his name now, Firth asked himself. That's right, Barclay.

Firth's path took him by a Redcoat kneeling over a French officer's body. At Firth's approach he jumped up, looking guilty about something and kept his hands hidden behind his back.

He was a small man with a pock-marked face that had a strange smile on it.

"We showed the Frogs, sir!"

"We did that, Private …"

"Good, sir, Private Good. There's nothing better than sticking steel into the bloody Frogs, is there sir?" Good then smiled a wicked smile showing broken and stained yellow teeth, "except getting a few treats from them that is."

"Treats, private?"

"Got a few rings and coins from them we did sir … 'cept we did need to use the knife on a few of the tight ones."

Firth didn't want to know exactly what this soldier meant and was about to continue past him when the Sergeant looked over.

"Good," Barclay barked, "stop that and get to the wall. If I see you carving rings off bodies again I'll have you on punishment you nasty little man!"

With that the private picked up his musket and scuttled off to take his place by the wall.

The Sergeant approached Firth and said: "Sorry about that sir, he's not one to let an opportunity go by."

"Sergeant Barclay, where are your officers?"

"All have gone, sir. The Colonel's dead, Major Way is captured, and all the rest are dead or wounded."

"Lieutenant Brook?"

"I'm not sure sir, he was last seen near Major Way. We haven't found his body, so we think he's been taken by the French."

Firth hoped he looked calm on the outside because his stomach had just knotted horribly.

"Orders, sir?" Barclay asked, in a tone that demanded rather than requested.

"Well …" Firth hesitated, "get some men to look after the wounded, others to collect weapons and keep an eye out for the Frenchies coming back. They're bound to have another go at us. And get someone to find any water around here."

There was a shout at the wall and the Redcoats readied their weapons as they formed a line behind the stones.

Firth moved quickly and saw what had sparked the alarm. The French had been rallied some 500 paces from his position and were being formed into an attack column to take back the wall.

He could see officers capering about, excitedly rebuilding the confidence of their men. They waved their swords and danced and, Firth had to admit, it seemed to be working as troops began their own shouts to add to the noise. By contrast the British stood silently, watching the performance with quiet determination.

Firth called both Needham and Barclay to him and told them to stand within earshot either side of him. They would not fire until the French were within 40 paces of the wall. Firth hoped that his men would then have time to reload and fire a second volley by the time the French reached the rocks. After that, he told the sergeants, it would be in with the bayonets. They moved into their assigned positions and Firth was left alone.

"Colours to me," he ordered and the giant yellow regimental symbol was brought up behind him. An equally large King's Colour - the Union Flag – soon joined its mate. Again Firth discovered that he was unconsciously rubbing the grip of his sword and, immediately upon noticing it, put a stop to it.

In the distance French drums began sounding their rhythmic call for an advance and the cheering from the bluecoats gained in strength.

"40 paces men, wait until then. 40 paces, remember, then reload like the Devil - for your lives depend upon it," Firth ordered.

"Here they come," a voice called and the shouting mass of French quickly closed the gap between the two forces. Strong sunlight flashed and sparkled off their bayonets and the drums kept up their incessant, booming beat.

At 300 paces the tramp of hundreds of feet could be heard distinctly. Every now and then the call of an officer broke through the drums and the crunch of boots.

At 200, the waiting defenders began picking their first targets. Very few of the Worcesters looked the slightest bit concerned at the approaching mass of men and watched the display with stoicism.

At 100 paces, Barclay and Needham called out for the regiment to get ready.

At 60, they shouted for the men to present.

The French column now seemed huge and to Firth appeared as if it was a human battering ram swinging towards the thin British line. The noise from the enemy was extraordinary, but above it all he could hear calls of "Vive l'Empereur".

At 50 paces, Firth unsheathed his sword and raised it high above his head. "Steady 29th," he called, "not long now. Wait for it … wait for it." He feared he had waited too long and that French would just keep walking right up to the wall and not be able to be stopped.

40 paces.

"Fire!" he yelled, an order echoed by Barclay and Needham, and the entire length of the wall disappeared in a mass of choking smoke. Screams were heard and then he called "Reload!"

Firth had no idea what was happening on the other side of the wall as the white smoke was worse than a late-autumn fog, but he could hear urgent yells in French and the screaming of wounded men. As the white veil slowly began to lift he saw glimpses of fallen men and tangled piles of bodies. The following troops were trying to stumble over their fallen comrades and while the attack had been put off balance enemy officers were surprisingly fast to steady the lines and urge their men forward. The French drums, which had been quiet for only a few seconds, began their irresistible beat again.

Looking at his nearest soldiers Firth noted they were well into their reloading process, with the ramrods already being used to tap down the next volley's projectiles. Even so, he knew it was going to be a tight race.

The leading enemy troops were now past their wounded and while shouting loudly lowered their bayonets. They were only five paces from the wall when Firth screamed out his command. "Fire!"

A second explosion of noise, smoke and lead erupted around the British and more awful cries of agony came back from the French.

"Now men, up and at them! Follow me you Vein Openers!"

Firth was the first over the wall and behind him a terrifying "Huzza" boomed out as the men of the 29th threw themselves at the French.

The enemy was so close the two forces collided instantly with the British bayonets rammed with brutal impact into those men immediately to their front.

Firth smashed the base of his sword into the first face he saw and heard the crack of breaking teeth.

A surprised grey-moustached corporal appeared to his left, but fell instantly as a slash from Firth sliced off his ear and left the side of his face hanging from the cheekbone. The first two ranks of French died within seconds and the third and fourth recoiled from the screaming savages who were throwing themselves at them. That backwards movement threw the following ranks into disorder and men tripped and stumbled as they tried to avoid the deadly spikes of steel being thrust at them.

The Redcoats were on them in an instant killing and maiming with vicious jabs.

A punctured jugular sprayed blood over Firth, but he quickly used his left sleeve to wipe it from around his eyes. Another blue uniform was sliced by his blade and the falling man pulled him, momentarily, off balance. A bayonet snaked out at him slicing his sleeve and ripping across his shoulder. There was a sear of pain, but the wild thrill of the melee kept him moving forwards.

Firth had never felt anything like this before and he had to fight the rush of excitement to keep his mind on what was happening around him.

The British charge was too much for the surprised soldiers of the Emperor who, only 30 seconds before, had been marching with utter confidence in victory.

The column broke like a porcelain pot hit by a chisel and the soldiers scattered like escaping grains of rice. It wasn't panic that took hold, but a strong desire for self-preservation and despite taking to their heels, most of the fleeing men held on to their weapons.

As soon as he saw the French breaking Firth screamed for the charge to halt. To his outnumbered men the wall meant safety and if they strayed too far from it there was a chance they would be overrun.

"Help the wounded, get them back. Come on men, hurry. And take the Frenchies' water … make sure you get their water."

Firth suddenly felt very hot and had a strong desire to open his woollen jacket, but knew that would be setting a poor example for his men. A light-blue wooden water barrel was handed to him and he accepted it gratefully and looked up to see Needham.

"Thank you."

"Pleasure sir. That was a grand move sir," beamed Needham.

"Move? Oh, yes, thank you. It certainly saw them off." Firth frowned and added "How many men have we lost?"

"Well, sir, in the 6th company at least 10 dead and a score wounded. As for the regiment it's more a matter of who's left. We've lost at least two-thirds of the men – in the gully and here – and you're the only officer … until Mr Ricketts and the others arrive."

Firth looked at the silent men around him and knew they were desperately tired and needed something to liven their spirits.

"Acting-Sergeant Needham, a song. Lead the men in a song."

The big redhead nodded, took a swig of water, cleared his throat and began the Worcesters' marching song.

"When I was bound apprentice in famous Worcestershire,
Full well I served my master for more than seven year ...
Till I took up to poaching as you will quickly hear ..."

At the start of the chorus more and more voices joined in.

"Oh 'tis my delight on a shining night, in the season of the year ..."

As the rendition got louder and louder Firth again jumped on to the wall and watched the French preparations. They would come again, all right, and very soon.

XIX

Rolica, 3.30pm

Across in the French positions Florian Bellegarde and his brother were ecstatic. They both had hold of Black Jack's bridle and were hurrying along to find their Colonel. The white-haired officer had two-days' growth on his leathery brown cheeks and his eyes looked red and tired. While he was full of praise for the brothers' opportunism, he had other things on his mind. Besides, what the hell did he need with a beautiful horse. He told them to take it to General Delaborde's staff and, he ordered gruffly, to not sell it too cheaply to those ponces.

It was only a short walk to a group of staff officers who took one look at Black Jack and began an impromptu auction.

As the drums began beating to announce a renewed attack on the British defending the wall, the Bellegardes returned to their unit with 6000 francs split evenly between them. A fine day's work, they laughed.

It was all noise and bustle among their fellow voltigeurs as they prepared to advance ahead of the main attack.

General Delaborde watched the preparations.

"Antoine," he said to his aide, "I made a mistake in not having skirmishers screening our column in that last attack. These British are not so easily scared as other armies," he said grudgingly.

"This time, however, we will test them with our voltigeurs and thin their lines out a bit, eh?"

The aide nodded.

"And then we will keep them so busy the Roast Beefs won't be able to deal with our attack until it is too late."

"Our hunters are deadly at 100 metres and we will force the British to attack us to clear them away. Then, when they are out from behind their wall, we shall strike hard and decisively," Delaborde said, hammering his fist into his palm as he did so. "They won't have a chance."

Opening his telescope Delaborde searched the British positions for officers. There was only one he could see. Snapping shut his glass the General turned to his aide. "We're in luck, there is only a boy in charge over there … we'll see if he falls for our bait."

XIXa

As usual the Bellegardes advanced side-by-side and while always eager to kill the enemy, greater concentration was spent on loot and looking after each other. Both were grinning like fools. Their new-found wealth was a God-send and both knew they had to redouble their efforts to stay safe.

They could hear the drums starting to pound behind them and they were close enough to see clearly the faces on the red figures ahead.

There was a slight rise to the wall and on it they could see a tall fair-haired officer. He was standing in the open with his sword lowered in his right hand and in his left was the pole of the British flag.

"That's the man for us, Ugo," the older brother said, "he's the only officer I can see. Let's stay back a bit and try at him from a distance."

"Does he have a horse?"

"Smartarse! Let's just stay well away from those bayonets."

While the rest of the skirmishers closed on the singing defenders, the pair halted and took aim as the officer called out something and his men stopped singing and fell silent.

"You go first Ugo, and remember to aim just above his head. I'm feeling rich so 100 francs if you hit him first."

"And the crackling off the next leg of pork, brother."

"You are a harsh man, Ugo, but it's a deal."

The Frenchman had a clear view of the young officer and knelt to make his shot. Looking along the barrel he made a mental note of the slight breeze and the need for elevation before lining up the figure. He aimed above his target and that should allow enough for the ball to drop and hit his chest. Slowly the finger tightened on the trigger and with a careful intake of breath he drew it back.

The smoke from the musket obscured his enemy for a few moments but then the older Bellegarde was tousling his hair and grinning.

"You missed. My turn."

Barely seeming to take any care with the shot at all, Florian knelt, aimed and pulled his trigger.

A laugh burst out from his brother. "That was very close, you could see he heard it fly by him. He jumped, huh?"

The pair moved forward while reloading and when they were ready stopped for the next shot.

Again Ugo went first and Florian noted that despite the near miss the officer had not got down from the wall.

"He's got guts, that one, but it won't save him," he added as he took his shot. The ball flew out of his barrel and towards Firth. It dropped as it travelled truly for 70 metres before it started to slow and was gently pushed off track by the breeze. If not for that it would have hit the young officer in the throat, but instead nicked the silver braid on his epaulette.

He may have been imagining it, but Florian could have sworn he saw the officer grin. His brother's next also missed the target, but the ball struck the face of a man to the rear of the intended victim, felling him instantly.

The drums behind them were now being given added weight by the crunch of boots and it was time for the skirmishers to give way to the column.

"Vive l'Empereur," the advancing French shouted in unison and the front rank levelled their bayonets.

They were now only 50 paces from the wall and expected at any stage to see a billow of smoke from the enemy lines and a gut-tightening explosion that would throw a wall of metal death at them.

"Vive l'Empereur!"

The officers were encouraging them with talk of all the gold coins they would be able to liberate from the corpses of the Redcoats. Others joined them with insults yelled at their enemies and there were many quietly spoken prayers uttered to the God of the battlefield.

"Keep calm my children, they'll be firing soon," an officer shouted, his shako on the tip of his sword acting like an improvised banner.

The French were now within 10 paces and they hadn't yet received a volley. They had caught the British napping.

A victory-confident shout of "Vive l'Empereur" rang out again and the men knew they had won this time. No soldiers had ever stopped them before.

Five paces from the wall the front ranks prepared to hurdle over it when a massive roar exploded from the Redcoat line.

Musketballs ripped into them at point-blank range tearing off fingers and hands and throwing men off their feet. It was as if Hell had reached out for those at the lead of the column with every man of the 80-man wide rank hit. The large British lead balls smashed through ribs, punctured skulls and caused massive damage to the frail flesh they punched through. One man was hammered backwards as the balls smashed through his upper arms, ripping muscle, sinew and shattering the bones. Wondering why he had so much difficulty standing the shocked veteran of three campaigns saw both limbs had been blown away and blood was pouring from the horrendous wounds.

He barely had time to call out for help before he passed out and died bleeding.

The French in the third rank tried to clamber over the bodies of their comrades in front but, under pressure from those following them, found themselves pushed off balance.

The smoke had still to clear when those pushing forward suddenly found themselves facing a red line of screaming madmen who came over the walls like a wave of barbarians.

Those French who tried to fight back fell instantly and panic filled the survivors.

"Save yourselves" came the cry and the formation disintegrated as men turned and ran.

The Bellegardes were no exception and joined the race to gain the safety of their own lines.

Watching on General Delaborde cursed both his lily-livered men and the young British officer he'd been watching through his telescope.

Like his troops, Delaborde had believed the Redcoat had misjudged the timing of his first volley and had been surprised by the lateness of it. Even more surprising was the immediate bayonet charge. The youth had timed it perfectly, Delaborde thought appreciatively.

"Send out the hussars, keep those Red Devils from advancing too far," he ordered his aide.

Ah well, he thought, with other British troops pouring up the surrounding gullies it was time to move again.

"Sound the retreat, Captain, we'll have to wait for the armies of Loisin and Junot to join us before trying again. And then, I promise, things will be different."

XX

Rolica 4.20pm

On both sides of the British wall it was a scene of carnage. Hundreds of red and blue-uniformed bodies lay in tangled heaps that spread as far as Firth could see. Moans from the wounded men created a continuous low hum that was punctuated by the occasional shriek as a badly injured man was moved. Firth looked down at a Frenchman he guessed was about his own age. The soldier's jaw was slowly opening and closing like a fish out of water and his hands were pressed tightly against chest. The brown eyes of the dying youth met his and Firth looked away. There was nothing he could do.

Barclay and Needham approached and the blood-stained Firth could see both had cloth strips wrapped around injuries.

"Are you hurt, sir?" Barclay asked.

"No, Sergeant, I'm not."

"Maybe you should sit down, sir and we'll have a look at that shoulder."

"Shoulder?"

Firth looked down to his right where Barclay was pointing and saw the torn wool on his jacket where French blade had caught him. "I'd forgotten…"

"Tends to happen a bit, sir, you find yourself too busy to worry about all but the worst of them. Shall I get some water for you to clean yourself? You're quite a sight, sir."

Firth supposed he was, but dismissed the offer, "Give the water to the injured. Our men first, but both sides, Sergeant."

He felt both elated and stunned by what had just happened. Looking around he could see that the proud Worcester regiment that had marched earlier that day was no more. Hundreds were wounded or dead. The Colonel was gone … and so was Brook.

"Where are you Sam?" he said softly and then dizziness hit. He knew what was coming and turned aside as his stomach heaved out vile-tasting sourness. A second time was followed quickly by a third.

"Now then sir," Needham said kindly, "take a rinse of water and spit it out. It's just the excitement sir. I've done it myself first-up and there ain't no harm in it. Better out than in my old Ma used to say."

Firth managed a bitter half-smile and took a mouthful of the warm water.

"Tell you what Mr Firth, have a sip of this … it'll do wonders for you," the Sergeant said and offered over a small flask.

Firth took the drink and the fire of the brandy seemed to wash away the bad taste in his mouth.

"Thank-you Sergeant. I'm fine now." Pausing, Firth looked around and said: "We need to find where our officers are so can you please detail the men to search through the dead and wounded."

"I'll get right on to it, sir. You've done a grand thing today sir. A grand thing."

Feeling as he was it didn't seem to Firth as if there was much grand about anything.

A shout went up that a lone French rider was approaching the British lines. He was leading a black horse with a truce-indicating white napkin tied on to the tip of his sword. "It's Black Jack," came a follow-up cry and soldiers hurriedly crossed to get a better view of what was going on.

Firth walked to where the Frenchman had halted next to the wall.

"Monsieur?" he asked.

"My General, General Delaborde, wishes to return this fine horse to its owner in honour of the way you British fought today. My General wishes it to be known that to be bested by such troops is no dishonour and he is looking forward to meeting again soon."

"Thank your General, sir, although I am sad to tell him the owner of this horse, Colonel Lake, is dead."

"My General feared as such," the French Major said, "and told me to then present it to the officer who commanded this action."

"That was me, sir, however, I cannot accept such a gift."

"My General will be very upset, Lieutenant …?"

"Firth. Joshua Firth."

"Then I suggest Lieutenant Joshua Firth that you take it on behalf of your regiment and present it to your next commander."

The tone in the Frenchman's voice told Firth he was not going to be deflected from his duty and so he nodded for a nearby private to take the proffered reins and lead the animal around the wall.

"It is a generous gift, sir," Firth said, "and it makes your General Delaborde an even more honourable soldier."

Smiling for the first time, the Major made a quick bow before whipping his horse's head around and spurring the animal away.

Five minutes later the private approached Firth with Black Jack. He took the reins with his bloodied hands and saw they were shaking. The more he tried to stop them the more they seemed to move. He was stunned at what had happened. Robert Gell was dead, so was Sergeant Major Richards.

Looking up at the smoke and blood-covered faces of his men he shook his head. So few left, so many dead. And this, he thought, after a small battle. The 29th had lost almost one third of its number – at least 250 men - and its Colonel.

He gave an involuntary shudder. He was still trying to get his mind around what had happened over the past few hours when a number of horses reined in next to him.

Looking up he saw Major Ricketts staring around and then down at him.

"Mister Firth, where is the Colonel?"

"The Colonel's dead, sir."

"Dead? Are you sure? Where's Major Way?"

"We believe he's been taken sir, along with four or five other officers and a half-company of men."

"Damn the men, who's commanding?"

"I'm afraid I have been sir … there was no-one else."

Ricketts' black eyes flared with barely concealed animosity.

"You?" he leaned forward and said quietly: "More like the sergeants, you mean. What would you know?"

Another thump of hooves sounded and General Wellesley rode up at a canter.

"Where's Lake? Who leads here?" he demanded.

Ricketts brought his horse around to face his superior and said: "Colonel Lake has been killed sir, I'm in command."

Wellesley looked down his hooked nose at the relatively clean uniform of the dark-eyed officer and his sweating horse, which had obviously been recently pushed hard, and asked: "Who led the fight?"

Ricketts looked stung by the question and was unable to respond immediately.

"I did, sir," said a weary Firth.

"Good God, Mr Firth, is that you under all that blood? I take it, sir, you are well?"

"Well enough, thank you sir."

"Damn fine action, Mr Firth, you did damn well. Bet the Frenchies didn't know what hit them. Was that you standing on the wall? Damned impudent if you ask me. Why did you do it, sir?"

"I felt it might lift the men, sir, that was all."

"Damn brave, Mr Firth, damn brave – and damn foolish. I don't want to see you do it again, do you hear me?"

"Yes, sir."

Turning to Ricketts, Wellesley said: "After all, we don't want to lose such enterprising young officers do we Major?"

"No, sir," Ricketts quickly agreed.

Looking at Firth again, the General said: "Damn fine work, Mr Firth. Be at my tent tonight for dinner – 8 o'clock sharp, hear me?"

"Of course sir," he replied.

"And get yourself cleaned up lad, you're a disgrace," he said light-heartedly. "Eight o'clock, Mr Firth – and don't be late!"

With that he twisted his horse around and set off at a trot back towards the East Norfolks.

Firth watched as the commander left and then felt eyes burning into him. He found Ricketts glaring at him with eyes that could have killed.

"Have you posted picquets, Mr Firth?"

"I was about to, sir."

"Well get on with it man, your tardiness could endanger us all."

"Yes, sir."

"And don't get big-headed, Lieutenant, I'm in charge of this regiment now and I don't impress easily. Understood?"

"Perfectly, sir."

As Ricketts slid off his horse and stomped off a party of junior officers who had just arrived with the 29th's reserve companies mobbed Firth, their eyes filled with a mixture of envy and admiration.

"You lucky dog, Firth," a fellow lieutenant said patting him on the shoulder.

"Bloody good job, Joshua," said another, "we saw the last charge from the ridge. You sure put those Frogs to flight."

"Fair shat themselves, I reckon."

"You better get on with those picquets, Ricketts is very unhappy. Watch yourself."

As if I wasn't going to, Firth thought, the Major is going to give me a very hard time of it.

XXI

British Headquarters
6pm

The small flames on the candles flickered as the evening breeze moved into the canvas tent. Putting his quill aside, General Wellesley stopped his writing for a moment and pondered the day's events. He had lost a lot of men – some 500 - and had had one regiment badly mauled. Bloody Colonel Lake, he thought, too impetuous. Could have got us in a lot of trouble. Retrieving the pen, he dipped it into the small crystal ink well and began to write to the dead officer's brother-in-law.

"I do not recollect the occasion upon which I have written with more pain to myself than I do at present, to communicate to you the death of your gallant brother-in-law.
"He fell in the attack of a pass in the mountains, at the head of his regiment, the admiration of the whole army, and there is nothing to be regretted in his death ... he deserved and enjoyed the respect and affection of the world at large ... he was respected and loved by the whole army ... he fell, alas! with many others, in the achievement of one of the most heroic actions that have been performed by the British army.
I am,
Sir Arthur Wellesley,
General

Reaching out for a small glass of claret, Wellesley drained it in one go and poured himself another. Five hundred men, he thought shaking his head. Far too many. He silently cursed Lake again and thought about re-writing the letter to the Colonel's relative but instantly dismissed it as being unworthy. It wouldn't be right, he thought, the man was guilty of being careless but then he'd paid for his folly. A cough at the entrance to the tent finished his internal battle and in walked the short frame of General Benton.

"Ah, Benton, what news?"
"No real reports of the French, Sir Arthur, they seem to be pulling back towards Lisbon. There are signs, however, that Junot, Loisin and Delaborde are moving to combine. No details yet, but we've patrols out."
"Time?"
"Not within the next three days, Sir Arthur, that's a certainty."
"Good."
"Reinforcements?"
"We have 7000 men coming from Gibraltar and Sir John Moore is bringing a similar number down from the Baltic."
Wellesley nodded approvingly, "they'll be enough to do the job. We'll need to keep close to the coast and find a good landing spot."
Getting up, he crossed to a large map of Portugal that stood on a frame in front of his writing table and beckoned Benton over.

"We need a beach no worse than Mondego Bay, preferably near a good defensive position. Junot will be looking to interrupt a landing."

Running his finger down the canvas he stopped at a half-circle bend. "There!" he tapped his finger, "that's the spot … Maceira Bay. It's large enough and here's a town, Vimeiro, not far inland. That'll guard the beach. Perfect! We'll march tomorrow. We don't want the troops getting comfortable, do we?"

"No, Sir Arthur, heaven forbid. Do I need to mention the fact that Sir Harry Burrard will be arriving with the Gibraltar force?"

"What? Oh, damn, yes of course he will. Typical of Horse Guards they replace me with a chap who hasn't done any fighting in 15 years - and then that was a cock-up." Wellesley paused for a moment wondering how he would get on with the man who was taking over the army and then brushed it out of his mind. He had too many more important things to do than ponder on political slights.

"Now, Benton, where are we at with that Spanish chap? What's his name again? Minus?"

"Minas, Sir Arthur, General Don Costanzo y Minas and he is just south of Cadiz with about 20,000 men."

"How important is he?"

"Well, they say 5000 of his men are cavalry and you know how short of horse we are."

Wellesley grunted with barely suppressed disgust. He had fewer than 300 cavalrymen to oppose at least five times as many Frenchmen. And the French were well led.

"Don't talk to me about cavalry, Benton, you'll upset me. So what else does this Minas offer?"

"Well … aside from the troops under his direct command, Minas sees himself as the popular leader of a revolution against Bonaparte."

"Is he popular?"

"As I said, he thinks he is and says he commands not only the loyalty of regular troops – though they aren't worth much – but he also has contacts with several large bands of partisans."

"Partisans?"

"Well, bandits is a more truthful description."

Benton paused. "There have been some rather distasteful rumours about Minas, Sir Arthur, he's a blue blood but, according to some, is a nasty piece of work."

"How so?"

"There are reports that he butchered three men in a street fight because they blocked his path."

"Go on ..."

"And it is said he killed a Spanish naval officer who complained about holding landing drills in dangerous breakers that drowned 30 sailors."

"And ...?"

"He's reputed to be one of the finest swordsmen in Spain with a liking for wine, fighting and pretty faces."

Wellesley's face darkened. "Do we need this Minus?"

"It's an unknown factor, Sir Arthur. If he is what he says he is he's valuable. If not … then we've wasted time."

"And some poor officer who has to try to reach him."

"True, Sir Arthur," Benton agreed. "Have you decided who'll go?"

"I was thinking that perhaps our best choice would be young Firth."

Benton's face betrayed his surprise. "Isn't he too inexperienced, Sir Arthur? He is only a Lieutenant and the new regulations don't allow promotion without two years' experience in the field," said Benton, a frown creasing the forehead above his shaggy gray eyebrows.

"Oh, he's a Johnny Newcombe all right, but the lad's got a bit to him. He captured that Frenchie on his first ride out … and look how he performed today. He's had more experience in a month than most would see in two years."

"He did very well, that's certain, but he showed recklessness by standing on that wall … you said so yourself."

"I did … but it was inspirational recklessness and I like that. Everything else was done exceptionally well. And he has another thing in his favour, he speaks French. If this Spaniard Minus doesn't speak some form of King's English, then like as not he'll *parlez-vous*."

"True, Sir Arthur, languages are not really a strong point among most of our officers. Well, when do you want to talk to him?"

"Soon, he's coming by for dinner. We can tell him then."

"I'll get everything prepared, Sir Arthur."

"Good, by the way, what happened to his friend?"

"Lieutenant Brook? I believe he's been captured … well, that's what we hope. We are still trying to identify some officers' bodies. There is one headless one - a Lieutenant in the 29th who came too close to a cannonball - and that may be him."

"It's too bad, Benton, the Worcesters lost a lot of good men today. Who's commanding them now?"

"Major Way was captured … otherwise he would have been given the regiment. Now it seems that Major Ricketts is the senior officer."

"Ricketts? We must change that as soon as we can … the man's a bullying buffoon. And most tiresome to boot … have you ever talked with him? Boring as a nasty old maid."

Wellesley pondered for a moment and then said.

"Let's get those Spanish maps organised, Benton, there's not much time. I'll finish these damned letters. Better make the meal brief, I've a lot more to write."

Picking up his quill he paused again. Would such an assignment be too much for the young man? Ah well, Wellesley thought, he'd also been dropped in deep water and had swum. It would be a good test.

XXIa

Two hours later Firth arrived at Wellesley's tent. He had washed, but with his other uniforms back with the army's baggage he'd been unable to change any thing. His boots were scuffed and scratched, the epaulette on his right shoulder was hanging loose above a wide cut and there were two rips in the long tails of his red jacket.

"The Frenchies didn't miss by much, sir," a voice said and Firth, glancing up, nodded in agreement at the smiling guard at the tent's entrance. From the rankers' grapevine the private had heard how a junior officer had held the line on the cliff-tops of Rolica and had seen off two heavy French attacks. The last of which he'd fought on a wall, in full view of the enemy.

"Bloody good job, sir," the soldier said, "you did us proud sir."

Adding a faint, embarrassed smile to another nod, Firth told himself he had indeed been lucky, those two holes – in the middle of the left coat tail – showed how close he'd come to either being badly wounded or left bleeding to death.

The idea of losing a leg had already crossed his mind, but he had determinedly put that into the background as his excitement calmed and he began thinking of Brook and all the others of the regiment lost that day.

Where was Brook? His body, thank God, had not been found and there was talk that more than 40 men of the Worcesters had been taken by the French. There were supposed to be several officers among that group, one of them being Major Way, and Firth hoped his friend would be with him.

His mind quickly cleared of that line of thought as General Benton emerged from the tent, his gray hair looking reddy-white in the setting sunlight, and beckoned him inside.

"Lieutenant Firth, good to see you again. I hear you've been giving the Frenchies a bit of what-for, eh?"

"Yes, sir … well, I suppose so, sir."

"Very fine work indeed. Come in."

The tent had the smell of canvas and crushed grass and was bathed in a diffused light that had taken on the dimming sky's pink glow. Firth glanced around the interior and noted large maps draped across folding chairs, the commander's bicorne balancing delicately on a tall, three-legged stand, and a table set for three. Nearby was a large flat board covered in a parchment map of Portugal and Spain.

Sir Arthur Wellesley emerged from a screened-off area at the far end of the tent and smiled at Firth as he walked over to the table.

"Ah, Lieutenant Firth, good evening. I trust you've recovered from your exertions today, sir?"

"Quite recovered, sir, thank you."

"How is the shoulder?"

"My shoulder, sir? Oh it is little more than a scratch …"

Firth felt the eyes of his commander on his uniform and began to feel uncomfortable. "I'm sorry about my condition, sir, but my spare uniforms have not been brought forward yet."

"Well, Mr Firth," said Wellesley, "I do like my men to be well dressed, it inspires the men, but I think Benton and I can probably overlook it … this one time."

"Thank you, sir."

"Port?"

"Certainly, sir."

At a signal from Wellesley, Benton handed Firth a small conical glass filled with the dark liquid.

"The King!" he said, and both Wellesley and Firth raised their glasses and repeated the toast.

"Hope you like beef," said Wellesley, "I'm rather partial to it myself. And … but don't tell anyone … I rather like the Frenchies' wine."

"Beef sounds wonderful, sir, I'm rather famished."

"Eaten at all today?"

Firth shook his head.

"Bit too busy, I expect," said Wellesley. Motioning the young officer to sit at the table, the British commander stared at him for a few seconds before speaking again. "You've had quite a career already, haven't you Mr Firth. Capturing that Frog and today smelling powder for the first time. Won't get to your head will it?"

"I don't think so sir, I'm just glad I was able to be of some use."

"Some use? Some use?" Wellesley gave his whooping laugh. "My boy, you saved the day. If it hadn't been for you rallying those men and seeing off the Frenchies we'd be having to attack that damned place again tomorrow. I don't see that that would be much fun, let me tell you. But thanks to you and your men we showed the Frogs the sort of thing they're in for."

Four white-jacketed soldiers moved into the tent carrying trays and proceeded to place full plates in front of the seated officers. One poured glasses of claret and then left the gold embossed decanter in the middle of the table.

Despite the delicious smell of roasted meat and vegetables urging him to wolf down the food, Firth ate at a deliberately slow pace. During the meal talk was kept to a minimum and Firth got the feeling that he was being assessed by both officers.

Later, over a third bottle of claret, Wellesley asked Firth to remind him about his background.

The Commander laughed as he was retold of the incident with the press gang, but frowned when he heard the captain of the ship was the brother of Firth's now senior officer.

His eyes narrowed and then he asked: "Do you speak Spanish, Mr Firth?"

"Ah, not Spanish sir. I've picked up a few words of Portuguese – and French, of course – but no Spanish."

"Would you care for a bit more adventure?"

"More, sir?"

"We have a task for you and I'll not lie to you and say it will be easy. Interested?"

"Of course, sir."

"Splendid."

Wellesley turned to Benton and nodded towards the mapboard. The older officer stood and moved to the easel.

Pointing to the left of the map Benton said: "We are here at the moment, with three French armies close by. We need to make contact with a general of the Spanish army called General Minas. He's just over the south-eastern Portuguese border with some 20,000 men. We need to get a message to him so he will move to block the French from escaping into Spain. That way we'll have General Junot and his fellows trapped between ourselves, the sea and the Tagus River. He'll have nothing to do but surrender."

"And how do I get to General Minas, sir?"

"We've ruled out going overland, far too dangerous at the moment, but a Navy sloop is available. There are a few Barbary pirates still about, but they usually don't try on anything with vessels much larger than a longboat."

"When do I go, sir?"

Wellesley interrupted: "In a few days, Mr Firth. We think it best for you to help your regiment get itself back in order. There's another thing, when you return to camp you can have the honour of telling the men that they are to rid themselves of those damn queues. Verminous, smelly things. Cut 'em all off. You'll be a very popular man for letting them know of that order!"

"Yes, sir."

"Well, that's about it Mr Firth. You'd better go and get some sleep. Your regiment needs its captains wide awake."

"Beg your pardon sir, I'm only a Lieutenant."

Wellesley smiled. "Not any more Mr Firth. As of now you are a Captain. Only a brevet rank, for the moment, as it will need to be confirmed by Horse Guards. Your regiment has plenty of vacancies - having seen the casualty reports I can assure you of that. You've done well, sir, I'll expect you to keep doing so."

Firth was stunned and mumbled his appreciation. Outside he shook his head in amazement and half-smiled. A Captain, he thought, wouldn't Brook be surprised. At the thought of his missing friend the smile died on his face and he felt as if he had been kicked in the stomach. Where are you Sam, he thought? Slowly making his way back to the 6th company's bivouac he decided to take up Needham's offer of a bottle of brandy. Perhaps that would ease his mind.

XXII

On the Lisbon Road,
South of Rolica

He was never quite sure which it was - the jolting of the hard floor of the wooden cart, or the horrendous screeching of its wood-on-wood axles - but Brook awoke from unconsciousness with a start. The sudden movement sent shards of pain through his head and he groaned. It was dark and he had a raging thirst. A hand patted him on the shoulder and he turned towards where he thought it came from but could see nothing. Sweet God, I'm blind, he thought.

"Who's that?"

"It's Major Way, Samuel."

The voice and hand were meant to reassure Brook, but in his pain and fear he got little comfort from them.

"I can't see, sir," he muttered. "I can't see a thing."

A wooden canteen was pressed to his lips and he greedily took a mouthful of the warm water.

"Take it easy, Samuel. It's a dark night and you took quite a blow to the head."

"But I'm blind, Major…"

"Calm down, lad," the older man said, and poured some of the water over Brook's forehead. "You've got a nasty cut there - a good and deep one - and I'd bet a tuppence to a guinea that once we get that cleaned up you'll be able to see well enough. You'll still have a headache though, I'll warrant."

Brook heard water being poured again and then felt a wet cloth wiping his face. Even light pressure sent more pain through him.

"You took a hell of a belt from a musket butt, young Brook, a hell of a belt. I have to say I thought we'd lost you for a while. You didn't move for three hours."

"What happened, sir?"

"Well, we were overrun by those Frenchies and brought back to their lines. There are about 40 of us. Most have wounds, but there's only you and a couple of others who caused us any concern."

"Where are we now sir?"

"The Frogs are retreating south, so I'd say we beat 'em. Damned if I know how, but after we reached their camp they did form several times for attacks. They made a hell of a racket, but seeing as they are now retreating, I take it they failed. Now hold still, I'm going to try to clean your eyes."

Brook prayed silently as the cloth rasped over the dried blood covering his eyes. He could feel it pulling his eyelashes but he dared not move or complain.

"Right, Samuel, I'm going to pour some more water over your eyes to see if that cleans things up. Keep them closed now."

The liquid dribbled across his face and then the cloth was reapplied. It took several minutes of careful work by Way to remove almost all of the caked blood and then he told Brook to slowly open his eyes.

The young man did as he was told and initially saw nothing, but his eyes soon became accustomed to the gloom and he could make out stars.

"It seems I've worked miracles, Mr Brook, I take it you can see?"

"I can, sir, I can. Thank the Lord."

"Indeed, indeed, and whoever it was who gave you such a hard head!"

Brook savoured his relief silently and then asked. "Where are we heading, Major?"

"To Lisbon, I'd say. That's the main French base and where they keep their supplies and prisoners. It's the prison hulks for us, I'm afraid."

"Could we not try to escape?"

"You may, Mr Brook, but I have given my parole and it wouldn't do to break it. The Frogs have treated us pretty decently and, in your condition, I'd just lie still and rest. There's not much we can do until the French are beat."

Brook shifted slowly in the wagon and got into a better position. Despite the rolling wagon's hideous noise he thought the night peaceful. Ahead of him men in British uniforms marched slowly and silently, while their captors walked beside them talking quietly in French.

He could have sworn he heard two of the men talking about a black horse, but weary and with little strength it didn't take long for him to fall back to sleep.

XXIII

Vimeiro 20 August, 1808

It was midday and the small village of Vimeiro was unusually busy in the heat of the sun. The locals were ignoring their siestas and hurriedly packing as many of their belongings as they could on to carts. Closing in on their homes was a French army and they had no wish to end up like their countrymen in Evora.

The village sat snuggly in between three low hills near a bend in the Maceira River. From his map Firth had thought it to be a major waterway, but in the stifling heat had dried to little more than a stream.

From where he stood, Firth could look down on the collection of small houses that was dominated by the towering steeple of a large church and a high stone wall enclosing its cemetery. Turning to his right he could see the fine mist that marked where Atlantic ocean breakers lashed up against the cliffs some two miles away.

To his left was a steep gully through which the Maceira flowed separating the hill he was on from a similar ridge. In front of that rise lay a small stream, the village itself and a low round rise known as Vimeiro Hill.

Having passed through the gully the Maceira then turned towards the ocean where the map showed it opened into a wide mouth. That, Firth had been told, was where some 4000 British reinforcements from Gibraltar were disembarking.

As he watched the villagers leave, Firth ate a handful of grapes taken from one of the many vines that covered the southern sides of the hills. Aside from the excellent fruit, a natural spring near the dwellings had given Wellesley's troops the opportunity to fill their canteens with some of the sweetest drinking water they'd had in Portugal.

It had only been three days since the clash at Rolica, but life had changed dramatically for Firth. He was now a Captain, although the rank had still to be agreed to by Horse Guards, but it was a promotion nonetheless. He had taken over command of the 6th company and did so with a heavy heart. The high number of casualties among lieutenants at Rolica meant he had no-one to assist him and Major Ricketts' dislike of him also meant the acting-commander of the regiment was in no hurry to make his job any easier.

Lt Coker had his leg broken by a ball during the battle, but was fortunate enough for it not to have needed amputation. It seemed to be healing and when he was fit enough to return to duty he would rejoin the regiment. Coker was not wealthy and could not afford to purchase promotion to one of the many now-vacant captaincies in the 29th, but he had told Firth he would be happy to serve under his once-junior lieutenant.

One of the company's new sergeants was Thomas Needham, who had quickly won back his stripes with his bravery on the ridge at Rolica and had asked to leave the grenadier company and join Firth. He had proved an enthusiastic helper and had used his scavenging abilities to ensure the men of the company had fared better from the supply wagons than most others in the regiment.

The rank-and-file men had enthusiastically embraced the young new Captain and were buoyed by his actions and bravery at the battle.

Both Needham and Barclay had smiled when they overheard Good's snide comment on Firth's youth being shouted down by others in the company.

"Shut your trap," Slater had told him, while the oldest men in the ranks - Siddle and Sweeney - told him to quieten down because Firth's actions were the bravest things they'd seen in years.

A sullen Good now sat with his back to his comrades cramming grapes into his mouth while the rest of the 6th watched the other regiments take up their positions. The bulk of the army was deployed on the western ridge to protect the troops landing at Maceira Bay.

There was a buzz about the camp at rumours French cavalry patrols were watching the British disembark and that somewhere to the south was a 16,000-man French army. It was said to be under the command of General Junot, one of Napoleon Bonaparte's best subordinates, who was aided by the ruthless General Loisin and General Delaborde, the man who had defied Wellesley at Rolica.

Excited junior officers talked loudly with each other on being given the news and the warning - be vigilant. All now knew that Junot would either have to break through the strong British position at Vimeiro, or else outflank them in order to disrupt the landings.

"That means reporting any signs of the French quickly," Firth had told them.

With the officers in animated form the men of the Worcesters' 6th company were pleased to be able to sit and rest. While the march from Rolica was not a long one, only some 15 or so miles, the journey had been difficult with the huge numbers of wounded men needing to be assisted.

There had not been enough carts to deal with them all and those that were used were of little real help. Soldiers sneered at the so-called wagons that were actually little more than platforms of wood on two wheels.

"Look at that," former farm hand Sergeant Barclay said in disgust, "the dopey beggars attach the yokes to the ox's horns … no wonder they jolt around."

Needham grimaced. "Aye and that bloody noise. Have they not heard of using grease? My head is splitting."

"You know Thomas, the local heathens say they don't use it because they believe the hellish noise will frighten off evil spirits."

Both men laughed, but knew it was no joke. The wagons only travelled at about two miles an hour, making the journey even more tortuous for the wounded on them.

Men who were not severely injured, or were lucky enough to be able to walk with some assistance, had made their own way behind their regiments. At nightfall they had finally been able to catch up with their comrades and enjoyed billies of tea and whatever leftovers could be found for the latecomers.

Having arrived some of Firth's men dozed, others cleaned their weapons but most just sat with their backs on their packs enjoying the sun - and the antics of artillerymen trying to haul six-pounder cannons on to Vimeiro Hill.

The blue-coated gunners swore at and beat their horses as the poor creatures struggled up the inclines and were forced to break their own backs holding the guns if the animals faltered or slipped. It was two hours of hell for the gunners, but much enjoyment for the watching British infantry.

Firth allowed himself a sympathetic smile and continued eating the sweet fruit.

"Better them than us, hey lads?"

There were smiles all round.

"Hope they stop the Frenchies when they come hopping over, Mr Firth," Good said.

"I'm hoping to stay out of the way today and just watch what goes on."

"What? And miss the pickings from their pockets? I can't believe that Good you wretched little weasel," Needham called, sparking laughter all round.

Good scowled. "Well better a live weasel than a dead hero. We did our bit back at Rolica and I'm happy to stay out of this."

And for once, most of the 6th company agreed with him.

XXIIIa

Overlooking the orderly British landing at Maceira Bay from the bluffs above the beach, Major Stanislaus Zapalski wished he had a few light artillery pieces with him. The disembarking British troops would have made a fine target – and one that could not fire back. Still, his mission was to estimate British numbers and he could go back to General Junot and report the British would slightly outnumber his men when they took the field. That would not deter the courageous and clever Junot who had beaten far larger armies in Italy, Egypt and Germany.

Zapalski admired the General, not only for his intelligence but for his courage. Zapalski had been near him when he was attacked by six cavalrymen and, before the Pole could get to his side, Junot had cut them all down. He had suffered a severe face wound, but that incident had inspired Zapalski. Junot was a fighting man he could follow.

The Major smiled. Junot was also one for the ladies and his headquarters in Lisbon was almost a Turkish harem. With half-naked women serving senior officers all the wine and food they could eat – and plenty more besides. Oh to be a friend of the Emperor.

"Well, Dezydery," he said to the Lieutenant next to him, "It looks like we'll be fighting the Redcoats at last."

Zapalski had long wanted to test himself against the men from the island nation. They had a reputation for being good soldiers, although their officers were said to be bad. Aristocrats and pampered sons of the rich, he thought contemptuously. Men who joined the army because they had nothing better to do. Not like the men of the Emperor's armies who fought to preserve a just cause. No the men wading through the waves below him and the rest of their army would be scattered quickly by Junot's men – as had every force that had ever opposed the will of the Emperor.

"We're moving against them tomorrow, Dezydhery, and will hit them before they can link with their comrades. There are more of the *bougres* on the way – a squadron of ships was sighted off Brest – so we need to deal with them now while the odds are good."

Chlapowksi smiled. He was also eager to fight. "It will be good to go up against real soldiers rather than bandits, Major."

"Let's go, Dezydery, we'll give the General the numbers and then find ourselves good women for the evening. It may be our last, huh?" he laughed

XXIV

Vimeiro 2pm

The coming battle was weighing on the mind of Sir Arthur Wellesley as he rode
slowly towards the British landing point with senior members of his staff. The
General was even more thoughtful than usual and Benton, moving beside him, knew
better than to break the silence.

Not only was Wellesley pondering on the positioning of his troops, but he was trying
to keep calm about his army being given to a more senior officer in Sir Harry Burrard.
"Do you know what infuriates me more than anything else Benton? Everyone knows
Burrard is not the man to face Junot. His last command was against the Danes and I
had to save the bloody man's career when he got caught out at Copenhagen. I mean
they were Danes, for God's sake, second-rate Prussians."

Wellesley did not expect any acknowledgement of his words and he dropped into
momentary silence then spat out: "That's not much of a recommendation for old
"Betty'' Burrard, is it Benton?"

Wellesley was damned annoyed and now had to meet his new commander and eat
humble pie. Still, he was confident about his positioning of the army and knew the
troops were eager to have another crack at Bonaparte's soldiers.

Having seen the way his boys had dealt with Delaborde's men at Rolica - when
attacking against strong positions - he had no doubt of their ability to see any French
attacks off. That was if he was commanding them, of course.

As the small party of his staff rode to the edge of the beach, Wellesley looked out at
HMS Brazen on which sat Burrard. The man should have been at the village
surveying the battleground, not sitting aboard a ship writing letters.

Another reason for Wellesley's bad humour was the fact that he would have to get in a
longboat, get out through the rough surf - praying he would not be tipped out - and
pay his compliments to Burrard when he had a dozen better things to do. "Bloody
Horse Guards," he muttered.

Fortunately, for the men around him, the boat trip was completed without incident
despite a slight shaky moment as he clambered up the side of the ship.

Wellesley bridled at the fact that Burrard was not there to greet him on deck and was
instead awaiting him in the Captain's cabin.

Composing himself before entering, Wellesley told himself to stay cool and not
become annoyed with his new commander. After all, it was Burrard's high political
connections that had got him the post and Wellesley, as a junior general, could not
afford to risk official displeasure.

Burrard stood when he entered the room and waved an aide out. Burrard was slightly
taller than Wellesley, his hair was a middle brown, his eyes a middle blue and
everything about him screamed middling to the younger general.

"Ah, Sir Arthur, you are well?" He didn't seem particularly interested in an answer
and immediately asked: "Are the troops well?"

"Very well, Sir Harry. I have positioned them at Vimeiro, a small village some two miles from here. They are screening the landings."

"Good, good … we'll base them there until the next transports arrive."

"I believe that Junot is in the area, Sir Harry, and is likely to attack us. Perhaps we should move out an intercept him once these regiments have disembarked."

"No, no, Sir Arthur. We don't have enough men. We'll wait until Sir John Moore arrives, that will give us another 7000 men and then we can move out."

"And when will that be, Sir Harry?"

"Within the week, I'm told …"

"But that will also give General Junot time to reinforce his army," interjected Wellesley. "If I may suggest Sir Harry, we already outnumber him and the troops are up for a fight after beating the Frenchies at Rolica. Now would be better."

"We will wait, Sir Arthur …"

"But if Junot decides against an attack and cuts and runs to Lisbon, then we will have a hell of a time dislodging him."

"No, Sir Arthur, we will wait. You must learn patience."

Wellesley could see by the look in Burrard's eyes that he was not prepared to listen to advice from a less senior officer, even his predecessor. He's just putting me in my place, Wellesley thought, and showing me he's in charge.

"Well then, Sir Harry, when can we have the pleasure of your company ashore?"

"I've decided to stay aboard until tomorrow, I've too many letters to finish. If you would organise a command tent for me and have it ready by noon I'll join you then."

"And should the French attack?"

"They won't, Sir Arthur, the French will skulk around and may observe us, but they won't move against us."

"Very well. Anything further, Sir Harry?"

"Yes, make sure I have a comfortable bed in my tent, Sir Arthur, my back's been giving me hell and I need something soft."

With extreme difficulty Wellesley bit back a sarcastic comment and hoped his anger was not betrayed by flushing in his cheeks.

"I'll have it arranged, Sir Harry. Something nice and soft."

He turned and left the room and stormed out on to the deck. You arrogant nonentity, he mentally fumed, a soft bed indeed. Pah! And with that he kicked out a bucket and sent it clattering across the deck. Sailors, Marines and Redcoats all looked up at the General and then quickly turned away. Wellesley stomped over to the side of the vessel and then climbed down into longboat.

"Get me back to land," he ordered harshly, "and be damned quick about it. And make sure we don't tip over or I'll have the lot of you flogged!"

One senior officer who was enjoying his day was Colonel Charles Taylor of the 20th Light Dragoons. The weather was beautiful and the prospects of imminent action stirred his excitement.

Heartily sick of patrol duties - intelligence gathering was for the Exploring Officers - what he wanted was a good old-fashioned charge at the head of his men into a mass of French hussars. Not likely to happen though, he admitted to himself, the British had too few horsemen for the campaign and Sir Arthur Wellesley was unlikely to risk them in a pitched battle.

Still, he thought, you can never know what was planned for you.

Taylor pulled up his troops near the Maceira River and gave orders to have the mounts watered and fed. He took off his orange-turbaned Tarleton helmet and wiped away a few drops of sweat.

"I'm just going to have a look around, Finlay," he told a young Cornet. "So, if I'm needed, I'm up there with the Foot Wobblers" and pointed to where the Redcoat infantry was resting on the western ridge at Vimeiro.

It wasn't a difficult climb and Taylor was glad of the chance to stretch his legs. He reached the flat top of the hill and looked around at the preparations for battle.

On the smaller hill across from him he saw artillerymen labouring away carrying barrels of powder and cannonballs to the summit where several big guns sat facing south. He smiled at their exertions and was glad the most strenuous thing he had to do was to order his servant to brush down his horse.

"The gun boys are having a bit of bother aren't they?" he commented to a young Captain near him.

"Yes, sir, but you should have seen them earlier dragging the guns up. My men thought it very fine entertainment."

Taylor looked at the youth who seemed somehow familiar.

"Have we met Captain?"

"I do believe so, sir, just out of Figueira. Your men took a French Captain off my hands. Rey his name was."

"Ah, yes, he's enjoying a period in a barracks at Gibraltar at the moment. You're Firth aren't you?"

"Yes, sir, Joshua Firth."

"A Captain I see. Weren't you a Lieutenant? By jove, that's fast advancement for a young man."

"Came as a surprise to me, sir."

"From what I hear, Mr Firth, you earned it. Fancy becoming a hero in your first action."

Firth felt himself colour at the comment and looked away.

"Don't be modest, Captain Firth, always accept praise when it's given. You'll get very little of it in this army, I can tell you."

"Yes, sir."

"I envy you, Mr Firth, you'll probably see more action than I will this day. My regiment is likely to be stationed in reserve, away from the fighting, and will spend the day watching the rest of the army getting all the glory."

Taylor looked to the south and gave an accepting sigh. "I'd give my right arm for a chance to be at the damned Frenchies."

Firth was about to make a comment when Sergeant Needham approached quickly. "Sorry to interrupt, sir, but Major Ricketts wants to see all officers immediately."

"Thank you, Sergeant, I'll be there." Turning to the Colonel Taylor, Firth offered his hand. "I hope you find action this day, sir. I truly do."

"It's very kind of you, Captain Firth, and I wish you all the best," he replied, shaking the young man's hand.

Firth watched as the Colonel moved down the hill and it was only a loud cough from Needham that returned his attention to the Sergeant.

"The Major, sir, is in a right tizzy and he's just aching for you to do something wrong. We'd better be going."

"Certainly, Thomas, I wonder what joys Major Ricketts has in store for me today."

"I did hear mention of a regimental rag fair, sir."

"A what?"

"A rag fair," Needham could barely suppress a smile, "is an inspection of the men's underclothes and necessaries, sir."

"What? Today?"

"Yes sir, he wants the men to be in good order for the enemy sir."

"Thank you, Sergeant - I've never seen one of these rag fairs."

"Begging you pardon sir, but I have a feeling you'll be seeing a lot more of them. You're to lead the inspection."

XXV

South of Vimeiro,
8pm, August 20, 1808

General Delaborde listened intently as the meeting wound down. He thought Junot had a good plan and - with the 15,000 veteran infantry, cavalry and artillery available to him - could not fail to throw the British back into the sea.

Junot's generals were experienced and Delaborde, who had won praise with his performance at Rolica, did not rank himself as being the best subordinate.

No that honour, Delaborde freely and realistically admitted, would go to the hero of the Battle of Marengo, General Francois Kellerman, son of the famous marshal.

Kellerman led Junot's cavalry and was a great tactical thinker. Small, he was also very clever, but in the way of a rat always trying to get more for himself, Delaborde thought. And … he was ugly.

A mass of densely curled hair, eyes too wide apart, a shapeless nose and thin unsmiling lips made up the face of a soldier whose on-field excellence was only matched by his ceaseless search for plunder.

Next to Kellerman was Junot, who could have almost been taken for effeminate, Delaborde noted, were it not for the long, deep scar that ran down the left side of his face. That wound had been gained during his celebrated fight with a group of enemy cavalrymen.

He smiled. Junot was not a man to mess with. On more than one occasion he had offered to settle his debts to creditors by running them through with his blade.

Needless to say, few had the courage to try to claim their money.

The General's financial problems were common knowledge and came about through a life of wanton extravagance and his latest uniform was a prime example of it. Instead of wearing the gold-decorated blue coat of most generals, Junot outfitted himself with an ostentatiously appointed uniform of a general of hussars.

The jacket and pelisse were both a stark white, liberally layered with enough gold lace to rival a Catholic church. His dark-blue pants were gold encrusted down the length of his thighs to his knees and even the tops of his bright red boots were intricately woven with the precious metal.

No wonder he was always begging his good friend the Emperor for more funds, Delaborde thought. Uniforms, whores and Romanesque orgies also hit the commander's purse hard and he was moving quickly, Delaborde judged, towards utter debauchery.

Despite having a hot-blooded young wife, Junot – who had been sent to Portugal by the Emperor after Bonaparte discovered he was having an affair with his sister Caroline - regularly dallied with low women at harem-style evenings at his headquarters.

He also had a ferocious temper when roused and was known as The Tempest. One night after heavy losses on the card table Junot had wrecked the gambling establishment and beaten up the dealers. The Emperor had been unimpressed and had asked his friend if he wanted to die a fool.

But, Delaborde did admire Junot's less-public side. It was one that completely contrasted with his reputation as a wild man. The Tempest loved rare books and took a portable library with him on campaign. He also had fine taste in food and wine and his chefs were the most respected in the Grande Armee. And behind his fiery temper there was an intelligence that came to the fore when he was dealing with the populations France ruled. As an occupying General he was just and fair and when he took to the field he fought without malice.

Delaborde knew that was more than could be said for the other senior officer present, General Loison, the one-handed butcher of Evora. He was a man who not only employed unnecessarily brutal methods, but enjoyed using them.

Only a month before, that small town in southern Portugal had made the mistake of rebelling against French rule and Loison had been sent to re-establish control. He had done so by killing every living thing in the village - its men, women, children, donkeys, chickens and dogs.

Delaborde looked at Loison with a loathing he usually kept for Germans. The man was an animal. The Portuguese called him Maneta, the one-armed one, and hated him with a passion. No surprise there.

All of the commanders examining the map on the large wooden table were years younger than Delaborde and each had their own vices.

The General smiled to himself as he wondered what they thought of him. Boring? Perhaps even an old woman? No matter, he had already given the English leopards a bloody nose at Rolica and the others had yet to face the Redcoats in the field.

That counted for something and so Delaborde listened to Junot's plans to defeat the British near Vimeiro with a contented look on his face. He knew that would irritate the others but that was their problem.

According to the scouts more Redcoats were landing at a bay to the west of the main British positions.

Junot tapped the map with his forefinger. "The enemy general has picked good ground, but ..." he paused, "only if we are going to march straight up to him and try to batter our way through."

He smiled and straightened up. "So we won't gentlemen, we'll try to use a few more brain cells than that," he added sarcastically.

Again stooping over the canvas he began tracing his finger over the area around Vimeiro.

"I think we should take a more sensible route and outflank these British. We'll begin before first light and while they are still yawning and brewing their tea we'll be on them, cutting them off from the sea and destroying them. Then it will be back to Lisbon for a hero's reception and honours from the Emperor.

Delaborde nodded with the others. He knew victory would earn a marshalcy for Junot, while he and Loison could expect small duchies as part of their rewards. Whatever, he thought, for all that mattered was beating the British and returning to the real war against the Austrians and Russians.

XXVI

Off the Coast of Spain,
Near Tarifa

The sloop cut through the heavy grey swells with a lightness that belied its size and the power of the waves. Spray burst over its bow and the full spread of sails slapped and strained the three masts they covered.

The Swallow was moving quickly – more quickly than its Captain would have wished – but the vessel was coping well with the demands placed on her. There was a reason for the urgency of the Swallow's voyage – three, in fact, and they were following the Royal Navy vessel at an uncomfortably close distance.

The lookouts had reported the presence of unidentified ships earlier in the morning. They were not flying flags and so, as a precaution, the Captain had crammed on all the sail he dared in a bid to outpace them.

As fast as the Swallow was, however, the smaller shadowing ships were staying in touch while the larger one, which had the shape of a Spanish frigate, was still within sight.

The Swallow was flush-decked and well-armed for its size, carrying 12 nine-pounder cannons and four 24-pounder carronades on its single gun deck. The gunners were quick and accurate, the result of daily practice sessions that kept their skills as sharp as a marlin spike.

In single-ship action, the Captain was confident his men could either out-run, or out-fight, opponents, but here he was facing three potential enemies and the odds were well against him.

Why on Earth were they following him, the master asked himself for the fifth or sixth time. We have no pay chest on board and the dispatches were little more than routine papers.

The only out-of-the-ordinary aspect of this voyage was the fact they were taking a small number of passengers from the fortress of Gibraltar to Portsmouth. Four men were from Portugal and would be dropped off at Figueria da Foz, while the remainder were traders returning to England.

Well, he paused, there was a woman ... not much more than a girl really, the 45-year-old Captain thought. Although on the few occasions he had spoken with her she had shown a remarkably mature grace and knowledge of not only the sea but, of all things, politics.

He tapped his closed fist on the weather-worn starboard rail and stared out at the pursuers. He let out a sigh and then felt a presence at his shoulder. Turning he saw the tall willowy form of the young lady and smiled.

"Do I interrupt your thoughts, sir?"

"Not at all my lady, how may I help?"

"I see we have company ... is that usual?"

"No, my lady, it is not but no cause for concern."

"I see they carry no ensigns … are they friendly?"

The Captain sighed again and said "To be truthful, my lady, I know not. But I suspect they are people we do not wish to meet. However, we are running fairly and are keeping our distance so, all being well, we shall stay away from them. Now is there something I may do for you?"

He looked again at the girl and realised she was older than he thought, probably near her 21st year. Her long reddish-brown hair was being blown from under the hooded cloak she wore and she carefully brushed it from her eyes that were, he noted, a striking green.

"I was interested in some of the other passengers – the men who are Portuguese. I do not believe they are what they say they are," she said in a soft voice.

"My lady?" the Captain questioned almost too quickly.

"Please Captain, my name is Constance. You see I speak Spanish quite well and I am sure their accents when speaking Portuguese are those of Castille. Why would they pretend to be from Portugal?"

His mind was racing now and he had already thought the same question.

The wind had freshened considerably and small squalls could be seen skitting across the ocean ahead. The weight of spray from the bow was becoming heavier and the pitch of the vessel was becoming more pronounced.

"I think we have worse weather approaching, my lady … Miss Constance," he corrected himself, "perhaps you would be more comfortable in your cabin."

She gracefully nodded and, with a glance towards the following ships, went below. Spanish? What would Spaniards want on his ship?

Suddenly the nationality of his passengers flew from the Captain's mind as a huge gust of wind hit the sails. He ordered the mainsail to be taken in immediately but, before the men could move up the ropes, the squalls hit in full force. The old mainsail was well patched and looked after, but the force of the winds tested its salt-spray-soaked strength. Unknown to the sailors of the Swallow there was a weak spot that had grown over the months and the extra pressure now placed on its tired seams took its toll. The rip began as just a slight parting of canvas and then within seconds had raced the length of the mainsail, the loss of which immediately slowed the Swallow. The Captain had no need to say anything as crewmen ran up the ratlines and began to rid the mast of its now-useless weight of canvas.

Others shouted and cursed as they moved to collect a replacement from below the deck. He did, however, look to the ships following him and thought they had instantly closed.

Within five minutes he knew they had. While his aloft sailors worked frantically to change sails the Captain had a feeling their efforts would be in vain. Still, he thought, he may just have been imagining a threat from trio of vessels.

That doubt was quickly dispelled when the lookout called down that the shadowing vessels had opened their gun ports.

Calling for drummers to beat to quarters, the Captain also signalled for the Swallow's guns to be run out and strapped on the sword that had been brought to him by a seaman.

There was a score of red-coated marines on board and they positioned themselves along the starboard railing.

"Double-shot," he called and the crew responded by adding an extra roundshot to the already loaded guns. He knew there was a danger that the additional pressure in the barrels could burst his cannons, but being outnumbered meant the British ship needed to make its first broadside a telling one.

"Mister Jones, at my side if you will. Lieutenant Chamberlain, also."

Both the Midshipman and First Lieutenant obeyed.

"Well, Mister Jones we have but a simple plan. Either outrun, or outfight."

Looking at the sailors struggling to re-sheet the Captain knew which would decide their fates.

"Make sure the gun teams are ready Mr Chamberlain and when I give the order fire like the Devil himself. Those smaller vessels are fast so we'll sink them if we can, then we'll try to outrun that frigate."

"Aye, sir," Chamberlain said, "Shall I ready a boarding party?"

"Not for the moment, thank-you Mr Chamberlain, but I like your confidence. No, we'll just pound them for a while."

The Captain knew his men should be able to fire four or five times faster than their opponents but the big danger was that frigate. He had to prevent it getting directly behind the Swallow, or else one raking salvo from its cannons could travel the length of the ship leaving her a shattered wreck.

By now the leading pursuer had edged close to the Swallow's port side and a puff of smoke was followed by the loud report of a cannon firing.

The cannonball fell some 50 yards short of the Royal Navy sloop and sent up a spout of water. A second shot echoed soon after and the adjusted range sent the ball splashing within a boat-length of the Swallow's bowsprit.

"We'll wait for them to close and give them all we can … right into their bellies," the Captain called, "and then fire for your very lives."

Now positioned beside the ship's wheel, he watched anxiously as the first vessel closed within hailing distance. Through his telescope he could see a senior officer approach the rail with a hailer and call across to him. At first he couldn't pick up the words being used but then made out the enemy's call to surrender. It was given in Spanish, but the message was clear enough.

The Captain cupped his hand to his ear in a suggestion he hadn't heard the command, but the bid to buy more time was answered by a third cannon shot that this time roared across his bow.

"It's almost time, boys, remember fire on the downward roll," he said, knowing well his crew wouldn't forget the basics of ship-killing shots - wait for the cannons' muzzles to start lowering before firing.

The Swallow and the leading attacker were now only 50 yards apart. The Captain thought the time right and as the railings started to dip towards the enemy he shouted "fire!"

The entire side of the Swallow disappeared in smoke and that announced to the enemy that several tons of metal had just been launched at them. The Captain heard the splintering of wood and the shrieks of men from the closest ship and the bellows of his gun captains screaming "reload!"

The enemy vessel sent out a ragged reply and immediately the Swallow seemed to be attacked by rushing winds and roaring objects that send chunks of wood flying around the deck.

The accompanying screams were much closer to the Captain's ears now, but his concern eased as he saw that all starboard guns were still operable.

"Gun crews fire at will," he shouted above the din and watched as within 30 seconds a second salvo of shots slammed into the opponent.

He knew the damage to the enemy must be considerable, but of more immediate concern was the position of the other pursuers.

The other smaller vessel was approaching his stern on the starboard side, while the frigate was approaching on the port.

The crippling of one opponent had given him confidence there was still a chance to escape, but the Swallow was being hauled in by the burning vessel's sister. Luckily for the British, it opened fire at long range. Several spars were brought down, but now the Captain decided to turn slightly and close on his attacker while the crew was reloading.

"Wait on my order," he called.

It would take careful timing and he reckoned the enemy would take at least two minutes before being able to fire again.

"Fire," he roared and the Swallow's answering salvo struck home with extreme brutality. The Captain watched as the enemy vessel visibly shuddered as the double shots hit, and again his hopes of escape rose.

Turning away the British crews worked frantically to reload and prepare for their next shots. Men sponged out the barrels while others stood handy with cannonballs and powder. The Captain knew it was crucial his men got off their next broadside before the enemy and was confident they would do so. There were few crews able to match his gunners.

"Fire!" he called and as his guns erupted. "Reload like furies, men, give 'em another blast."

He was silently counting the seconds. He had no idea how much damage he'd caused the enemy but he knew there was return fire coming very soon. Hopefully, the Swallow had knocked a lot of their guns out.

"Faster boys, faster, we'll beat these bastards."

He watched as one by one his gun captains raised their arms. They were all ready.

"Fire!" and again smoke and death belched from the British ship just as a ragged salvo came back at them.

"Clear away the decks," the Captain called, "Reload and fire when ready!"

All of a sudden his world erupted in a maelstrom of noise, screams and flying wood. A broadside from the frigate had hit the Swallow sweeping away much of the deck including the ship's wheel.

The Swallow's main mast took a direct hit and splintered half-way up its towering height. Falling wood and canvas crashed on to the deck and at least half of the sloop's guns were out of action. Sailors hurriedly tried to move the wreckage from on top of their cannons cutting through wood and rope with axes and machetes.

But the Captain now knew in his heart the battle was done. He couldn't manouevre, couldn't fire back and would just be sitting there waiting to be smashed to pieces by the frigate.

It hurt him greatly to have to give such an order, but he had his men's lives and those of his passengers to consider.

"Haul the colours down," he called to a blood-stained sailor. "We've done all we can."

He called a Midshipman over and told him to retrieve the packets of documents from his cabin. The boy returned presently with a canvas bag and handed it to the Captain who placed a heavy grapeshot ball in it before retying the top and dropping it over the side. He watched it quickly disappear trailing a chain of bubbles.

A longboat was now in the water from the victorious frigate and quickly pulling towards the Swallow.

Behind him the Captain heard a scream from below deck and as he moved towards the sound a door opened. Through the entry came two of his Portuguese passengers followed by the British woman and then two more Portuguese. All of the men carried swords and pistols.

"You," he called, "unhand her."

His command came with the backing of half a dozen Marines who had survived the carnage on deck and they levelled their muskets at the men.

"What are you doing?"

The leading stranger moved his pistol to Constance's temple and pulled the hammer back. "Silence!" he hissed.

"Sir?' a Marine asked, wanting directions from the Captain.

"Wait man, wait," he responded. "Leave the woman alone and tell us what you want."

"It's simple … we want her. She is safe from any harm unless you do not do as we say."

Looking at the woman the Captain asked: "My lady, what is this about?"

With tears in her eyes she shook her head "I know not, sir, I know not."

"What do you want with her?"

"It is of no concern to you. Tell your men to put down their weapons, let us take her to our ship and you will not suffer further."

"We would never abandon a lady in danger …"

"Don't Captain," Constance said, "you mustn't risk your men further. I have no idea what these men want, but even if you wished you could not protect me. There are too many of them."

Fighting back screams of frustration the naval officer knew she was right. His men could overpower the pirates on the Swallow, but the young lady would almost certainly die in the attempt.

"My lady," he said in a distraught tone, "I am so sorry. Forgive me."

"There is nothing to forgive sir, you have done all that could possibly be expected of a gentleman and your crew has suffered greatly."

Helplessly the Captain turned and watched as a longboat pulled next to his vessel and a well-dressed officer in Spanish uniform smartly clambered on board.

"I must protest. We are a British ship and I demand to know what is happening here."

The officer just smiled and, without answering the question, said: "We seem to have what we are after."

"Who are you?" the Captain again demanded and once more the query was ignored.

"Answer me you Spanish bastard, why are you taking her?"

The officer silently turned his back on the Captain and took Constance by the arm as he led her towards the side of the ship.

The Swallow's Marine Lieutenant arrived at his side: "We can't just let them take her. For God's sake she's an Englishwoman. We must protect her. We must fight them."

The Captain looked at the soldier and said simply "How? If we shoot at them she will be killed."

He watched as the longboat pulled away from the side and stroked evenly to the waiting enemy ship. Shame at his inability to defend Constance burned his cheeks and scorched his guts. He would have to return to Gibraltar and report the incident and face what penalties would come his way.

The Captain was too distracted by Constance's kidnapping and arrival aboard the enemy vessel to notice the enemy frigate had now taken position behind the Swallow's stern. It towered over the sloop with its two decks of gun ports open.

The first the Captain knew of the broadside was the horrendous explosion as 24 large guns spewed out a metal wall of death and destruction.

The 16-pound balls ripped through the rear of the Swallow, smashing through wood and gouging pathways of death the length of the body of the ship.

Within the ship the devastation was horrendous. If not bludgeoned to pieces by the force of the cannonballs smashing into the sailors' flesh and bones, the men were speared by metre-long shards of broken oak. The force of the roundshot would be denied by nothing and destroyed anything in their way. Walls and tables were obliterated, cannons overturned and chunks of wood flew around the dark interior. In a matter of seconds the innards had been ripped out of the British sloop.

Had he been alive the death of his ship would have hurt the Captain even more deeply than the kidnapping of a passenger. But his headless body lay in a pool of blood near the remnants of the wheel, along with that of the Marine Lieutenant, his helmsman and 10 sailors.

The damage to the Swallow was so severe it began to sink beneath the grey waters almost before the smoke from the broadside had cleared. It went to the depths silently, as if already mourning the 120 men who died with her.

XXVII

Vimeiro
August 21, 1808

It had been an early start to the day for the troopers of the 20th Light Dragoons. They had been roused by Cornet Finlay and several sergeants before first light and ordered to prepare themselves and their horses.

Some of the men, who had left their horses saddled overnight, were now crouching around small fires trying to boil tin containers of water into which tealeaves had been thrown. As they sat and watched the steam begin to rise from the dark brew, their comrades worked quickly and quietly to get their mounts ready for action.

They were excellent troops and regarded themselves as the equal of any in Europe, but they were pitifully few in number.

The regiment could only muster 240 troopers and, until yesterday, only two-thirds of them had mounts. Even for a young officer new to campaigning it was obvious that the lack of horses was a major problem in Wellesley's army. And, Finlay knew that had it not been for the generosity of the Bishop of Oporto, a highly regarded horse breeder who had sent the British 80 of his own creatures, they would have been unable to provide any meaningful form of cavalry for Sir Arthur Wellesley.

Patrols that had come in the previous night had told the British senior commanders that General Junot's army had more than 2000 horsemen in its ranks and the men of the 20th had no doubt the French would not be struggling to find mounts.

To bolster his cavalry, Wellesley had ordered some 240 Portuguese dragoons and some mounted Lisbon police to join the 20th. The Portuguese were well-presented men on very fine looking horses and even the old hands of the 20th nodded in approval when they had entered camp the previous afternoon.

Like the British troopers, their jackets were dark blue although the Portuguese ones were much simpler in design and had none of the intricate silver braiding that covered the fronts of the 20th's uniforms. Their breeches were grey, contrasting with the 20th's dark blue, and their helmets were similar in style to the British leather Tarleton ones, although the plumes were far thicker and higher.

The Portuguese too were rising from their blankets, although the chatter and noise of their preparations were markedly different to that of the quiet British. Still, thought Colonel Taylor, they doubled his strength and - from a distance - they could be taken for British troopers. If nothing else they would make the French a little more wary.

Sipping his strong tea, Taylor looked around him and nodded in appreciation. He thought Wellesley had positioned the army well and his regiment was deployed slightly above the village of Vimeiro and just behind its hill.

Looking up at the light blue sky he knew it was going to be another warm day and it was one he had been looking forward to for most of his military career.

After all his years in the army he had only seen action twice - in the West Indies and South America - and both of those campaigns were mainly infantry affairs where his horsemen had delivered dispatches rather than joining any fighting.

In fact during the embarrassing expedition to Buenos Aires just the year before his regiment had had even fewer horses than they had now. No horses, tied to the Foot Wobblers and having to surrender as well.

The desire to avenge that humiliation burned deeply within Taylor and there was only one way he could see to do it and that was on a proper field of battle leading his beloved regiment into action.

Taylor's musings suddenly ended as trumpets sounded on top of the two hills to his rear.

Shouts accompanied the call to arms and by the amount of activity on the British right wing he knew the French must have been sighted. But where were they coming from?

XXVIIa

By the time the bugles sounded Firth was already moving with his company towards the eastern ridge. Long French columns had been sighted to the east and most of the army's right wing was quickly being moved to counter the threat.

Riders had galloped up through the regiments relaying orders that demanded instant redeployment and within minutes the campfires had been extinguished with the contents of the smoking kettles being poured over them and the men formed for march.

There were plenty of curses as thirsty men watched as their looked-forward-to drinks were wasted, but they quickly subsided with the excitement of another chance to come to grips with the enemy.

The 29th was at the westernmost tail of the 11 regiments ordered to redeploy and Firth watched as more than 6000 Redcoats disappeared from view in the gully between their original positions and their new objective.

"Fine morning for it, sir," came the now-familiar voice of Sergeant Needham. "Seems like the Frogs are trying to turn us."

"You're right, Sergeant," Firth agreed and when he looked down from his horse to nod to the red-headed man was surprised to see him shaving while walking. "Sergeant?"

"Oh, don't worry about me sir, never nicked myself once. The lads would love to see it and there's a bit of money going on when that will be."

Firth smiled as Needham quickly finished his work and was about to wipe the remaining soap from his face when a red-faced Major Ricketts rode up.

"What the hell are you doing, Mr Firth," he demanded.

"Sir?"

"We are marching to a battle, not a dance! What do you mean by allowing your men to dawdle along shaving?"

"It's a trick sir, it helps the men …"

"We don't want tricks, Mr Firth, we want men ready to fight. I can see we'll have to instill a bit of discipline around here after this day's efforts. Move your men along and be quick about it, damn your eyes! You are supposed to be an officer."

Firth felt a flare of anger surge in him and he was about to issue a protest at such a comment, when he thought better of it. Although insulted by Ricketts' treatment of him the man was still his commanding officer.

The Major turned his horse and cantered back along the column berating his men to march faster.

"Don't worry about him sir, looks to me like he has the wind up," said Needham. "And, if I may say sir, he's not got over your handling of the regiment at Rolica. Showed him up good and proper it did."

"That was not my intention, thank you Sergeant," Firth responded coolly, gently letting the enlisted man know he was about to step over an unspoken line of respect for senior officers. But silently Firth wondered if Needham was right.

Since Rolica Ricketts had been even tougher on him and the 6th company. While he would never openly admit it, if another opportunity came up to outshine the Major, Firth was looking forward to doing so.

XXVIIb

Sitting on the brow of a hill observing the French, Wellesley had been surprised by Junot's flanking move, but felt he had countered the move quickly enough to negate any advantage the French may have got.

"Thought they'd catch us napping, eh Benton?" he said. "Well, by God, we'll show them."

Benton smiled and put his brass telescope to his eye. He could see columns of French troops in long white summer coats sending up clouds of dust as they marched towards what had been a weak British left wing.

"Well, Sir Arthur, they'll be in for a bit of a shock if they expected to surprise us."

"Now Benton, you did tell Generals Nightingall, Fergusson and Bowes to keep their men out of sight behind that eastern ridge didn't you?"

"Of course, Sir Arthur, they'll not be spotted."

It had only taken half an hour, but the British army had now realigned itself and was drawn up along a north-south axis. Wellesley was silently delighted with the way his army had made the redeployment with little fuss.

On the extreme right of his lines was General Rowland Hill, one of his most dependable men who, with his 2600 troops, would guard against a French move there. It was unlikely, Wellesley conceded, but if it occurred then Hill was more than capable of dealing with it.

In his centre, on the slopes of Vimeiro Hill, sat the brigades of Generals Anstruther and Fane - some 5000 men backed by 12 cannons. With cavalry for support, rough terrain for attackers to cross and the village's church as a strongpoint against an attack on his rear, Wellesley felt the position secure.

Between the village and the newly reinforced left wing - now with some 6000 men set to defend it - was General Acland's 1500 men.

Wellesley allowed himself a small smile. Junot had revealed his hand and the British aristocrat was sure he would soon give it one hell of a slapping.

The Frenchman had also made a basic mistake, Wellesley thought, in that he had seemed to split his force in two. There was a strong French presence to the south of the village and another to the east in the flanking force, but were there others? Wellesley's confidence dropped for a moment. Did Junot, who was undoubtedly a clever fellow, wish him to believe he had split his army? Was there another French force in between the two, one waiting unseen in the undulating ground for the right moment to make a move against Acland and by doing so cut off the British left wing? Wellesley took a depth breath and went over his deployment again in his mind. No, it was strong he told himself and while Junot's plan of attack showed the sort of bold manouevre that had beaten many European armies this time the French would be meeting British soldiers.

"Hah, they'll not find winning a battle so easy," he said to no-one in particular. Snapping his telescope shut, he smiled again. Bring them on and we'll remind them how Englishmen fight.

XXVIII

Vimeiro 8am

General Delaborde took the news that his division would open the French attack on
the British centre with both pride and a sense of wariness. It was good to have been
chosen to lead the way, but it would be a difficult assignment.
Delaborde ignored Junot's confidence that the Redcoats would be quickly brushed
aside, as experience had shown him these Englishmen knew how to fight. Observing
the enemy lines he was impressed by what he saw. Not only were they drawn up with
pin-point precision, but the only things moving along the whole hill were the giant
regimental flags. Everything else was still as the enemy sat patiently waiting for the
attack.
His main push would be made against the south-eastern slopes of Vimeiro Hill and
success there would allow a move into the village behind the flat-topped rise. If all
went to plan General Brennier's flanking force would push past the British left wing
and link up with his own division, hemming the British in against the ocean.
To accomplish his part of the strategy, Delaborde had a little more than 2000 men,
although he would receive support on his left from a brigade from Loison's division
under General Charlot.
Altogether, some 3000 seasoned troops would take on the defenders and while they
were outnumbered Delaborde was the confident his troops, who had taken on greater
odds and won, would prevail.
As the troops formed into their attack columns, the drummers began to beat out the
pas-de-charge, a staccato message to French troops that now was their chance to win
glory for La Belle France. Delaborde also took it as a signal for those opposing the
Emperor to prepare to meet their maker.
As usual a host of sharpshooting voltigeurs moved out in front of the columns their
yellow pom-poms appeared bright in the morning sun and moved rhythmically on top
of their shakoes.
In all of the French victories in Europe these men created mayhem in defenders' lines,
wounding and killing as many as they could to thin the number of muskets against
their columns.
Delaborde watched as the small wiry voltigeurs easily outstripped the main body and
closed in on their targets. Few nations had as many of the sharpshooters as France and
rarely did the voltigeurs ever find themselves at a disadvantage against an enemy.
This day, Delaborde knew, they were up against a foe that had learned the light-
infantry trade the hard way, in the forests and woods of North America fighting
Indians and American rebels.
The crackle of gunfire echoed from grape vines below the British positions and by the
amount of white smoke drifting upwards Delaborde knew his men had met stiff
resistance.
So, he thought, they had been lying in wait for us. He tapped an aide on the shoulder
and told him to send forward more skirmishers.
In the plentiful cover offered by the lush vines Lieutenant Henri Delort was finding it

hard to keep an eye on his men. He could hear calls in English and the nearby sound of whistles, but spotting where the enemy lay was proving difficult. Still, Delort knew his men well and was sure they would not let him down.

They were running forward in pairs with a confidence born of having beaten the best Europe could throw against them when suddenly they were hit by fire from what seemed like hundreds of muskets. Dusty white coats were splattered with red as musketballs tore into flesh, smashing bones and creating gaping exit wounds. Officers were hit first, then sergeants, then corporals.

Delort ducked as a ball passed by his head and then his sword was knocked from his hand. Wringing his fingers he looked to see if he still had them all and then picked up his blade and continued forward.

Next to him a private grunted and fell with a bullet in his throat. He thrashed around with his eyes pleading for help as he tried to stem the blood pouring from the wound. A sergeant stopped to assist and that gave an unseen British soldier time enough to drill a shot through his head. He fell without a sound.

Now ignoring the cries and moans of their comrades, the French returned fire through the increasing smoke. Their enemies were mainly in red, some in green, and they came at the voltigeurs with no fear pushing bright bayonets ahead of them as they screamed out blood-curdling cries.

Delort parried one thrust from a bayonet and before the man could recover his balance he had shot him with a pistol. A second green-jacketed figure leapt at him, but Delort's height and agility allowed him to fend off the charge and strike back with his sword. It cut into the wood of the man's short rifle near his trigger hand and he yelled in fear.

The Frenchman was about to deliver a killing strike when he was felled by a massive blow in his side. The pain was intense, but Delort was not willing to lie helplessly waiting for someone to kill him. He tried to rise but the effort sent waves of agony through him. He put his arm back feeling for where he had been hit and gasped as new spikes of pain exploded. He was bleeding badly from just below his ribs and knew the shot had gone into his vitals. Delort was dying and he cursed it.

Around his prone figure the battle raged with the British pulling back slightly in the face of the extra voltigeurs sent against them. Soon, however, their tactic of first taking out officers and sergeants paid dividends. With few leaders left, and under extreme fire, the confidence of the French attackers waned and they began to pull back towards their main force.

Positioned with the right column Delaborde was surprised by the level of resistance offered by the British.

Usually the voltigeurs opened the way up for the massed formations to exploit, but today the main body would have to assist their comrades punch through the enemy light infantry.

He ordered the pace increased and his officers began to shout and wave their arms about in an attempt to fire up their men's eagerness for battle. The troops responded with yells of their own that became ever more energetic the closer they got to the vines.

The extra troops were enough to gain control of the firefight, Delaborde was pleased to see, and the British slowly withdrew to their main lines.

Now there was nothing between his men and the British and the pas-de-charge boomed out with new urgency.

Delaborde watched his men with pride and knew that if any troops could show the British how to fight it was them. The mass of white-coated soldiers seemed unstoppable and their step never faltered, even when they moved on to rougher ground at the lower slopes of Vimeiro Hill.

An orderly suggested the General move to the rear of the attack, but he spat a curse at the suggestion. A General should lead his men, not follow ... and he would wait until the men were much closer before dropping back – but only into the middle of the formation.

To his left Charlot's soldiers were making faster progress, but then they faced fewer obstacles along their line of march and, as yet, the British had not attempted to delay them.

Delaborde watched as the white column pushed up the hill towards the lines of red with a precision that resembled being on the parade ground of the Champs de Mars. Suddenly a cannon fired from the hill, then another and another.

The solid metal balls clearly struck home as Charlot's formation seemed to ripple after each belch of flame and thunder. The General could see dozens of men left lying on the ground along the paths of the cannonballs but, despite the disruption of men having to step over their fallen comrades, the column quickly regained its shape and pressed on.

The drums pounded louder and Charlot's troops set off a mass of cheering. As the column got within 100 paces of the enemy, the red ranks disappeared in a burst of smoke and a second later the roar of the muskets hit Delaborde's ears. The front rows of the French folded, but the momentum of the attack didn't change.

Again the British muskets fired and more white coats fell. The front French ranks were now returning fire, but the shape of the formation meant only the two leading ranks of troops could actually use their muskets, while the defenders could bring every weapon they had to bear on the mass of men. Deploy some of your men into line, Delaborde silently urged his comrade, but he feared it was too late.

The column had now closed to within 50 paces and, although its speed had slowed to a barely moving crawl, cheering could still be heard through the gunfire.

What worried Delaborde was that against most armies French columns petrified defenders and by the time they had got as close as Charlot's men had the enemy's resolve had faltered and they had broken and run away.

These British just stood their ground and reloaded their weapons. There was no appearance of worry, just a professional determination to load and fire as quickly as they could.

More smoke poured from the front of the now-stopped French, only to be consumed by an avalanche of smoke from higher up the hill. Dozens of men in white had fallen and the head of the column writhed in obvious agony.

Then Delaborde was stunned as one regiment in the British lines pushed out, gave a clearly heard shout and threw themselves forward on to Charlot's stationary men.

Like a red tide the enemy closed on the now disorganised French troops, while a second body of men attacked them in the flank. Delaborde could see the mounted Charlot desperately urging his men to stand, but within seconds they had broken and were fleeing down the hillside.

Delaborde was shocked at the scene. Never before had he witnessed such a rapid repulse of an imperial force – even at Rolica his men had fought with more determination and against troops in hard cover. He set his jaw firmly knowing he could still finish the matter with his own attack.

Free from the harassment of enemy skirmishers, the voltigeurs again moved out in front of Delaborde's men and nimbly made their way up the steepening slopes of the hill. Operating in pairs they found themselves good cover just below the British and began to fire into the infantry lines.

Those defenders are holding their fire, Delaborde noted with admiration, for he could see many of the Redcoats falling to the increasingly accurate musketballs sent flying towards them by his voltigeurs.

As the British light infantry had done, so the voltigeurs went after the enemy commanders. Several officers were thrown backwards from their horses as balls struck home.

The French drummers were belting out the *pas-de-charge* and officers in white again danced about trying to encourage their men. As the volume of shouts and jeers increased, so did the confidence of the attackers who were sure the defeat of their comrades had been just bad luck. No line formation had ever stood against a column and their General had fought the British before and would see them through this time. Ahead, Delaborde could now see the waiting figures standing confidently in front of this display of imperial power. While most British troops seemed to have yellow collars and cuffs on their uniforms, these had jet-black facings. He didn't want to admit it, but the commander thought it gave them an extra measure of menace.

As he watched, that part of the defenders' line began to move forward and advanced some 50 paces from the main body. His own leading ranks began to shoot and Delaborde wished he had been allowed to have taken them forward in lines.

Once again the defenders crashing first volley utterly destroyed the first two ranks of his column.

Training came to the fore, however, and the white coats just stepped over their injured friends and continued up the hill.

A second volley spat another deadly wall of lead and felled even more men within the compacted French. Worse followed as British light companies moved in and fired into their flanks.

By now the confidence of his men was badly shaken and so ignoring the dangers Delaborde spurred forward to raise their spirits.

A third defensive volley stopped the attack in its tracks and then a wild cheer went up from the British.

Again the men in red threw themselves forward with bayonets lowered and the head of Delaborde's column simply melted in front of the terrifying threat.

The General found his horse being pushed around as his fleeing soldiers ran from the wild men and he struggled to stay mounted. Delaborde struck at troops with the flat of his blade and shouted curses at them, but it did little to stem the flow.

Suddenly Delaborde was almost knocked from the saddle by a blow to his sword arm and had it not been for the sabre-knot around his wrist the weapon would have fallen. His aide immediately grabbed his uninjured arm to steady him and shouted that it was time to pull back and reform. With bitterness Delaborde reluctantly agreed and turned his horse down the hill.

His face burned with shame as he made his way to the starting position, the loud "huzzas" from the British adding insult to his injury.

XXIX

Vimeiro 10am

On the flat plateau of Vimeiro Hill, British staff officers broke into tension-releasing smiles and thought the job well done. One who was not outwardly pleased was Sir Arthur Wellesley, who just nodded and patted his horse's neck.

"There's still plenty more of this day's work to be done, gentlemen, so I'll ask you not to slap each other on the back until we've seen all the Frenchies turn tail and run," he said gruffly.

Wellesley motioned to one of his young aides who edged his mount closer to the commander. "Compton, I want you to go to generals Anstruther and Fane and give them my compliments on fine actions."

The young Captain spurred away down the hill just as another party of riders came up behind Wellesley.

"Sir Harry is here, Sir Arthur," a low warning came from Benton.

Wellesley stiffened and scowled, but by the time he had turned to greet his new commander a half-smile was on his face.

"Ah, Sir Harry, welcome. I was about to report to you that we have been attacked by Junot and have seen off his first efforts. As you are the senior officer, I presume you would like to take over command of the army?"

Sir Harry Burrard looked down at the mass of white-coated bodies in front of the British lines and shook his head.

"Not at all, Sir Arthur, you and your men are doing a very fine job of it. It would be presumptuous of me to take over when you've begun the battle. Please carry on, sir, with my blessing."

Wellesley looked about as pleased as he could without wishing to show it and nodded to his senior general.

"Thank you, I believe we'll be seeing some more action rather soon. We've got a French force to our east over there," he said pointing with his telescope, "and I do believe we'll face a bit more trouble from those troops in front of us."

"Will we beat them, Sir Arthur?"

"I certainly have every intention of doing so, Sir Harry. Now, gentlemen, I believe it is time for a sherry!"

XXIXa

Not far from where the staff officers were drinking a Royal Artillery colonel was making sure his cannons were in readiness for the next French assault.

The two companies of guns had barely been used in the opening clash, but Colonel

William Robe was determined that should they be needed his crews would be able to respond immediately.

His six-pounders were heavy 2.5 ton brutes made of bronze that could throw a solid metal six-pound ball as far as 1300 paces. He patted one lovingly.

The better killing range, however, was only half that and Robe smiled as he remembered how his men had cheered when they had sent the shot into the left-hand French column.

Files of men had been smashed bloody by the cannonballs as they had bludgeoned through the packed bodies. Solid shot was good, he thought, and so was canister - if the Frenchies got that close.

At 400 paces the thin tin casing of canister would explode open to spray a deadly shower of metal balls and iron that would shred an attack.

Beautiful stuff, the Colonel thought.

Robe looked with anticipation at a pile of new ammunition just behind the cannon trail.

"Will they work, sir?" a young gunner inquired.

Robe looked up "Let's hope so …"

"They look just like shells, sir."

Robe agreed that the ammunition, sitting on wooden bases, did look similar to ordinary shells.

"But these are much more effective," he said. "Imagine six pounds of gunpowder exploding in the air above you sending musketballs and pieces of metal all over the place. Anything within 70 paces is likely to get hit."

"Have the Frenchies got them sir?" the young man said nervously.

"No, lad, they're new and they're ours. We'll be firing them at the French and thankfully not the other way around."

"God bless us, sir!"

"No, lad, God bless Sir Henry Shrapnel – he's came up with the idea."

The gunner moved away and Robe turned his attention back to the slope in front of him. The trick was to decide how long the fuse should be. If he wanted the shell to hit troops at some 650 paces it needed to be a quarter-of-an-inch long and almost twice that for targets closer to 900 paces.

In the opening French attack the guns had not been heavily used because British skirmishers had been operating forward of the main lines. They had now been forced back to the main body and so his guns now had a clear field of fire.

Robe ranged his guns for 650 paces and ensured his men had at least three rounds of Shrapnel shell fuses cut for that distance. The rest of the ammunition was set for closer in – in case the French hadn't been dissuaded from carrying on the attack.

The Colonel looked at his gunners calmly going about their business and was satisfied. They were good crews who knew what they were about and would give their infantry all the support they needed.

The men of the 29th had seen nothing of the clashes as they sat in their new position on the eastern ridge.

They did hear the sounds of the British musket volleys rolling back over Vimeiro Hill, but apart from the rising cloud of smoke that masked the forward portion of the hill's flat top they didn't know how the battle was progressing.

The Worcesters were the rearmost regiment of new Allied left wing and unless things changed dramatically the men felt they were in for a quiet day. Most were happy about that following their exertions at Rolica, but Major Ricketts was eager to be at the French.

His standing among the regimental officers had suffered as a result of not arriving at that battle on time and he wanted to show them he - and not just that jumped-up Firth - would have held the line.

Bloody Firth, he muttered to himself, a Captain after only a few weeks. He had made the upstart's life difficult by ordering him to do the most menial of tasks he could set for officers, but the young bastard had accepted everything with an annoyingly good grace. Mind you, he had shown signs of being upset at the last comments made to him so maybe it was getting to him, Ricketts thought a bit more positively.

Somehow Firth had found favour with Sir Arthur Wellesley and that stuck in Ricketts' craw. He was the senior officer of the regiment and yet Wellesley had chosen to single Firth out.

Firth was also the darling of the enlisted men and while many officers could barely raise more than a "yes, sir" from the soldiers, the scum actively sought conversation with their new-found hero.

Well, Ricketts was going to change that today and he was determined to keep presenting himself to Wellesley and show he was a keen and intelligent officer ready to serve his King.

"Mr Firth," he roared, "What are you looking at?"

Firth turned and crossed the brownish grass towards him.

"Major Ricketts, sir, I was just watching that French column to our left … over by that village."

"Well I am damn sure, Mr Firth," Ricketts sneered, "that everyone has seen its approach and that's why we are now facing in this direction."

"Yes, sir," Firth responded, "but I thought I saw a second body of troops moving to our right. I can't be sure, but I think it left the main road and is coming through that broken ground over there."

"And you saw this without the aid of a telescope did you?"

Firth cursed himself again for not having got a 'scope.

"Yes, sir, there were white coats moving towards us from the north-east. I am sure of it. Several thousand men, sir."

Ricketts drew himself up and looked at the taller youth. "I think, Mr Firth, you would be better advised looking after your company rather than worry about things that do not concern you. You, sir, should be an officer to your men and ensure … " Ricketts paused, "that they do not crap in their lines."

Firth was stunned, "Sir?"

"Just bloody look man, look at that dirty beast there," said Ricketts, pointing his finger at Good who was just unbuckling his pants preparing to squat. "Keep your men in order, sir, or you'll find yourself in serious trouble."

"Sir," Firth said, and then hurriedly made towards the 6th company.

Ricketts gave a savage grin at the Captain's discomfort. That'll teach him. Thank God Firth was leading the 6th and not one of the regiment's better companies. The dregs of the 6th would allow him plenty of opportunities to make Firth's life even tougher.

XXX

Vimeiro 10.30am

General Delaborde winced as the metal probe pushed against the musketball lodged in the biceps of his upper arm. His intake of breath made the nervous surgeon stop and look up hurriedly, but a quick nod from wounded man gave him permission to continue.

The velocity of the ball must have almost been spent by the time it hit the General as it had not gone deep enough to hit the bone. Still, the surgeon would have to dig it out. His hands, slippery with the blood of the scores of men he had already dealt with, took up the small knife and eased it into the wound.

A few quick cuts loosened the ball and he then took out the slim tongs with which he would try to pull it from the flesh. A small pop signaled its successful extraction and the surgeon took a bottle of high-proof brandy and poured it into the wound.

Delaborde hissed, but made no other sound. Then the doctor wrapped a clean bandage around the area to immobilise the limb.

"There you are General, you'll be ready to use that sword again in a few days' time."

"A few days? Merde. I'm needed now, doctor. I'll carry my sword left-handed if I have to."

Delaborde stared over the surgeon's shoulder as a gun team noisily passed through the massing troops. At last the guns are here, he thought.

He'd asked for artillery support before the first attack, but the request had been rejected by Junot. The commander had said it would be faster to go in with the infantry without cannon and he had learned to his men's cost that the British were not easily surprised, nor moved. This time around there would be eight cannon to soften up the Redcoats.

Standing to have a sling placed around his shoulder, Delaborde summoned a just-arrived messenger to him. He took a note from the rider and looked at it.

The graceful handwriting was from Junot himself and informed Delaborde that he would lead the next attack and receive support from two battalions of the grenadier reserve. The original assaulting troops were hurriedly being re-organised and would soon be ready to make another attempt on the British positions.

As the General got the messenger to write a reply to Junot, he could see the artillery crews unlimbering their guns. There would be a short bombardment before the attack and the artillery officers were under orders to make sure they began as quickly as possible. The big guns needed to fire a few rounds to warm up their barrels and extend their range. Delaborde hoped that by the time the next attack was ready the cannon should be landing their deadly projectiles with precision. Anything to disrupt those British lines, the General thought.

His injured arm made climbing on to his horse difficult and his arthritic knees did help either. I'm too old for this, he told himself, and then shook his head. "No I'm not, I bloody love this ..."

After issuing final orders to his officers, Delaborde took his place on horseback behind the leading regiments and ordered the drums to begin.

He was always amazed at how quickly his troops could recover from a setback and as he looked at his pocketwatch realised it was only 40 minutes since they had poured down the hill in disorder. Now, once more, they were arrayed in perfect formations and eager to strike back.

The drums thundered, voices called and cheered and the white-coated columns tramped up towards Vimeiro Hill. They followed the same path as before and barely took notice of the wounded forms and dead bodies of their comrades who had fallen so recently. The smell of crushed grass mingled with gunpowder was strong as the sun sparkled off their bayonets.

On and on they pushed up the incline. Above them the British infantry waited. A crash of heavy guns boomed out from the hill and Delaborde waited for the cannonballs to whip through his men. However, instead of aiming directly at the troops, the British seemed to be firing way over their heads. Are they after our guns? The General watched as the British shells exploded in the air ahead of his men. They're firing badly he thought, very badly indeed. More and more of the shells burst in the air and one exploded almost directly in front of him. Delaborde could hear the crack, then came a hissing and screams from the men. Several fell to the ground with their hands over their faces, while others staggered and dropped their muskets from bleeding and damaged hands.

Each time one of the shells erupted in a cloud of smoke it was more of the same. Men were dropping more quickly now as the distance between them and the British lessened. They must have a new type of shell, Delaborde cursed, and encouraged his men on with a wave of his sword.

Issuing a cheer he spurred his mount forward and was about to catch up with the leading regiments when all hell appeared to break loose. The French were about half-way up the hill and within British musket range. As more and more shells showered down pellets and metal pieces, the Redcoats began a methodical fire that moved rapidly from right to left along their lines.

White coats were now dropping by the scores and Delaborde recoiled as his knee and thigh were stung by flying metal.

"On, on," he cried but the impetus of the attack had stopped. He could see his officers pushing men forwards, but they could not deal with them all.

"Forward for the Emperor," he screamed as the almost continuous musketfire tore great holes in the ranks of his men. Fear was now appearing on the faces of his troops and the men were casting around looking for a way out of this scene from hell.

"On, get forward," he screamed again, but it was of no use. Some troops were firing back at the British, but Delaborde knew his men would not stand and that hurt as much as the pain from yet another wound.

Within minutes the mood had changed from one confident of victory to a panic focusing on saving one's skin. Delaborde again used his sword to beat at fleeing men, but it mattered little.

"Do you call yourselves Frenchmen?" he yelled. "Remember the Emperor, do this for the Emperor. Remember the Emperor!" he almost pleaded.

A fleeing sergeant looked up at him as he passed and shouted "We do sir ... Vive l'Empereur" and continued his flight at an even faster pace.

Everywhere it was the same and Delaborde's disgust grew as more and more men turned their backs on the heights and ran downhill.

Another overhead explosion sent shards flying and took the cocked hat off his head and gauged across his forehead. His horse's left ear was sliced open and it bucked and whinnied in pain and terror. With blood trickling into his eyes Delaborde slowly turned his horse and reluctantly followed his retreating soldiers.

XXXa

Colonel Taylor could barely contain his excitement. Underneath him his horse shifted restlessly and even his soothing words and gentle patting hand could do little to calm the creature. It could hear the crash of musket volleys and artillery fire and, like its master, the smell of the powder wafting into its nostrils stirred something deep within. Taylor kept flipping the silk tassel hanging off his sabre's guard and it annoyed him that he couldn't make himself stop. He was too edgy and the adrenalin of expectation was running fast through him. Surely today he and his men would see real action. The infantry were having all the fun of it so far and he hoped they hadn't done their job too well and forced the French into retreat already.

He looked along the lines of his men and could see most were as excited as he was. What a fine-looking bunch of fellows they were, he thought, and their mounts immaculately presented. Several horses were skittish and he supposed they were some of those sent by the Bishop of Oporto and were not used to the noise or smell of musket fire.

To each side of the British cavalry sat squadrons of Portuguese troopers. In Taylor's mind they were still of doubtful quality and so he had placed them on the wings where they could do little damage if their nerve failed.

So far most of the action had been obscured by Vimeiro Hill, but from his position on the lower slopes of the western ridge behind Vimeiro itself, Taylor had a good view of the church and the main road leading into the town.

The third French attack had been driven off some 10 minutes before and while most of the field was silent Taylor could hear French drums still sounding somewhere. The *pas-de-charge* meant only one thing, another assault was coming, but it was hard to see where as smoke still drifted thickly across the undulating terrain.

"Sir," Cornet Finlay said and pointed to the slopes of the hill. Taylor followed the young officer's arm and saw hundreds of British troops moving quickly down towards the church.

Snapping open his telescope, Taylor could make out the white regimental facings on the uniforms and guessed they were the 43rd, the Monmouths, a light-infantry regiment that had only just arrived in Portugal.

"Looks like someone's seen something, Mr Finlay."

Taylor moved his 'scope on to the church, but could see no sign of anything other than the positioning of the 43rd. He swept up the main road and then, from out of the smoke, came a French attack column. Tricolours flew within the tightly packed formation that was moving at a surprisingly fast pace.

What a target they presented to Taylor. The Colonel could think of few better things than to thunder into the heart of such a formation and lay it waste beneath horses' hooves and slashing blades. But the village was no place for a cavalry attack and so once again all the 20th Light Dragoons would do is sit and watch as a battle slipped by.

On Vimeiro Hill artillerymen quickly swung their guns around and began firing shells that exploded over the French column. Numbers of white coats fell, but those unhurt by the flying pieces of metal continued on their way. As the attackers passed the first houses in the village Taylor could see puffs of smoke appearing at the windows and doors as British troops within them fired at killing range.

More Frenchmen fell and while some moved away from the formation to clear the houses the remainder - probably some 1000 strong, estimated Taylor - pushed on towards the church.

The 43rd had arrived just in time to prevent the strongpoint falling into enemy hands and a fierce fight developed.

The height of the cemetery wall stopped the French being able to climb over it without help and any that tried were quickly dealt with by the defenders, who were able to shoot over the wall by standing on barrels placed at its base. Once they had fired the men from the 43rd used their bayonets to discourage the white coats, or swung their weapons around and clubbed them with the heavy wooden stocks.

Watching through his telescope Taylor admired the bravery of all concerned as their vicious life-and-death struggle raged.

From a distance it became hard to follow the engagement as clouds of thick smoke soon obscured the eastern cemetery wall. At the opposite end of the church he could see more Redcoats running to join the fight and being hauled over the wall by the welcoming hands of the defenders.

Other British troops were moving down the rear slope of Vimeiro Hill and began to pour fire into the great mass of Frenchmen. Despite an increasing number of casualties the veteran French Grenadiers continued fighting for possession of the church.

The arrival of a mounted officer distracted Taylor from the action and he was passed a note.

"Here are your orders, Colonel Taylor," the man said, "ready yourself to move against the French near the church."

Taylor couldn't believe it. At last his men were going to be allowed to show what they could do.

"Now 20th, threes about and forward!" he called, pocketing the note.

The British and Portuguese cavalry moved off at a brisk walk and moved several hundred paces along the slope. To their right the battle for the church raged, but Taylor's men now ignored it. At their new position a Staff Major waited and told them to form into half companies.

Looking towards the main French positions, Taylor could see another large body of French troops moving into the fray. A brigade of cavalry - twice as many men as the

British horsemen could muster - guarded them and thick clouds of dust behind the infantry suggested the presence of cannon being hauled.

Suddenly, a loud huzza rang out from the British in the strongpoint and as if by magic the attacking Grenadiers lurched backwards. They knew what was coming - hundreds of red-coated demons thrusting their bayonets forward and the resolve of the French infantry failed. They turned their backs on the church and fled towards their own lines. Volley after volley poured into them from the rear and sides, dropping scores at a time.

Taylor heard his name being called and looked to his left. There was Sir Arthur Wellesley, cocked hat in hand, waving it over the top of his head shouting "Now Taylor, now's your time!"

The Colonel needed no further encouragement and called for his bugler to sound the advance.

"Now 20th, now!" Wellesley shouted again.

Putting his heels into his mount Taylor took the regiment forward at the trot. He took care to ensure all of his men could accelerate into the open ground where the French had taken to flight. One hundred paces from the enemy cavalry that had dashed in to cover the retreat he jabbed his spurs into his horse's sides, drew his sabre and let go a wild scream.

To Taylor it seemed like an eternity in slow motion, but the ground was closed in a matter of seconds.

The excited yells of his men could be heard over the pounding of hundreds of hooves and then they were on the French horsemen.

The shock of the two bodies colliding was extraordinary, but the bigger and heavier British mounts smashed into their foe bowling dozens over with the ferocity of the charge. Those enemy cavalry not unhorsed found themselves trying to fend off blows delivered by strong arms and wickedly curved sabres.

Taylor was almost thrown to the ground himself as his horse stumbled during the first collision, but quickly regained control and chopped back-handed at a dragoon. The blade of his weapon smashed the brass helmet in and knocked the enemy to the ground.

The Colonel didn't have time to wonder if it was a killing blow as he swung his blade at a second green-jacketed dragoon to his left. That man went down screaming as the steel bit into his shoulder almost severing his arm.

Within seconds the French cavalry had been routed and now it was time for the infantry. Clouds of dust were thrown up during the clash, but white coats could be seen nearby. Some of the French managed to turn and fire their muskets, felling several of the Portuguese horsemen. More of the white-breeched troopers fell and within seconds they had turned their horses around and were fleeing for safety. A number of the mounted Lisbon police remained, but the charge was now effectively an affair for the 20th.

With a battle rage born of years of frustration Taylor's mind screamed at him that this was what he had become a soldier for. This was true exhilaration and he dealt out fearful blows at the almost defenceless and panicking Frenchmen. Another fell under a low backwards cut and then Taylor found himself surrounded by the enemy.

He parried a bayonet thrust, then killed the man who had delivered it. Another's soldier's head was crushed under a mighty blow and third's skull was split almost to his chin. Urging his mount on Taylor broke through the pressing infantry. He had lost count of the number of men he had killed but his sword arm was covered in gore to his elbow.

"On, on," he screamed and his men followed with blood-curdling cries.

For the routing French infantry it was pure hell. The dust was choking and demonic horsemen seemed to be everywhere. There was only one place of safety and that was behind the fast-approaching reinforcements.

Taylor noted the new troops too and saw them as being more trophies for his regiment's battle honours.

Again spurring his horse on he charged at the French. As he closed on them he realised his mistake. These French were not panicked but were waiting in square. The hedge of bayonets loomed at him and he furiously hacked down with his blade. Three bayonets struck out at him from the second line in the square. One caught him in the thigh, while the other two speared into his mount.

The creature reared in pain and panic, but Taylor's magnificent horsemanship kept him in the saddle.

"Back," he shouted "back ..." and as he wrenched his reins around he found himself looking straight into the eyes of a young Frenchman.

Even from the height of his horse Taylor thought the musket barrel was extremely large. It seemed like an age before he realised it, but he was falling just in front of the French square. He tried to struggle to his feet but was unable to move. He could hear yells in French and then the enemy soldiers nearest him broke out of the square. Taylor watched helplessly as they stood over him and pressed forward with their bayonets. He was surprised he didn't feel any pain as the blades sliced into him, or when they were withdrawn and plunged in again. He didn't know it but the shot that had smashed his chest to a pulp had glanced off bone and traveled up his backbone, severing his spinal cord as it went. He didn't feel the pain as more bayonets stabbed in at him and died wondering why.

Cornet Finlay was horrified by the fall of his Colonel and the situation in which the 20th now found itself. The French muskets were taking a toll of the regiment and he could see more enemy cavalry forming to charge.

"Beware cavalry," he called and looked to find a way back to British lines. To his right there was a low fence with gaps in the railings, large enough for several horses to pass through. "To the right, to the right!" he screamed.

Leading the regiment through the fence Finlay suddenly noticed that there were Frenchmen lying on the ground. Although he passed through unscathed some of the following riders had their horses disemboweled as the prone soldiers jabbed their bayonets into the mounts' stomachs. Many were thrown and relied upon their comrades lending an arm to have them climb up behind them.

Spurring on through the dust, Finlay discovered that his path was no gateway to freedom - in fact it led to a sunken area of ground that made the fence impossible to jump. He and the 20th were now trapped within the natural corral with French infantry moving to turn the area into a killing pit.

He heard a captain yelling "out, out" and made for the gaps in the fences. The once-prone enemy soldiers were now standing, however, they faced men fighting for their lives. Within seconds the French were all cut down, but the 20th still needed to escape the muskets being levelled at them.

With tired horses and weary sword arms, the light dragoons steeled themselves for a breakout battle to the death with the enemy.

It was not to come, however, as to Finlay's great relief a roar of British cheers sounded to his left and the welcome sight of a Redcoat infantry charge cleared the way for the horsemen to escape to safety.

"God bless the 50th," he almost sobbed as he picked his way back to safety through hundreds of dead and wounded bodies.

XXXb

Wellesley's aides heard the commander give an audible curse as he watched the disaster overtaking his only units of cavalry.

"My God," he said to no-one in particular, "that could do us in."

Whipping around, Wellesley asked Benton if he could count how many of the 20th were returning.

The elderly General had been watching the retreat through his telescope and was ready with the answer.

"I believe we've lost about a quarter of them, Sir Arthur. All of the Portuguese seem to be ready for action, however."

"Portuguese? Portuguese! Bloody Portuguese, I say, Benton. They're damn cowards the lot of 'em. A couple of shots and they turned like cowardly dogs and ran for safety. I should shoot some of the scum!"

"Probably not a good idea, Sir Arthur, and I should point out they seemed to have reformed. Maybe they will be of use later in the day."

"Bah!" spat the commander.

A rider came up to Benton who saw it was Ricketts. "A word with Sir Arthur if I may General Benton," he said.

Wellesley turned and his face wore the warning signs of an approaching thunderstorm.

"It's Major Ricketts, Sir Arthur."

"What do you want Major Ricketts? And why are you not with your regiment?"

Ricketts squirmed uncomfortably in his saddle. "Ah, things are quiet on the wing sir and I was wondering if you needed my 29th elsewhere?"

"Elsewhere, sir? I have placed your regiment on that wing for a reason ... there's a large brigade of Frenchmen somewhere east of you ..."

"We haven't sighted it sir and I thought we could be of more use ..."

Wellesley cut him off. "When I want your opinion Major Ricketts on the dispositions of my army I shall ask for it. An army could hide in the gullies of this region and be up on you before you'd know it. Now get back to your men, sir."

As the clearly shaken Major rode away Wellesley uttered a foul profanity that had some of the younger aides blushing.

In a quieter tone he said to Benton: "That man is an ambitious fool ... keep him well away from me or I shall not be held responsible for my actions."

Taking a deep breath Wellesley turned back to the central battlefield and put his 'scope to his eye.

"Cavalry aside, we've done well gentlemen. It seems the Frenchies have decided they have had enough. That'll show them that they'll need to do a bit more than march straight up to us shouting and cheering like schoolboys.

Send my thanks to generals Fane, Anstruther and Acland. They and their men have done us proud today. They've given the Frenchies a damn good kicking."

Wellesley allowed himself a smile that belied his real thoughts.

There were still some 6000 Frenchmen wandering around on his left flank and if that idiot Ricketts was right then they were lost to view. That meant they could be anywhere and could appear at any time. He needed to know where those men were.

XXXI

Vimeiro, 11am

Some miles from where Colonel Taylor died, Zapalski's Poles were riding slowly ahead of the flanking force Junot had sent out under General Antoine Brennier. Encumbered by heavy nine-pounder cannons, Brennier had decided to stay on the main road towards the town of Lourinha before swinging west to occupy his target - the farm buildings at Ventosa. The stone and wood structures were near the edge of the British left flank on top of the undulating hills and ridges that made the terrain so difficult for guns.

Despatch riders had just informed Brennier that the British had seen his 4000 men on the march and had swung the axis of their army around to face it. What the enemy didn't know, and this made Zapalski smile, was that a second force of some 2000 men under General Jean-Baptiste Solignac was currently crossing the rough ground to the farm to reinforce the attack.

Even from the back of his horse, Zapalski could not see the ridge that the British were defending and that pleased him, because that meant they could not see the approach of the main assault columns.

It was a stunning day, the Major thought, just perfect for a battle. The breeze had strengthened slightly and that took the edge out of the sun's heat. Still, he had to feel for the infantry marching behind his regiment, they must be footsore from the stony roads and their throats must be parched from the dust thrown up by his horses.

Uncapping his canteen he took a small mouthful of the warmish water and wished he had remembered to fill his goatskin, that would have kept the water much cooler.

Zapalski was looking forward to the coming action as he was sick of patrolling and escort work. A cavalryman existed to draw blood in battle, he thought, and the idea of running his blade into British troops appealed to him.

He had heard the noise of battle off to his left and every now and then the faint smell of powder reached his nostrils. He wished he was leading a charge rather than plodding along the road, but he had no doubt his time would come.

Zapalski had been surprised by the way the distant fire had started and stopped on several occasions, normally it was a continuous roar that echoed like a severe storm rolling in over the meadowlands of Poland.

Perhaps Junot had already driven in the main British line and the stop-start nature of the firing was an indication that the enemy was conducting a fighting retreat and pulling back a short way before making another stand.

No matter, the Major thought, that would mean plenty of Redcoats to hunt down and that would make fine sport for him and his men.

XXXIa

Less than a mile to the west of Brennier's column, Firth and the men of the 29th were sitting down eating flat bread and olives. Some of the luckier ones adding to their fare with local cheese liberated from the abandoned village in Vimeiro.

Commissaries were slowly making their way around the British regiments dispensing the daily grog ration, but few soldiers among the seven regiments on the British left wing thought the wagon drivers were doing their job fast enough. Almost all were anticipating the fiery belt the gin or rum would give them and it would help take their minds off what lay ahead.

Needham watched the progress of the wagons around the fields at the base of the hill. Every now and then they would disappear behind trees and, for a painfully long period, a splendid farmhouse.

"Oh the buggers are taking too long," he moaned out loud, "Lord quicken them up a bit will you!"

Needham was sick of the waiting and not just for the drink either. The lack of action was getting to him and he wished he could have gone with the light companies sent to the east of the farm to give an early warning if the French came into sight.

Firth's men were also ready for action. He had personally inspected each of them and that not only were their weapons clean, but each man was eager to use them.

Other regimental officers had not yet checked on their men, but then they didn't have the spectre of Ricketts breathing over their shoulders as Firth did. He knew that if he didn't do things before anyone else, he would be criticised by the Major for not being up to the task.

His brother officers knew what was going on and gave him knowing and sympathetic looks, although that knowledge didn't help Firth when Ricketts was trying to humiliate him.

Firth looked around trying to find his dark-haired nemesis but he didn't seem to be with the regiment at the moment.

He stood up and strolled over to where the surgeon Dr Geoffrey Guthrie was preparing his instruments. Twin One and Twin Two were assisting, to the best level they could with their single arms, and the pair was bickering over how best to roll bandages.

"Morning Mr Guthrie," Firth called as he approached.

"Ah, Mr Firth, how is our youngest Captain this fine day?"

"Well thank you, Mr Guthrie. All in readiness?"

Guthrie looked up from the amputation saw he was sharpening and smiled. "Getting there Mr Firth. This is as sharp as a razor - but by the time I've sawn through 10 or 20 limbs it will be blunter than a spoon."

"I hope not to need it, sir."

Guthrie smiled, he liked Firth and his matter-of-fact attitude towards army life.

"I wish you all the best Mr Firth, but if you come before me I'll try to deal with you first."

Firth gave a half-smile.

"Have you seen Major Ricketts about?"

"No, I've not seen him these last minutes. I believe he was setting off again to see if we could be shifted more into the action. It's the second time he has made a personal visit to headquarters, the last time was not well received I believe."

Firth looked up the hillside and nodded.

Guthrie stopped his work and also looked.

"And if the French come this way," he said, "being in the reserve we are not likely to see much action."

What Guthrie said was true, Firth agreed, the 29th was being held in reserve along with the 6th and 32nd regiments. Ahead of them were three other formations and unless things went very badly there was not much chance of the Worcesters joining the fight.

Just then a rider came over the ridge at full speed and made his way to where the brigade commanders, generals Fergusson, Nightingall and Bowes, sat at small camp tables. The three men instantly leapt to their feet and gave orders to their aides who immediately moved towards their various regiments.

"Form up, form up," came the calls. "Form lines, gentlemen."

Taking his leave from Guthrie, Firth ran back to the 6th company where Needham was getting the men to their feet.

Other company captains were also organising the troops on their own initiative as there was still no sign of Major Ricketts.

They could all hear musket fire from over the brow of the hill and it was followed by the deep menacing sound of drums being pounded.

The French had arrived.

Firth marveled at just how quickly the resting men had taken positions in two ranks of perfectly straight lines. Gone were the relaxed smiles and laughter, replaced by stern faces and utter silence.

Mounted officers rode up and down the ranks and ushered the now-returning light infantry to fill the gaps between the regiments.

The drums became louder and louder and then the tops of tricolour flags could be seen on the ridge. They were soon followed by variously coloured pompoms on the French shakoes, faces and finally dusty white coats.

The leading French soldiers had pushed back the British light troops without a care in the world, but when they crossed the ridgeline they almost stopped in mid-step. Instead of pursuing retreating light troops, the French now found themselves up against long lines of formed British soldiers.

From where he stood Firth could almost feel the confusion in the minds of the officers and men on the hill and it wasn't until the appearance of a senior officer, a general he supposed, that the French spread out to form their own lines.

They began shouting and jeering at the British, taunting them and shaking their muskets. The Redcoats stood impassively and waited for the order to advance. That didn't take long to come and the first line moved off at a steady pace with their bayonets at the ready.

Watching from the reserve Firth was quick to see that the French were vastly outnumbered as the British lines extended well beyond those of the waiting enemy. White-coated French skirmishers in front of the main body began to fire and their accuracy stopped many of the attackers in their tracks.

Ignoring the threat, the red line continued its march up the hill. At 100 paces orders rang out, the march stopped and 1500 Brown Bess muskets came up to shoulders. Another call and the line disappeared in a bank of smoke, followed almost instantly by an ear-splitting roar.

As the men of the Prince of Wales' Volunteers, Glasgow Highland Light Infantry,

Herefordshire and Somerset regiments reloaded, Firth was astounded by the damage done to the French.

The dangerous skirmishers had been blasted away to a man and gaps had appeared in the formed ranks behind them. The general who had been issuing orders only a moment before had disappeared from his horse. The French line then exploded in smoke and noise as they returned a volley upon the reloading men below. Few of those shots hit, however, as many of the defenders had not adjusted their aim enough for firing downhill and most balls fluttered over the heads of the British.

With their weapons again primed for killing, the Redcoat line advanced silently. A second volley spat down from the hilltop dropping only a few men in red.

As the British closed on the ridgeline the French resolve broke and they fled out of view. With an enormous "huzza" the attackers sprang forward and pursued them out of the sight of the men waiting in the second line.

Given the order to advance to the left, the Worcesters moved up the hill to join in the victory pursuit.

XXXIb

Firth rode Boadiccea slowly at the front of the 6th company and felt comfortable with her easy rocking. The regiment's musicians, positioned with the Colour Party behind the line companies, were playing *The Worcestershire Poacher* with the confidence of men who knew they were celebrating a battle victory and were determined to put on a good showing for their comrades.

Boadiccea had behaved admirably during the last French attack and, although she had skittered a little at the roar of the volleys, had settled beautifully. Firth gave her an appreciative pat on the shoulder and softly told her he was proud of her.

He was also very pleased with the cut of his company and the disciplined order in which the men had formed lines instantly and with little fuss.

Of course sergeants Barclay and Needham, who now marched at his side, had a lot to do with that and Firth was pleased he had such experienced hands to help him.

Almost all within the ranks had taken quickly to their newly promoted Captain and those few, such as Good, who thought to moan about him being too young were loath to make their opinions public for fear the sergeants would roughly deal with them.

On either side of Firth the regiment's more senior captains were also at the head of their troops. In the absence of Major Ricketts, the grenadier company's Captain Samuel Gauntlett had temporarily taken command of the regiment and his men were being led forward by a lieutenant. No-one had seen the Major for some time although it was known he had gone back to ask Wellesley to give his troops a taste of action instead of being held in reserve. Unfortunately, for Ricketts, the order to move against the French had come while he was away from the line.

From over the brow of the hill Firth could hear the bang of irregular shots, but no quick counterfire. He presumed the French were being shot at while continuing to retreat and had yet to make a stand. If, of course, the British advance allowed them time to reorganise.

The Worcesters moved over the ridgeline and Firth's beliefs were confirmed. In the distance he could see hundreds of Frenchmen running into a valley between two hills, pursued by a swarm of British light troops.

Behind the Light Bobs came the formed infantry who would halt when the skirmishers were clear and fire at the enemy if they gave the slightest hint of stopping and reforming.

The pursuit was being done rapidly and the men of the 36th, 40th, 71st and 82nd were almost a mile ahead of the Worcesters. Firth could see them overrunning three cannon that the French had brought with them for the attack, but which had now been abandoned as the gunners sought safety. Firth knew capturing enemy guns was a bonus for a victorious army, particularly one such as Wellesley's where they had come to the Peninsula with too few artillery pieces.

He wasn't quite sure how to feel about the battle, because he and his men had seen very little of it and had yet to burn powder themselves. Still, after the exertions at Rolica, he was sure the men were content to watch other regiments shoulder some of the hard work.

Reaching for his water barrel, Firth was about to uncork it when he could hear shouts to his left. Immediately he saw the light company's Captain turn his horse and gallop across the regimental lines calling "Beware left, 'ware left". Firth looked in that direction but could see nothing. Bugles called urgently yet Firth was unsure what had sparked the alarm.

"There sir," Barclay said, pointing to the hill under which the guns had been taken, "Frenchies on the hill!"

Following the direction of the Sergeant's outstretched arm, Firth could see a body of white coats moving on to the skyline.

"There's cavalry with them, Mr Firth," said Needham, "and it looks like our men haven't seen 'em."

Instantly Firth could see the Sergeant was right. While the 36th and 40th continued their pursuit, the men from Glasgow and the Prince of Wales Own Volunteers had stopped to secure the captured guns. They were too occupied with the cannon to notice the imminent threat above them.

To his right Captain Gauntlett had just finished giving orders to the 7th company and cantered over to Firth.

"My compliments, Joshua, but it seems the lads ahead have forgotten about that French column. If the Frogs catch them in the flank there'll be hell to pay ... so it is up to us to do something about it. We'll double-quick forward and give them a hand. Straight forward now and let's give them a taste of Worcestershire ball."

Firth nodded in agreement.

"They've also got cavalry, Joshua, so we need to be wary of the horse moving against us. Keep your men going forwards quickly, but get ready to form square."

As Gauntlett spurred off to the other company commanders, Firth looked down to Barclay and Needham.

"Well, let's get the men on sergeants ..." Firth said and then paused and thought about what he should say next. He knew that he should present a confident and decisive manner when ordering the move out, but he had not faced cavalry in action and wanted advice from the vastly experienced Needham. Would it lessen the Sergeant's confidence in him? Firth felt he had no choice but to take the risk and spoke directly to the veteran.

"I have to say that cavalry worries me ... and I'll be happy to take suggestions."

"They're devilish quick, Mr Firth," Needham said without a hint of anything other than suppressed pleasure at being asked his opinion, "and can move like the wind. In India we occasionally formed four ranks - that would keep us moving fairly quickly, but poked enough bayonets at the brutes to keep them off us."

Firth considered Needham's words and smiled.

"I appreciate that Sergeant. Form the men in four ranks."

Around them the regiment's companies moved off at double pace towards the increasingly large French force that had begun to spill down the slope towards the unsuspecting 71st and 82nd regiments.

The relatively clear terrain allowed Firth to watch the potential disaster unfolding ahead of him. It astounded him that the British commanders had not seen the French and it wasn't until the white coats were half-way down the slope that they realised something was amiss.

Spouts of smoke erupted from the French muskets and numbers of redcoats fell as shots struck home. Instantly there was chaos in the British ranks as surprised officers tried to form their men to face the threat.

There was no time to get organised and so they abandoned the cannons to the French and withdrew across the small valley forming up as they went. They rallied on the foot of the far slope but were outnumbered by almost three to one and were in danger of being overwhelmed.

The Worcesters had closed to within 400 paces of the clash and were still advancing at the double. Firth looked about hoping for a sign from Gauntlett to reform into line but the grenadier Captain was nowhere to be seen.

"Beware cavalry," came a call from his left and instantly Firth's attention was on the lines of dark-blue horsemen with square-topped helmets advancing down the hill.

They didn't look as if they were about to charge but, as Firth knew from experienced veterans that could change in seconds from a possible threat to a deadly danger.

Firth's right hand felt for the hilt of his sword and he realised his palms were wet and slippery. In fact he was sweating freely and he was sure it wasn't all due to the late-morning heat. Where was Captain Gauntlett? And where was Major Ricketts?

Then came an aristocratic voice from behind and, with no small relief, he instantly knew who it was.

"29th ... close ranks," shouted Sir Arthur Wellesley, "Captain Firth's company form on the left."

The well-drilled Worcesters made the moves smartly and within 30 seconds had formed a broad, thin rectangle of four ranks with Firth's 6th company now on the left wing of the regiment.

"29th advance and volley fire at 100 paces," Wellesley ordered.

With the fifes and drums picking up again the regiment moved on the now open flank of the French attack. Some of the white-coated figures had turned and were firing at them, but the Worcesters would not reply until they were close enough to make out their targets' faces.

At 100 paces the regiment stopped and began a rolling fire that moved down the line from left to right.

"Reload," came the orders and then the men closed to within 50 paces of the enemy before letting loose another devastating burst of fire. "Reload."

"Mr Firth," shouted Wellesley, pointing to the hill, "Your job is to guard the flank against those horsemen."

"Sir!" Firth in turn called to Needham and Barclay, "move 30 paces to the left and set us at 45 degrees to the line."

Again the manouevre was carried out rapidly and the 6th angled itself to offer the best protection it could to the left of the regiment's position.

Firth placed himself on the right, with Needham on its left and Barclay in the middle of the rear rank. He decided it was better to stay on Boadiccea as it gave him a better view and allowed his men to see him.

A few French musketballs whistled around Firth, but he was too busy concentrating on the cavalry to care much.

Behind him the regiment let off another series of volleys and as he heard the cries of "they're running" the men under the square-topped helmets began to move forward with their sabres drawn.

"They're coming lads, front rank kneel - but hold your fire, they won't close," he called.

The Polish cavalry walked down the slope towards the 6th and when they got within 150 paces they began to trot.

Firth could only guess at their number, but he put it at about 300 men and they made an impressive sight. At 100 paces they increased their speed and with a loud hurrah threw themselves forward.

"Steady boys, steady. Don't fire. They want us to run, but if we stand they won't close," he said, praying he was right.

The drum of the hooves was louder than Firth expected and huge sods of earth were being thrown high into the air. At 50 paces the troopers bent low over their horses' necks and pushed their sword arms forward.

"Hold now, lads, hold."

To his left came a shout and Firth saw a handful of red-jacketed men peel off from the rear rank and start to run towards the main body of the regiment.

"Stop you fools," he screamed, but there was no halting them as they fled for perceived safety. Most were young troops who, like Firth, had never faced a cavalry charge and the idea of standing in lines under the swords and hooves of the attack was too much for their courage.

The first of them had barely gone 10 paces when the leading Polish troopers were on them. The first went down spitted on a blade, while another had his head almost severed by a brutal backswing. The others threw themselves on to the ground in a bid to avoid the cuts and several were badly injured as the riders deliberately trampled over them.

Firth and the 6th company were now cut off from the main regiment and sat out in the battleground like a small red island in a swirling blue sea.

"Rear two ranks about face," he screamed, and moved Boadiccea as close as he could to the ranks. He ordered the front-rank of the rear-facing line to kneel and again called for every soldier to hold his fire.

"Wait lads, I want only the standing men to fire. Pick your targets. As soon as you have fired reload as quickly as you can and keep firing independently. You men in the front - do not fire! Sergeants … deal with the first man who does. Ready lads … standing men fire!"

The men obeyed his orders to the letter and volleys erupted from each side of the ranks downing a dozen enemy horsemen. The next 20 seconds passed like an eternity for Firth as he mentally counted and waited for the next volleys from his company. Shots crashed out again and more riders fell. One was tipped off his horse and landed under the hooves of one of his comrade's horse, which tripped flinging the man to the ground. He landed near one of the prone Worcesters who had run from the ranks and was quickly stabbed in the neck by a well-aimed bayonet.

Boadiccea was now nervously turning in a tight circle at the noise of the muskets and the whirling horseflesh. Struggling to control her Firth shortened the reins and held more tightly with his knees. Some of the men who had run were now trying to get up despite shouts of warning from their friends.

A gold-braided Polish officer saw their movement and spurred towards them, barely straining as he delivered killing blows. Three more Redcoats rose and sprinted towards Firth. The enemy officer saw them and darted forward. Firth didn't think his men would make the ranks in time and so set his own heels in Boadiccea to intercept the attack. He drove his mount hard into the gap between the hunter and his prey.

The enemy Major saw Firth and spurred his horse harder. This one would be worth killing Zapalski thought. He aimed his horse's head straight at the chest of his enemy's beast and, at the last possible moment, dragged it to the left so that the animal's shoulder would hit home. The two mounts collided at full gallop and it took all of the Pole's skill to stay on his horse.

Firth was less fortunate and despite Boadiccea being large and powerful she was thrown sideways by the impact. As she lurched over Firth was unable to drag his right foot free. He hit the ground with a breath-expelling force and instantaneously felt Boadiccea's weight on his leg. As she tried to get on to her knees Firth had the presence of mind to pull his foot from the stirrup. Unfortunately the leather strap had twisted and he could not pull free.

Above him the enemy officer was balancing himself and preparing to make a killing strike with his sabre. Firth's sword had landed within his reach and he grabbed at the hilt. He missed with the first attempt, but then made a further lunge and grabbed hold of it. Knowing he had little time to save himself Firth held the blade over his head just as Zapalski's sabre cut down.

There was a clang of metal on metal and the force of the blow jarred the nerves in Firth's arm. As the Pole swung his sword back Firth took the chance to slash at the stirrup strap and half-severed it. Kicking his right foot he cut again and this time the leather gave way allowing him to roll out of the way as Zapalski aimed at his head. Firth now had a chance to get to his feet and his mind raced as to how to save himself from both the swinging blade and the horse's hooves.

The enemy officer was right-handed and had his arm raised over his left shoulder. Firth grabbed at the bridle and moved across the animal's face smelling its snorting breath and avoiding its biting teeth. He was unbalanced and that resulted in his own sword swing lacking the power and accuracy he would have liked. It grazed the horseman's thick leather sword belt that diagonally crossed his back and did little more than scuff the white surface.

Zapalski felt the hit and was determined to shake the youth's hand from his horse's bridle. Forcing his mount to back away from the British officer gave the Pole another chance with his sabre and he sliced it down viciously. Again he missed his nimble enemy who was exceptionally quick on his feet. Immediately Zapalski had to arch his body as his enemy's slender blade passed by his stomach.

This boy is fast, he thought, and again backed up his mount to give his sword arm enough room to strike.

Firth could hear the snorting of the horse loud in his ears and the heavy breathing of his opponent and while focusing on the man's cocked arm he forgot about his boots and received a painful kick on the nose.

Stumbling again he found the bridle ripped from his grasp and then the mounted man was above him ready to strike. Firth threw himself sideways and heard the steel whistle past his head. He leapt to his feet returning a cut of his own. The blade bit into Zapalski's forearm and forced a gasp of pain. Firth jabbed a second time and almost shouted with glee at the accompanying feel of it striking home.

Zapalski was surprised by the stinging wounds, but he was now too enraged to let them stop him killing this boy. He jagged his mount's head to the right and then instantly pulled it hard to the left.

Firth had jumped with the first change of direction, but had not anticipated the second and he found himself looking full into the face of the blue-eyed man above him. He only had time to pull his head back as the sabre cut down through the front of his bicorne and sliced across his brow.

Firth's quick reactions saved his life as a full blow would have split his skull. Instead the tip of the blade sliced a gash on his forehead and through his left eyebrow almost instantly blinding the eye beneath it with blood.

As Firth fell backwards Zapalski grinned and was leaning forward to finish the Captain off when a number of British soldiers, led by a red-haired Sergeant, fired their muskets at him and broke from the isolated formation in a bid to save their officer.

With a loud oath, Zapalski turned his horse and spurred to where his men were reforming. More musketballs flew around him but none came close enough to worry him into ducking. He was needed elsewhere and personal duels did little to cover the backs of the now-retreating army of General Junot.

Zapalski looked at his arm and knew he would need to see the surgeon - but he took some consolation knowing so would that young British officer.

XXXII

British Headquarters,
Vimeiro,
August 22,1808.

The overcrowded British headquarters was in early morning pandemonium as staff officers paced and clerks scurried around with hands full of papers.

Burrard had taken over the largest and least damaged of Vimeiro's buildings, but it was still choked with aides and waiting dispatch riders. Adding to the seeming confusion few knew who was actually in charge of the army as it now had its third commander in two days.

Sir Hew Dalrymple, formerly governor of Gibraltar, had superceded Sir Harry Burrard but was still to arrive.

Wellesley was still fuming at the snub given to him by Horse Guards and Benton was astounded he was keeping his temper under control and not showing too much displeasure. Of course, Benton knew just how angry the General was through the venom of his mostly quiet asides. The older man thought himself wise to keep agreeing with everything the commander said to him.

Burrard himself, however, was not displeased at being out-ranked. Ordered and meticulous by nature he was beginning to fret as the strategic situation for the British had changed markedly over the past 12 hours.

It was true the French were beaten – and he had Wellesley to thank for that – but then the man wouldn't stop pushing for a pursuit. Burrard shook his head and wondered if Wellesley had ever doubted himself. Probably not, he thought with a measure of envy. Then the memory of Wellesley's tirade against him came to mind and any reasonable attitude towards the younger man died.

Burrard had never heard such words from a subordinate before but, in view of Wellesley's fired-up temper, he ignored them.

To add to his headaches Sir Harry knew a Russian fleet had just arrived off Lisbon and its ships were sitting at anchor within firing distance of the Royal Navy's vessels. Burrard feared Russia's Tsar Alexander might have sent an army on the vessels to assist his ally - Napoleon Bonaparte - deal with Britain and that would really make life difficult. Fortunately, Sir Harry sighed, that was now Dalrymple's problem as the new commander was due to arrive soon and then everything could be passed over to him.

Burrard was looked forward to acting as a second-in-command, a position he preferred and one where he could use his organisational ability.

Firstly he would oversee a medical evacuation of the British wounded – thank God very few – and getting in supplies and ammunition.

Vimeiro had been a stunning success and Sir Harry had thought Wellesley's handling of the army was superb. For the loss of 700 men, only 135 of them dead, he had beaten the French killing, wounding and capturing at least 2000 of them.

"Damn," he cursed softly. He had forgotten to include the prisoners-of-war in his calculations for needed food and medicines.

154

As he looked out the open window of his room, Sir Harry saw three more dispatch riders heading for the outer office and he sighed. Too much to do and too little energy. He half-heartedly picked up a quill, took out a new piece of parchment and began writing a note to his wife. There were plenty of more important official things to be dealing with, but Sir Harry felt the need to write to his lady of more than 30 years and while a letter was not the same as being with her it always raised his spirits. He had only put down a few lines when his aide knocked on the door, entered and informed him that General Dalrymple was about to reach the village. The Captain said Dalrymple had sent him ahead with a request for lunch for himself and his staff. Well, that's that, Sir Harry thought and gave his assent to the Captain. "Oh, by the way," he said almost as an afterthought, "you'd better inform General Wellesley of Sir Hugh's imminent arrival … he may like to lunch with us."
And won't that be a pleasant meeting, he added silently to himself.

XXXIIa

As Sir Harry had feared the meal was not one filled with good humour, or celebration. Wellesley was quiet and when he answered questions he was cold-of-voice, while Sir Hew Dalrymple said very little and seemed more than a little distracted.
Dalrymple was an elegant man with well-styled grey hair and large side-whiskers. He carried himself well, Burrard thought, and was known for his intelligence and sensitive handling of delicate political matters.
Wellesley could learn from him in that area, he noted.
Burrard could understand Wellesley's disappointment, but Sir Hew Dalrymple was the perfect man for the army. He had been Governor of Gibraltar for the past two years and had close contacts with the Spanish – their new allies.
Burrard almost choked at that idea. Spain had always been after regaining Gibraltar, the great fortress at the southern tip of their country that sat guarding the entrance to the Mediterranean Sea. We must never let them have it, he almost said out loud and hoped he hadn't. But Burrard knew that even if it had been said he would get agreement from Sir Hew.
During Dalrymple's tenure at Gibraltar the fortifications were strengthened even further to protect it against both an attack from the sea - and anything that may come from the Spanish side.
Looking across the table Burrard noted Dalrymple had barely touched his food and his glass of wine remained almost full. He was musing on a letter he had just received from Lord Robert Castlereagh, the minister in charge of the military.
What's in that? A suddenly curious Burrard wondered.
Dalrymple was annoyed at the words he was reading. He had to take notice of them, they did come from his chief after all, but he did have to like them. Castlereagh was suggesting to him that he would do well to listen to the advice offered by Wellesley. When he first read them Dalrymple had taken Castlereagh's comments as good sense. Now, however, he was of the opinion they smacked of unwanted political interference in army operations. Wellesley may be good but clearly the man was a politician's

lackey, he bristled. And not even 40 to boot!

Folding the letter and placing it in his jacket, Dalrymple took more notice of the conversation around the table. It was constant, but low of volume, and was little more than repeating the events of the previous day and finding out who had been killed or wounded. He reached for his glass and took a sip.

"Well, Sir Hew, when are we to move on from this place?" Wellesley asked.

Dalrymple was initially unaware that he was being spoken to, but finally looked up.

"Leave, Sir Arthur? Why?"

"Surely we must follow the French and make sure we keep them off-balance."

"I think not, Sir Arthur, Sir Harry disagreed with your suggestion for pursuit and I completely concur."

"And what about food and the likelihood of disease, Sir Hew?"

"Disease, sir?

"We have hundreds of French bodies lying in and around this village, sir, and if this nose is not mistaken they are already beginning to putrify. If we stay here too long we'll find ourselves badly weakened by disease. Besides which, the army has eaten all its food stores and we are without means to get new ones while we sit here."

"Thank you for your opinion, Sir Arthur, but we'll move when I see the time is right. The men need rest and I need to get better acquainted with the situation."

"The situation, sir," Wellesley answered in a way that exuded frustration, "is that the men are ready to take on the French and give them another damn good hiding. Attacking or defending it's no matter. If we move out now we'll clear their damn army from Portugal within a week!"

Dalrymple visibly stiffened at the obvious lack of respect, although he didn't change his manner or tone.

"And what, Sir Arthur, of the fortresses at Almeida and Peniche and Elvas? We have no siege guns to batter them down. The French can sit in them and laugh at us until Bonaparte dies of old age. We must prepare ourselves and move forward when we are suitably equipped."

Seeing Wellesley was about to answer him Dalrymple held up his right hand and added "and I will have no more discussion on it here, gentlemen. We move when we are ready".

An uncomfortable silence fell upon the table but was quickly broken by the sound of bugles and shouts from nearby sentries.

XXXIIb

Firth left the regimental staff tent with several other captains who had just been given orders from Ricketts. As usual, the 6th company had drawn night sentry duty.

He didn't care about doing the task himself, but he was annoyed his men seemed to be being punished because Ricketts didn't like him. It wouldn't make the men happy but, as Firth had found out, they were prepared to wear the extra duties.

Ricketts had been in the most foul mood Firth had ever seen, the result of a thorough dressing down by Wellesley for his missing of the 29th's part in the battle at Vimeiro.

The Major had attempted to put his case - that he was in fact seeking orders at the time – but every time he tried to interject the commander just screamed louder. He had been told in no uncertain terms that his time in the army was now limited and as soon as a replacement could be found he would be given other tasks.

Wellesley did not detail what his plans for Ricketts were, but hinted he would not like them.

The Major took comfort from the fact that Wellesley could not summarily dismiss him from the regiment - that was the prerogative of Horse Guards.

The bright sunlight made Firth squint and did nothing to ease the discomfort of his head wounds. The cavalryman's blade had left its mark on his forehead and eyebrow and, despite the best efforts of Surgeon Guthrie in tying small stitches, would leave him with a scar.

He had been taken to Guthrie's makeshift surgery by Needham, who had used a neckerchief to stem the flow of blood pouring from the slash. When they arrived at the canvas-topped area, Guthrie had been under extreme pressure removing badly damaged limbs from wounded soldiers.

The harried medical man was covered in blood and bits of what Firth presumed was flesh. His arms were red to the elbows and the rolled up sleeves of his cotton shirt were soaked. His formerly off-white apron was similarly stained and when he wiped sweat from his brow he left bloody streaks.

Guthrie was conducting his operations on three portable wooden tables and he would move to each in turn as the previous patient was dealt with. Next to each of the trestle tables was a pile of hands, arms and legs.

Firth was shocked – and not a little sickened – by both the sight and smell of the heaps, which in the heat of the day were attracting large numbers of noisy blowflies.

Twins One and Two were there to lift the amputees off the tables and take them outside where they were laid on blankets. They then helped the next soldier on to the bare but bloodstained wood, gave him a pint of rum to swallow before holding him down so Guthrie could begin his work.

The grog eased the men's fears and dulled the pain, Guthrie had once told Firth. The surgeon favoured quick amputations believing the shock of the injury meant the tissue around the wound was so traumatised that pain was minimised.

Unlike many of his army colleagues, Guthrie was a man who would treat casualties on their merits and if that meant an injured Frenchman was operated on before a Redcoat, then so be it.

This led to Firth witnessing one incident where a Scottish private used his own just-cut-off arm to hit a Frenchman he felt was moaning too much.

It was an hour before the doctor got to him, but once the wound was washed Guthrie had it sewn up within 15 minutes. "It'll give you a dangerous look for a while, young Joshua," he said, "but the ladies of London will think you a hero."

Firth smiled at the thought, but the attention of the group was drawn to the thump of hooves and the arrival of a French troop of horsemen under a white flag. The dozen officers and men were halted by sentries and then allowed to pass.

Firth could see one of the men was the officer who had wounded him. He stared at the figure as he rode next to a small ugly general and took a good look at his face. He's a hard man, Firth thought. The French passed next to where he was standing and when the Polish officer noticed Firth he pulled up his horse quickly.

"Aaah, the Englishman I met yesterday. I see I marked you well."

Firth looked up at him and responded, "And it appears that I was also successful, sir."

Zapalski raised his bandaged arm and smiled. "You did, but I will not live with the scar to show my defeat."

The comment stung Firth who felt anger rise in him. "Well perhaps if I had had the advantage of being on a horse, I might have acquitted myself better."

The Pole's smile turned cold.

Firth continued "And in fact, had I been on horse and allowed a mere infantry officer to survive I'd consider I had not done my duty properly."

The jibe stung Zapalski whose hand flew to the hilt of his sabre. Firth's hand also moved to his sword and he stared unblinking into the Major's eyes.

The other British officers closed between the two. "Steady on Firth," one said, "we don't want another fight."

"Don't we?" he said, "I don't see why we should put up with such comments from men in an army we've beaten twice within four days!'

Zapalksi spat out the curse "merde" and half-drew his blade. But by that time Firth's steel was out of its scabbard and at his throat.

"I warn you, sir, that were it not for the flag of truce I would run you through on the spot. Keep your damn airs to yourself, sir, or I'll take great pleasure in teaching you some manners."

"Hold back Joshua," Captain Gauntlett said, "you can't do this."

Firth was about to reply when another voice sounded.

"He's right, monsieur, this would do little good."

Firth saw it was the ugly General who now spoke and as he did so he patted Zapalski's arm and the Major pushed his weapon back.

"We are hear to talk, not fight, and while Major Zapalski may not appreciate the courage of British soldiers I have learned to do so over the past week."

Firth could only nod at the courteous General and withdrew, then sheathed, his sword.

The Frenchman went on "by the way, I am General Francois Kellermann. Your name is?"

"Captain Joshua Firth, 29th Regiment of Foot."

"I did not witness your fight with the good Major, Captain Firth, but I did hear of it. He is a very fine soldier and you did well against him. I have a feeling your comment on him being on horseback hurt his pride. One day maybe the two of you can meet again on, how shall we put it, more equal terms. And now, I'm afraid, we must be about our business. It was good to meet you Captain Joshua Firth."

Kellermann leaned over and extended his hand to the young officer who reached out and reciprocated the firm grip.

"The honour was mine General," Firth said truthfully. He knew of Kellermann's battlefield heroics and was thrilled to have met a man of such ability.

Zapalski said nothing, but his face was dark with fury as he wheeled his horse and spurred off with the General and his escort.

"Lord, Joshua, we must keep an eye on you," said Gauntlett. "What on Earth made you react like that?"

"I have a bad headache," Firth said, although that was not the reason at all. He had taken an instant dislike to Zapalski and his arrogance. He was forced to accept it from people like Ricketts, but he'd be damned if he took it from an enemy.

Gauntlett looked at him in a strange way and nodded. "Fair enough, Joshua, but let me tell you I have never before seen anyone whip a sword out that fast - or look more likely to fillet someone over such a trifle."

XXXIIc

A cavalry colonel strode into the room and stopped at Sir Hew's side. He bent over and whispered into the commander's ear something that clearly shocked the General. He turned and looked into the man's face. "Are you sure?"

The Colonel shook his head. "No sir, however, the Navy believes it is the case. Your daughter's ship has sunk."

"My God," Dalrymple said, "Oh my God. How can this be ...?"

Wellesley stood. "My regrets, Sir Hew, is there anything we can do?"

Fighting back tears the senior officer shook his head in the negative. "Thank you Sir Arthur, but there is nothing you can do. It is God's will."

"Sir Hew, I have a fine young officer about to sail towards Gibraltar, he can watch out for survivors. Do you have anything that will help us recognise your daughter?"

Dalrymple paused. "I have a painting of her in my belongings ... oh, and a small portrait that I carry with me."

He reached into his jacket and removed a pocketwatch-sized oval frame.

"This is Constance."

"She looks delightful, Sir Hew. Most fair."

Before Dalrymple could answer the Colonel quickly returned.

"Sirs, I believe there is a French party here carrying a flag of truce. The man carrying it is General Kellermann."

"What do they want?"

"They have a message from General Junot and they say it is urgent."

"Is it, by God," Wellington muttered, "well they'll just have to stew until Sir Harry, Sir Hew and myself have dealt with a more pressing concern than anything a pack of bloody Frogs want to say."

The Colonel recognised Wellesley's tone and quickly exited to let the French know the meeting would be delayed.

"Sir Hew," Wellesley said, "We will do all we can to find out what has happened to ... Constance."

"You are most kind, Sir Arthur," Dalrymple said. "Now if you would indulge me for a time, I need to collect myself before we engage the Frenchmen."

Wellesley's dislike of Dalrymple eased, here he was facing the horrible thought of the death of his daughter and yet he was ready to continue on with his duty.

Burrard said: "Sir Arthur, what if this truce move is just a ploy on the part of the French? What if they are moving on us now as we sit here?"

Wellesley could see the sense in Burrard's concern. He sent a servant to recall the Colonel and when the man arrived said: "Please send all senior officers back to their brigades and have them call their men to arms. We need to be prepared, just in case the Frogs want to try their luck again on the field."

The Colonel immediately understood the situation and hurried out leaving Britain's three senior generals alone in the room.

One was thinking about his beloved daughter, another was focusing on the French, while Wellesley cast his mind to the problem of the Russian fleet near Lisbon. Had it attacked the Royal Navy there? Had Junot been reinforced by new troops from France or, worse, by Russian infantry?

Whatever their thoughts the trio sat silently. The sudden tightening of stomach muscles meant finishing their food was out of the question. Wellesley downed his glass in one long gulp and sat waiting for Dalrymple to speak. Burrard was happy to take short sips, while Sir Hew left his wine untouched.

"Well, gentlemen, what're the French up to? Sir Harry?"

"I have no idea, Sir Hew, it may be they want to recover their wounded."

"A possibility, a possibility … What do you think Sir Arthur?"

"I wonder if they might be after terms, sir."

"Terms? Do you think they want to surrender? Good God man they've an army of 15,000 men, they'll fight."

Wellesley ignored the tone of the comment and continued.

"I disagree, Sir Hew, they are not in a good position. It is true they occupy Lisbon, but that is a hostile city and Junot wouldn't want to be fighting us while looking over his shoulder and avoiding an uprising.

"Secondly, he won't want to have us on his tail if he decides to retreat into Spain. It is a hard trail over the Estremaduran mountains at the best of times, let alone when one is running like a cur.

"I believe Junot is caught between us and a hard place, Sir Hew, and if he wants to get out of Portugal he will want to talk peace."

"And so what do you suggest we do?"

"We listen to his terms and keep in mind that we are in a better position than they."

Dalrymple nodded to show Wellesley he had heard the points and then raised steepled fingers to his lips.

After several seconds he stood and spoke. "Gentlemen, we must meet with this General Kellermann and I suggest we do so in full-dress uniform. If nothing else it will show this looter that we are men of substantial means and have a breeding that he can only pray for. I have no idea what he is after but, knowing the French, we'd better keep our wits about us. We'll meet the devils here in an hour."

When the three generals returned at the appointed time the area had been changed from a senior officer's dining area into a scrupulously clean and spartan meeting room.

The long, wooden table had been covered up by a thick white-cotton cloth and along each side of it sat three chairs. Behind the trio nearest the large window were two large King's Colours that had been placed in heavy metal stands. Dalrymple took the middle chair, while Burrard took the position to his right and Wellesley the remaining spot.

Two secretaries entered and each, armed with parchment and quills, sat at separate small wooden desks near the unused fireplace. Their job was to note down the matters as they arose and keep track of the conversation.

The British commanders stood and waited for the French party to arrive and were amazed when Kellermann strode in alone. All three men were also surprised at how small the redoubtable General was. He was a good head shorter than Wellesley, the smallest of the British trio, and was positively dwarfed by Dalrymple.

But Kellermann's presence was clearly felt in the room and his swagger left them in no doubt he was a man confident in both his cause and ability. After the men sat down a servant came in to inquire about drinks and served glasses of madeira to all.

There was a long silence as each side summed the other up and then Dalrymple began to speak.

"Good day General Kellermann, I have to say this meeting is somewhat irregular."

"You are correct, General Dalrymple," Kellermann began in heavily accented English, "and I must say I am a little, how do you say, confused. I had been led to believe that General Wellesley was the British commander and now I find he is in fact not.

"No matter, my task is to deal with whoever is in charge and that is now you." Kellermann went on.

"My own commander General Junot, the Duke of Abrantes, wishes to come to a sensible arrangement about the situation in Portugal. We have a large army and control not only Lisbon and the major cities, but also all the fortresses in this country. We would, however, be prepared to withdraw - subject to reaching an amicable agreement with you."

Kellermann pressed his thin toad-like lips tightly together. In fact, Junot's last words to him had been rather less neutral. He had said he expected nothing less from his negotiator than "getting his army out of the mousetrap".

More like right out of the merde, Kellermann had thought.

"Good, good," muttered Dalrymple – much too loudly for Wellesley's liking, who saw at once the Frenchman had noted it well.

Kellermann smiled in a way that made his face slightly less ugly and went on.

"General Junot has a proposal that will see you take control of Portugal with no additional loss of life and in as fast a time as is possible."

"You will withdraw then?" said Dalrymple, again too eagerly.

"We wish to, but before we do we want certain guarantees."

"Such as?" asked Wellesley.

"Well … we have produced a suggested list of terms for settling the issue," and with that he reached into his dark-blue jacket and pulled out an envelope.

"Here are four main articles that we see as being both fair and reasonable."

"And what are they?" growled Wellesley.

"Firstly we will hand over Lisbon and all the Portuguese fortresses in their current conditions."

"A good start …" Wellesley butted in. A sideways glance from Dalrymple let the disgruntled General know that his comments were not appreciated.

Kellermann went on. "In exchange we will be transported back to France in British ships, will not be considered prisoners of war, and will be allowed to take our arms and baggage."

Dalrymple leaned forward. "Who will pay for using our naval vessels?"

Kellermann smiled. "You will."

Wellesley let out a laugh and was about to add some more colourful words when Dalrymple held up his hand.

"I have to say General Kellermann that the terms seem sensible, at first glance, but we will need to satisfy ourselves as to their *bona fides*. In the meantime, we will grant you a two-day suspension of hostilities during which time representatives can meet and work out a proper list of terms."

"I hope we can, General Dalrymple, although there are many within our forces who would prefer to fight on. We have large armies operating in Spain who can move over the borders if necessary."

Wellesley let out another derisive laugh. "Hah! Then why have they not already done so? The truth is, General Kellermann, that they are unable to come to your aid because they are too busy dealing with their own problems."

"You may take that view, General Wellesley," said Kellermann with another smile, "however, should the need arise they will move."

Dalrymple broke in: "I think we see your point General and will take everything into account when considering your proposals. I think, sirs, that will be all for now. You will have our response soon General Kellermann."

With that the British commander stood and offered his hand to the Frenchman. It was taken and then in turn shaken by Burrard and Wellesley.

"We look forward to your response, General Dalrymple."

XXXIII

Junot's Headquarters, Lisbon
August 22, 1808.

The small group of British officers at the entry arch into the noisy dining hall stopped and tried to let their eyes take in the spectacular sight that lay before them.

The huge room was a moving tapestry of colour and sound as scores of elaborately dressed French officers talked and laughed. Thousands of candles in massive crystal chandeliers reflected light off the cavernous marble ceiling and the glittering braid of a host of brightly hued uniforms sparkled and shone.

The walls were also of marble and rose twice the height of a man, along each of them were enormous blue-tile azulejos murals. Moving in front of the nearest one Brook was astounded at the artist's ability to create such highly detailed pictures on tiles. In between the murals French tricolour flags were hung and in the centre of those were the famed regimental eagles.

Groups of senior officers sat at long dark-blue clothed tables where they were being served glasses of wine. In between the men were some of the most beautiful women the British had ever seen. Their hair was styled in the fashionable ancient-Roman way with it braided and tied on top and their gowns were pale with plunging necklines. Brook was still marvelling at the overall sight when he heard Way splutter beside him.

"My God, those dresses are see-through!"

Brook looked quickly at the closest woman and was embarrassed to discover that the Major was probably right and turned his eyes away even faster.

"It's un-Christian," came a voice from behind, although another quickly chimed in with "well God bless the pagans!"

The British officers were all from the 29th and included Major Way, several captains, Brook and four other lieutenants. They had been invited to the dinner, guests of General Junot himself, as an early celebration for the expected successful end to negotiations currently underway for an evacuation back to France.

Way looked at his men. "They don't look like a beaten army do they Patison?" he said to a Captain next to him.

"That they don't, sir," he replied, "although those are the rumours."

"Well beaten or not, they certainly know how to put on a feast," the Major said admiringly. "We must remember this for our own mess gentlemen."

The officers smiled and looked at the roasted meats and bowls of fruit adorning the tables.

"Can we get some of the women too, Major Way?" a voice behind him asked.

"That wasn't you was it, Mr Brook? Way asked.

Brook looked shocked and then by his senior officer's smile knew he was once again being teased. "I don't think so sir, although it could have been."

"That's the spirit lad," Way laughed.

Brook, still sporting a large bandage around his head, thought how very different this treatment was to that handed out just after they had been taken at Rolica. Only the courage of a French drummer boy had saved Major Way's life. Twice the lad had stood between his own comrades and the British prisoner and stopped them from bayoneting him to death. Other officers had been roughly handled and most suffered bruises and cuts from being punched upon reaching the French camp. Brook remembered little of being taken, or of the long journey to Lisbon, as his head wound had laid him low for several days.

Once in the Portuguese capital the British officers had been separated from the 45 rank-and-file men – they were sent into a guarded barracks – while the officers were made welcome at the enemy headquarters.

In return for giving their parole, Brook and his fellow officers were allowed to keep their swords and were given permission to walk about Lisbon within a mile of the headquarters. They of course had to do so with an escort, but Brook had found the junior French officers charged with accompanying them pleasant and agreeable.

The attitude among the officers was one of confidence as they had heard rumours of the French defeats at Rolica and Vimeiro and all were delighted the 29th had performed so creditably.

Brook was excited to hear of a young officer who was said to have held the line against two French attacks at Rolica. News of the action was scarce but, from the description, it sounded to Brook as if it had been Firth. A hero already, he thought with pride.

Details from Vimeiro were few, all they would be told by their captors was that a treaty was being organised that would see them returned to their regiment within a matter of days. They had only received the welcome news that morning and the resulting air of good humour was still apparent in their demeanour.

The officers came to attention as a limping General crossed the highly polished wooden dance floor and approached them. They recognised him as General Delaborde, the man whose troops had captured them.

"Good evening gentlemen, I hope you have been treated well. I would very much like you to join me at my table," Delaborde said with a smile.

Major Way stepped forward and replied "thank you for your invitation General we would very much like to enjoy your company and …," he hesitated, "some news perhaps?"

Delaborde smiled and nodded. "Assuredly."

"You will have to forgive my appearance, but this sling is the remains of a present given to me by one of your men at Vimeiro."

The Frenchman stopped suddenly and looked at the swords the British were wearing. "You are armed?"

Way shook his head and explained: "It is our tradition, General, that we never dine without swords. A bad experience in the American colonies … We would beg your indulgence in allowing us to wear them."

Delaborde nodded. "I understand Major. There will be no problem. Now we must get you some fine wine."

And very fine it turned out to be. Brook had never tasted the like before and marvelled when told it had come from Junot's own 5000-bottle travelling cellar. And it was not the first time the young Lieutenant's tastebuds had been treated since his capture, the food they had been served was better than any meal he had ever sat down to and Brook ensured he ate heartily of almost everything on the mess table.

The British were seated at the head of the hall on Junot's left-hand side. The senior General had raised a half-full glass to them as they prepared to sit and in turn had received a return of the courtesy.

"Hope they don't expect us to toast bloody Bonaparte," Major Way muttered. "I'll be damned if I wish him any good health."

A wounded Captain Pattison coughed gently into his hand and said: "Perhaps, sir, we could stand – if a toast be offered – and not raise our glasses."

Way thought about it for a few moments and then nodded. "Fine idea, Andrew, fine idea. That's what we will do, gentlemen, we'll stand for a toast - but not drink."

But when Brook saw what was being put before him on a silver plate he forgot anything of toasts and even wine. He'd eaten quail back home, but the honey-glazed pair that he now saw was almost a work of art. And the aroma that rose from the plate … Brook was mindful that while his heart belonged to King George - his stomach was definitely beginning to show signs of being Bonapartist.

Taking his lead from watching Delaborde, Brook dispensed with his knife and fork and gently broke the birds up with his fingers. The meat was cooked to moist perfection and almost melted in his mouth. Lemon too, Brook thought, as the new tangy flavour increased the sweetness of the crisp-honeyed skin.

He was so taken with the quail that it was only when he was nudged by his neighbour that he realised Delaborde was talking to him.

"I see you are enjoying that Lieutenant …"

Brook squirmed and flushed red. "Yes sir, I am. Very much." He looked around the table and saw that he was almost finished while most of the officers had yet to start on their second bird.

"I'm sorry sir, it is just that these quail are heavenly."

Delaborde threw his head back and laughed. "I am glad to see someone enjoying their food ahead of polite conversation. Your health Lieutenant," and raised his glass.

Again Brook blushed and quickly looked at his brother officers who all wore big grins on their faces – particularly Major Way.

"To Gurgling Brook," the British toasted, using Brook's nickname for the first time in public.

The young man was mortified and was unsure how to react.

"Gurgling Brook?" Delaborde questioned.

"It is a name I have been given, sir, since witnessing a flogging. It made me ill…"

Delaborde looked intently at Brook and smiled. "I would be … ill … as well young man. Whipping a man for a mistake of judgment is barbaric," the General said. "What do you do in your army, sir?"

"If it is serious enough we shoot them, Lieutenant Brook. Some of your fellow officers may regard that as brutal, but it works. Anyway, young man, here's to your health."

Again glasses were raised and laughter broke out at the table. Brook squirmed in his seat but felt better when Way gave him a fatherly pat on the back. "Never mind us Samuel, we're only pulling your leg. You've done well, lad, enjoy yourself."

More wine followed and further silver trays loaded with glorious-tasting food appeared. The conversations grew louder, laughter was almost constant, and at several tables French officers were becoming amorous with their female companions.

At Junot's table, several scantily clad women had draped themselves around the French commander who was clearly enjoying their company. Brook and the British were not sure whether they should be offended, or jealous of the white-uniformed hero.

Much later in the night Junot finally rose unsteadily to his feet and called for silence in the hall. He poured himself another large glass of red wine, spilling at least a quarter of it on to the tablecloth, and held it high.

"Brothers and ladies," he slurred, "A toast to our Emperor."

Around the room everyone rose to attention and raised their glasses.

"The Emperor," they roared.

Junot drained his wine and looked across to the small band of red-coated officers. They had not drunk the toast.

"You sirs, you have not drunk to the Emperor!"

The hall fell silent and eyes tried to focus on the British.

"Why, Major Way, do you not join our toast?"

Delaborde moved to intercede, but Way signaled to him not to interfere. He stood tall and looked at Junot.

"General, I regret to say we are uncomfortable at toasting your Emperor. We mean no disrespect to you or your men, but that is how we feel."

Junot looked quizzically at the Major, then his face hardened and he took a bottle of wine and moved to the British table. Delaborde feared his senior officer was about to lose control of his volcanic temper and was hoping Way would back down.

The British officers stood behind their Major and waited to see what would happen next.

"So, Major Way, you will not drink a toast to our Emperor."

"No, General Junot, we are unable to."

"So, Major Way," Junot said coldly, "who will you drink to?"

"We would drink to our King, sir," came the reply.

Junot's eyes closed slightly and then he turned, waving glass and bottle in the air, and called out "these men will not drink to our Emperor, but instead to their King – are they not our guests?"

"Yes," came a loud response from the French.

"Well then, my brothers, there seems to be little for it other than to make them toast." He spun back to face Way and said: "Let us toast – your King. To King George of England!"

The surprised British could barely be heard among the uproar as the French officers took up the cry and drank to the health of their most implaccable foe.

Again Junot turned to Way and said: "Major, you are brave men and I would willingly drink to you. We will be friends soon – France and England – and tonight we will celebrate. Your health, sir."

"And yours, General," said Way.

Brook also drank to the officers' health, and then his own and then the chef's and then slowly sank back into his chair before falling into sleep.

For the others in the room, however, the night was but young and there were many hours of celebrating to be completed before thoughts turned to bed.

Part Two: The Search for Constance

XXXIV

Off the Coast of Spain
August 24, 1808

Firth was having the time of his life sitting astride the bowsprit of the 38-gun Dragon as it carved through the post-storm swells. His eyes were focused on the fifth-rater's bow in an attempt to spot the pod of dolphins that had been racing them since they rounded Cape St Vincent on the southern tip of Portugal.

Firth guessed there were at least two dozen of the creatures powering along with surprising speed and grace. Along the rails off-duty seamen laughed as the dolphins leapt out of the dark-blue seas.

Firth was not only enjoying the animals' antics, but also the thrill of being at sea again with the smell of salt water thick in the air.

It had only been a few weeks since he and Brook had arrived in Portugal and he had not realised how much he had missed the ocean – particularly on a warm, sunny day such as today.

He turned as he half-heard a shout from the deck behind him and looked to see Wren beckoning him back from his precarious perch.

Firth waved and made his way to the safety of the sloop.

"You're mad," Wren called and Firth grinned.

"It's wonderful out there Chris, you really should try it."

"There is no way, I'd slip off and get eaten by a shark."

"And you a Royal Marines officer?" Firth teased, "How long have you been in the service?"

"Well, that's as may be, but the ships I am used to are usually bigger than this."

Both grinned as they looked about. The Dragon was fast and well armed, but it was dwarfed by most of the Royal Navy's main fighting vessels, even fourth-rate ships of the line.

"Still, she rides well," said Firth, gazing to the port side at a large dark mass several hundred yards from the ship.

"So that's where the dolphins have gone ... there's a big shoal of fish out there Chris ... they're probably sardines."

"I could do with some of them now, Joshua, I'm famished."

"Let's get a net, I'm sure Captain Allison will be more than happy to stop for a bit of fishing," Firth laughed.

"I don't think so, he's a bit proper our Captain ..."

"I was aboard the Victory, you know ..." Firth said as he pulled a very serious face and almost collapsed laughing as he did so. Wren couldn't contain his glee at the mimicking of the Dragon's Captain who had indeed been with Lord Nelson three years before at Trafalgar.

Captain Allison was a pleasant gentleman, Wren thought, but very straight-laced and by-the-book. It seemed an almost daily occurrence that he somehow managed to mention the fact of his time with the great naval commander to all and sundry.

"Chris," came a shout from Firth, "Look over there. About 60 degrees to starboard." Wren quickly followed Firth's pointing arm. Initially he couldn't see what his friend was indicating but then his eyes picked up some shapes on the water about a mile distant.

"What is it Joshua?"

"Can't tell from here ..."

"Shame you haven't got yourself a telescope Joshua, make life a bit easier."

Climbing on to the rigging of the ship Firth easily worked his way up the ropes. The higher he climbed the more he could see a spread of debris on the water.

"It's wreckage, Chris, there's timber and I think some sails."

Firth's shouts had drawn the attention of the ship's lookout who spun his view around 180 degrees and immediately called to a midshipman who told a drummer to beat to quarters. Within seconds the Dragon went from a quiet running vessel to what seemed to Firth like a madhouse. Sailors ran up the rigging, others to their gun posts while the ship's Marines and those of Wren's detachment lined the rails, muskets at hand.

As Wren walked briskly towards his men, Firth looked around to see where Captain Allison was and spotted him by the wheel.

Amidships a longboat was being hoisted and a crowd of eager hands prepared to crew her when she was dropped on to the ocean. As the Dragon closed on the floating objects it became apparent to Firth it was ship wreckage and by its wide spread – he could see tell it had not happened that day, but within the past few.

Barrels and chests bobbed among scattered broken planks and spars that still trailed tarred ropes and pieces of canvas. Crafting their way into the debris the men watched the half-submerged objects and kept their eyes ready for any survivors.

A small wooden locker was hooked by a long spike and drawn in, while the discovery of a woman's dress raised some mirth. The Dragon's longboat had been away for about 20 minutes when a cry went up from it and the sailors on board dragged something over the gunwales.

Captain Allison's telescope snapped open beside him and he heard the officer mutter something under his breath.

"She's British," he said with a sigh. "They've just brought in her ensign."

"Launch another boat please, Mr Weaver," he said to his first officer. "We may find some of our people out there."

He looked in Firth's direction and half-smiled.

"Someone's had some bad luck, eh?"

"Was it the French, sir?"

"Not likely, Mr Firth, we've got them bottled up. Could be privateers, the bloody Americans frequent these parts hunting our merchant ships. Then again, maybe it's just bad luck."

Bad luck indeed, thought Firth.

"Do you know her size sir?"

"I'd say she was a sloop Mr Firth and, if that's the case, I want to meet the brute that did this. As soon as we've finished looking for anyone left alive we will hunt these devils down. However, I don't wish you or Mr Wren to be prevented from your mission."

"Thank you, Captain" Firth said, "but I want to find those who did this." Turning back to the search scene he added: "Let's hope we find some of the crew …

Allison spoke before he thought of the full consequences of his thoughts.

"Sharks will have had them, is my guessing, Mr Firth. Still, we'll spend another hour or so checking and if we haven't found anything by then we will have to move on."

Firth nodded in an accepting way.

Then came another shout that had them both looking around. A figure in the bow of the longboat held up a piece of plank and shouted a name but it was lost on the breeze. A midshipman then raised a hailing trumpet and the phrase was much clearer.

"It's the Swallow."

"My God," Firth said.

"What's the matter Mr Firth?" asked Captain Allison, "You've gone as white as a sheet sir."

"The Swallow was the ship Constance Dalrymple was on …"

XXXV

Near Huelva, south coast of Spain
August 25, 1808

As the Dragon continued its progress southwards, Firth could not shake the thought of what could have happened to General Dalrymple's daughter.

The likelihood was she'd drowned but if the ship had been attacked by privateers they might have captured her. That led to even more terrible thoughts about how she was being treated. Sleep had been almost impossible and so now he was on deck as the early morning sky lightened.

Taking the image of the woman he was to find out of his pocket, Firth looked at the painted face. She certainly was worth a portrait, he thought. The colour of her hair appeared light red-brown, but it was something about her eyes that grabbed Firth's attention. What an amazing colour, he thought. He had seen it before and with horror he realised it was the woman he had bumped into those long weeks ago at the market. It was with difficulty he wrenched his mind away from her and switched it to his mission.

It was simple enough, he thought, deliver the dispatches to General Minas and then wait for any response. Benton had thought he may be with the Spanish commander for two days and told Firth just to accept any hospitality offered to him.

Enjoy yourself, Benton had said, but don't make a fool of yourself. That turned Firth's thinking towards Brook and the knot of despair returned in his stomach. Inquiries before he had left had not turned up any news of his friend, but Benton had promised to contact the French about British prisoners taken at Rolica and Vimeiro. Firth thought the past week had been one of the hardest of his life as Brook had been an almost constant companion since they were boys and he missed his cheek and humour. He didn't want to think about his friend being dead, but it was a possibility. He hoped Brook was one of those captured and had not been wounded.

Firth's own cuts and bruises were healing well and he was very glad the blow to his head hadn't been any worse as the stitches over his eye were beginning to itch. Wren had thought the stitch pattern was warrior-like and that until it healed properly would give him a look that would both frighten the enemy and entice the ladies. That comment set them both off into fits of laughter that were both unseemly for officers and made Firth's wound stretch painfully.

It was a beautiful morning and Firth appreciated both the view in front of him and the quiet of that part of the day. There were only a few hands on deck as the bell tolled four times. Firth looked at his watch it marked 6am on the dot.

"Sail ho," came the call from above in the rigging. "Sail astern."

Astern? Firth silently queried. He had been looking in that direction only five minutes before and there had been no masts in sight.

As the ship beat to quarters men emerged from just about every part of the frigate and took to their assigned posts with practiced ease. Firth watched as Marines climbed up to the platforms on the masts where they could be used to fire into a vessel - should the need arise.

Clambering up the nearest lines he looked behind the Dragon and there was definitely a three-decker flying the Spanish colours not two miles distant. How on Earth did he just appear like that? He could see back to the horizon down the coastline and he had seen no sails out to sea.

On the quarterdeck Firth could hear Captain Allison demanding answers as to how the vessel had got so close before he was informed and eased himself down the ropes and made his way up its wooden steps.

"If that man was asleep I'll have him flogged," an irate Allison said harshly. "No lookout on my ship will let us down like this again."

"Begging your pardon, sir," Firth interjected, "I have been on deck for an hour or so and saw nothing of that ship until just now."

"Ah, well … that may change things. Thank you, Mr Firth. Midshipman Thomas, I'd like to talk to the lookout. Bring him to my cabin later."

"Aye, sir," the young man said as he touched his hat and ran to the main mast.

"Well, well, well, she snuck up on us sure enough," said Allison, "Let's hope she really is Spanish I'd hate to get a broadside from that up close. By the way," he said to his First-Lieutenant, "We'd better open the gunports and ready the guns. Just in case it's under a false flag."

It hadn't struck Firth before – and certainly in not a so dramatic a manner - but while the Dragon was a powerful vessel an enemy line-of-battle ship would tower over it and, if it opened fire at point-blank range, there would be very little of the fifth-rater left.

With renewed interest in the flag Firth hoped he was showing as much indifference to the situation as Allison and his officers, who were silently watching the closing vessel.

A small figure in a cocked hat aboard the unidentified trailing ship moved up to the figurehead and called out in passable English through a speaking trumpet.

"Hello English, we are the Queen Maria-Luisa from out of Cadiz. We would like to escort you into a port."

Taking his own trumpet Allison welcomed the Spanish offer and suggested the Maria-Louisa may like to take the lead.

Waving a hand the Spanish officer turned to his colleagues and orders could be heard being barked at the crew. The shape of the ship's sails changed and slowly she began the preparations for turning about.

Allison watched the smooth manouevre by the Queen Maria-Luisa, appreciating its discipline and ordered the Dragon to follow suit.

"Do it right now lads," he called, "Don't want the Dons showing us up."

Firth later thought Allison needn't have worried as the Royal Navy sailors swung the Dragon around with a perfect display of seamanship that soon had the frigate tucked in behind the Spaniard.

Looking around for Wren, Firth saw him with his sharpshooters on the mainmast's large platform and moved towards the ratlines leading to it. Scampering up the tarred ropes he pulled himself on to the black-painted wood and crossed to his friend.

"Great view up here," he said.

"Stunning," came the reply, "You can see for miles."

"That's what concerns me a little, Chris. It's a perfect morning and you can see for miles and yet they were on us out of nowhere. There must be an inlet around here."

"I was below until the general quarters," the Marine Captain said, "I saw nothing."

"Well I was on deck and the only thing I noticed was a small bay about two leagues back. But it wasn't big enough for a ship of that size to hide in."

"At least it has got my men up and about," Wren said, "They are mighty grieved by the cramped conditions between decks. I've got 50 men with me – normally we should only fit half that number."

"Have more inspection parades," Firth suggested with a smile.

"Oh yes," Wren retorted, "and sleep on the deck. I can just see Captain Allison being happy about that."

"So why so many Chris?"

"It seems, Joshua, that I need to take extra care of the British army's new rising hero." Firth looked quizzically at Wren who punched him lightly on the shoulder.

"You, Joshua, I don't think Wellesley wants to send you off into the unknown without a bit of support."

Firth smiled again. "You are having me on. This is a quick delivery, wait for the reply and then back to Portugal."

"I wonder," said Wren, frowning a little. "It may be wise not to take everything we see at face value."

"Do you really think something is not right?"

"I, like Captain Allison, am worried about that ship and where it came from. It can't have appeared out of nowhere … that just doesn't happen. So there must be a reasonable anchorage along this coast."

"We may have passed something in the night," Firth mused, "but I have only seen that cove this morning."

Opening his telescope Wren began examining the coastline ahead. "How far up Joshua?"

"I think it was around the next headland … that one with the trees."

Both now watched the Queen Maria-Luisa more closely waiting for signs of a change in sail or direction.

They came upon the promontory sooner than they expected and lost sight of the Spanish ship as it made its way around the rocky outcrop. By the time the Dragon had also passed that point the Queen Maria-Luisa was turning towards the small cove Firth had dismissed.

It was surrounded on each side by high cliffs and was longer than Firth had initially registered. As their own vessel manouevred to enter the sheltered water Firth's eyes sought to see where the Spaniard had been earlier, but it was not until they had sailed several hundred yards into it that the bay revealed its secret.

There was a larger estuary to the left and possibly another to the right, but the Dragon followed a port turn by the Queen Maria-Luisa into the hidden inlet.

"No wonder we couldn't see it," Firth said, "Those cliffs hide everything from the view at sea. And look how deep the water is … a ship-of-the-line could use this as an anchorage."

Both vessels reduced sail as they followed the water seemingly inland and after another bend and set of cliffs Firth saw an unexpected harbour-side port busily going about its business.

There were several merchant ships waiting to be loaded, three frigates sitting at anchor and a large ship-of-the-line being provisioned by a stream of small boats.

"You'd never have guessed would you Chris?"

"My word, no, Joshua. This is amazing. What a perfect spot."

Wren's eyes looked at the cliff tops around the harbour and noted artillery batteries covering the town and anchorage.

"Very good defensive placements too," he said. "Well, Joshua, I had better shake the men up and get a guard ready. Have to make you look important," he laughed.

"I'd better clean up as well," said Firth, "I have a general to impress."

XXXVI

Minas' Spanish Base
August 25, 1808

As he left the Dragon's gangplank with Captain Allison and Wren, Firth did feel important, but in an embarrassed sort of way.

He had his letter to give to Don Minas, but felt far from comfortable dealing with a Spanish general.

The British officers walked between two lines of perfectly turned-out Marines standing at attention and towards several Spanish officers in front of a company of infantry in pristine white coats and yellow waistcoats.

Heading to the officers Captain Allison, as highest-ranking British officer, took the lead. Stopping in front of the Spaniards he touched his hat and gave a small bow.

"Gentlemen I am Captain Peter Allison of His Majesty's Ship Dragon and am here on a mission to give dispatches to General Don Costanzo y Minas. This is Captain Firth of the 29th Regiment of Foot and this is Captain Christopher Wren of the Royal Marines."

All the officers touched hats and made slight bows towards each other.

The oldest of the Spaniards issued a greeting in his native tongue and then turned at the sound of approaching carriages. The first, an ebony-coloured carriage drew to a halt near the group and a soldier quickly dismounted from next to the reinsman, opened a door and folded out shiny brass steps. A ring-bedecked hand reached out and grasped a polished-wood rail and the portly form of Don General y Minas emerged. Another officer alighted from a second, open carriage.

Firth was impressed by the General's uniform and aristocratic bearing as the Spaniard moved towards them.

"He's no oil painting," whispered Wren, who instantly received a cold stare from Allison.

Minas' aide stood at the General's shoulder and waited for his superior to speak.

Minas looked serious and gave a bow before saying: "I give you greetings, sirs, from His Most Catholic Majesty King Ferdinand of Spain. Welcome to his lands."

The three British officers returned the bow and Allison said how pleased he was to meet such an eminent Don of Spain.

Minas looked pleased and nodded. "Gentlemen I would like to invite you for some refreshments at my headquarters. My aide Major Bland will be only too happy to get you whatever you require. After all he is one of your countrymen."

Looking at Allison, Bland shook his head slightly and said: "Major Connor Bland and I'm actually Irish gentlemen."

Peering at the three men in front of him Minas' small eyes narrowed to the point of disappearing. "And from which of you will I receive the letter from General Wellesley?"

Firth took a half-step forward with the leather case containing the document. "I have General Wellesley letter, sir, my name is Captain Firth."

A fleeting flash of annoyance passed across Minas' face, but it was so fast Firth thought he imagined it.

"A Captain ... I would have thought a major might have been more appropriate in dealings between generals."

Firth shifted uncomfortably, but returned Minas' stare. "I believe General Wellesley has every confidence I will be able to perform my duties, sir."

Minas smiled through shapeless lips. "Of course, Captain, of course. I will meet you later and read General Wellesley's letter." Turning to Bland the General shot out a burst of Spanish and returned to his coach.

The Irish Major indicated for Allison to follow him and led them to the carriage.

Firth found the ride to the headquarters an interesting journey through wide streets of white two-storey houses. They all looked similar with green arched doors leading on to small balconies, although Firth could see the occupiers used a selection of colourful plants in earthen pots to add their own style.

In the older part of the town on a small rise behind the waterfront the buildings took on a different look with tiles and mosaics distinguishing various buildings.

Wren was having a wonderful time pointing out aspects of architecture that showed Moorish origins and subtle blends of both Arabic and Spanish styles. Firth could not bring himself to lessen his friend's passion and so nodded with interest.

People thronged the streets. Women with heavy-looking cane baskets, peddlers trying to sell food and gentlemen walking slowly engrossed in animated conversations or smoking long cigarillos.

Several times their driver had to slow their progress as people pushed across the cobbled streets in front of the horses and Firth noted that somehow the General's coach was always free of such annoyances.

Crossing an open plaza Firth could see a large walled building ahead. Its bell tower initially had Firth thinking it was a church, but then he noticed soldiers guarding the entrance, some sitting smoking next to a cannon, and supposed this was Minas' barracks.

The guards snapped to attention as the carriages passed and equerries ran about to ensure some sense of purpose was delivered to what seemed a chaotic situation.

"All seems in order here," Allison sniped through sarcastic lips, "I hope their ships aren't run the same way."

Realising he had thought out loud, Allison turned to an impassive Bland and smiled. "I'm sorry, I did not mean to insult you Major Bland."

"It is not an issue Captain Allison I, too, think the Spanish should take a bit more notice of how things should be run – such as in your Navy and Army. It will take time, however, and so we must do with what we have. General Minas is working very hard to rectify that and I think you'll find his soldiers are some of the most highly disciplined troops in Spain."

Allison looked a little relieved at the generous response from the Irishman.

"Major Bland," Firth began, "I was wondering what this place is called. You would never know it existed were it not for being led here."

"The town doesn't really have a name – it is entirely the property of General Minas. We are, however, not far from Huelva and Palos de la Fronterra, where Christopher Columbus departed on his voyage to discover the Americas."

"General Minas owns the whole town?" Firth asked in amazement.

"It is his family's winter retreat," Bland stated. "They are of an old and proud family that is linked in the past with kings of Castille."

Both Firth and Wren looked at each other and tried to imagine the sort of wealth that could afford such things. Neither could.

Inside the compound was a small parade ground flanked by three-tier buildings and their covered stone external walkways. Ahead lay a grand house with wide marble steps leading up to its multi-coloured tiled doors. A squad of a dozen soldiers stood outside the entrance and came to attention as Bland walked by and eyed the British officers as they made their way in.

Inside the building it was cool and the tinkling of water could be heard from somewhere in the large hall.

"My God, it's beautiful," murmured Wren as he followed Bland. "I don't suppose I could do some sketches could I, Major?"

Bland said he thought Wren would be welcome to do so and suggested he may like to gift one to the General.

Wren happily nodded assent.

"Now gentlemen, can we offer you some refreshments? Water, wine, some food?"

"Water will suffice thank you Major," said Allison.

"Then after that I will show you to quarters set aside for you during your stay," the Irishman responded.

"I'm sure that will be fine for Mr Firth, sir, but both Captain Wren and myself have duties aboard my vessel that require our presence during evenings."

"Of course, Captain Allison, that will not be a problem. The General is having a celebratory dinner tonight to mark your visit and offers you and your officers seats at his table. It is a great honour," he added pointedly.

"And we will be pleased to take up General Don Minas' generous offer, please thank him for us," came Allison's reply.

While the trio drank cool water from glass decanters, Major Bland excused himself and went to arrange a meeting time for Firth and General Minas.

It was well after noon when Bland returned. Allison had gone to the Dragon, Wren was seated with pad and pencil capturing aspects of the interior and Firth was eyeing a just-laid table of fruit, cold meats and olives.

"The General will see you now, Captain Firth," said Bland. "Please follow me."

The pair walked up another grand flight of stairs and into an ante-chamber fitted with desks and cabinets. An officer seated at one of the desks stood up and saluted Bland who went to a door behind the man and knocked once.

A barked reply had the Major opening the door and then turning and beckoning Firth inside.

Minas sat at a massive wooden table covered with papers and maps. On the floor was a decorated woven rug and hung on the walls were Spanish flags interspersed with weapons.

The General stood and when Firth handed over the satchel Minas indicated it should go to Bland, who quickly took it, unfastened the ties and passed the letter on to his commander.

The corpulent General sat down and opened the seal on the parchment. His eyes ran over its contents and he grunted softly. While reading he reached for a glass of red wine and drank slowly.

"I find reading your English a little tiring, Captain, it is such … an unromantic language," Minas said looking intently at Firth. "But I suppose it is more the language of traders than our more sophisticated Castillian."

Firth said nothing, as he wasn't sure if the General was trying to insult him or whether it was his natural aristocratic way.

"No matter," said Minas, "I have read the letter and will deliver my response to you in due course. I take it you are being looked after?"

"Very well indeed, sir, thank you for your hospitality."

The General waved aside the comment as if it meant little.

"Tonight, Captain Firth, you will see how Spaniards entertain. Until then …"

Firth knew instantly he had been dismissed and came to attention in front of the General before following Bland to the door.

"It will take quite some time before you get your letter, Captain," Bland said once it had closed. "The General is not known for quick decisions. It may be some days so I would suggest you enjoy the sights of the town. Take a stroll around and I will ensure any items you want from your ship are brought here. I will show you your quarters now and then please feel free to enjoy your visit. There is a wonderful market not two streets from here that is well worth seeing."

After seeing his spacious rooms, complete with bath and balcony overlooking the water, Firth went downstairs to find Wren. He chanced upon him seated on the floor in an alcove.

"It's the only way to get the right angle for that beautiful archwork there," he explained, much to Firth's amusement.

"No, look, it is a rare use of marble and Arabic tiles within stone. Just look at it," he said pointing.

As much as he could Firth tried to spot this astonishing architectural treat but, for the life of him, he couldn't.

"Come on Chris, we've apparently got plenty of time so let's go for a walk. Maybe we'll see some more rare uses of marble and Arabic tiles."

Laughing at himself, Wren rose and left his papers with a guard asking him to take them to Firth's rooms.

It didn't take long for the pair to near the market. Along the way their distinctive red jackets either drew looks of admiration or scowls from the locals. Firth had a feeling that while allies, in name, the Spanish had little time for Britain's soldiers of the King. They heard the trading area a street before they saw it and when rounding a corner were amazed at the spectacle. Everywhere there were barrows and carts filled with all kinds of colourful fruit, vegetables, hung chickens, fish, blankets and clothing. Voices were raised in an excited way as prices were seriously haggled over and then smiles broke out with even more accompanying enthusiasm. Spice stands had baskets of dried powders and leaves and Firth swore he had never smelled anything so interesting in his life.

Wren seemed to be having the time of his life as he looked at all the people in the marketplace and occasionally stopped to indicate a spectacular donna of Spain.

"Look at those dark eyes," he said, "My God these are some of the most beautiful women I have seen. Look at her hair," he added gazing towards a black-maned lady.

Firth could see they were very beautiful indeed, but his mind had moved back to Constance Dalrymple and her fate.

He should have asked Major Bland if he had reports of a sunken British ship and see what he could do to track down any survivors.

"Hang on, Joshua," Wren said, grabbing him by the arm, "Look at these!"

Firth stopped and looked at the stall that had taken Wren's attention. Its items were small hand-carved buildings and replicas of churches.

"These are marvelous," Wren admired.

The small one-armed vendor moved to the pair with a practiced smile and greeting.

"Ah welcome English," he said holding his right arm out as if for a hug. "You are our great friends now and I wish you well."

Taken somewhat aback by the reception Firth smiled at the man while Wren pored over the carvings.

"Did you create these?" he asked the vendor.

"Yes, senor, I did. It was a little difficult but, luckily for me, I'm right-handed."

"I'll say and for me, too," Wren said. "These are very skillfully done. You have great talent, sir."

"I'm glad you like them senor."

"I'll take them."

"Which one, sir?"

"All of them, they are just so very fine."

While Wren was given the price and handed over some gold coins Firth looked at the stallkeeper.

"Your English is very good, sir."

"Yes, thank-you," he replied with a broad smile. I was in the Spanish Navy and fought Nelson and your ships at Trafalgar. I was on the Santisima Trinidad.

"What a fight," he said with a sparkle in his eyes.

"We fought hard, but you are sea demons and would not be stopped. I lost my arm in the fight – a cannonball whisked it right off. I was lucky to survive as the storm that followed sank my crippled ship and I was thrown overboard by a friend who then strapped me to a barrel."

"May I ask then, why you like us?" said Firth.

"It's easy, English, your sailors saved me - and hundreds of others."

A deep frown now creased his face "but only half were saved … less maybe. It was terrible, nearly 600 of my shipmates died in the winds and seas."

"I'm sorry to hear that," said a genuine Firth who was now shifting uncomfortably from foot to foot.

"It is the past, senor. I was a prisoner for more than a year and, with help, managed to learn a bit of English."

"You have, sir, very well indeed. I don't suppose you get to speak it much."

The man laughed. "No sir, not until recently, when there was a young Englishwoman here."

"What?"

"An Englishwoman, very tall, very pretty. She came in off one of the boats."

"When?" Firth demanded.

"Less than a week ago. Is there something wrong?"

"I'm sorry, no," said Firth. "Your name, sir, is?"

"Hector, senor."

"Tell me Hector," Firth said quietly, "Who was she with and where did she go?"

"With the soldiers, to the headquarters."

Firth was stunned. How could it be there had been no mention of an Englishwoman?

"Thank you Hector, thank you," and he handed a coin to him.

His mind was racing. It probably was nothing more than Minas' bad manners, he thought, but when he explained it to Wren he urged his friend to keep the knowledge quiet.

"Let's have a walk by the docks," Firth said, "I'd like to look at those Spanish ships for a while."

Encumbered by the basket containing the miniature buildings, Wren found it harder to get through the throng of townsfolk.

"I'll be glad to get these on the Dragon," he said, quickly steering around an oncoming donkey and cart.

At the ship he gave the trove to a bemused Marine guard and then caught up with a striding Firth.

Across the harbour were the Spanish warships. The larger vessels included three two-deckers – heavy frigates - and the ship of the line Queen Maria-Luisa. A large transport ship called the San Cristobal sat alongside at anchor. The procession of small boats rowing between them and the docks seemed to have become busier, thought Firth.

"Look at that one, Chris, on the right. If I'm not mistaken that's been in a fight recently. Look at the work being carried out on her."

Wren agreed. Sails were being replaced, carpenters hammered on her hull and railings and men were hauling hard on lines holding up a new mizzen mast.

"She's been in a bit of a scrap, that's for sure Joshua, but let's not stand around here we stick out like sore thumbs ... let's keep walking. I think if there is something amiss then there'll be eyes on us."

"And Chris, I believe that transport is sitting even lower in the water than when we first arrived. They sure are packing her with supplies."

"And there are lot more guards on deck than on the other ships. Must be a valuable cargo," Wren added.

The pair continued to a loading area where sacks and barrels were being passed on winches from a large warehouse to the waiting bumboats. Neither stopped to watch the activity as Wren was becoming warier of being followed.

"I think Joshua we need to return to the ship and think this out. We have been told there is an Englishwoman here and know that ship has been in a fight. That's all. The Spanish are our allies and I can't see any reason for us to think ill of them."

"But ...," started Firth, who was about to mention Hector's description of the woman.

"But nothing, my friend. We have a brief description of a pretty Englishwoman."

"Very tall, that Hector said."

"A lot of Englishwomen would be tall to him, Joshua, and there could well be one living here married to a local. We don't know. One thing is for certain, we need to keep our heads clear this evening at dinner."

Firth nodded and fingered the portrait in his pocket. "But I know she's here."

XXXVII

Minas' Headquarters
August 25, 1808

It was a very tired Firth who left the dinner party and carefully made his way up to his rooms for the evening. The clock had just struck 11pm and Firth was feeling the effects of bottles of wine and rich food.

His stomach was full to bursting and negotiating the stairs was taking a little more concentration than he would have liked. He nodded to the guard at the top of the stairs and entered the large quarters.

Inside it was dark and rain beat heavily against the glass panels in the doors and on his small balcony.

Hitting his shin on his wooden chest Firth cursed softly and tried to remember where he had left the wax-coated matches and tinderbox. And where was the damned candle, he muttered impatiently? Figuring the effort was not going to be worth it, Firth instead turned towards the bed, took off his sword and belt and, without removing his boots, collapsed on to it.

He awoke some time later with a noise on his balcony. Through his just-roused mind he dismissed it as the rain, but then the sound came again. It was a sharp knocking. Opening his eyes Firth could hear it was still pouring down outside and through the dim light he could see a figure trying to peer into the room. Reaching for his discarded sword he swung on to his feet and with hand on the hilt moved to the balcony doors. He recognised the person immediately and unbolted the doors.

"Chris? What on Earth…?"

Firth stopped his inquiries when Wren put his finger to his lips and indicated silence. They moved inside, shutting the doors.

"What's going on Chris?"

"Something strange, Joshua, and not a little concerning."

"What?"

"Well you know how I cried off early from the dinner …"

Firth nodded.

"I wasn't sick, I just wanted to take a look at that second inlet – you know the one we passed on the way in."

Again Firth nodded.

"You have to see what's going on there and we have to go now, while no-one is around."

"But …"

"No time Joshua, we've got to get there and back before first light. We do not want to be seen."

"Okay, Chris, lead the way," said Firth and moved towards the main door.

"Not that way, we'll go the way I came, there's a pipe leading up here that makes it an easy climb. And don't forget your greatcoat."

Peering at Firth Wren asked: "Are you all right?"

"Could have done with more sleep … and you missed an excellent meal."

"Wake yourself properly, we need to go," he said to his friend with some urgency. "Come on."

Firth carefully followed Wren over the wrought-iron balustrade and slipped his way noisily down the pipe.

"Quiet Joshua," Wren whispered.

Mumbling his apologies Firth followed as Wren made his way to the shadowy side of the street and moved off quickly. As the pair rounded the first corner and disappeared from sight a cloaked figure emerged from a pitch-black doorway. Pausing momentarily to check the surroundings the figure then carefully moved off and began to tail them.

Avoiding lit areas, Wren led Firth away from the dockside until he reached a muddy road that continued to follow the water's edge. It was not until they had gone a mile or so from the last building that Wren allowed himself the luxury of speaking aloud.

"You have to see this Joshua … they've got a full-blown invasion force sitting in this other inlet. No ships-of-the-line, but they have at least six transports and hundreds of longboats."

"They are at war, Chris …

"Yes, but with whom?" Wren responded pointedly. "Why hide them away when the warships are in the other harbour?"

Firth had no immediate answer but matched Wren's urgent pace.

"It'll take us about an hour to get there and you'll need to watch out for patrols. They are irregular, but the Spaniards are out and about."

The strength of the rain increased and despite the turned-up collar of his coat Firth felt the discomfort of water running down his neck. As he walked Firth wondered if Wren's suspicions could amount to something although, he reasoned, why would the Spaniards mention the flotilla to newly arrived foreign officers. He was sure there was a good explanation – if indeed the force was as large as Wren said it was.

At a small crossroads Wren turned left into a much-rutted track. It was clear lots of heavy traffic had passed along it, but again that was nothing to be concerned about, he thought. Soon after the turnoff Wren moved on to the grassy verge and crouched.

"Over that hill, Joshua, is a pier and a guardhouse. There are at least two soldiers in the hut but, when I was here earlier, they did seem to be rather involved in dealing with a wineskin."

Firth smiled then winced a little as the dull ache in his own head came to the fore. He could feel a large trickle of water flow down his neck, hit his already-wet collar and he felt like cursing.

"Chris … I hope we are not on a wild goose chase."

A large muddy puddle splashed dirty water almost up to the top of Firth's boots.

"Bloody hell."

"What's up, Joshua, feeling a bit poorly are we?"

Firth muttered something that Wren couldn't quite hear but he could tell from the tone it was not wishing him good morning.

They walked on in silence before Firth asked "Any tents?"

"Sorry?"

"Are there any tents? If there are lots of boats they'd need to have a camp for men to fill those boats."

"I didn't see any but, you're right, there should be ..."

As they approached the ridgeline the pair crouched lower and slowly moved over the brow before settling down below the skyline. It was still very dark, but the sound of hooves coming from the distance ahead had them quickly lying on the wet ground.

Below them was a small wharf, a guardhouse and scores of boats.

Firth estimated the vessels were about 20 feet long. Further out in the cove Firth could see the tall masts of transport ships. Lamplight shone on to parts of the ground around the hut but, after watching the structure for several minutes, neither Firth nor Wren could detect any movement in the area. Then, through the now sheeting rain, Firth could see four riders trotting from over the brow of a distant hill and down the road towards them.

Pushing himself down as far as he could he took a deep breath as the men rode by. Their horses' hooves kicked up great dollops of watery mud and rain flowed from their oilskin-covered bicornes and down tightly wrapped cloaks. Waiting until the sound of the animals receded behind Firth looked over to Wren who instantly nodded and whispered: "Let's move to that next hill."

Again keeping low the pair made their way to the hill where they dropped to the ground and wriggled over the ridgeline. What they saw made Firth look at his friend and nod as if to say he was beginning to agree with him about questioning the Spanish intentions.

Below them spread an expanse of large tents in neat rows. Firth estimated the size of the camp was similar to that of General Wellesley's before the battle of Rolica.

"There must be room for 10,000 men," Firth whispered. "And look, they've got guns."

Wren followed the direction of Firth's gaze and silently agreed. There were at least a dozen cannon in the force.

"We'd better get back Joshua," Wren whispered.

"Right, but I want to look at some of those longboats as we head back."

"Time's running out Joshua."

"I know, but I'd still like to check one out."

While keeping their eyes and ears open for more horsemen, Firth and Wren skirted the guardhouse where they could see one figure sitting in a chair by a slit brazier. From a distance the guard appeared to be sleeping. The pair eased their way over small sand dunes and, after checking it was safe, went down to the water's edge.

The closest boats had been dragged above the high-tide mark and were covered in canvas sheets. Most were flat-topped, but there were enough of them with raised areas to make Firth curious. As quickly as he could with cold hands he untied a thick rope holding the cover down and pulled it back. Sitting on the bow of the longboat was a small cannon and underneath it were at least a dozen roundshot to fit it.

"It's a grasshopper gun. They're using these as gunboats!"

"Just perfect for landing troops, Joshua. They could fit 20 men in each of them."

Replacing the canvas Joshua's mind was racing as he turned to Wren.

"Okay, I've seen enough ... it does look suspicious," he admitted. "Let's get back. We'd better let Allison know."

"I'll tell him. You'd better get back to Minas' headquarters, they'll be expecting to see you this morning."

Looking at Firth's wet and muddy outfit he added: "And I hope you have spare uniform."

Firth smiled and self-consciously rubbed his hands over his greatcoat. "Luckily this wore the worst of the rain, but I do have a second uniform in my trunk in the rooms." The pair walked as quickly as they could back to the town.

"We need to keep our eyes open and wits about us Joshua. There is something definitely not right about this place. Let's meet at noon ... best in the market."

Firth nodded.

"And, Joshua, be very careful ... there will be eyes watching you."

"I will Chris. Hell it's cold, I hope the fire is still going in my rooms."

"Lucky dog, I've got a damp ship to try to sleep in."

It was still dark when Firth reached the street under his balcony and made his way back up the drainpipe and into his room. Taking off his saturated greatcoat he hung it between two chairs by the fireplace and threw two logs on to the embers. His red jacket, shirt and breeches went on to wooden hangars. Pouring himself a port from a decanter he sipped the sweet drink before arranging his spare uniform on the table. Looking at his boots he knew he should clean them but, after a very long night, couldn't be bothered and sank on to the bed seeking sleep.

XXXVIII

Minas' Headquarters
August 26, 1808

As soon as he awoke Firth immediately knew it was several hours too soon. His head was thick and buzzing, but his mind jumped to what he and Wren had seen the previous night. His clothes were everywhere and he recognised the need to pack away his uniform from potentially prying eyes. Thank God no one had woken him, as he didn't want the state of his clothing to be reported back to senior officers.

Looking at his pocket watch he could not believe it was 10am. Cursing himself for his tardiness, Firth hurriedly washed with water from a jug, dried himself and changed into the shirt, breeches and red jacket he had placed over the table. Looking in a mirror he thought he was presentable enough, but he shook his head at the state of his boots. Mud reached almost up to the top of the usually shining footwear and it took five minutes of washing to make them semi-presentable. First thing was first, he thought, and left the room to seek out Major Bland.

A guard at the top of the stairs saluted and handed him an envelope. Firth opened it and read the note on the parchment.

It was from Major Bland and he requested Firth join him in his office for breakfast. The young officer looked at the soldier and nodded. "Si."

The Spaniard beckoned for him to follow and took Firth down the stairs, across the foyer and into an ante-room. He spoke quickly to the officer sitting behind the polished wooden desk who rose, nodded to Firth, and tapped on double doors on the wall next to him.

A voice answered, the officer went in and spoke and then re-emerged.

"Captain Firth, Major Bland is waiting for you. Please go through."

Firth thanked him and entered Bland's office.

The tall Irish Major smiled at him and proffered his hand. Firth shook it and said:

"Good morning, Major."

"Good morning Captain, please sit down. I hope you are hungry."

"I am, sir, thank you."

"Have you eaten much Spanish food?"

"No sir, last night was my first real taste and it was delicious. After my time in Portugal I quite like their omelettes and spicy sausage."

Bland laughed. "Ah, yes, but things are different here in the morning. The Spaniards like smaller breakfasts before having a lunch that would feed a family back home for the entire week."

A servant knocked on the door and Bland fired some rapid Spanish at him.

"Coffee?" he asked Firth.

"Yes, please."

"I would recommend the churros. They are lightly fried dough topped with honey. Sweet and delicious, they take the edge off my servant's coffee. Try as I might I just cannot even begin to have him get it right."

Firth looked at the churros and thought he wouldn't need a second invitation to try them. They were indeed delightful.

"I hope the food is to your taste?"

"It certainly is, sir," he said, biting into the delicious morsels.

"Now Captain Firth, I regret to inform you that General Minas has been unable to look at General Wellesley's letter as yet, he is in the middle of training manouevres and is currently outlining his plans to senior officers. He assures me he will get to it as soon as is practicable.

"In the meantime, he wishes me to convey that you are welcome to stay in the headquarters for as long as you like."

"Thank you, Major Bland, for letting me know. I will await General Minas' response whenever he chooses to give it. It gives me time to explore the town's market again."

Later Firth stood, gave a shallow nod to the Irishman, and said: "And thank you for breakfast, it was very tasty."

Walking towards the door Firth heard Bland's chair scrape back.

"Oh, Captain Firth," Bland called, walking over to the English officer. "Do you need someone to look after your uniform?"

Turning, Firth shook his head. "No thank you Major I'll have it seen to back at the ship."

"Oh, it's just I noticed your boots and they look as if they need a bit of attention."

Firth's heart skipped a beat as he looked at Bland and hoped his face didn't betray the shock he felt. Think fast Joshua, think fast, he told himself.

"You are so right major, I'm rather ashamed of them this morning. I made the mistake of leaving them out on the balcony last night and it seems that during the storm mud from the planter boxes splashed out on to them. I did a bit of a cleanup this morning but, it seems, not a very good one."

Bland's eyes narrowed and then he smiled. "Those sudden rains catch me out too, Captain Firth. I hope you enjoy your time at the market, it certainly is the safer part of town."

Firth instantly wondered if that was a warning from the Irishman.

"A word of advice Captain Firth. In this town," Bland continued, "there are many eyes. Very little that goes on is not seen and noted."

Firth smiled. "I appreciate that Major Bland and, again, thank you for your company at breakfast."

The Major bowed and Firth left the headquarters with his mind racing to work out if Bland knew of last night's journey to the guarded harbour?

XXXIX

Town Market

The clamour and smell of the market at midday was far more exciting than Firth had ever experienced back home in Yorkshire and he wondered how Wren could ignore the noise while working on his drawings. He had caught up with the Marines officer in the food-stall sector finding him seated at a table with sketchpad and pencil in hand.

A small cup of black coffee sat in front of him, as did a small penknife and a pile of shavings.

"Morning Captain Wren."

"Ah, good morning Captain Firth. How have you recovered?"

"Pretty well thanks Chris, courtesy of some very tasty churros with Major Bland."

"How is the good Major?"

"He looked well. He's very pleasant. But he may know what we did last night."

The pencil in Wren's hand stopped its movements. "What did he say?"

"He didn't say anything, just suggested I be careful as the town has eyes. Damn it, it was my boots. I couldn't clean them well enough and he noticed them. I thought I had put him off the track but ... now I'm not sure."

Wren looked at the younger man.

"Don't worry, Joshua, if he didn't confine you on the spot he probably doesn't know much. You know how these Irish officers are in Spain. They don't like us, but they don't get respected by the Dons and so they tend to keep to themselves and their own counsel."

Wren waved a coffee seller over. "One more please," he said in what he thought was a Spanish-sounding English. "Joshua?"

Firth nodded.

The man poured out two cups from a silver container he had around his shoulder.

Wren slipped him some small coins and sat back in his seat.

"All right," Firth agreed, "but we do need to be careful until we find out exactly what's going on."

"So," said Wren, "When do we head back to the other inlet?"

The question came as Firth began to sip his thick black coffee and he almost spat it out in surprise at the question. "What?"

"Just kidding ... don't take on so."

"You're not funny Chris, I almost drowned in coffee ..."

"You mean you almost drowned me in coffee."

The pair laughed, but quietened down when they received dark looks from nearby Spaniards.

"What are you sketching?"

"Well, amid the spots of coffee," he began with a smile, "I have rather taken the fancy of a little church down that street a bit and then down a few alleyways. It's Santa Maria - St Mary's, if you like - and it is quite lovely."

"You don't want the cathedral then," Firth turned and looked at the grand building near the waterfront.

"No, too big and too ... well ... Catholic for my taste. It's all chanting and incense waving. The stonework is very good, but it just seems to lack a bit of spirit. You should go and check out St Mary's it is much more intimate and quite dark. Good for the soul."

"Ah my English friends," came a loud voice. "How are you today?"

Firth looked up and there was the one-armed stallkeeper they met the previous day.

"Hector," said Firth, "Buenos dias, senor."

"I am full of the health, gracias. I was able to put a lot of food in the cupboards because of your generosity sir," he said to Wren.

"They were very fine pieces, Hector, you have a true talent."

"Gracias senor. I'm slower than I used to be, but craftier no?" he laughed. "It is a beautiful day senors, just perfect for shopping and being in the market."

"What else can we see, Hector?" asked Wren.

"Down that way there is a swordsmith, but his work is not of the best quality. For your wives and sweethearts there are linen and embroidery stalls. Some very fine lace work."

"Umm, no thanks," said Firth, "We wouldn't know what to buy?"

"That is a shame, senor, because I am sure I saw your lady of the green eyes there a little earlier."

"What?" said Firth, a little too loudly drawing eyes to their table. "Are you sure Hector? The Englishwoman?"

"She did not speak, senor, and she had a shawl wrapped mostly over her face but I recognised her eyes. She had two soldiers with her. They seemed to be guarding her, but she did not seem to be a prisoner."

"When was this Hector? Hurry now," Firth urged.

"Not quarter past the hour ago," the Spaniard said. "Down that street. She was wearing a dark-green cloak and it had a hood."

Firth began to stand when Wren reached across and pulled him down again.

"Wait up, Joshua. Let's think about this. If this is Constance Dalrymple why is she here? Why is she not at Minas' headquarters?"

"She's alive Chris, we have to get her."

"Slow down my friend. There must be a reason for Minas to want to keep her away from British officers. That means she will be being watched and we don't want to tip our hand without knowing what we are up against."

"I can't just sit here Chris, if nothing else I want her to know that I'm around."

"And how are you going to manage that Joshua?"

"I don't know," Firth said as he stood, "But I'll think of something."

"It's against my better judgment, but I'll come with you ..."

"No Chris, you go back to the Dragon and let Allison know what we've found out. We may need to leave here with, or without, a message from General Minas. I'm sure Hector can show me the way to the linen market."

The Spaniard nodded his assent and Wren sighed.

"All right, I'll wait here a few minutes before going back to the ship. Just keep your wits about you Joshua. This place seems friendly enough, for now, but there are one hell of a lot of Minas' troops around here. Not to mention all those warships. I'd not like to have to force our way out."

"I have an idea for that, Chris, I'll explain when I get back to the Dragon."

Firth left his friend and followed Hector as he eased his way through the packed crowd. He knew he stood out in his uniform but, as he was a good head taller than most of the shoppers, Firth figured that didn't matter much anyway. And the shadows of the alley ahead would help him be less obvious. Thinking it an idea to look as if he was actually shopping, Firth stopped to buy some apples and he momentarily lost the former sailor. Hector quickly doubled back to find him.

"Senor Captain, the linen market is down the end of this alley. Let me see if I can find what you seek."

Hector disappeared in the crowd and Firth pulled out one of the apples he was carrying in his bicorne and bit into it, enjoying the crispness and taste.

He was down to the core when the Spaniard appeared hurriedly. "She's coming senor. She still has two soldiers with her."

"Is she carrying anything?"

"Senor?," Hector queried.

"Does she have any packages of bags?"

"Yes she does senor, why?"

"Never mind, Hector, you'll soon see."

Firth stepped as close to the wall of the alley as he could and waited to see the Englishwoman. He hoped against hope he was right and this was Constance.

At the alley entrance he saw two uniformed men enter followed by a tall figure in a green cloak and hood. He couldn't see the face until she turned slightly revealing luminescent green eyes.

"My God it's her," Firth whispered, his heart now pounding.

He knew his plan was risky, but it could work.

Firth waited for the soldiers to pass him then he walked straight to Constance and bumped into her side.

She yelled in shock and indignation as her parcels and Firth's apples fell to the ground. Then Constance looked at his uniform, then his face, and a flicker of recognition crossed her features.

"Watch what you are doing, sir!"

"I'm terribly sorry, my lady. May I help with your packages."

"No I can do it myself," Constance said in an irritated tone. "It's all right," she said to the soldiers who appeared at Firth's shoulders. "It was an accident. I can manage."

Constance bent down to get her items and Firth did the same to get his fruit. Their heads were very close and he noted she smelled of roses.

"St Mary's, 8.30pm," Constance whispered.

"I am so terribly sorry, my lady, it was dreadfully careless of me," he said loudly and gave a barely perceptible tilt of his head.

Taking her hand he helped her up and handed over one of her packages.

"Captain Joshua Firth, my lady, 29th Foot."

Constance didn't get a chance to acknowledge the introduction as Minas' soldiers moved between the pair and moved the Englishwoman on.

As Firth watched her go he could still smell the slight trace of roses.

"Senor, senor," Hector said urgently.

"Do you think they noticed anything," Firth queried.

"It looked to me like a clumsy young Englishman, senor," the Spaniard grinned.

"Hector I cannot follow her now, that would be too obvious."

"I would be happy to Senor Captain. I will see where she goes and will find you later."

"Gracias, Hector."

XXXX

The Dragon

Firth, Wren and the naval officers were crowded around the desk in Allison's cabin. They were looking at a hand-drawn chart of the inlet into which they had sailed to get to Minas' town.

Letter Xs marked Spanish ships at anchor and circles showed where gun batteries were positioned along the edge of the water and on the opposite heights.

"My ... the Dons have placed those guns very well," Allison said grudgingly. "Any ship trying to get out of here against Minas' wishes will have a rum old time of it, there's no doubting that."

His lieutenants agreed with assessment, not relishing the idea of being such a target.

"Still, Captain, there would be ways to deal with that would there not?" asked Firth.

"It would depend upon the tide and wind, Mr Firth, as you would know. Other than that a spell that would make us invisible perhaps?"

The officers all laughed.

"At night then," Firth suggested. "What time will the tide be with us?"

"My guessing is about midnight, Captain Firth. There is a strong tidal current that would reduce the necessity of a good wind to take us out."

"Meaning we could do so without sail and with little noise?"

"Should we be needing to sneak away, sir, then I believe we could it without sail. But why the plan?"

Firth shifted uncomfortably. "I don't know why Captain, but things are not as they seem here. We have several damaged Spanish ships in the harbour and we know the Swallow was sunk. We know Constance Dalrymple was aboard the Swallow and I've seen her in this town."

Allison looked surprised.

"I saw her just today," Firth said.

He continued: "That large transport ship they keep taking the boats to is sitting very heavily in the water ... so she's loaded with something. In a harbour, just a few miles from here, we have hundreds of longboats - some with bow cannon - transport ships and an army in training for goodness knows what."

"But Captain Firth," Allison interjected, "They are at war with the French, not us."

"That is true, Captain, but why then have we been kept at arms length. Surely they would want to impress us with their training if they were our friends?"

Firth continued: "And then there is the matter of Miss Dalrymple. Why have we not been told of her, or been allowed to meet her? If she'd been rescued then wouldn't they be celebrating that with us?"

"What do you think Captain Wren?" Allison asked.

"Joshua is on to something. The situation is not right here. Something is building. I think we need to be ready to move quickly if needs be."

Wren frowned. "The problem is we don't want the Dragon stuck here on the docks. She needs to be at sea, Captain Allison, so she won't be bottled up."

Allison and his officers nodded.

Firth spoke up again. "It is only a few miles across land to the sea from here and there are a number of good beaches where someone can be picked up by longboat."

"What are you suggesting Mr Firth?" Allison asked.

"I'm meeting with Miss Dalrymple tonight at St Mary's church. She asked for the meeting. I believe she knows something about what Minas and his men are up to."

"But she is a woman," Allison said, "And she has been in London for months ..."

"But her father was Governor of Gibraltar, Captain. She speaks Spanish and she has been here in Minas' headquarters. If anyone knows what could be happening it will be her."

The officers fell silent thinking on Firth's comments.

Firth broke the moment. "If she is being held against her will here then we need to help her. I will wait with her and, if needs be, I will carry her to the ocean beach to await your arrival."

Allison responded. "That is very brave and commendable Captain Firth, but we have yet to know for certain that the Spanish here are anything other than our allies. I suggest you meet with Miss Dalrymple and then gauge the situation. In the meantime, we will invite the Spanish to a party on board the Dragon tomorrow night."

"Tomorrow?" asked Firth.

"If they think we are still going to be here tomorrow night, Captain Firth, they may not look so closely at us this evening," said Allison. "Gentlemen, I believe we need to cover our options and be prepared to sail tonight."

Looking at the young officer he said: "Joshua, I am of the mind that you and Captain Wren are correct in your assessment of the Spanish. You must meet Miss Dalrymple, talk with her and see if she is in danger. But you must not do anything at the church. Chances are she will be being watched."

Firth nodded. "I believe I will know where she is staying by then Captain and, if needs be, can wait until she has returned there before acting."

Allison continued: "If she is imperiled you must protect her. However, if she is only here as a guest then you must let us know before 11.30pm - for we will have little choice but to sail by midnight. Understand?"

Firth nodded.

"If you do not come back by that time we will know that something is awry and we will slip our cable and run out on the tide."

Allison smiled kindly.

"If we are gone when you return you must try to reach the Atlantic coast. We will have to sail away for a time to avoid those vessels coming after us but, rest assured, we will return for you. Make sure you have a tinderbox and flint. If we see three fires in a row we shall come inshore and send a longboat for you. Be assured Joshua, we will not abandon you."

Wren looked at his friend. "Joshua, such a course means you will almost certainly be in danger. When you go, take your weapons."

"I can hardly waltz into a church with my sword, Chris."

"Yes you can, and your pistols too. It never hurts to be prepared ... as one of the 'Ever-Sworded 29th' would know."

Firth smiled at the jest.

Allison folded the map over and looked at the officers. "Well, we know what we must do. Let's get an early dinner and ready ourselves for whatever is to come. May the Lord watch over us."

"Amen," came the collective response.

Santa Maria Church

The evening was balmy, but Firth wore his grey greatcoat as he walked towards Santa Maria's church. Not only did it hide his red jacket, but also the pistols he kept within its pockets and the sword on his belt.

His heart was racing at the potential danger of the upcoming meeting and - if he admitted it - at the thought of seeing Constance again.

The twilight had turned the stucco white walls of the church into a cold grey, but the warmth of candlelight coming from its doors and windows was welcoming.

Firth paused at the corner of a nearby building and watched for any unwanted sets of eyes and, seeing none, he steadily walked up the small flight of steps into the holy place.

Inside he quickly saw there were about a dozen people sitting in pews, but there was no sign of a green cloak.

Moving to the right of the entrance he stood in shadow beside a tall column.

Firth stood there quietly for five minutes as worshippers arrived for the evening service. Constance was not among them.

The smell of incense tickled his throat unpleasantly and he wished he had water to wash it away. He knew it was now past 8.30pm and there was no sign of the Englishwoman.

Firth shuffled his weight from foot to foot in a bid to keep pins and needles from settling in either limb.

"Captain," a voice came from behind him, "Stop moving so or you may draw attention to yourself."

It was a soft English voice accompanied by the scent of roses and he resisted the urge to turn.

"Lady Constance?" he whispered.

"I am here."

"Are you well?"

"I am for the moment, thank you Captain Firth."

"I am so sorry for bumping into you my lady, but I did not know how else to attract your attention without doing so."

Firth could hear a slight laugh.

"You seem to enjoy bumping into me sir. I believe that was the second time."

He blushed and was glad he was facing away from her. "I regret that ... please take no offence."

"Captain, I have never been so happy to have been bumped into by a handsome officer."

Firth's blush deepened. "My lady ..."

An awkward silence followed as Firth regathered his thoughts.

"Lady Constance, what is happening?"

"To put it simply, Captain Firth, you are in the Devil's Den. Minas is no friend of Britain. He attacked and sank the vessel taking me to Gibraltar."

"He what?" a shocked Firth responded, barely able to resist turning. "Why?"

"He knows I am well known in the fortress and that I am familiar with its defences. He wants to make use of that."

"But why, my lady?"

"He aims to take advantage of France invading Portugal to right what he sees as wrongs," she paused. "He means to take Gibraltar back from us."

Firth was stunned. Such a move would be disastrous for Britain's naval control of the Mediterranean Sea. It would seal off any British forces in the region and cut contact with Egypt.

"How do you know this?"

"I've heard he and his senior officers boasting of the plan. They did not think I speak Spanish and so have arrogantly talked when I have been nearby."

"So that is what the longboats are for, to land on the beaches at Gibraltar. But they would first need to destroy our Navy there."

"He has it all planned. And he has supporters within the garrison."

"Traitors?"

"Treacherous Irishmen. There was a plot only a few years ago that was foiled, and now it seems they are trying again. My father suspected it, but could never gather enough evidence to arrest the ringleaders."

"My lady ..."

"Please Captain Firth ... Joshua ... call me Constance."

"Constance ... you must come with me to the ship. We must leave this place."

"If I leave with you now they will seize your ship, or sink it as we leave."

"We have a way, Constance, everything is ready."

"I'll not come with you. I have given my word and that is why I am allowed a little freedom. Everything has to seem as normal. If your ship is trapped here then we have no way of preventing an attack upon Gibraltar."

"Now I must leave, Joshua, as must you."

Firth turned and looked at her face. "Constance I will come for you tonight at 11pm. We are inviting the Spanish on to the ship tomorrow evening for an event, but that is just to throw the Spanish off. We mean to sail tonight."

He could see the indecision in the Englishwoman's lovely eyes. "Parole given to a man such as Minas is not binding Constance. If we leave you will be in even more danger than you are now. I cannot do that. I will also stay."

Constance looked as if she was about to say something else, but stopped and then relented.

"I'll be ready. I'm in an ochre-coloured building to the east of the market. It has a blue door and window surrounds."

"I have had someone following you so I will find you. Until 11pm, my lady."

She looked at him and smiled. His heart leapt. Then she rose on tiptoes and her lips brushed his cheek. "Thank you Joshua."

He blushed and stammered "There's no need to thank ..."

But she was gone, walking out of the church and into danger.

Firth stood still, forcing himself to remain where he was. It would be ill advised to leave so soon after Constance, just in case someone was following her.

His mind went over the plan again. It all came down to the Dragon leaving the port.

Without the ship everything else would come to nought.

If necessary he would have to stay behind and take Constance to the coast. There were plenty of small dinghies on the water's edge and years of practice going out to his father's vessels had made him a good oarsman. Failing that there would be no moon, but he could take a bearing on the stars and all he needed was a westerly course to walk to the Atlantic.

Firth felt for the tinderbox into the top of his boots. It was there. I mustn't lose that, he told himself, signal fires don't start themselves.

It had been five minutes since Constance had departed the church and Firth felt confident prying eyes would have also disappeared.

He made his way to the entry and paused. There was still some warmth outside and he loved the warm evenings of the Peninsula, far better than those of Yorkshire when the temperatures dropped quickly after sunset - even in summer. The steps clattered under his boots and he was about to reach the cobbles of the square when a voice sounded.

"Good evening, Captain Firth.

Firth stopped still and turned towards the familiar voice. Walking towards him was Major Bland, his face wore a smile, but his hard eyes did not.

"Ah, Major Bland, how are you this evening, sir?"

"I am well, thank you Captain. I see you are a religious man."

"Well, not really Major. I'm more of a type to pop in and see what's going on. It's a lovely church."

"It certainly is Captain. A lot of leading citizens regularly take Mass here. Are you Catholic?"

"No, Major, I come from a long line of Church of England folk. Although we do have many Catholics on my father's estates and in his business ventures."

Bland smiled, but Firth saw it was cool.

"Sometimes, Captain Firth, when we search out what's going on, we land ourselves in areas we shouldn't."

"That is true," the younger man responded, "but, by doing so, we learn from our mistakes."

Bland's smile warmed a little.

"True, very true. What are your plans for this evening, Joshua? I have a very fine bottle of muscat that really needs two to finish."

Firth laughed. "Would that I could Major. But I believe we are having a party on board the Dragon tomorrow for our gallant Spanish allies. I fear I have been given the task of organising seating ... on a man of war ... at night."

It was Bland's turn for humour. "I'll not swap assignments with you ... my job is just to get General Minas there in a good mood. Then again ... can we trade places?"

The Englishman laughed and shook his head. "I do not think your General would approve. He does not seem to like my countrymen."

"Ah, you picked up on his subtlety then, Captain Firth," Bland smiled. "Enjoy your evening, sir."

"And you yours, Major Bland. Thank you for your, how may I put it, understanding."

Bland's teeth showed in a bright smile. "It is a pleasure, Captain Firth."

XXXXII

The Dragon

The walk back to the Dragon seemed an eternity for Firth. The light was dropping, but he felt as if there were dozens of eyes upon his back. He was sure Bland had cottoned on to the fact he had met with Constance, as his sudden appearance could mean little else.

What would come of that? He kept running the question through his mind as he made his way to the docks.

The ship was a lively sight as seamen were hanging the red and yellow colours of Spain to the rope lines, while others were making plenty of noise playing music and dancing while swigging rum from big containers.

The tunes were a tortured form of Spanish songs as the crew followed orders to practice melodies that would make their hosts feel welcome.

In a pile of sails on the seaward side of the vessel a sailor played a pennywhistle to which his colleagues sang a subdued version of *Heart of Oak*.

"Come, cheer up, my lads, 'tis to glory we steer,
To add something new to this wonderful year;
'Tis to honour we call, you as freemen not slaves,
For who are so free as the sons of the waves?
Heart of oak are our ships, jolly tars are our men,
We always are ready; steady, boys, steady!
We'll fight and we'll conquer again ... and again.
We ne'er see our foes, but we wish them to stay,
They always see us and they wish us away;
If they run, we will follow we will drive them ashore,
For if they won't fight we can do no more.
Heart of oak are our ships, jolly tars are our men,
We always are ready; steady, boys, steady!
We'll fight and we'll conquer again ... and again."

Captain Allison came out of the cabin and sternly ordered "quiet lads, no more of that. There'll be a lot of the local Dons who fought off the coast at Trafalgar and they'll not take kindly to that song."

A voice called out "How about *Spanish Ladies* then Captain?"

The ship erupted in laughter.

"No, Jenkins, that would be even worse."

Again more hilarity broke out as the sailor called Jenkins received heavy slaps of congratulations on his back.

Firth walked to the Captain and Allison's eyes narrowed.

"Anything to report, Mr Firth?"

"Yes, Captain, and I need to do so immediately."

"Right, I'll summon the officers. We'll go straight to my cabin."

When the men arrived Firth decided there was no point honey-coating his news and so came right out with it.

"Gentlemen, the Spanish are planning to attack Gibraltar."

Firth could hear the air being sucked out of lungs and there was silence.

"You are joking," the ship's Second Lieutenant exclaimed. "Why would they do that?"

"They see it as their territory."

Wren broke in. "How do they expect to do it Joshua? And when?"

"It's imminent. In the next few days, I'm thinking."

Firth turned to Allison. "Captain, how would you attack Gibraltar?"

The older man shifted his feet.

"To take the fortress you would need to besiege it. Cut off supplies with a naval blockade and starve it out. But that would take months and we'd send a fleet in to clear them away so I don't think that's what Minas is planning.

"The Spaniards would have to hit everywhere at once. That means land forces applying pressure from the north. They will never be able to overwhelm us there, but it would mean men being diverted from the seawall and harbour areas."

Wren chipped in. "And that would mean fewer soldiers holding off the troops arriving by those rowboats."

"Even so, getting past our anchored ships would be impossible for that flotilla. They'd be blown out of the water," Allison responded.

"Unless, sir," Firth said, "Our Navy wasn't there. What if it was called away?"

"They'd never leave Gibraltar without a covering fleet, Mr Firth, it would weaken the defences too much."

"Of course, sir, I was ... oh my God ..."

"Mr Firth?"

"What if they destroyed our fleet at anchor?"

All eyes turned to Firth. "Captain Allison, what if they sank our ships there? What if they sent in fireships against us?"

"They've tried it before Mr Firth in 1780," Allison explained. "We spotted the vessels, the Saint Fermin hooked them and towed them away. They got nowhere near the rest of the fleet. It's highly unlikely they'll try again, Mr Firth, they'd need ..."

Firth pointed out the wardroom window towards the man of war sitting low in the waters of the harbour.

"Unless they had a ship loaded with powder and set it off in the midst of our ships, sir."

Every officer in the room let out a low profanity.

Captain Allison looked stunned. His mind raced as he sought to weigh up Firth's suggestion. "It's outrageous, but possible," he said.

Firth spoke again. "And after our ships are destroyed they can just row straight in and land their forces."

"I think Joshua has a point, Captain," Wren said. "It is a devilish plan, but one that could gain the Dons Gibraltar."

Allison nodded. "I fear you may be right."

Looking squarely at his officers he said: "Gentlemen, our schedule is tight. I want all crew in quarters within one hour. Lights out within two hours. That gives us an hour to present any prying eyes with a ship quartered down for the night.

"And half an hour after that to ready ourselves for the ebb tide. At midnight we will cut the anchor rope and, hopefully, be out from under the guns before the Spanish know what is what."

"Captain, I must get Constance. I've promised her I'd reach her by 11pm."

"I am reluctant about that, Captain Firth, the likelihood is you'll both be taken."

"It is a risk, sir, but it is one I must take. I cannot sail away leaving her in the hands of Minas."

Allison looked at Firth with a heavy heart. "Very well, Captain Firth, but remember the plan. If you reach the coast, three fires and we will come for you. But we can only wait until mid-morning, after that the Dons will have sent their warships after us and we cannot risk being caught by them. We must warn Gibraltar."

"I understand Captain Allison. We will be there."

The house in which Constance Dalrymple said she was staying was quiet.

There was little inside movement that Firth had observed and there had been no arrivals at its blue door. Lantern light flickered in several rooms on both levels and the lack of ground-floor curtains made it easy for him to see the room directly across from where he stood was empty.

It was clear that despite the late hour people were still up and about inside and that had taken Firth a little by surprise.

He turned to Hector and whispered: "Why are they still up?"

"Families often stay up eating and drinking late, Senor Firth," the Spaniard replied.

Firth whispered a swear word. He was getting nervous and patted his right coat pocket to feel the outline of a pistol.

The pair was standing in shadows, made blacker by the lack of any moonlight.

"Senor Firth, there has been no one visiting the house since 10pm. No one in, no one out."

"Have you any idea about where she may be in the house, Hector?"

"I think she may be in the upstairs room by that balcony, senor."

Firth turned to the small man next to him and offered his hand. "Thank you for all your help, Hector, but this I must do alone."

A protest began, but Firth shook his head. "It is too dangerous for you to be seen with me any more, Hector. God knows what will happen here in the next few minutes and so I want you to go."

There was hurt in the Spaniard's eyes, but he nodded.

"Go with God, Senor Firth," he said, then he turned and, within seconds, had disappeared down an alleyway.

Firth felt a pang of uncertainty at being alone, but knew he had made the right decision. He didn't want the friendly Spaniard to endanger himself any more than he had already done.

He turned his eyes back to the house. It was time to move.

Briskly crossing the street he walked to the window of the lit room and looked inside. It was empty. Firth then moved to the front door and put his hand on the latch. His thumb released the catch and he gently pushed the door ajar, hoping the hinges were well oiled. There was no noise and he eased himself into the darkened hall. His heart was racing and he pulled the pistols from his pocket, cocking them as quietly as he could.

There were tiled steps at the side of the hall and Firth took his time climbing them. Easy does it, he told himself, take your time.

Firth stopped when he could see the second floor hallway. Pressing his back against the wall he held the pistols out straight while scanning the area. Is no one here, he asked himself?

The doors to the rooms on his left were closed but, as there was no light coming from them, he risked not checking them. He had to find Constance and get out of the place. A floorboard creaked underfoot and he stopped instantly. Picking his foot up slowly he eased towards the front room.

Firth was sure anyone in the room would be able to hear him breathe and so he held his breath as he approached the doorway. Pistols again at the ready he sidestepped into the lit doorway and gasped at what he saw.

In the middle of the room, tied to a chair, was Constance. Her green eyes were wide open in surprise and she was shaking her head from side to side. Firth launched himself into the room and swung his weapons to the area behind the door. Nobody was there. Putting one of the guns into his coat he used one hand to untie the gag around Constance's face.

"It's all right Constance, I'll get you out of here," he whispered.

Firth's efforts were not helped by Constance continually moving her head and trying to speak. Frustrated with the gag Firth placed his weapon on the floor and took out a small knife from his coat.

"Please stop moving."

He slid the blade carefully between the material and her neck and gave it a sudden pull, cutting it cleanly and removing it from her mouth.

"Oh, Joshua, you shouldn't have come. It's a trap. They've been waiting for you."

"Quiet now, Constance," Firth said as began cutting the ropes binding her hands. "I couldn't leave you. My father would not be best pleased if I left a beautiful damsel in distress."

She laughed and gave him a pained smile.

"They've had me tied here since I returned from the church. There was a group of soldiers and officers, including Major Bland. They knew you'd be coming for me."

"Bland will answer for this," Firth said.

"No, Joshua, he was a gentleman and apologised for having to do it. He was under orders from Minas. He made sure I was not in discomfort."

As soon as her hands were free Constance began rubbing her wrists to get the circulation working again. Standing, she looked at Firth and grabbed him by the face and kissed him full on the lips. "You are my knight in shining armour."

"Well, while this knight wants to be thanked like that again. He also thinks it is time we get out of here."

Handing her the pistol from the floor, Firth took out the other with his left hand and unsheathed his sword.

"I'll go first and let's hope they've fallen asleep."

The pair moved down the stairs and stopped at the front door. There was a solitary figure standing in the street.

"Good evening, Captain Firth, or is it morning now?"

"Major Bland! You are a brave man coming here to stop me by yourself," Firth challenged.

"Well, I am brave enough ... but I'm not alone," the Irish Major said with amusement in his voice. "I have 10 men here with me and they are more than enough. Even to deal with you, Captain Firth."

Bland moved closer. "But to resist will be to endanger Miss Constance and I don't think you would do that, would you sir?"

Firth drew her to him. "No, you are correct Major. I'll not fight you. We will place our pistols on the ground."

"And your sword, sir. We don't want any possibility of moments of madness, do we?"

Firth bridled, but Constance squeezed his arm.

"And my sword too, Major."

"You are a gentleman, Captain Firth, and if you promise not to try to escape as we go to General Minas' headquarters then I'll not put you in irons."

"Are we not returning to the Dragon, Major?"

Bland gave a short laugh. "Unfortunately, Captain, it seems your friends have flown the coop. The vessel slipped out of the harbour before we could stop her. So, in answer to your question, we will not be returning you to that ship."

Firth hid his relief that Allison and Wren had got away, but he knew his options were limited and so nodded. "I'll not try to escape on the walk to your headquarters, Major."

Bland looked at Constance and asked: "My lady, are you well?"

"Quite well, thank you Major. Although I'm not sure about the hospitality of this town."

"I regret, Miss Constance, that fate has turned out the way it has."

With that the Irishman snapped his fingers and from the dark soldiers appeared to pick up Firth's weapons and form a two-wide column behind the prisoners.

"Follow me please Miss Constance, Captain Firth."

The thick rope cable slid into the water with barely a noise. Almost instantly the Dragon began to move with the current away from the wharf.

A sailor climbed back over the side of the vessel and on to the deck, sheathing his large cutlass as he did so.

Everyone was still and silent on the deck, nerves tensed for an alarm cry that could send Spanish cannonballs hurtling their way within minutes.

Wren and Allison were at the wheel of the Dragon.

The Captain had the wheel himself and eyed the waters ahead intently. Wren looked around at the faces of the men on deck. They were all nervous. There were two watches ready to jump into action should the vessel be seen. One watch was to unfurl the sails to speed escape, while the other would clear away and man the readied guns for action.

Wren noted however that the hilltop batteries would have a huge advantage in firing down on to the Dragon, while its guns would be unable to elevate enough to hit back. The Marines officer wanted to say something to the commander but didn't, fearing it could jinx their efforts. He watched the older man skillfully use the current.

Earlier that day Allison had taken a stroll along the shoreline he was now navigating and had noted potential trouble spots.

There were no major ones within the harbour and the Captain's confidence rose. The problems would be the gun batteries.

The first one they would have to contend with was sitting across the water from where they lay at dock. If that fired on them they were immediately in trouble as the others would be alerted and the Dragon would have to sail the gauntlet of all five bastions.

In total the Spaniards had three gun posts on the heights overlooking the inner harbour, evenly spaced along its length to the channel out to the Atlantic Ocean. Covering the exit channel was a small fort and, on the far heights of the estuary, sat another battery.

Allison knew the most dangerous guns were in the fort. An alert from there would mean receiving fire from not only its stone ramparts, but also the guns atop the cliffs. His hands gripped the wheel tighter. He could feel the tensions rising and was glad God had been kind with no moon. He took time to look away from his course to scan his sailors and officers. He was proud of them all. No Captain could hope for a better crew. Here they were under strict orders of silence and he had not heard as so much as a whisper. Not even a footfall. Now they stood ready for action if the Fates called upon them to do so.

The Dragon was quickly under the guns of the second battery and nearing the line of sight of both the third emplacement and the fort. Allison could see a solitary brazier lighting the gunpost and took comfort in knowing they'd have one for each gun glowing brightly if they were ready for action.

He estimated the ship was floating along at about two to three knots and in the next 10 minutes he would need to take her out from hugging the land to a course that would allow for turning into the ocean channel.

During that manoeuvre he would unfurl the sails and head for the open sea. Allison knew that meant increasing the size of his silhouette, which could make being spotted much more likely. It would also present the Dragon's stern to the fort's guns. Those 24-pounder cannons could then rake the length of his ship or, possibly worse, destroy the rudder and cripple the vessel.

Best not to dwell on those things, Allison thought, just keep her steady and, above all, quiet.

The faces of the men around him were starting to show the strain and he hoped their discipline would see everyone through.

Checking his timepiece, Allison noted it was nearing 12.30am and he wondered how Firth was faring.

Brave lad that he acknowledged and Firth would need his courage for what he was trying to do.

Bloody Dons. He had no time for them. Clinging on to their pompous ways as if they were still a major empire. Worse than the French, he thought, at least the Frogs had good wine and food.

The roar of a cannon far behind him jolted him out of that train of thought.

"Quiet still lads," he hissed.

Another gun fired and then the bells of the church started clanging.

Allison stared up at the third battery. Still one brazier. On his port side there seemed to be no activity at the fort.

"Must be Joshua," Wren suggested.

"I think it more likely they've discovered we've slipped the noose, Captain. But we are not out of harm's way. Nearly," he said, "but not fully."

"Lieutenant Weaver," he called softly, "Run out the port guns. We may need to deal with that fort."

"Unfurl the sails."

The crew ran about the deck and up the ratlines in relative silence, but the cannons gave a deep rumble as they were pulled into position.

"Lights sir," a sailor pointed to the third gun emplacement. "And in the fort now."

Allison turned his gaze to the main danger. Lights were being lit inside the main building and at least one door to the battlements was open sending a beam of yellow light into the darkness.

Above there were four braziers now burning and Allison knew that they had little time before shots would start falling around them.

"Guns ready Captain," Weaver called.

"All right boys, let's get the first shots in," Allison shouted. "Fire!"

The ship lit up as flames belched from its gun ports. The Captain watched as chunks of masonry were blasted from the fort.

"Load and fire as fast as you can lads. And roll out the starboard guns."

The bark of guns above caused a moment's anxiety but the splashes were too far from the Dragon to worry about yet.

"Just ranging shots from above, lads, fire on that fort. Quickly as you can."

Barely 60 seconds after the first broadside the Dragon's guns sent forth more destruction. Allison noted with satisfaction that at least one enemy gun was knocked off its carriage, but they had plenty left.

Eyeing the channel to freedom he knew he had to begin his turn soon.

"One more round before we turn, boys. Starboard guns can you reach the battery?"

Lt Weaver responded: "No sir, guns won't elevate to that height."

Unsurprised, Allison shouted: "No mind, we'll be out of here soon."

Above the deck the Dragon's sails began to fill with the breeze coming off the land. A ragged series of shots rang out from the fort but all fell short sending up plumes of white water.

"Guns ready, sir," Weaver called.

"Fire again, Mr Weaver."

The Dragon rocked as the gun captains pulled the cords attached to the cannons gunlocks. They roared into action again.

Now the Spanish guns on the far side of the channel came into play and as the ship picked up speed it was surrounded by waterspouts from all three batteries.

Long after they were out of range the Spanish guns kept firing in the hope of a miracle.

"That's it lads, we're clear," Captain Allison called.

"Huzzah!" came a ringing chorus from around the ship. "Huzzah!"

Wren offered his hand to Allison who shook it warmly.

His cabin boy appeared at his side with a small tray with two cups on it. Wren was offered the other. The coffee was hot and laced with rum. Both men raised their cups in a wordless toast.

Smiling, Wren said "Well let's hope we were right about Minas being an enemy, otherwise we are going to be shot for declaring war on an ally."

Allison laughed out loud. "I'll blame you, Captain Wren, and Captain Firth as well. Let's hope we find him on the coast in a few hours time so I can do so."

Wren smiled. His friend would find a way to get himself and Constance safely away. Of that he was sure.

Allison tapped a seaman on the shoulder and indicated that he should take the wheel. The Captain then walked to the port rail and reached up. With a dagger he cut the lanyards holding the Spanish flag to some rigging and crumpled it up. Carrying it to the taffrail at the Dragon's stern he leaned over and threw the emblem into the white wake of the ship. Allison watched as the flag floated, refusing to sink. His thoughts turned to what the coming day would bring. Possibly death. Possibly glory. Definitely it would be action filled.

Minas HQ

As the couple walked along towards Minas' headquarters Constance pressed herself against Firth. The young officer felt slightly uncomfortable, but cautiously put his arm around her.

"It will be all right Constance. They'll not harm you."

She looked up at him and asked: "But what about you Joshua. Will they treat you well?"

Firth was pretty sure of that answer, but decided to lie.

"I'll be treated well, my lady."

Major Bland had nothing to say to the pair as they approached the headquarters, he seemed lost in his own thoughts.

Firth felt a little sorry for the Major, who he thought was a decent man caught up in something he could not control.

That didn't stop him looking for every possibility of getting out of the situation though. He'd given his word not to escape - on the way to the barracks - but that didn't preclude him from plotting a later one.

Near the church he got a smell of the sea and hoped the Dragon had made its way unnoticed out of the harbour. It was vital the ship got its warning to Gibraltar. If that meant his death and - he dared not contemplate it - Constance's, then that was a price that had to be paid.

He stole a look at the woman next to him. She was truly beautiful and he could think of nothing other than protecting her. Drawing her closer he whispered: "I will be here for you."

She acknowledged the sentiment with a slight bow.

'Thank you Joshua."

Bland saw the exchange and felt shame in the pit of his stomach. He felt no enmity towards Firth and certainly not towards a young woman caught up in a plot hatched by a brutal General.

Reaching their destination Bland ordered the soldiers to take the couple to his office and seat them. One soldier was to stand guard inside and the rest were to occupy the corridor.

Soon after they were settled a grim-faced Bland entered. He sat down at his desk and looked at the pair.

'General Minas is coming, I would suggest you answer his questions honestly ... and quickly."

Firth began to stand. "Is that a threat Major, because I am an officer in His Majesty's Army and I am on a diplomatic mission.”

Bland hissed: "Sit down Joshua and for God's sake shut up. General Minas is a murderer. He is an evil-tempered killer and if you provoke him there is no hope for either you, or Miss Constance."

Firth was stunned: "Do ..."

He will kill both of you horribly so shove your bloody diplomatic office anywhere you like. Stop trying to be a brave hero and just shut up. When he asks a question answer it and do so truthfully. I have seen him do the most terrible things, Joshua, and I do not wish to see them done to you. I want to see them done to the lovely Miss Constance even less."

Fear crept into Firth at those words and when Constance looked up at him he could say nothing. All he could do was move closer to her.

"Major Bland you are a soldier, you cannot allow this," he said.

Bland looked him straight in the eye and said: "Joshua, this man is evil. He answers to none. I beg of you, please play the game. There is no other way."

The sound of striding boots entered the room and when the doors were swept open there stood General Minas.

Constance shrank into Firth and kept her gaze from the man. Firth looked him in the eyes and hoped for the best.

"Ah, Major Bland, you have succeeded in bringing these people to me. Well done," he said in his heavily accented English.

"Excuse my language please," he told the couple, "I have little time for using such a barbaric tongue."

Firth bit back a retort while fighting to look impassive.

The General seemed disappointed Firth did not rise to the bait. He looked at Firth with his head tilted slightly, as if judging him.

His mouth opened to launch another jibe when a cannon roared from nearby.

Minas turned to Bland and ordered him to see what was going on.

The Irishman walked briskly from the office and summoned several soldiers to go with him towards the docks.

At the sound of the cannon Constance started and Joshua held her more tightly.

"It's okay, my lady, it's okay."

The church bells began to chime and she cried out "What does that mean Joshua?"

He squeezed her hand and said matter of factly: "It means trouble for us, Constance."

Minas moved behind Bland's desk and sat down.

"So, my doves, what is happening here?"

Constance spoke first. "General, we have no idea what is going on. Captain Firth came to my house to ensure I was safe."

Minas sneered: "Safe? In the middle of my town? No one would harm you here ... without permission."

"What have I done to you General?" she asked.

"Nothing, my dear, but when has that ever mattered?" he responded through rubbery lips.

When she felt Firth move to stand she squeezed his thigh to remind him of not aggravating the Spaniard.

Minas noticed the gesture and smiled tauntingly. "Ah, so the brave boy is set to challenge me is he?"

Anger was coursing through Firth, but he was trying his best to hide it.

"No, General," he responded, keeping his voice as even as possible. I am unsure as to why we are being treated as we are."

Minas rose and stood over Firth.

"You are here because your King believes he can occupy Spain's sacred soil.

"You are here because ...

Minas stopped as Bland burst back into the room and whispered to him.

"And you are here because your ship has fled leaving you both behind."

Noticing the couple's apparent relief Minas laughed.

"You know, they will not get very far. If they make it out of the harbour and the channel they will face a squadron of my ships between here and Gibraltar.

"They have no hope ... nor do you," he added viciously.

Firth's anger burst forward. "So what do you hope to achieve you damned Spanish traitor?"

Minas smiled and taunted Firth: "Ah, he finds his angry voice ...

It is easy ... boy ... I am going to take Gibraltar back for my most Catholic Majesty and my country. And you and your friends are not going to be able to stop it."

He moved to Firth and pressed his face forward. "My forces will sail to your fortress, destroy your fleet and then regain Gibraltar for his most sacred Majesty."

"And how will you manage that?"

Minas laughed. "Aha, I think you have already guessed that Captain Firth. Have you not been admiring my floating bomb? We will sail that directly into Gibraltar's Rosia Bay among your warships and then detonate her. After that we will bombard your gun batteries and then send in our gunboats and troops."

The General smiled at the thought of being the first Spaniard to capture Gibraltar in almost a century. He grinned at Firth. "A big bomb. Lots of dead Englishmen. Boom!" he said spreading his hands. "No more Royal Navy!"

"Bastard!" Firth called and Minas laughed. "I am no traitor, you upstart, I am a patriot!"

With that he plunged a dagger into Firth's thigh.

Firth did all he could to stifle his cry of pain. His head spun and he wanted to throw up with the agony of the blade.

Constance screamed and tried to stem the flow of blood that was already coming through Firth's breeches.

"Stop your noise," Minas demanded. "He will be all right."

He lent close to Firth and added: "That was for calling me a bastard, you English mongrel."

Then he grinned as he ripped the knife from its fleshy home and laughed as Firth fell to the floor without making a sound.

Floating back into consciousness Firth sensed he was being held while hands pressed on his thigh. He momentarily struggled then heard: "Ssssh Joshua, lie still ... you are being treated."

He then felt and smelled the rose scent of Contance's long hair beside his face and momentarily forgot about the throbbing wound.

"I'm sorry," he said weakly, "didn't mean for that to happen."

"What?" Bland's voice sounded near him, "To get stabbed?"

Firth shook his head slowly.

"To pass out?"

Again he silently signalled no.

"And sorry ... for bleeding on your floor."

"Ah well," said the Irishman, "I suppose it adds to the character. "Now the doctor says you are not to make any sudden moves with that leg."

"I'll do my best to remember that Major, thank you."

Firth winced as the hands pulled a bandage tight. "Where's the glorious General?"

"He's making plans."

"Bet he's in a bit of a vapour."

"He is not a happy man, Joshua, your actions and those of Captain Allison have somewhat angered him."

"Did the Dragon get away?"

"I shouldn't be telling you this but, yes, she got away. It did some damage to the channel fort on the way out as well."

"That's good," Firth smiled. "Thank you Major, for being such a gentleman."

"I would expect the same, Captain. Possibly more so. You see I would be expecting a large brandy to ease my pain."

"Would you?"

"Yes, one very much like this one," Bland said, passing a tumbler to Constance who took it and brought it to Firth's lips. The fumes off the potent liquor made his eyes water and taking a gulp he felt its fire running down his throat.

"Oh that is good," he said, and took another mouthful. It wasn't long before the effects of the brandy coursed through his body. "Best I've felt in ages," he smiled. "Can I have another?"

Bland obliged.

"Make the most of it Captain," he said, "it may be the last you'll get for a while. General Minas has ordered you and Miss Constance to sail with us when we move south. I am truly sorry, Miss Constance, to have to do this."

He looked at her stroking Firth's head and saw she smiled resignedly at whatever would be in the future. "I understand, Major Bland, I do not blame you at all. You are not the monster in this."

Bland gratefully nodded, but felt no better. There was no honour in this escapade that he could see.

"Come on Joshua, I think it's time we put you back on that chair."

With the help of the doctor and a soldier the trio grabbed an uninjured limb each. "Are you ready Joshua?"

Firth nodded and held his breath waiting for the command that pulled him up and sat him down. Bland looked as Firth's colour drained, but the young Captain made no complaint. Then, helping Constance to her feet, Bland moved another chair next to Firth's and gestured for her to use it.

"I must go now. There is a guard outside the door and I'll leave one here if you need anything. I hope I don't need to ask the pair of you to not try to escape."

Firth retorted blackly: "I'm not in any bloody condition to try am I?"

Bland half-smiled and said: "I will return presently."

Constance's hand found his and their fingers entwined. "How is your leg Joshua?"

"Barely a scratch," he lied, "But the brandy has made it much better. God what did that doctor do to my breeches?"

Firth was looking at his sliced open pants that had a bloody bandage wrapped around his leg within them. "That won't do on parade," he joked.

"You are not funny, Joshua ..."

"I'm feeling amusing, my lady, I think my wound is making me lightheaded."

"I think it's the brandy ... Captain Firth," she smiled.

He smiled back and looked into her eyes. "I'm better than I have ever been, Constance."

"What are you thinking?"

"Well, I have to say first-off that I think you are the most beautiful woman I have met."

"Stop it, you're embarrassing me," she said in a thoroughly unbelievable way. She brought her face closer to his. "What else?"

He thought about kissing her, but instead said: "I was also thinking how enjoyable it will be to kill General Minas ..."

The sun was bright when Firth and Constance were led from the headquarters down to the docks. Their wrists were bound in front of their bodies. Four soldiers marched ahead of them and four to their rear.

Firth was having difficulty keeping up the pace and when he got too close to one of the soldiers behind he received a musket butt in the back for his efforts.

A crowd of locals lined the cobbled way and while most stood in silence there was the occasional heckler who yelled a tirade of what Firth presumed was abuse at him.

Constance walked with dignity and her head erect. She looked at the crowd and maintained a small smile throughout her ordeal.

The bottom of her full-length white dress was showing brown dust from the street and her green cloak was too warm in the sun, although she knew once they were underway the sea breeze would quickly cool her.

Another musket blow thudded into Firth and Constance turned to the soldier and said "For pity's sake sir, leave him be."

"I'm all right, Constance, I'm fine," he said. "There's not far to go" and indicated the dock with a nod of his head.

"I'm picking we'll be accompanying Minas on his ship and I don't think that will be the bomb ship ... more likely a frigate – like the one you ran into while on the Swallow."

Firth could see a shadow of regret flit across her features.

"I'm sorry, I did not mean to remind you."

"There's nothing to be sorry for Joshua, what is done is done. I pray God gave the Captain and crew mercy and hope he punishes Minas."

"I'm hoping he leaves him for me," Firth said savagely.

The frigate was laid alongside the dock along with one of the smaller sloops. There were no signs of the army of workers that had loaded the vessels as both looked to Firth as if they were ready to sail.

"They must just be waiting on the tide," Firth said to Constance.

The pair were taken to the gangway and moved carefully in single file up to the deck. Sailors moved aside as they went aboard and a group of naval officers stopped their conversation and bowed briefly in Lady Constance's direction.

She smiled and nodded in return.

"Ahh," came a voice from above them. "My officers have keen eyes for a beautiful woman, do they not Captain Firth?"

Firth looked up and saw Minas at the rail of the quarterdeck.

"It seems they do, General. They have very good taste."

Minas smiled. "Of course, of course."

Looking at Constance he said: "My lady I think you have big feelings for this boy. Maybe even *el enamoramiento* - falling in love with him."

Constance blushed.

"Well, then you should say your farewells to him as he will not be sailing with us."

Constance spun around and looked at Firth with shocked eyes.

"What does he mean Joshua?

"I think it means you will be safe, Constance."

Firth lowered his head and gently kissed her on the lips. They were so soft he felt he would melt into them. He could taste the salt from her tears.

"I'll not say goodbye to you Constance. We will meet again. My thoughts will be with you."

He kissed her again as she pushed closer into him.

"Don't let me go, Joshua, don't let ..."

Minas broke in. "I'm afraid, my doves, it is time for you to part. Lady Constance you have been given our guest cabin, courtesy of Lieutenant Torres. My servant will show you to it when Captain Firth has departed. You are to remain there until we have raised sail and then you may come on to the deck."

"What about Captain Firth," she asked, "Where is he going?"

"We need his abilities elsewhere. He will be part of our little adventure on another ship.

"Separate them," he commanded the officers.

Constance struggled as the Spanish officers pulled her from Firth. He watched as he saw tears pour down her cheeks.

"Harden up, man," he told himself, "You need your wits about you."

He put on a false smile for her and addressed the Spanish General.

"So where am I to go General?"

"We have a berth for you on the San Cristobal," he said and pointed across the harbour.

Firth looked and was not surprised by what he saw. The San Cristobal was the bomb vessel.

"No," he heard Constance cry out, "No... Joshua ..."

"Take him away."

There was none of the gentleness shown to Constance as Firth was manhandled by sailors to the harbour-side rail and forced to a small rowboat underneath. Slowed by his leg Firth was helped on his way by a barefooted kick to his chest that dropped him several feet into the dinghy.

Winded, he sat up as quickly as he could and waited for the sailors to put their oars through the rowlocks and pull quickly away from the frigate.

Firth looked back, but could not see Constance.

He knew there was little likelihood of ever seeing her again.

XXXXVIII

The hold where Firth was tied was below the San Cristobal's waterline.
It was dark, hot and stank of fetid water. He could hear the slurp of bilge contents and the occasional scurrying of small feet. There was also a smell of gunpowder.
Hardly surprising that, he told himself, as the vessel was crammed from deck to keel with barrels of black powder. Hundreds, maybe thousands of the things.
From the feel of the way the ship was rocking he gathered they were now in open waters, outside the protected inlet and its harbour. The Spanish fleet had got underway while Firth was still being rowed to the bomb ship. Minas' frigate and the sloops left first, presumably to guard the way and, in the distance, Firth could see the sails of the transport ships being released.
Lying off them were lines of tarpaulin-clad gunboats that would be towed to the invasion spot before being manned by men from the larger ships.
Had it been a British force assembling Firth would have been impressed, but as it was the enemy he was worried instead.
Minas' plan had a very good chance of succeeding and there was little he, now stuck in the hold, could do about it.
To keep from being bored Firth ran possibilities through his mind.
How could the attack be thwarted?
Obviously, he told himself, the most sure way was to destroy the bomb ship. That however would leave him either floating alone in the Atlantic, or blown to pieces.
And, would the destruction of the San Cristobal be enough to stop Minas' attack. He still had a number of warships and several thousand soldiers who could, with the advantage of surprise, pull off the audacious plan.
Was it possible to destroy both the bomb ship and the other vessels?
Firth shook his head, he couldn't even see his way to getting out of the hold, let alone capturing the ship he was on.
It was only manned by a skeleton crew but, even so, that was at least 20 men - 20 men who weren't tied up, he reminded himself.
Firth could just make out the rope around his wrists. At least they were still in front of him, enabling him to take a drink and eat a bit of the bread the Spanish had left.
He'd tried to weaken the ropes by rubbing them along the sides of the water barrel, but it soon became apparent that was not going to do anything quickly.
Firth thought he could use his tinderbox, which he had secreted in the top of his boot before being taken, to start a small fire and burn the bonds away - but immediately reckoned it was not such a good idea when surrounded by a shipload of powder.
His penknife had been taken from him and he wished he'd slipped that into his boot when he had the chance.
As he munched on some more bread he figured his best hope was to overpower the guard who came to check him every couple of hours. Then he could get the sailor's blade. He'd have one, Firth thought, every Spaniard seemed to own a knife of some sort.
He must have dozed off as echoing steps in the distance woke him. Firth could see a

dim light from a safety lamp working its way towards his position and readied himself to act if the moment presented itself.

The man was moving quickly and Firth tensed. This was it. He was now within three paces when Firth saw he was carrying a wrapped object under his arm - or rather stump of an arm. The lantern was raised and Firth saw him looking into a face he knew.

"Hector? What are you doing here?" Firth gasped.

"It is me, senor, I am here to help you."

"Bloody good job, Hector. Quick, cut these ropes off ... they are killing my wrists."

The Spaniard rapidly did as he was bid. His razor-edged knife made short work of the bonds.

"There we go senor, how is that?"

"Much obliged. How did you get here?"

"Ah, senor, I heard you had been captured and thought you may need a bit of help. So I joined the crew of this vessel. There were not many volunteers and so it was easy."

Firth chuckled quietly. "You are a brave man, Hector, you live up to your name."

The Spaniard beamed.

"And," he said, "I have brought along a friend of yours."

Firth peered past the man, but saw no-one else.

"No senor, your best friend," and patted the bundle he was holding.

As soon as he touched it Firth knew what it was.

"My sword! How did you get this Hector?"

"I have been sworn not to tell, senor, but it is from a friend. One who hopes you will soon be free and can maybe stop this madness."

"I don't know who it is, but I'll be glad to thank them if we live through this. Tell me, Hector, how many crew are on the San Cristobal?"

"I'm not exactly sure, senor, but I think maybe 15. One man to steer the ship and others to ready the sails. They are all on deck as it is forbidden to go below unless it is to check on you."

Firth's mind was racing. There were 15 men on to the two of them – and Hector only had one arm. The odds were too great. So how to deal with them? Then it dawned on him.

"Hector, we need to get them off the ship!"

"How senor?"

"I'm not sure yet, but it will come to me."

Firth started thinking out loud. "We are outnumbered and have a sword and a knife between us. Not good odds. We can't beat them in a fight, but we need to get them off the ship ...

"How do we get them to want to leave the ship?"

Looking around the hold his eyes settled on a water keg.

"Oh my God, that's it. I know how we can make this work Hector."

The Spaniard was lost for a moment, suddenly wondering if the young Englishman had taken one blow too many to his head.

"We need some fuse, Hector, some slow-burning fuse. We'll attach it to an empty water barrel and take it on to the deck near the wheel."

"And pretend we will blow everything up if they do not leave the ship?" the Spaniard asked.

"Exactly."

"But what if they instead decide to try to take the barrel off us?"

"Ah, yes, well that could happen. Okay, we need a short length of fuse - say two feet - for the barrel and another fuse running down to the main hold."

"To blow up the ship?"

"Yes."

"With us on it?"

"Yes."

"I like the one making them get of the ship better," Hector said. Firth nodded his agreement. "Me too."

"Hector, how far behind the frigate are we?"

"We are a few miles away from her."

"Can we close that gap?"

"We are astern and have a slight wind advantage, but we are very heavy and slow."

"So we can't catch them then?"

"Well, senor, it will be difficult while they are sailing, but they will want to attack Gibraltar fortress just before dawn and that means they need to stop for a few hours somewhere at night."

"Let's hope they halt long enough for this ship to get close enough to them to do some damage then."

Hector looked alarmed: "But what about Lady Constance?"

"I've already thought of her, Hector, after we have got the crew off this vessel we will rope the wheel so it runs straight at Minas' fleet. We will light a long fuse and then we take a longboat to his flagship, rescue Constance and get out of the way before the ship blows up."

Saying it out aloud did not make it seem a sensible a plan to Firth, but there was little choice and, the brave little Spaniard nodded his assent.

"The time to strike will be when they – and you – are about to eat. Then you'll all be in the same spot. Is the longboat tied alongside the ship?"

"Si, senor, it is there in case the sailors need to leave the vessel quickly."

"Well, Hector, we will just have to ensure they want to … now let me put together a bomb.

"Oh, and one other thing, are you the only person who will come down here?"

"Si, the others don't want to. They say it smells bad here."

"Ha, it must be I've got used to it … ah well, at least I won't be disturbed. And Hector, next time you come down could you … er, bring a bucket please."

The Spaniard looked at Firth in a confused manner and then understood.

"Of course, senor, of course."

Firth was very proud of his bomb. The small keg looked exactly how he had envisaged it … dangerous.

And the short fuse sticking out from the lid made it seem even more so.

Firth had decided on a very short fuse just in case the Spaniards thought they might be able to snatch the bomb away from him before he set off an explosion.

Now as soon as he touched it with a match the sailors would fear almost instant death and want to head overboard.

The real fuse was more problematic. Firth knew the approximate burning rate of the cord, but he had only Hector's best estimates as to how long the thing needed to burn before the San Cristobal was among Minas' ships.

The key thing, Firth thought, was to err on a longer time rather than shorter. He wanted the explosion to be right among the enemy vessels to do the most damage. Damaged? No way in Hell, he thought. Firth wanted them obliterated and all the men sent to the bottom of the sea.

There was only one person he needed to save and that was Constance. He was sure he could still smell her scent of roses.

Dragging his mind back to the task at hand he knew the first part of the plan was about to be attempted. Hector had visited him an hour before telling him that all was in readiness on deck. The longboat was tied up, he was at the helm so he could subtly steer the bombship towards the fleet and then he would tie the wheel up and go and join his fellow Spaniards on deck for their meal of cold cuts. One that was unlikely to be finished when Firth appeared with his keg. Oh, and he told Firth, he had presented the sailors with bottles of wine to get their evening off to happy start and make their ejection from the ship easier.

As he carried the keg up through the decks the sounds of revelry got louder. It took him longer than he had reckoned because his wounded thigh was throbbing and had stiffened, making it both difficult and painful to bear his weight up the steps. But Firth was determined to carry on, because he knew that if he and Hector failed, then the likelihood was that Gibraltar would fall and Constance would die.

Ahead there was laughter, toasts to everything under the sun and more laughter. One of the sailors began to sing what sounded to Firth like a Spanish shanty.

As he approached the last entryway Firth got his first breath of sea air for some time and he inhaled its fresh saltiness with pleasure.

Pausing to collect himself he drew breath, lit a length of fuse to use as a match and climbed up to the main deck.

Taking a moment for his eyes to adjust to the light Firth instantly focused on the noise coming from the sailors to his left.

He did not know how many, but there was a large party of them, all completely surprised by the sudden appearance of their prisoner.

Some dropped their drinking cups and began to stand, but were stopped by Hector's warning.

'He's got a bomb," he shouted and the sailors froze in position.

Firth took advantage of the moment to advance upon them with the lit fuse in his hand near the keg's wick.

"You," he shouted at Hector. "Tell them what I am saying."

Hector pretended to be cowed by the Englishman and said to his comrades: "Friends, halt, this man could blow our ship to the heavens."

Sailors turned and put fearful eyes upon Hector, then Firth.

A man with grey hair urged Hector to talk with the Englishman.

"Tell him we do not wish to die."

The other sailors nodded agreement.

"Tell him we will do what he wants."

Hector acknowledged the man and spoke to Firth in English.

"Please, do not fire the bomb senor. What do you want us to do?"

Firth gave each of the men a hard stare and said: "Tell them to leave this vessel and row away from it in the longboat."

As Hector translated his order Firth could see a relief passing across the Spaniards' faces.

"Do not do anything other than get in that boat. If you do so I will blow this ship to kingdom come."

Hearing the order the sailors shook their heads and raised their hands in surrender.

"You," Firth said forcefully to Hector, "get the men into the boat."

It didn't take long for the sailors to clamber over the side and settle into the rough wooden benches on the longboat.

Once they had done so Firth told Hector: "Slash the sail."

Hector did as ordered and ripped his knife through the yellowed canvas, making it impossible to try to use.

"Now cast off," Firth shouted.

As the longboat moved from the side of the San Cristobal Hector leaped on to the ropes hanging from its side.

Initially his one hand seemed to lose its grip, but he held on before gaining control.

As he clambered over the railing Firth held his hands out to drag him to safety.

There were protests from the sailors, but Hector only gave them a brief salute before turning to the young Englishman. He watched as the boat quickly fell behind.

"That's the easy part, senor. Now we have the battle on our hands."

"And we have no time to waste, Hector," Firth said, "It's up to us – and only us – to foil Minas' plot. And, dear God, I pray we can do so while saving Constance."

The older man crossed to Firth and put his right hand on his arm and squeezed it.

"We will save her senor. We will save the beautiful lady."

Firth couldn't reply. He turned from the Spaniard.

"Of course we will," he said in a faltering voice, "but this is no time for being soft Hector. We need to prepare the other longboat, line up the fleet and fire the fuse."

The Spaniard smiled at the young man's distress and outwardly ignored it.

"Aye, aye, Captain – is that not what your Navy says?"

Firth laughed and put his arm around the man's shoulder.

"Against men like you Hector, how ever did we win at Trafalgar?"

"Aaaah," the Spaniard said lightly, "There were not enough like me …" and joined Firth in his laughter.

Together they went to the ship's mighty wheel and checked the lashings that held its course towards Minas' fleet. It seemed set true to Firth. His task was now to recheck the fuse leading to the ship's powder, while Hector made sure their longboat was ready to take them to the enemy General's flagship.

Twenty minutes later Firth extinguished the lanterns aboard the bombship and set a match to the cord leading to the powder barrels below decks.

He then the made his way to the side of the San Cristobal and down to the boat and helped Hector set the small sail.

"This is it, Hector. Now is our chance to save Constance and kill an absolute bastard."

"Si ... Captain."

In the inkiness of the night, Firth could make out the faint pinpricks of light from lanterns on the larger Spanish vessel.

He and Hector were sailing along at a reasonable speed and Firth hoped the wind that propelled the San Cristobal towards its target would continue.

He knew it was highly improbable that he would achieve what he wanted – sinking the attacking force – but destroying Minas' main weapon would be victory enough. The most difficult part of the plan was finding Constance aboard a large enemy vessel at night.

He guessed she would be somewhere near the Captain's cabin at the stern of the ship, but her exact whereabouts were anybody's guess.

Then there was the crew and any soldiers Minas had placed aboard his vessel.

He and Hector had a brace of pistols and a sword each. Enough for a brief fight, but not the firepower needed to take on the whole crew of a frigate.

Firth was steering the longboat silently, while Hector hummed a tune and occasionally broke into the chorus in Spanish.

The young Englishman's nerves were strained. Not only did he have to think on his mission, but he had to force from his mind all thoughts of Constance. He cursed the Devil for putting her in this situation.

She deserved a life in society, not being held for ransom – or worse – by a deranged Don.

At that moment Firth just wanted to ram his sword's blade straight through Minas' face. He didn't care at what cost to himself.

Hector sat at the bow of the longboat and watched the young officer and his internal struggles. He understood both the attraction of a beautiful woman and the desire for revenge. He also knew his task was to help the Englishman in whatever way he could to save his lady. Hector had lost loved ones and did not want the same pain forced upon a youth he had become fond of.

Their small craft was closing on Minas' sea-anchored vessels and Firth could see more lanterns on the Spanish ships. Though dull, they made steering towards the fleet easier.

Looking behind, Firth could see the closing outline of the San Cristobal. He couldn't say with any certainty how long it would take the ship to reach the Spanish or, in fact, if it would actually make it. A dozen problems filled his mind – the wheel ropes could slip, or snap, the wind could die away leaving the vessel becalmed, or a change in wind direction could send it off on a very different course.

It was in God's hands, he thought, and unwittingly spoke aloud "Thank God he is an Englishman."

A soft laugh from Hector brought Firth out of his thoughts.

"I said that aloud didn't I?"

The Spaniard laughed. "Si, Englishman, you did."

Firth smiled back and gave a half-shrug.

"You suit that shade of red on your face, senor, it matches your coat."

Firth grinned and returned to watching the distant shapes.

He was nervous … really nervous. This was worse than the lead-up to a battle. At least on a battlefield, Firth thought, you had some idea of what the enemy could throw at you. In this situation he was both blind and in unknown territory.

He had discussed with Hector the broadest of plans of what to do when they reached Minas' flagship and even as he outlined them he knew they sounded like the delusions of a madman.

One person climbing aboard an enemy man of war armed only with a sword and two pistols, up the side of the ship, at night, without sentries spotting him – or the small boat beneath him - and then trying to find a prisoner. All without knowing the exact layout of the vessel.

In his favour, Firth believed Minas would keep Constance in, or near, his cabin at the stern of the ship. And there was usually a second apartment reserved for any senior officer who may be travelling with the Captain. Either of those two could be easily entered from the main deck and, if the ship were like most, there would be a small amount of cover offered by the steps leading up to the ship's wheel.

Then again, he argued against himself, she may be in the gunroom, which was usually one deck below the Captain's quarters. Worse still if she was a further deck down in a junior officer's room.

"Captain Firth," Hector deliberately broke into the officer's thoughts, "we should sail up directly behind the cabins. That way we may be lucky and we may get to see who is in there."

"Of course, Hector, that would make my task easier."

If the room's had a lamp lit, he told himself, and if anyone was standing and …

Firth told himself to shut up and fell into an unthinking silence.

His eyes, though, never left the target, which had edged ever closer.

Firth estimated it was probably only 20 minutes later that Hector loosened off the sail and the craft began to slow. They were a about a mile from Minas' vessel, which lay at the rear of the Spanish flotilla.

The outlines of masts stood out against the sky and to his relief Firth saw a faint glow from the officers' windows. Please let Constance be there, he intoned, as Hector reduced speed further almost slowing to a stop.

The Spaniard knew his stuff, he recognised, and was allowing their sailboat to drift slowly on the current. And with no sail they would be very hard to spot from the top deck of the warship. It would also allow time for the San Cristobal to move closer to the Spanish fleet.

Both men were now staring at the windows. They could just make out figures in the lower row, which Firth thought was the gunroom where officers would gather after dinner to smoke, or drink, or read. Above that was less of a glow, possibly the light from a single lamp. That had to be the room in which Minas was holding Constance, he concluded. If it wasn't, then it would still be the best place to start his search.

What troubled Firth was if she had been placed somewhere else, how long would it take him to find her? He decided to worry about that if it happened and sat back in the boat trying to clear his mind.

Looking astern he saw that the bombship had closed the distance more quickly than he would have realized. This could take a lot of luck he thought.

A quarter of an hour later Firth could hear the slap of water on the underside of the frigate. It was now looming large and Firth went over his plan again in his mind. Then he tapped Hector on the shoulder and pointed to the starboard side.

"That's where I'll get off. Just under the first cannon. When I'm on board I want you to stand off where it is safe and look out for us. When we come it will likely be fast so please, Hector, don't be too far away."

The Spaniard nodded. "I will be there for you Joshua … and Miss Constance."

"Wish me luck," Firth said as he stood carefully and looked at the wooden wall near him. He had hoped there would be ropes available for him to climb, but Minas' sailors were obviously more disciplined than most crews and there were no obvious stray ropes. The lower gun ports were closed but Firth reckoned the wooden covers could give him a reasonable handhold. From there he could pull himself up and then reach a tarred covered ratline and then pull himself up to a narrow wooden platform that ran the length of the ship just below the top deck of guns. That's the way, he told himself, and moved as soon as a wave lifted the small boat.

His jump was ungainly, largely due to his injured thigh, but effective. He thumped against the wooden hull and almost lost his grip but held on as his right foot sought something to support itself on.

He pushed his boot into the junction of the side of the ship and angled outer wall of the officers' quarters. While not terribly secure it allowed him to take his right hand off the gun hatch and reach for the ratline.

Taking hold of it Firth pushed off with his foot and grabbed at the cable with his left hand. Holding tightly he then went hand over hand up the cable until he was able to rest his feet on the gun cover. Firth breathed a sigh of relief and paused. His ears were searching for any noise that would tell him of a sentry's presence but they heard nothing. He could hear muffled voices from the gunroom to his right, but nothing above him.

The ratline was fastened to the hull through an iron ring and Firth picked that as his next foothold. From there the move to the platform was an easy one. Crouching down by the deck's rail he steeled himself for the next part of his mission.

Raising his head he peered around the rear deck area. There were no sailors to his left that he could see, although he could hear two men talking on the deck above and to his right. They'll be guarding the wheel, he thought, and hopefully will be too busy with their chatter to move around and look in his direction. By the steps to that deck he could make out the Captain's cabin door. A crack of light eked out of the bottom gap between the door and the deck.

He was about to clamber over the rail when he heard footsteps. Staying still he watched as a musket-holding sentry paced slowly from out of the near shadows and across the front of the entryway. Damn, he chided himself he hadn't seen that man. The sentry turned after 10 paces and moved back towards his starting point. Firth froze, knowing that to move would likely give himself away. He held his breath and watched the sentry complete his route before turning and retracing his steps.

A silent wish the soldier would move elsewhere proved a false hope and after another few passes Firth decided he had to act before others came along. When the guard was at his furthest from him, Firth slipped over the railing hoping his sword wouldn't scrape against anything. Making himself as small as he could in the shadows of a lashed down rowboat, he waited for the chance to pounce. That came when the man began back towards the cabin's door. Firth reached into the deep pocket of his coat and pulled out one of the heavy pistols. He didn't bother cocking the weapon, as that would instantly give him away. Instead he held it by the barrel and quickly closing the gap to the sentry and brought the wooden butt down across the back of his head. The man barely gave a grunt as the blow slammed home and he crumpled sideways on the deck, his musket – luckily for Firth – landed on one of his outstretched arms rather than the rough wood.

Grabbing the limp body by the white crossbelts of his uniform, Firth dragged it back to boat's shadows. Then he retrieved the musket and slung it over his shoulder. He knew he now had to move quickly and after cocking the pistol he placed his hand on the cabin's door handle. Taking a deep breath he eased it open and, holding the weapon in front of him, slipped inside before pushing the door closed behind him.

Once inside the cabin Firth instantly knew the room was empty but for one figure standing by the lamp near the windows. He looked down the long barrel of the pistol and over the front sight. His finger tightened on the trigger and then eased off it.

"I believe you may need some help, my lady," he said and half ran across the room. Constance stood stock still, her hands to her mouth as if to stifle a scream. Her green eyes flashed and began to water. Then she threw herself into Firth's arms and kissed him fully on the mouth. He melted into her taste and almost crushed her with a desperate embrace.

"Oh Joshua," she whispered, "You are mad. I thought you were dead. Oh my God, I thought you were dead."

Tears were now pouring out of her eyes. "How did you get here? How ever did you find me?"

"I'll tell you later," he said, easing her away from him, "because right now we have to get out of here and off this ship before the Dons know I'm here. And they'll know fairly soon … as there is one of them lying outside with a cracked skull."

He tried to give her a reassuring smile but he felt it came across more like a grimace. She nodded quickly and grabbed his hand. She squeezed it and held to her wet cheek. "I'm ready."

Leading her to the exit Firth then released her hand, raised his pistol and slowly opened the door.

He stepped through sideways, weapon ready, only for a loud shot to go off and a musketball splinter the wood of the door surround.

He dived back into the room and a quick-thinking Constance shut it and bolted it. Getting to his feet, Firth went to Constance and said: "I guess they know I'm here." Then he heard a voice that set his hackles rising. It was Minas.

"Captain Firth, I am surprised to see you again. You just can't stay away from that woman can you? Don't bother answering because I'm not interested in what you say anyway. I will tell you this, however. There are more than 600 men upon this ship and any chance you had to get away disappeared about two minutes ago.

"I'm not even going to ask you to surrender, because I am going to kill you. I am going to run my sword through you several times, before you depart this world." Firth had enough and shouted back.

"Shut up you fat Spanish pig. I will gladly fight you, but you will need to come in here to do so."

The English couple heard laughter, then orders being barked out in Spanish.

"Joshua, we could go out the window," Constance suggested. "We can jump and try to swim away."

"Hopefully Hector is close by and will see us, but there doesn't seem to be a choice," he agreed.

Using the butt of his weapon he smashed the thick glass panels and felt the cool of the breeze push in. When he had cleared enough for them to get through he looked outside and stopped.

"We can't go that way. Not any more."

Puzzled, Constance peered out. She saw darkness and the shape of a ship sailing close by.

"Is it one of theirs?" she asked.

Firth shook his. "No it's ours, but it's about to blow up and take everything around with it."

Stepping back he ran his eyes around the room. There was a loud thumping on the door and a piece of parchment slid under it.

Written in a good hand – and in English – was a brief note.

"Give yourselves up or we will come and get you. You have two minutes."

Constance looked up at Joshua and asked: "Why would they give us two minutes?"

"Minas is just playing with us. He wants to drag this out, like a cat does with a mouse. He's a sadist."

Firth looked at Constance and he swam in those eyes. "You are the most beautiful woman I have ever seen, Constance."

She returned his look: "And you are not only the most handsome and brave man I know Joshua. But you are also utterly mad to try to save me."

"I would be mad not to, the world needs a beauty like you," he said, meaning every word.

She put both her hands on his face and kissed him again. A long kiss that he felt throughout his body.

When their lips parted he held on to her. He wasn't sure if it was to comfort Constance, or himself.

"I will do my best to get us out of this but, whatever happens, I will do my damnedest to kill that Spanish bastard before he lays a finger on you."

Constance put her right forefinger on his lips. "Ssssh, my sweet, what will be, will be. I'm thankful to have met you and I pray God will somehow save us from our predicament."

A part of Firth was hoping for divine help, but he would have preferred a handful of Royal Navy frigates appearing on the horizon. "Please do as I ask and go and crouch down in that corner."

He indicated the area to the left of the door he knew the enemy would come through. "They will blast the door down and then come through. They will fire at anything to their front. I will shoot the first few who come through."

Then Firth added: "I only hope that Minas comes before my blade ..."

"But Joshua, he is a master swordsman, he will kill you."

Firth recalled what he said in front of Hector. "But God, I hope, will remember that he's an Englishman," he laughed.

Constance took a pistol and went and huddled in the corner.

Firth saw two naval pistols hanging in bucket holsters on a hook in the wall. Picking them up he checked to see if they were loaded with a ball. They were, but not primed. Opening the tin powder flask he had in his coat pocket he tipped a thumbnail of the dark dust on to the pan and closed the lock. He repeated the moves with the second firearm. He laid both naval pistols on the Captain's desk and added the ones he already carried. He unslung the sentry's musket from his shoulder and unsheathed his sword. Then he ducked down.

"Come in Minas you bastard," he said to himself, "and I will send you to Hell."

Then all Hell erupted as a three-pound cannonball smashed through the door sending shards of wood across the room. Blinded by the smoke all Firth could do was aim a pistol at the first shadowy figure he could see.

He fired and no sooner had the pistol kicked in his hand than a scream sounded out. Picking up a second pistol he fired it at another silhouette. Another scream.

"Stay down," he called to Constance and without waiting for a response he shot the next man through the door, laying him flat on the floorboards.

He had a musket and two handguns left and after they were fired it was purely down to his skill with the blade.

His adrenalin was pumping, but Firth knew he had to stay as calm as he could. Cold anger filled him and guided his next shots.

The first took the top of a Spanish soldier's head clean off, splattering his brains across the wall. The second hit a man in the stomach and he fell screaming, leaving a bloody mess on the floor as he writhed in agony.

Firth now screamed himself: "Come on Minas you fat coward. Fight me, man on man, blade on blade."

For a few seconds no Spaniard entered the cabin, then the doorway was filled with his nemesis.

Minas' bejeweled sword flashed through the air as he whipped it from side to side.

"Come on puppy," he taunted Firth, "show me your teeth."

"Bastard," Firth yelled, and ignoring his last pistol launched himself at Minas. His blade struck down, but the Spaniard easily parried it away.

"You are too eager, boy," Minas said. "Maybe you should have waited a few years before you have yourself killed."

Again Firth's sword struck, but Minas knocked it aside with little effort.

"Such temper, such youthful energy … it is almost a shame you won't live for long."

Firth leapt at the General with fury in his heart but his charge was stopped as Minas put a deep cut across his left shoulder.

Firth grunted and Constance screamed.

That fired up the Englishman even more. Their blades collided time after time. Firth could see Minas was tiring, there were streams of sweat pouring down his face. His breathing was heavy and, Firth thought, his sword strokes were slowing.

That's when Minas jumped forward and smashed his sword's handguard into Firth's face. The blow sent the young Redcoat sprawling, reducing his vision to a blur through the tears pouring from his eyes. He needed a moment or two to clear his head but Minas moved surprisingly quickly and hit him again.

Firth was sent flying and lay on the cabin floor. The Spaniard grinned as he closed on him and raised his blade for the killer blow.

What happened next Firth could not explain. The walls of the ship seemed to ripple, bend, then break apart. Constance's scream was near, but oh so far away, while Minas was thrown heavily into the cabin wall. Firth felt the floor of the room warp and buckle and tried to cover his face as splinters showered around him.

When the boards under him regained their solidity he tried to stand, sword in hand and sought out Minas. The Spanish General, however, was not only tough but very fast for his size. He again had Firth at his mercy and with a snarl moved to kill the young man. The blow was to be an overhand thrust down through the top of the rib cage into the lungs leaving Firth to drown in his own blood. Minas picked that so he could taunt the irritating officer as he died slowly. His sword tip was aimed true, but an excruciating pain stole the power from the thrust. Minas looked down in surprise as six inches of steel emerged from his own chest. The pain was immense and he instantly collapsed to his knees.

Seeing his chance, Firth rose and jabbed his own blade into the fat man's neck. His thrust has missed crucial arteries and Minas eyes widened in bewilderment. Rising to his feet Firth stared down at his badly wounded enemy and struck again. The point of his sword punctured Minas' sword arm and he followed that up with a second. If he gets up again, Firth thought grimly, he'll be a hell of a lot slower with that sword.

Firth had no mercy in him as he stood over a now subdued Minas who was desperately looking around for assistance.

"You Spanish swine," he said coldly, "this is for …"

"Joshua," Constance called out, "be merciful. Do not stain your hands further with his blood."

Firth stopped. He looked at his bloodied blade and then at the man who had acted like a heathen when he was in his power.

He gazed across to the beautiful woman who wanted him to show mercy to a dangerous killer and knew she was asking him to stay his blade.

His heart softened.

Then he again rammed the blue metal into Minas' throat and took pleasure in the splash of blood that erupted from the butcher's neck.

He kept his arm ramrod straight waiting until the fat general's body had stopped twitching before pulling his steel out.

"That's the mercy he showed his victims," Firth said.

"Enough Captain Firth," called a voice and the young officer finally saw who was standing behind Minas.

It was Major Bland and Firth could see the dripping weapon in his hand.

"You?" he said. "You stabbed Minas?"

"I had to," the Irishman said, "otherwise you would have joined your ancestors."

"Why?" a stunned Firth asked.

"Well," Bland said, "I work for General Wellesley. How else do you think your Spanish sailor would be able to give you your sword?"

"Oh my God," Firth muttered and sank to his own knees. Constance flew to help him. "You've been on our side all along."

"I'm pleased you have finally recognised that," Bland said flatly. "I have watched that man kill at whim and he would have destroyed one of the great bastions against Bonaparte's godless ideas.

"And," he added, "We need to get off this ship because it is about to join the San Cristobal."

"Can we get across the deck," Firth asked as he wiped his blade clean of Minas' blood on his fallen enemy's coat.

Bland shook his head.

"There are still plenty of Spaniards out there wanting our heads at the moment and the only thing I can suggest is that we get off here as fast as we can."

Firth sheathed his blade and looked at Constance. She nodded. "Let's go out the window," he said to the Irishman and he and Constance leapt out the gap in the cabin's windows.

As he jumped, Firth hoped Hector was close by and waiting for them.

Defying the sting of the salty sea, Firth opened his eyes underwater. He could vaguely see a red glow above and the flicker of indistinct flames as he hauled himself to the surface.

When he broke through the thin layer of reflection his first reaction was to take a gulp of air. The second was to start searching for Constance. Her hand had lost its grip with his when they hit the water and now he was desperate to find her.

The scene about him was one of carnage. Minas' frigate was floating, aflame, without two of its masts and much of its superstructure.

Sails lay across the decks on which fires burnt. Their flames lit the area and, for as far as he could see, Firth saw overturned gunboats and men thrashing in the sea. Cries sounded all around him and then he heard his name.

"Joshua!"

It was Constance.

"Over here."

He looked around and saw her clinging to what looked like a cross-spar dragging a length of ripped canvas. Next to her was Bland. Firth swam over to them.

"Lord, did we do this?"

Bland laughed. "I think you did Joshua. You've made a hell of a mess. I would suggest we get away from this spot as quickly as we can because if that ship explodes I want to be as far from it as possible."

The trio kicked out and propelled their wooden floating haven towards the darkness. Firth hoped Hector had survived the blast and knew that if he had then the Spaniard would be seeking them out amid the chaos wrought upon the waters.

While the sea had washed away Minas' spray of blood, Firth still felt its warmth ... and savoured it. He would never confess it to Constance, but he had been thrilled ending that bastard General's life. He knew he had done the right thing and, for all those Minas had killed, Firth was glad it was his blade that had taken the final revenge.

And Bland, he thought, who would have known he had been such a friend. He so played his part well, the young officer thought admiringly.

He must have been so strong to have witnessed Minas' actions and not done anything about them earlier.

Then there was Constance. He looked at her and his heart raced. Her long hair was draped half across her face and she looked fatigued by what she had been through but, to Firth, Constance could have been sipping tea at Clifton Hall, rather than clinging on to wreckage to survive a shipwreck in Mediterranean waters.

Firth was glad of the spar as the weight of his boots and sword were wanting to pull him downwards.

"Constance, are you faring well?" he asked.

She nodded, but he could see the weight of her sodden dress was beginning to drag her down.

"Hold on," he said, "Hector will be here soon."

Firth did his best to conceal his fears, but he was sure Hector had perished, like so many others, when the San Christophe had exploded.

Putting his arm around her waist underwater, Firth used his strength to help keep Constance afloat.

"We will survive," he told her, and himself, "It won't be long before Hector is here." He thought that by remaining stoic and confident he would keep her spirits buoyant in what even he thought a damned mess. On the other side of the spar Bland nodded to him. Firth took some comfort in that.

He and Bland continued to kick away from the burning frigate ever mindful of the potential for its gunpowder magazine to explode.

Many of the men on board the ship had leaped into the sea, but the more disciplined among them were in a bucket chain trying to douse the flames.

Firth admired those men, trying to save both the ship and their comrades. There were cries in Spanish as explosions burst out and senior crewmen directed the fire-fighting operations.

Suddenly there were more shouts, this time with an urgency Firth had not heard before.

His eyes could not make out what was happening, but his ears heard the slam of wood on wood as the crippled ship's gunports were pulled open.

"What the ..." he exclaimed, before an ear-bursting noise erupted from his left.

Firth felt the air move around him and heard a terrible ripping sound before the side of Minas' frigate disappeared into a storm of shattered timber and smoke.

Constance moved as close to him as she physically could and buried her head into his body. Her question was drowned out as another roar of flame and smoke flew overhead and more of the Spanish ship exploded in every direction.

Trying to ignore the screams, Firth was doing his best to work out what was happening.

Then a small number of cannons on his right discharged their iron balls into the blackness.

Firth heard distant cries and then another crash of guns that silenced those to his right and sent a visible shudder through its timbers.

Who the hell is that, he wondered?

Being in the water between two vessels firing over their heads was a punishment for Firth's ears and he hoped that whoever was to his left would not close on the enemy ship and crush them in between their hulls.

But to his eardrums' detriment another broadside flew out of the darkness to his left and ripped apart the already mortally wounded Spanish vessel.

"Dear Christ, we are going to die," he thought.

Constance let out a scream and Bland muttered what Firth thought was the start of the Lord's Prayer.

"Hold on senor," he heard nearby, "Raise your arms."

Recognising Hector's voice he hauled Constance's arm out of the sea and pushed her out of the water. A rowboat appeared and a strong hand grasped on to her helping her into the boat.

"I am here senor," Hector said. "Quickly, into the boat, we need to be away."

Bland hauled himself up and flip over the side of the rowboat with comparative ease, but Firth's grasp slipped and it took both the Irishman's and Constance's assistance to drag him on board.

"Thank you," he gasped, "now let's get out of here."

No-one argued and as another salvo erupted from the night the four pressed themselves down below the side of the longboat and prayed its shallow sides would give them some protection from the storm flying overhead.

"Hector," he yelled, "what is happening?"

"Your friends are here, Senor Joshua. You are saved."

"Saved? What on Earth do you mean man? Saved by whom?"

"Why us of course," shouted a familiar voice. "You are an impudent youth Captain Firth!"

Firth laughed and responded: "And you are a delight to hear again my friend."

As relief took the energy from his body he pulled Constance into him. "We are safe, the Marines have arrived."

Constance looked up in a confused way until she saw a smiling face above her. "Oh Captain Wren," she said joyously, "you are a sight for very weary eyes."

"And you lady," he said, "are a vision that any man would sail the seas to rescue."

Firth heard the sailors on the Dragon bemoaning the slow pace of the journey back to Lisbon and thought about telling them to lose a sail to make it even slower.

For him, the voyage in warm sun over sparkling waters was too fast.

On the ship he had a lovely woman near him and he only wanted to spend more time with her. Apart from the delight of her arms and lips, his body also needed time to recover from the battering it had at the hands of Minas.

His thigh was still sore and each time it pained him it brought back memories of the agony of the Spanish general's dagger plunging deep into it.

The wound from Minas' sword blade was less of a discomfort as it had not been anywhere near as deep.

He was lucky there had been no infection, but there were bruises that he could not recall from where they came. They slowed him like an aged man.

And he had collected another scar or two.

Damn Minas, he cursed. The fat Spaniard had deserved to die and Firth felt no remorse about dispatching him to Hell.

He could still feel the spray of hot blood over his hands and face as he stabbed the man through the neck and told himself he would do the same over again.

His regret was that Constance had been there and had seen him kill Minas.

She had asked him not to and Firth felt that by going against her wishes she would think less of him.

He leaned his head back to enjoy the sun more.

Her gentle kiss upon his forehead made him open his eyes.

"You were deep in thought my Lancelot," she said.

Firth laughed.

"I was hoping the sails would be blown away and we would be weeks returning to Portugal."

It was her turn to smile. "I wish for that too, but don't tell the Captain."

Firth turned his head and looked up at the ship's wheel where Allison stood. "No, he wants to get back and report what has happened here."

And a lot had.

The exploding San Cristobal had crippled Minas' frigate, which was later sent below the waves by the Dragon. Scores of gunboats had been sunk and several other transport ships badly damaged. The death toll among the Spanish was unknown, but both Wren and Allison said they had sailed through hundreds of floating bodies on the way to rescue Firth and Constance.

Gibraltar was safe and Firth was regarded as a hero.

He groaned.

"I'm sorry my darling, did I hurt you," Constance asked.

"No," he said, "I was just hoping that the official reports don't mention me in this."

Her gentle laugh rippled over him.

"You mean don't mention one of the main people?'

"Well, yes …"

"Like the fact you uncovered Minas' plan ..."

"Well, no ..."

"Or the fact you foiled that plan ..."

"Well, no ..."

"Or the fact you sank a huge invasion force ..."

"Well, no ..."

"Or killed him ..."

" ... well ... no," he said guardedly.

She looked at him and saw a shadow of doubt pass over his face.

"Or the fact you rescued me?"

"Ah, well, yes I did that ..."

"And would do so again?"

"Any time, my lady ..."

"Any time?"

"Well, give me a couple of weeks before you get kidnapped again!"

Her gentle slap made him smile and he said: "My lady, you smell like an English rose."

She kissed him and responded: "A red English rose?"

"Never that!" he said. "You have the sweet scent of a white Yorkshire rose."

Firth stared back up at the rigging's dull white canvas contrasting against the sky. He wasn't the reason Minas' plot failed.

There had been many hands involved in foiling the attempt.

Wren, Allison, Bland, Hector ... and Constance herself. He had been merely doing what he thought was the right thing to do. And, Firth told himself, he was never sure of exactly what that was. He had only been following his instincts - for better or worse.

He saw Allison look down at him and raise his hand in acknowledgement. He nodded in return.

What would happen when the ship berthed back in Portugal? It would be back to regimental life and, with the French on the run, it may be ...

Wren sat himself down next to Firth, interrupting his thoughts.

His friend smiled and said: "Don't worry my lad, it isn't going to be boring you know.

Firth looked sideways. "Have you been reading my mind?"

'Didn't need to," Wren said, "I was just recalling the first time I headed back to land after a mission."

'What was it like?"

"Well," the Marine Captain said, "it wasn't much. Despite what we had gone through, nothing had changed there. We arrived back and it was same old thing."

He patted Forth on the thigh and saw him wince.

"Oh, sorry old boy, didn't mean to do that. Is it okay?"

Firth gave a shrug. "It could be worse."

Wren laughed: "Yes, you lucky blighter, you may not have the best-looking woman in England as your personal physician."

He stood and said: "Don't worry Joshua, all the excitement is over."

And Firth hoped that, at least for the next few weeks, Wren was right.

Lisbon, October 30

After all his adventures of the previous weeks Firth could have regarded his arrival in Lisbon as barely worth a second thought.

But the mighty river Tagus on which the Dragon slowly sailed down on a light breeze was impressive.

The waterway was huge – although a river it looked more like an ocean harbour to Firth.

Filled with ships of all forms and sizes, the Tagus stretched into the distance and the closest the right-hand bank got to Lisbon was about a mile and a half, Firth thought.

The brick-tiled roofs of Lisbon pushed back from the water's edge rising gently up low hills that were crowned by the huge dome of a cathedral and then, further up, the ramparts of a fortress.

The city looked worn and uncared for and, from a distance, it exuded a feeling of power ebbed away, but Firth still stood at the railing taking in the exciting new vista. He couldn't wait to explore its streets and cathedrals.

No doubt Wren had already had plans to sketch them all and he was certain Brook would have checked out almost every eatery in the city.

Brook … Firth cursed himself. He had barely thought of his friend for weeks.

Such had been the turmoil of his life. He had lost track of how many times he had been hit or stabbed since leaving on his mission to deliver a message to General Minas. The late General Minas, he thought with some satisfaction.

The last he heard was that Brook had been wounded and captured by the French. No-one knew if he was alive or, well, not alive. He gripped the rail tightly with both hands and felt an arm move around his middle.

By his side stood Constance, wearing a high-waisted pale green dress. Firth was sure it was fashionable, however, he wouldn't have known if it was or was not.

It looked very fine and fitted her form beautifully. He slipped his arm around her knowing that it was likely to be one of the last times he would be able to do so in public.

Her father, after all, was a General, a Knight of the Realm and the former commander of the fortress of Gibraltar.

Firth, however, was a mere Captain – and an ungazetted one at that – and would not have standing enough for Dalrymple's approval.

"What troubles you Joshua?"

"If only it were one thing, Constance. First and foremost, I have to confess to you, I want to see my friend Sam again. I need to know that he is safe. He was taken by the French and nothing has been heard of him since."

"I'm sure he is fine, if he wasn't word would have got out."

"That is what I am placing my hopes on," he then stopped, as if to steel himself. "But I have seen a lot of men die in recent months. I have seen good men – who deserved long and easy lives – taken in an instant.

He continued: "Sam is my best friend, Constance. I have known him since I was a lad. It has always been him and me."

Constance looked at the man by her and saw how young he was. She drew him closer. "I understand Joshua, he will be all right," she said with certainty.

Firth barely nodded, but pressed gently into her side.

She reached up with her right hand and brushed his fair hair from his forehead. Then she traced her finger down his cheek to his chin.

"What else worries you?"

Firth was silent for a few moments.

"Please tell me, Joshua, is it me?"

Firth looked into her eyes. "Yes, but not in a way you may be thinking."

"Well what way?" she asked quietly.

Firth didn't know how to put his concerns to her and so just went straight into what he thought was the problem.

"As soon as we walk on that dockside you are a General's daughter and I am just an unconfirmed Captain."

'And?'

'I doubt Sir Hew Dalrymple will say 'and?' He will more likely say 'he's beneath you,' 'he's only a Captain' and …"

Now she moved her finger on to his mouth to quiet him.

"He could also say 'he saved the day at Rolica.'"

Firth looked surprised.

"Yes, Joshua, I know of what you did there. Most of the army does …"

Cupping his chin to quiet him she added: "Or he could say he saved the flank at Vimeiro."

'That was General Wellesley …"

'What? The same General Wellesley who said it was a young officer from the Worcesters who held the line when it mattered."

'It was nothing, Constance …"

'What? It was nothing to hold off cavalry attacks while formed in line? Wellesley didn't think so. Nor did he think it nothing when a red-coated officer held his own against a mounted cavalryman."

Firth flushed. "Well, yes, I agree I did well in that encounter – but I was lucky."

Constance looked up with her intoxicating eyes.

'Joshua, my father is a fair man. He always wants what is best for me."

"Does that include a young officer from Yorkshire? Has he ever been up north?"

"I'm sure he has. He was born in Scotland," she smiled, then added: "Joshua, he admires courage, men who follow their duty and those who fight for what they believe. You certainly fight Joshua …"

He smiled at last. "Ay, that I do."

"And," she said before he could stop what she was wanting to say, "You saved me. You saved his daughter. That would count to any father and it certainly will to mine."

He nodded.

"And you have protected me …"

"Always."

"And I don't want to be apart from you …"

"That's enough for me, Constance. Even if we are separated I will hold on to that."
She got up on the toes of her shoes and kissed him.
"You are tall, my Captain."
"And you are beautiful, my lady."
Constance's eyes watered, she looked away. In her heart she knew they would be soon parted. Not necessarily because of her father, more likely the demands of war.
Firth also had to look away. He wasn't used to such close attention and it made him uncomfortable.
As he held Constance close he saw small craft busily going about their business from ship to shore. Even for a port there was a lot of movement.
"Looks like an army is moving out," he said.
She sighed: "Yes, I'm afraid we will be separated again Joshua ...'
He squeezed her waist and drew her tight.
"My duty is to the King and I must serve where he sends me, Constance."
She gave a light laugh: "Not that I'd know would I Joshua?"
He instantly blushed. "I'm sorry I did not mean to ..."
"Insult the daughter of a General? No, I should think not ... Captain."
He drew back to look at her and saw a smile. Then she laughed. "Oh Joshua, I understand army life. I do know what being an officer will mean for you and anyone who is with you."
Firth was saved from more embarrassment when Wren arrived.
"Isn't this such a beautiful city. Just look at those domes ... my God, look at that cathedral!"
Firth rolled his eyes. "Chris is there anything in your life other than buildings?"
"Not just buildings, Joshua. Great buildings. Homages to man's creativity."
"Oh dear God," he said, as Constance laughed.
"I was thinking those tenders are having a busy time. That looks like an army on the move."
"Joshua," his friend answered, "is there anything you think about other than armies?"
Firth bridled. "I was thinking about Sam ... and of course you Constance ..." he added, just a little too late for his liking.
It was her turn to tighten her arm. Then they both laughed.
"Have I missed something?" Wren asked. "If I'm being a third leg please tell me and I'll go and chat with some ... midshipman ... somewhere else."
Giving the Marine officer her most stunning smile, Constance touched him on the arm and said: "If you leave Captain Wren I shall report you to my father."
"I'll not even move my eyelids, my lady," he responded, causing the three of them to crack up.
Watching a large gun being winched aboard a merchantman Wren narrowed his eyes.
"That looks like a Gribeauval ... sorry Constance, a French cannon. We must be taking them back to England."
"Well there are a lot of them on that dock," Firth said. "I'd be happy with them not firing at us again."
He remembered Rolica and how those guns punched great holes in the Worcesters' ranks as they advanced. The fewer of those killers the Frogs have the better, he thought.

Firth remembered the faces of his old comrades and, of course, Brook's. He had only been gone a short while but if felt like a lifetime ago. Colonel Lake was dead, Captain Gell too, hundreds of other men of the regiment had been killed or wounded. And that was just at Rolica. More fell at Vimeiro.

While he was sure Brook was wolfing down a huge meal somewhere, there was also the black shadow of realism nagged at him that his friend was dead. He shook his head and tried to think of something else.

Ahead was a space in the wooden docks and the helmsman skillfully steered the Dragon towards it.

As they closed Allison joined them at the rail.

Wren asked Firth: "Joshua do you have a 'scope?"

Firth looked at the Marine officer who instantly recalled the infantry Captain never had a telescope.

Allison slapped one open and handed it to Wren.

'Damn my eyes, those are French horses being loaded," he muttered.

The group could now hear clearly the calls and instructions of those on the dock. There were English yells, excited Portuguese calls and … French commands ringing out.

"What the …?" Firth blurted out. "There are bloody Frogs there!"

Each of the British officers looked at each dumbfounded and then back to the quay. Allison and Wren yelled out at almost the same time "Beat to quarters" and within seconds the deep call of the drums had sailors and Marines running to retrieve muskets and swords from their racks.

At the same time other seamen poured out from below decks and ran to the rail.

"What's going on Captain?" Firth asked Allison.

"I'm not sure, Joshua, but there are definitely Frenchies working on those docks."

Wren joined in: "And they are not under armed guard … what the hell is going on?"

Satisfied his crew was prepared for a rush of the enemy Allison watched as his bosun brought the vessel into the quayside with a barely noticeable bump.

"Captain Wren how are your Marines?" Allison asked.

"Armed and ready, Captain Allison."

"Keep the ship secure, sir, until we find out what is going on."

"Aye, Captain."

"Captain Firth would you care to join me on shore?"

"Certainly, Captain."

As Constance moved forward Allison said with authority: "Not at present my lady. Let's us find out what is afoot."

He and Firth moved down the gangway and on to the wooden dockside.

To Firth's eyes the wharves looked like any of those he had often visited with his father. They were busy with movement everywhere and the energy was added to by the loud calls of orders ringing out.

To his right Firth could see horses being lifted on to a British transport. Their long tails instantly told him they were French but the men hauling them up and over the railing were cursing in very British language.

Ahead he could see a company of Redcoats resting with their muskets in vertical stacks while, to his left, wagons were lined up next to another British vessel. Wooden crates were being passed down from the back of the carts and carried slowly up the gangway to be tied down on the deck.

A warning shout from the nearest cart rang out and the men waiting to receive a box jumped out of the way. The crate hit the dockside and broke open. Firth was astounded to see silver goblets and plates clatter across the ground.

A barrage of abuse in French was screamed at the men involved as they hurriedly tried to recover the shiny metal and throw it back into the chest.

Firth and Allison looked askance at each other.

A carriage drew up next to them and Firth heard a familiar voice.

"Captain Firth, a moment sir."

The door swung open and the slow-moving figure of General Benton emerged.

"General, so good to see you … but what is going on here?"

"What you see, Captain, are the results of caution, inaction and, well, damn stupidity."

"Sir?"

"I'm sorry, Firth, I'm frustrated by what has happened here since you left.

"You have me confused General Benton, what has been going on?''

The usually amiable General gave a sigh. "Ah, dear boy, we won a war and then talked it away."

Firth was confused and had no idea what the General was referring to.

Then Benton straightened up and shot him a big beaming smile.

"But that doesn't matter, young Joshua, what matters is that you are home safe and you have done us proud."

He grabbed Firth by both shoulders and gave him a gentle shake.

"Wellesley is so pleased with your efforts in the mission to Minas. So, pleased …"

"I'm delighted General," Firth almost stammered, his mind whirring to try to work out what was going on around him.

"Yes we have had a dispatch of your exploits, although I am sure there are more interesting details to share.

"I will be able to give a full report sir."

Benton peered at Firth's face. "You've a scar or two more than the last time I saw you Joshua. And a limp too."

"Ay, I have sir. I'm hoping the leg will fully heal soon."

"The French?"

"No, our Spanish allies, sir. My leg was courtesy of the dagger of General Minas."

"What? Bless my soul. No … "

"I'm afraid so, General Benton."

"Firth, did you find out what happened to Sir Hew Dalrymple's daughter?"

"I did, general. Her boat was sunk by Minas' navy …"

"Upon my soul …" he gasped.

"And she was taken prisoner and held by him …"

"The brute …"

"He was sir, of the worst kind. But Captains Allison and Wren, as well as myself, were able to rescue her … and deal with Minas."

"I'm glad, Joshua, she is a pretty young thing. Was she … harmed?"

"No, general, she is safe and well and is aboard the Dragon not 200 paces from here."

"Is she now?" he asked. "There's something I must tell you about her father."

"Is he ill, sir?"

"No, Joshua, he is being recalled to England – along with Burrard and Sir Arthur - to defend themselves over the signing of the Convention of Cintra."

"Cintra? The one that was signed with General Kellerman?"

"Yes, that shameful treaty forced upon Sir Arthur by Dalrymple and Burrard. We had the damned devils by the throat and those timid men let the Frenchies hoodwink us into allowing them to escape."

Benton looked up with a shadow of shame and anger passing across his face. "What you see is the result. We are evacuating the French in our ships and they are taking with them their cannon, their weapons and, worst of all, all the loot they have stripped from this impoverished region."

"We allowed this?"

"To our shame," Benton said, "and the fury of the Portuguese. Can you not hear them?"

Now the General mentioned it he could hear the clamour of a crowd away from the dockside.

"It is getting worse Joshua," he said, "imagine this ... we are having to protect our enemies from our allies at the points of our bayonets!"

"Dear God," Firth exclaimed.

"But I will give Sir Hew credit for standing by his treaty. He personally led two brigades of men up to Elvas to rescue a French garrison that was being attacked by a Spanish force."

"Spanish?"

"They had crossed the border and were making a nuisance of themselves. Not only were they preventing the French from leaving by besieging them, they were also stealing food from the Portuguese villagers. That turned the locals back to our side because at least we ask for supplies – and then pay for them!"

"When do the Frogs leave?"

"Today, my boy," he said, "and it can't come soon enough. There has been bloody murder through the streets of Lisbon over the past week or so. Any French soldiers caught alone have been brutally done away with.

"It was so bad they had cannons out in the streets protecting any pathway to where they were quartered. Generals like Loisin, the butcher of Evora, daren't move without a company of dragoons escorting them. We are sitting on powder keg."

"General, one of the French crates spilled from a wagon just there and out poured silverware ... is that the loot you were talking about?"

Benton shook his head and looked downwards. "It is my boy, they have pillaged this land and we are letting them take it with them."

"How can we allow it?

"We have tried to limit it, Joshua, we even have been searching through officers' baggage to try to determine what is personal and what is just theft."

"And ...?"

"Most of it is straight out theft. General Junot, who has already gone, sent his aide-de-camp to Paris with 14 volumes of manuscripts of a 15th Century Bible. Lord knows what that is worth.

"And that is just a fraction of what he took. He had 53 large chests of valuables. You know, Joshua, I doubt there is anything left of value in any of the cathedrals and churches in his city. The French leaders were like vultures and picked the place clean."

"They clearly have no honour, sir."

"No, they don't. But they do have more than 25,000 pounds in gold coin and have not paid any of the bills they have built up since being here."

"How can that be, General?"

"It's in the terms of the Convention and we have to stand by it. Much as it chokes me to do so," he added.

The pair had been walking towards the entrance to the docks as they had been talking. Ahead Firth could see British Redcoats lining the street, their muskets held slanted across chests. They faced out at thousands of civilians who were shouting abuse at them.

Then Firth heard a sound that he knew would ignite the fuse to Benton's powder keg. In the distance he could hear the pas-de-charge - the French army's call to arms. The distant drums boomed out their rhythm. On the field of battle they were meant to intimidate an enemy army. The solid beat telling the foe to move or suffer.

It was a deliberate challenge from the French and Firth could hear the anger of the Portuguese crowd rise.

The closer the drums got the more agitated the Portuguese were getting.

"We need some men here General, when the dock gates open that crowd isn't going to be stopped if things turn bad. I need to get Captain Wren and his Marines here and sailors from the Dragon as well."

As if called by a mental link Wren arrived on the scene leading his men.

"Thought you may need a bit of backup Joshua ... again."

"Thanks Chris ... how do you want to deploy?"

"I thought about half on each side of the road, but that seems to me a bit too much like an official farewell. I think we should have the men lined up in front of the Dragon."

"I agree," Firth said, turning to Benton.

"General, if I may suggest, it may be better for your carriage to be moved by the Dragon. We can protect it there.

Firth realised he was ordering about a General and stopped. "Forgive me General Benton ... would you command here, sir?"

"I'm honoured, Captain Firth, "but I believe you two have everything in hand. I will let you younger men have the ... fun."

Wren's Marines quickly moved into position and Firth could see Constance watching from the deck of the Dragon. Allison stood at her side. She waved at him and he tipped his bicorne in response.

Benton saw the gesture and looked sideways at Firth.

"A conquest of the heart, Captain?"

"Miss Constance and I have become close, General."

"You are a lucky man," Benton said fondly, "she is the fairest lady I have seen in this country. But, Joshua, remember her father ..."

Firth hadn't wanted to think of Sir Hew. Not only was he one of the authors of the current situation, but he was now more likely than ever to take Constance back to England with him.

"Thank you General, I am mindful of him … and the possibilities."

"Good lad, Sir Arthur has plans for you."

Firth nodded, but didn't dwell on that comment. The gates to the docks were now being swung open and even the power of the drumming couldn't drown out the howls of fury being aimed at the departing French.

"Where do you want me Chris?"

"By my side Joshua …"

"And mine, Captain," Constance said from his left.

Firth spun and was about to tell her to go back to the safety of the ship but knew it would be futile and so shrugged his shoulders instead.

"I knew you would see it my way, Captain."

"As if there was any choice," he said.

A few scuffles were breaking out near the entrance as British troops pushed civilians back from breaking their red line.

In the meantime the French column continued its procession. At its head was a squadron of lancers in the deep blue uniforms and czapkas of the Poles. The man leading the way was familiar to him and Firth's hand immediately flew to his sword grip.

Wren's hand clamped down on his shoulder.

"Leave it be, my friend, leave it be."

Zapalski saw the movements and broke from his men to walk his horse across to Firth. Reining in two paces away from the British officer he looked down and smiled.

"Ah, boy, you are here to wave me off?"

Firth said nothing he just looked up at the Pole with anger.

'I see you have another scar to go with the one I gave you," Zapalski baited Firth. 'Where is your handkerchief for you to wave goodbye with?"

Wren's hand tightened and Constance placed hers upon Firth's left arm.

'Ah, you are being kept safe by a beautiful woman …"

Firth's anger was building quickly. "Shut your damned mouth or …"

"Or you will what, boy? Do you forget what happened at Vimeiro?"

"How could I? It was a battle where an infantry officer dealt with a mounted cavalryman."

Zapalski's eyes narrowed. "I should have killed you."

"True," Firth countered, "But clearly you weren't good enough."

"Joshua," Constance and Wren warned together.

But Firth's blood was now up. "How embarrassing was it to not be able to kill a man even when you had the advantage of being on horseback?"

Zapalski growled, his hand flexing its gloved fingers. He turned his gaze to Constance. "She is lovely … but maybe she would prefer a real man?"

Firth had moved before his friends, or even Zapalski, could react. He covered the distance between the Pole and himself in an instant and swung his elbow into the nose of Zapalski's horse.

The creature whinnied and reared to get away. By that time Firth had his sword cleared from its scabbard and as the horse's front hooves touched the cobbles he again smashed the creature on the nose – this time with the weapon's handguard.

Caught off balance, Zapalski could only try to hold his mount upright. Failing to do so he leapt off drawing his own blade as the horse galloped away bleeding heavily from its nostrils.

Slashing his sword in front of him, Zapalski advanced on Firth. The young English officer wasn't holding back and ignored further pleas from Constance and Wren.

The ring of steel on steel sounded clearly above the drums, whose rhythm faltered as the musicians were stunned by what they were seeing.

Zapalski was slightly bigger and more experienced, but Firth's sword skills and his cold anger countered his opponent.

"I told you, you Polish bastard, what would happened if we met on even terms," Firth called.

"I will slice you open," Zapalski hissed and aimed a waist-high slash at Firth's stomach. Firth avoided the blade and leaped forward. He parried the return slash from the Pole before spinning and smashing his right elbow back into Zapalski's face. He felt cartilage give way and the Major gave a grunt of pain.

"Bastard," the Pole spluttered, as blood ran freely down his face and into his moustache and mouth.

Firth closed again. This time he jabbed at his enemy, forcing him backwards. Zapalski stumbled and went down on one knee, his sword raised in defence.

Both French and English voices were yelling at the pair. The men in blue were calling on Zapalski to stand and fight, while Wren's Marines were calling for Firth to finish the cavalryman off. Firth advanced on the Pole.

"Captain Firth!" a voice bellowed.

Firth stopped.

"Put away your blade, sir."

Firth hesitated.

"Now, Captain!"

The young man took a deep breath and reluctantly eased the steel into its leather sheath.

He knew that voice and he dared not disobey it.

"Yes, General Wellesley," he said.

Looking in the direction of the Commander's voice he saw the General on his horse staring down at him in anger.

"You sir, will return to your ship and let these men leave in peace. And you will await my presence."

Firth straightened and returned to the Marines who parted to allow his access to the gangway.

The men offered him quiet congratulations and a series of "well done, sir" as he boarded the Dragon. Allison shook his head as he passed. "My cabin, Captain Firth."

Sitting on a small chair in Allison's quarters Firth stared at the wooden floor. His heart was still pounding with adrenalin and he would have loved to have walked the surge off, but Firth knew he was in trouble. He pressed the palms of his hands to his eyes and shook his head. The French drums were booming again and he could hear the occasional cat call of "bugger off Johnny Crapaud" and "see you soon in Paris." A quiet knock at the door came before the latch lifted. "Senor Joshua, can I get you something?"

It was Hector and Firth smiled at his companion. "A brandy would be good, Hector." Seeing the puzzled look Firth added: "If nothing else, how about a cup of tea?" "Si, one moment."

Firth had taken on Hector as his manservant following the destruction of Minas' invasion flotilla. The one-armed Spaniard had nothing to go back to and so willingly accepted Firth's offer.

Sitting there alone Firth had the chance to think about his actions. Could I have done better, he asked himself. Yes, the answer came back, I should have killed the bastard. While he was sipping the tea Hector had brought him, Firth thought that of the great qualities the Spaniard had tea-making was not one of them. The brew served up was like coffee and subtlety of flavour had been smothered in an overabundance of tealeaves. Still it was hot and helped the young officer calm down.

On a number of occasions he heard voices in the chamber outside but no-one came in. Looks like people were avoiding the condemned man, he thought. Then the latch sounded and in walked Wren followed by Constance. Firth stood and accepted the hug she gave him.

'Oh Joshua, what have you done?'

'Well, Constance …" he began.

'Don't say anything Captain Firth," she said, "about duty, or country … even me … you attacked him because you didn't like him."

He looked down at her and signaled his agreement.

"You are right, Constance. I do not like that Polish major because he killed a number of my men at Vimeiro. And he tried to kill me there too. I was probably lucky he didn't manage it then. And yes today his arrogance towards you – and me – delivered a challenge that needed to be answered."

"So you answered it," she said flatly.

"I did, Constance, and would do so again. Particularly if someone insults you the way he did."

She looked up and smiled, a little sadly Firth thought.

"Your eyes are even greener when you are angry. Did you know that?"

She stifled a laugh and put her head on to his shoulder. "Well, at least he didn't cut you up this time. I want to keep you with me for some time Captain Firth. Preferably in one piece."

Wren broke in. "He is highly likely to be with you for some time if Wellesley feels that way inclined. Our General did not looked happy with you Joshua."

"Maybe he'll cashier me and send me back to England …"

"More likely you'll be on the next merchantman to New South Wales. I'm told they need good men out there."

"I'm hoping for England," Constance said.

"I'm hoping for promotion to major," Firth said … and burst out laughing.

The others couldn't help themselves and broke into laughter too. Constance pushed her face deep into the hollow of Firth's shoulder and held on tightly to his uniform.

"It will be all right, Constance … one way or another. It's not as if I need my army pay," he added and kissed the top of her head. Her hair still smelled of roses.

The cabin door swung open and a grim-faced General Benton entered. He stared at both Constance and Wren. "I must ask you both to leave, Sir Arthur is here to see Captain Firth."

Constance kissed Firth on the cheek and Wren patted him on the shoulder.

"Blighty or Botany Bay, my friend."

After they left and closed the door Firth checked his uniform buttons. They were all done up. He looked at his bicorne. It was marked with dust from the docks' cobbles. He gently tried to brush it clean with his hand.

He could hear voices and footsteps outside and braced himself. The door swung open and in walked Wellesley and Benton.

Firth stood ramrod straight. He looked at Wellesley and his now-cold eyes.

"General Wellesley, I regret what I have done and …"

Wellesley's right hand shot up chest high, instantly silencing Firth.

He looked at the young man for almost a full minute without saying a word.

Firth had never felt more uncomfortable in his life. He was sure his career was over and the longer Wellesley stood watching him the more certain he became.

Then Wellesley spoke, without shifting his piercing hawk-like gaze off his victim.

"Are you injured, Captain Firth?"

Firth was taken aback. "I do not believe so, General Wellesley."

"Good, good."

"Sir Arthur …"

Again the hand shot up.

Wellesley crossed over to Firth and looked up.

"Well done, my boy. Well done."

Firth was stunned. "Sir Arthur?"

"I watched that incident on the dock and thought you did bloody well, young Firth. Bloody well indeed."

"But …"

"Here we were all lined up as those bloody Frenchies marched off thumbing their long noses at us. Pockets filled with Portuguese treasures and we just had to stand and bear it.

"But you, my boy, you showed them what we think of them and what we are capable of.

"It is a lesson they will not forget. I am so proud of you, your temper and your sword."

With that he patted Firth on the left shoulder and beamed. "And you knocked over his horse … his horse! Did you see that Benton?"

"I did, Sir Arthur," Benton said, "I could scarcely miss it - as the damned thing nearly stood on me in its hurry to get away from Captain Firth here."

Wellesley laughed his whooping laugh then brought his finger to his lips. "Mustn't be congratulating you too loudly, Joshua, everyone thinks I am here to cashier you!" Then he placed both hands on Firth's shoulders and said: "Nothing further from the truth, my boy. The men love you for it ... I heard what they were calling out to the French.

"It was a bit too polite for my liking, but there you go. Sent them scurrying off with fleas in their ears."

Benton appeared at Wellesley's side with a tray of glasses.

"Port? Excellent idea Benton, excellent idea."

Wellesley threw down the port in one gulp and proffered his glass for a refill.

"Damn I shall miss this stuff while in England. I can only take a gross with me and that won't last long. Come on Captain, drink up, you've a long story to tell me I believe."

"Well," Firth began.

"Come on lad, hurry up I've been waiting for this for a week!"

So as to keep track of everything Firth started with the trip down the Spanish coast, his initial meeting with Minas, catching sight of Constance.

Wellesley stopped him there. "This Constance, she's "Dowager" Dalrymple's gal isn't she?

"She is, Sir Arthur."

"Bit of a looker," he added.

"That she is, Sir Arthur," Firth responded.

Benton broke in. "It seems, Sir Arthur, that young Firth here and Miss Dalrymple struck up a ... friendship."

Wellesley looked at Firth. "Did you now? On the King's time?"

"Well, it just sort of happened ..."

"It always does, young Firth, it always does," Wellesley said and let out another whoop of delight.

"She's a brave girl then?"

"That she is, Sir Arthur."

"And she's taken a fancy to you?"

"Ay, I believe she has."

"Well," the General said, "She will need courage if she is to be with you. I'm not going to give you an easy life young man. If you want action then you'll be getting plenty of it I can assure you of that."

"I am ready for it, sir."

"That you have proved ... now on with the story."

Firth explained how Wren had discovered the Spanish invasion fleet and the plan with Allison to both free Constance and escape the hidden harbour in order to warn the garrison at Gibraltar. Firth told Wellesley how he had fallen into Minas' trap.

"I'm told Minas stabbed you?"

"He did sir, in the thigh. Then he bound me and put me on the bomb ship."

"How did you escape, lad?"

"I was helped by Hector – a Spaniard - who is now my manservant, Sir Arthur. And

Major Bland … he gave Hector my sword."

"Damn good man that Bland," Wellesley said. "Damn good man. Been with me for years, although serving with the Spanish."

"Yes, in the end he saved my life. On the bomb ship Minas was about to kill me when Bland ran him through."

"He killed him?"

"Ah, no Sir Arthur."

"Well who did kill the treacherous scoundrel?"

"I did, General. I stabbed him through the throat."

"Good lad, Captain Firth, he deserved nothing less."

Wellesley smiled at Firth. "You have done better than either Benton or I could have hoped, young man. You saved Gibraltar and quite possibly the war. If the Dons had got that place back they may have had second thoughts about staying with us against Boney."

Wellesley was interrupted by a quick rap on the cabin door. Benton stood and went to see who it was.

He turned to look at Firth with a broad smile on his face. "There's someone here to see you Captain."

Firth stood and looked to see who it was. As soon as he saw he broke into a massive grin.

"Sam!"

With the departure of the hated French Lisbon was in celebratory mode. Nine months of occupation had ended and the Portuguese were delighted.

Fireworks and spontaneous street gatherings kept most of the city's inhabitants happy, while the nobility and members of high-ranking society attended lavish dinner parties. A low-ranking temporary Captain like Firth would normally have no chance of attending such soirees and dinners, but not only was he the preferred escort for Constance Dalrymple – regarded as being a perfect example of an English rose – but he was also the man who saved Gibraltar.

Firth was famous – and he hated it.

Both Wren and Brook reveled in his discomfort and ribbed him unmercifully, but other officers of the 29th were less generous.

The worst was Major Ricketts. With Major Way on sick leave in England, Ricketts was the senior officer of the regiment and had taken up his dislike of Firth as soon as the young Captain returned. If a menial duty was to be officered then Firth was first in line for the opportunity.

Ricketts never outwardly criticised Firth, but he whispered terms such as "Wellesley's lapdog" and "pet" when he was around.

It was never within Firth's hearing as the Major was mindful of the younger man's low flashpoint and reputation with the blade. Rickett's cronies within the Worcesters – such as the rich wastrel Captain McGuire - would laugh, but most of the older officers would show no reaction. Among the rank-and-file men Firth was a hero. They revered him.

Most of them had fought with Firth at Rolica – where he held the line against a strong French counterattack – and again at Vimeiro where his quick thinking had stopped the regiment being overrun by Zapalski's lancers.

Many of those soldiers owed Firth their lives and they were willing to repay him with unconditional loyalty.

Brook was delighted to be reunited with Firth and couldn't be with him enough. Firth's boyhood friend was still getting over the serious head injury he received at Rolica and there were times his memory was not what it once was. None of his companions worried much as he was still the same always happy Brook, but they could see he was frustrated by his at-times slow responses.

Dr Guthrie had privately told Firth that, with time, Brook would return to normal. The blow he received had been fearful, but Brook was showing every sign of slowly getting over it.

When given time off from duty, the pair could be seen strolling with Constance and Wren around Lisbon's key buildings. Unsurprisingly Brook knew all the places to eat, while Wren picked those with the best views of cathedrals.

Firth would admire the vista and then look at his lady. She only had eyes for him. But both knew those days were coming to an end. Her father was in London to face an inquiry over the Convention of Cintra. Wellesley and Burrard were also back in England to face the same scrutiny.

Constance didn't know when, but her departure for London was imminent. She had not gone with Sir Hew because she said she needed to pack their belongings properly. Her father knew the real reason and grudgingly obliged. Before he left Lisbon he had taken her aside and told her: "Firth is a personable young man, my dear. He is intelligent, brave, well off and cares for you. But be careful, he likely won't live to an old age."

Constance knew exactly what her father was saying. Firth was brave to the point of foolhardiness and would almost certainly die on a battlefield in some foreign land. Her head knew the sense of what her father said, but her heart was filled with the gallant young officer who had not only saved her from Minas, but also knowingly risked himself against Zapalski over her honour.

How could one not love a man like that, she asked her father?

He had just gazed at her, smiled sympathetically and said: "You can't."

In that moment Constance doubted she had never loved her father more. He had been criticised for the Convention of Cintra, but had seen that as a way to quickly rid Portugal of the French succubus that was pillaging everything of value the impoverished nation had. The pressure on him had been immense, but still his concern was for her not himself. She knew Firth agreed with Wellesley over the matter – he would have pursued and wiped out the threat posed by Junot's demoralised French.

Sir Hew, however, was at heart a diplomat and Constance admired his standing by a principle to save as many lives as he could.

She was grateful Firth had not made any unseemly comments about her father, although she hadn't expected him to. Her young man had a code of honour that held such pettiness in contempt.

He was a fine friend but, as she had seen, an unforgiving enemy. Minas had discovered that, as had the Polish major.

Having witnessed a number of occasions when Major Ricketts had baited Firth she was amazed the senior officer was still alive, or at least unchallenged. She knew dueling was banned in the British army but enemies still found a way to settle their differences with weapons. A matter of honour … Constance shook her head … there was no honour in dying over a perceived insult. It was just stupidity, but then she was not a soldier.

She could only hope that Firth would keep his blood cool when dealing with such an annoying man. Constance found Ricketts repugnant, the symbol of much that was wrong with England. She was glad Wellesley disliked the Major and even more so that the regiment's senior soldier, Major Way, had little time for him. But Way would not be back for some weeks and that left Firth at the mercy of Ricketts.

Firth could always rely upon Wren, but he was soon to sail for new assignments. Brook, bless him, meant well but was no Wren, she thought. He was almost Firth's conscience – a social barometer whose reactions gave Firth another view on what was happening. Bless Brook, she thought, he is still a boy while Firth was hardening into a weapon.

She loved him, and wouldn't change him, but her father's words were a warning. Not against Firth, just pointing out the likely outcome of his life as a soldier.

Constance hoped she was a part of his plans. She wanted so, she prayed so, but when she returned to England, as she must soon do, would his feelings for her temper his devotion to duty?

It wasn't up to her, she knew, and what would be would be. She could only love him, tell him she did and be there for him. But not forever.

If his army life with the Worcesters was more important she would understand, she hoped, and would let him be.

No matter, Constance told herself that was way in the future. Tonight was a regimental dinner and Firth had asked her to accompany him to the occasion. And she had dressed to impress. The gown she had chosen was made of a delicate silk that fitted her like a skin. Her shoulders were revealed and its pastel green hue not only showed off her eyes, but the red in her long tresses and her pale skin.

When Firth saw her he slowly bowed his head and called her "my Venus." She smiled and he brought his hand up to her cheek and gently kissed her.

"You are stunning Constance. I would sing it to all who would hear."

Having heard him croak out *Over the Hills and Far Away*, a popular military air of the time, she quietly said "let's just leave it to your heart!"

He chuckled and winked. "Whatever my lady desires."

She stopped and looked at him in the eyes. "Joshua, please do not let Ricketts provoke you."

"Oh he will provoke me, Constance," Firth said, "The only issue will be do I take the bait?"

"My love, ignore his barbs. You are a far better man than he and he is just jealous."

"Ay, my lady, that's why it is so hard to ignore. Turning the other cheek is fine for Methodists, but where I am from a blow is returned with a blow."

Turning her green eyes to his she placed a gloved hand upon his and squeezed. "Enjoy the evening with me, ignore all barbs and take pleasure in the fact most officers in that room would love to have done what you have managed."

"Constance, I will do as you desire."

The moment was broken by Brook, who slapped his friend on the shoulder and said: "About bloody time. Listen to the lady, sir, she knows of what she speaks."

"Thank you Lieutenant," Firth said lightly, "Let's go in and see what Ricketts has in store."

The candlelit banquet room was dominated by four tables arranged in a giant square. Every officer from the regiment was present, as were any ladies they had invited. A string quartet played in one corner, Handel - Firth guessed.

When he entered with Constance on his arm the talk around the tables stopped instantly. The men were struck by Constance's appearance, while the women eyed Firth with a regard that should have sparked a score of duels – had the men looked away from his companion's beauty.

Ricketts raised himself from his chair at the head table and called: "Ah welcome Lieutenant Firth, fashionably late I see."

Firth knew the Major was trying to rile him by ignoring his unofficial rank of captain but before he could stop himself, he responded: "About as late as you were at Rolica .. sir."

Constance's fingers clawed into his arm. "Joshua, be nice."

The Major seemed to ignore the jibe. "And greetings to your lady ... it's a shame her father wasn't in town to be here as well."

The fingers dug in harder.

"Thank you Major," Constance said, "your thoughts are appreciated."

Ricketts tipped his head in a condescending way. "Well, since you are finally here, Lieutenant, we can begin to eat."

Holding a retort back Firth drew back Constance's chair and settled her in before sitting next to her. Brook was to his right.

The meal was sumptuous. Roast pheasant, grilled sardines, and a roasted pig that Firth thought was the best he had ever tasted.

Throughout the evening Ricketts kept staring at Firth and Brook. Firth noted the attention, but focused on Constance. Later, as the last of the post-dessert ports had drained, Ricketts staggered to his feet.

"Lieutenant Firth," he slurred. "It is unfortunate but I need someone to oversee the cleaning of the latrines tonight."

"I'm sorry, Major Ricketts, I'm not sure I understand you."

"It is fairly simple, Lieutenant, I want you to make sure the latrines are cleaned properly."

"Tonight, Major?"

"Yes, Lieutenant Firth, tonight."

Firth stood and glared down the table at Ricketts. Fortified by drink, the Major stared back. Everyone in the room expected there to be trouble.

Firth's hand touched his hilt and every officer in the regiment and their ladies drew breath.

"Major," Firth directly addressed Ricketts. "I have always obeyed your orders, but this is one I will not."

"Shame, shame," shouted McGuire.

"There are a few here who have no liking for me and that is their problem, not mine," Firth continued.

"Get out Firth," McGuire yelled again.

Firth stopped what he was saying and turned his gaze upon the overweight lickspittle. "Captain McGuire, I have often thought it is better to be silent and be thought a fool, than to open one's mouth and remove all doubt. I bid you keep silent, sir."

Laughter broke out around the table.

Ricketts said: "If you do not do as you are ordered sir, you will be thrown out of this regiment to your everlasting shame."

Looking back at Ricketts' black eyes Firth said: "Major, I will not leave this room, nor will I leave this regiment. I have shared the field with many here and I have spilled my blood on the regimental colours at Rolica and Vimeiro."

"Hear, hear," Brook shouted, only to be quietened by Constance.

"I am as much a part of the Worcesters as you and will be forced out of the 29th by no man.

"We have a campaign and a war to win and no matter our mutual dislike I will do my best for the regiment."

Firth looked around the room and picked up his glass. He raised it.

"The King."

Everyone stood, Ricketts reluctantly, and returned the toast. "The King."

"England," Firth cried.

"England!" came the return shout.

"The ever-sworded 29th."

"The 29th!" the room echoed.

Firth took his time to look around the gathering. "Ladies and gentlemen, I am – and always will be – a Vein Opener."

"The Vein Openers!" was shouted back once.

Then it was shouted again.

And then, finally, a third time.

As it resounded around the room Firth knew, as did Ricketts, the regiment was his for as long as he wanted it.

The End

AUTHOR'S NOTE

In setting out to write The Vein Openers I had a basic concept – my very loose plan was to follow one British regiment through its campaigns of the Napoleonic Wars.

I knew I wanted to start at Rolica, followed by Vimeiro and then cover each major clash the Worcesters were involved in.

However, I also wanted to include wider adventures for Joshua Firth and the ones I have planned will see him involved with plenty of action outside of Spain and Portugal and meeting some very interesting figures.

I also wanted to have various characters through which the reader could see different aspects and attitudes from opposing sides. Few of the characters are perfect – I did not wish them to be – and the less-likeable characters are not all bad. Well, except one ...

Firth's journey began a very long time ago but he was regularly set aside so I could pay the mortgage, build websites and raise children.

One of my websites is The Napoleonic Guide (www.napoleonguide.com), which came into being in the early days of the Internet because I couldn't find enough information on the Napoleonic Wars and so built an online resource myself.

Most authors have a fairly tight framework in which to develop their storyline however, while working within the historical confines of where the 29th had to be at certain times, I let my characters develop with no pre-ordained plan for them.

Why the 29th Regiment of Foot? Well, picking a regiment was no easy task and took a lot of bookwork before I decided upon the Worcesters.

The more I read about the 29th the more they seemed to fit my ideas. The battles they fought in, their previous history and, of course, that fabulous nickname The Vein Openers.

They also had a lot of clashes with the Polish forces of Napoleon's army and there was no love lost between the men of the Worcesters and the Poles. Hence one of my main enemies of Firth had to be Polish.

I have tried to mesh fictional characters with real people who featured in the Peninsular War and keep the historic storyline and battle details as accurate as possible.

While the focus of Joshua Firth's adventures will be the Peninsula, he will have other tasks that will touch on wider parts of the Napoleonic Wars.

One of my aims was to bring to life the age of Napoleonic warfare in a way that would interest people other than those devotees of the Napoleonic Era.

I hope I have managed that.

-     Richard Moore
richard@richardmoore.com

MAIN CHARACTERS

+ Denotes a historical person.

The British

Joshua Firth: Son of a wealthy Yorkshire businessman and estate owner.

Samuel Brook: Firth's best friend and son of a successful chandler.

Jonas Ricketts: Royal Navy Captain.

Colonel Denholme Firth: Yorkshire squire and Firth's father.

Captain Christopher Wren: A Marine officer who loves architecture.

General Benton: Senior aide to Wellesley.

Lord Edmund McGuire, Captain, 29th Foot, rich wastrel.

Major Edward Ricketts, 29th Foot, brother of Captain Jonas Ricketts, RN.

+ Surgeon George Guthrie, 29th Foot's regimental surgeon.

+ Colonel Charles Taylor: Commander of the 20th Light Dragoons.

+ Sir Arthur Wellesley: British commander in the Peninsula.

+ Thomas Needham: British soldier.

+ Colonel the Honourable George Lake, commander of the 29th.

+ Black Jack, his horse.

+ Major Gregory Way, 29th Foot.

+ Garret Dalton, a poacher from Kent.

+ Jonathon Siddle, William Sweeney, 40-year veterans.

+ Sgt Absalom Barclay.

+ Private William Good, a troublemaker.

- Sergeant-Major Richard Richards, a veteran soldier.

- Twin One and Twin two, medical orderlies with one arm each.

- Captain Peter Hodge, 29th.

Captain Robert Gell, 29th Foot.

- Lt TL Coker, 29 Foot.

Private Reardon, 29th Foot's armourer.

Private William Slater, 29th Foot.

Cornet Finlay, 20th Light Dragoons.

Constance Dalrymple, daughter of Sir Hew Dalrymple.

- Sir Harry Burrard, British commander after Wellesley.

- Sir Hew Dalrymple, former British commander of Gibraltar and army commander after Burrard.

- Captain S Gauntlett, 29th Foot, grenadiers

Captain Peter Allison, HMS Dragon.

The Portuguese

+ Bernardo Zagalo: Leader of Portuguese student force from Coimbra who seized Figueria da Foz from the French.
The Chef: a Portuguese bandit leader.

The French

+ General Louis "One Hand" Loisin, brutal French general.
+ General Henri Delaborde. French commander at Rolica.
+ General Jean-Andoche Junot. Senior French general at Vimeiro and friend of Napoleon Bonaparte. Known as the Tempest for his volcanic temper. A rapacious looter, but a man who loved both the arts and good cuisine.
Captain Hippolyte Rey: A junior French officer. Captured by Firth in Portugal. Fought with Marshal Louis Davout at Austerlitz and Auerstadt.
Major Stanislaus Zapalski: Senior officer in Polish lancers of the Vistula Legion. Courageous, single-minded and brutal when needs be.
Citoyen Charles Tabbard, imperial notary.
Lieutenant Dezydery Chlapowski, deputy of Zapalski.
Sous-officier Florian Bellegarde, French soldier.
Ugo Bellegarde, his younger brother.
Captain Hippolyte Rey, French aide de camp.
+ General Francois Kellerman, skilled French general.
+ General Antoine Brennier, French general at Vimeiro.

The Spanish

General Don Costanzo y Minas, Spanish general.
Hector, one-armed Spanish stallholder.
Major Connor Bland, Irish adjutant to Minas.

MILITARY GLOSSARY

Abatis:
Barricade of logs.
Aide/Aide de Camp:
Assistant to senior officer.
Amalgame:
System that mixed experienced, regular troops with conscripts in France's revolutionary armies.
Atiradore:
Portuguese sharpshooter.
Banquette:
A parapet's firing step.
Barrelled Sash:
A hussar's girdle with lace barrels.
Battalion Company:
Centre company in a battalion.
Battery:
Six or eight-gun emplacements.
Blackening Ball:
Nugget-like substance to blacken equipment.
Breastwork:
A parapet.
Briquet:
French Infantry sabre.
Brown Bess:
Common name for the British Long Land Pattern muskets.
Cacadore:
Portuguese rifleman.
Cadnettes:
Plaits dangling from the temples of cavalrymen.
Caisson:
An artillery ammunition wagon.
Canister:
Close-range, anti-personnel ammunition for artillery. Made up of a tin container filled with musket balls, canister was designed to break apart on leaving the cannon's muzzle.
Cantoniere:
Female canteen keeper accompanying army.
Carabinier:
A heavily armed cavalry trooper.
Carbine:
A short cavalry musket.
Carcass:
Incendiary to illuminate dark areas.
Cartouche:
Cartridge box.
Cascabel:
Knob at touch-hole end of a cannon.
Case-shot:
Similar artillery ammunition to canister.
Chasseurs:
Light troops (hunters).
Chasseurs-a-Cheval:
Light cavalry.

Chasseurs-a-Pied:
Light infantry.
Cheveux-Legers:
Light cavalry including lancers, chasseurs and hussars.
Chosen Man:
Corporal in the 95th Rifles.
Club:
A short powdered queue of hair at back of head.
Cockade:
National colours worn on hats.
Colours:
Large regimental or King's flags used by British regiments.
Commissaries:
Officials who organised supplies of food and equipment for armies.
Conscription:
System where able-bodied men between certain ages were called up for military service.
Cornet:
Cavalry equivalent of an ensign or second-lieutenant.
Corps d'Armee:
A balanced miniature French army that contained its own infantry, cavalry and artillery.
Corps d'Observation:
A body of troops split from a main army to cover an opposing army.
Crapaud:
Derogatory British word for French troops (Toads).
Czapka:
Square-topped cavalry hat, mainly used by lancers.
Dents de Loup:
Wolf-teeth cloth edgings to a shabraque.
Division:
Infantry or cavalry body that included several thousand men.
Divisional Column:
A battalion-wide column of attack.
Dolman:
A short, tail-less jacket.
Dolphin:
Lifting handle on cannon.
Dragoons:
Medium cavalry capable of fighting on foot with carbines.
Eagle:
French army unit symbol.
Eclaireurs-a-Cheval:
Mounted French scouts.
Embrasure:
Opening in defensive wall to fire cannons through.
Enciente:
Stronghold's walls.
Enfilade:
Flanking fire that can hit anything within an enemy position.
Ensign:
Infantry second-lieutenant.
Facings:
Colours worn on collars, cuffs and turnbacks to identify various regiments.
Fascine:
Wood bundles used as cover in defensive lines.
Fixed Ammunition:
Artillery shell with wooden sabot base still attached.

Flank company:
Grenadier or light company of a battalion.
Flanquers:
French light infantry, usually of the Middle Guard.
Fleche:
Arrow-head shaped earthworks.
Forlorn Hope:
Volunteers to conduct first attack on fortifications.
Frog:
Looped leather belt through which a sword scabbard is hung.
Fusil:
Light musket.
Fusiliers:
General infantryman.
Gabion:
Dirt-filled cane basket used for defence works.
Glacis:
Slope up to a fortification.
Goddams:
Nickname given to British troops by the French.
Gorget:
Small, metal crescent worn by officers around their necks.
Grapeshot:
Another close-range artillery shot made of a bag filled with large metal balls.
Grasshoppers:
French nickname for the green-uniformed British riflemen.
Grenadier:
Elite infantryman.
Grenadier-a-Cheval:
Heavy cavalry trooper in the Guard Cavalry.
Grognard:
Affectionate French term for "grumblers" of the Guard infantry.
Gros-Bottes:
French nickname for the Grenadiers-a-Cheval (Big Boots).
Guidons:
Standards used by cavalry units.
Halberd:
Axe-headed polearm used by soldiers protecting the Colours.
Half-pay:
Unemployed officers (including naval lieutenants or above) were entitled to half-pay allowances despite not being on active service.
Horse Artillery:
Highly mobile, horse-drawn cannons.
Imperial Guard:
Napoleon Bonaparte's elite infantry. Later split into the Young, Middle and Old Guard.
Kurtka:
A Polish lancer jacket.
Lancers:
Lance-carrying, light cavalry.
Levee-en-Masse:
Conscription.
Light Bobs:
British nickname for light infantrymen.
Light Infantry:
Units trained for harassing duties and skirmishing.
Limber:

Used to move artillery pieces.

Line Infantry:
Regular infantry that made up the bulk of an army.

Line of Communication:
An army's link to its supply base. Includes the route reinforcements and commissaries would travel to the army.

Line of March:
Direction an army is marching.

Line of Operations:
Direction an army is marching in enemy territory.

Line of Retreat:
An army's direction of retreat, preferably on its Line of Communication.

Mamelukes:
Turkey's elite cavalry.

Masse de Decision:
Reserve troops kept out of battle until the decisive moment of the fight.

Masse de Manouevre:
French force used to outflank enemy army.

Mirliton:
Hussar cap with flying wing.

Necessaries:
Personal kit issued by army.

Old Trousers:
British nickname for French drumbeat the Pas-de-Charge.

Ordenanca:
Portuguese militia.

Ordre Mixte:
Flexible attack formation mixing units in column and in line.

Palisade:
Wooden-stakes fencing.

Parados:
Rear-facing parapet.

Parapet:
Front-facing wall of fortification.

Parole:
Surrendering officer could give their word not to escape before being exchanged.

Pickers:
Wire implement to clear musket touch holes.

Picquets:
Army outposts or patrols.

Pontonniers:
Engineers who could build, or improve, bridges.

Queue:
A soldier's powdered and tightly tied pigtail.

Redoubt:
Independent defensive position.

Roundshot:
A solid metal cannonball of varying sizes and weights.

Sabot:
Wooden base for fixed ammunition.

Sabre:
A curved cavalry sword.

Shabraque:
Ornamental horse equipment.

Shako:
Cylindrical head gear for most armies.

Shrapnel:
Fused explosive shell filled with musketballs and pieces of metal that would rain down on troops when it burst in the air.

Spontoon:
A short, half-pike.

Steel:
Frizzen.

Stovepipe:
British shako without false front (Belgic).

Tirailleur:
A French sharpshooter.

Triangle:
A frame of lashed-together spontoons on which a flogging was carried out.

Tricolor:
The French flag of blue, white and red.

Vedette:
A cavalry scout.

Velites:
Trainee light infantry.

Voltigeur:
Elite French light infantry.

Yeomanry:
Volunteer British cavalry.

Printed in Great Britain
by Amazon

44181054R00154